D0962190

BURY THE LEAD

BURY THE LEAD

A Joe Gunther Novel

ARCHER MAYOR

Minotaur Books
New York

BURY THE LEAD. Copyright © 2018 by Archer Mayor. All rights reserved. Printed in the United States of America. For information, address St. Martin's Press, 175 Fifth Avenue, New York, N.Y. 10010.

www.minotaurbooks.com

The Library of Congress Cataloging-in-Publication Data is available upon request.

ISBN 978-1-250-11328-3 (hardcover)
ISBN 978-1-250-11329-0 (ebook)

Our books may be purchased in bulk for promotional, educational, or business use. Please contact your local bookseller or the Macmillan Corporate and Premium Sales Department at 1-800-221-7945, extension 5442, or by email at MacmillanSpecialMarkets@macmillan.com.

First Edition: September 2018

10 9 8 7 6 5 4 3 2 1

In memory of Eric Buel,

a friend and valued resource, but far more, an inspiring human being.

It was a privilege knowing you.

THE LEAD OR THE LEDE?

The title of this book, *Bury the Lead*, may need explaining for some. It is a phrase from news reporting, highlighting a long-standing journalistic concern about telling the reader—usually in the opening sentence— the primary aim of the following article. To bury the lead is to leave the reader wondering about the point of the piece. In Great Britain, the spelling, for the purists among you, is often "lede."

My usage of this phrase is predictably more complex. During almost every investigation I detail in my novels, the lead will remain elusive. Even when, as in the pages to come here, it appears as if the facts are apparent, straightforward, and conclusive. But stay with me. Appearances can be deceiving. My lead may indeed be buried, for good reason.

ACKNOWLEDGMENTS

My thanks, as always, to those who helped me beyond value in getting the details "right." They are listed below with gratitude, and hopes that they won't be appalled by how I've used all their hard work and advice.

Kevin O'Connor

David Gartenstein

Jan Cohen

Scott Tighe

Bob Palmer

Marilyn Cipolla

Eric Buel

Margot Zalkind Mayor

Elizabeth Bundock

Castle Freeman Jr.

Ruth Marx

Julie Lavorgna

Chris Huston

Kristopher Radder

James Maxwell

Clem Nilan

Kevin Gordon

Jim and Cherie Boucher

Mike Mayor

John Martin

Ray Walker

Tracy Shriver

Dan Davis

Hunter Brooks

Timothy Hunter

Matthew McClain

BURY THE LEAD

CHAPTER ONE

Joe entered the autopsy room unnoticed, stepped to one side of the broad door, and leaned against the wall to watch. The recently deceased Jane Doe he'd followed to Burlington through morning commuter traffic, behind the funeral home's unmarked minivan, lay inside an unzipped body bag on the nearest of two steel operating tables.

The room was at its standard level of activity for a homicide. Fortunately, Vermont didn't get too many of these—an average of eleven a year.

But business had just been delivered a pick-me-up.

That's why he was here. Joe Gunther was head of operations for the state's independent major case unit, the Vermont Bureau of Investigation, or VBI, which one of his own colleagues had once irreverently labeled "the FBI in barn boots." Nevertheless, it was responsible for situations like this: a young woman found dead—as someone had quaintly suggested— through "unknown misadventure."

It was early yet—the body had been discovered by a hiker only this morning in southwestern Vermont, by the side of a trail at the peak of Bromley Mountain, eleven miles northeast of the popular and affluent town of Manchester. But things were already looking ominously elusive, starting with a complete lack of identifiers. She was just a girl, probably in her twenties, clothed in a light sundress and sandals. Appropriate to Vermont's early summer weather at noon, perhaps, but hardly suitable for a mountainous hiking trail in the dark of night.

Joe continued watching as the medical examiner and her assistant—called a diener in the trade—worked together, the former scrutinizing the body's hands and collecting its fingernails for later analysis, while the latter separated the body bag from the white sheet on which the young woman was actually resting, placed there at the scene by investigators to keep potential evidence from being lost.

In the meantime, the state trooper assigned as the office's law enforcement liaison got ready to collect fingerprints, take photos, and eventually gather the clothing for analysis by the forensics lab in Waterbury. Additional personnel in the room consisted of an assistant medical examiner, two medical students on their pathology rotation, and another cop shadowing the trooper to learn the ropes.

They were in the basement of the University of Vermont Medical Center, the state's largest, also its highly regarded primary teaching facility. There were often extra people at autopsy as a result of this latter role, brushing up on one of medicine's least appreciated disciplines, but Joe suspected that a young female homicide victim's appearance on the day's caseload calendar also played a part.

He, by contrast, largely ignored the distracting bustling. His attention was on the medical examiner—tall, slender, and blond—whose back was currently turned. She was Beverly Hillstrom, the chief ME, Joe's trusted associate for decades, and—more recently, unexpectedly, and happily—his romantic partner. That development had certainly made all professional visits to this corner of the state much more pleasant.

Todd, the diener, blew Joe's cover. Looking up from his labors, he delivered a friendly nod and asked, "This one yours?"

Hillstrom turned at the inquiry. Even obscured by plastic glasses and a mask, her eyes betrayed her pleasure. "Joe," she said. "There's a treat. I was hoping you'd be tagging along. Typical that you didn't give me a heads-up."

"You would've worn something more fabulous?" he asked.

Everyone laughed, since they were all garbed in shapeless pale green scrubs, including Joe, who'd changed in the office's small locker room. In fact, Joe's comment wasn't entirely off the mark: Whether by design or oversight, Beverly was wearing an elegant gold necklace, which looked all the more glamorous in this incongruous setting.

He left his spot to stand at the other side of the autopsy table, putting the dead girl between them like an inconsiderate intruder. Neither Joe nor Beverly paid any attention. They'd been in this same place too many times to count.

"You know me," he explained. "All that cell phone and texting stuff. I prefer to just show up."

"I do know that," Beverly said, circling around to let the others prepare things for her turn.

She stood close enough to give him a little bump with her hip. "Good to see you," she said very softly.

"You, too," he replied in like style. "It's been a long four days."

"You were counting," she chuckled. "How sweet."

They stood studying the case before them, each subconsciously noting telling details as they surfaced, their combined experience in this realm allowing them a seeming insouciance, when in fact they were utterly focused.

Beverly spoke first, as Todd expertly removed the sundress and slipped off the thong underwear beneath it, placing both on an adjoining table—again on a clean sheet—for Beverly to refer to as she worked. Jane Doe was wearing nothing else besides the sandals. "I realize it's warming up," Beverly commented, "but that's not much. Where was she found?"

"Top of Bromley Mountain, beside a combination hiking trail–dirt access road." He leaned into her slightly before adding, "So you're right: The clothes are wrong."

"Any evidence that she was brought there after the fact?"

"Crime lab's still on-site. It probably is a dump job, but why there, I have no clue. Makes no sense at the moment. It's in the middle of nowhere, but like I said, near two well-traveled paths." He shook his head slightly. "That's one reason I'm keeping her company: I'm hoping you'll find something I can use."

They were silent for the few minutes it took Todd and the cops to finish. Then Beverly said, "Well, let's see what she has to tell us."

They resumed their places across from each other. The deceased, nude on her back, her shoulder blades supported by a small metal block that made her head tilt back, looked relaxed, uncaring about her audience. Her ink-stained hands lay curled beside her; her eyelids were half closed, ready for sleep. She was slightly built, with shoulder-length fair hair and no piercings, tattoos, or visible scars from random past injuries—or any self-cuttings increasingly common among the young. Her pubic area had been shaved, as was currently trendy.

To Joe's eyes, so used to such sights, there was an additional detail, one he found slightly disturbing. Studying the girl's face, he couldn't but think there was a remaining luminance still in place. It wasn't anything as bland as beauty, but a lingering radiance. He couldn't help imagining that she'd been someone others had noticed, and enjoyed keeping their eyes on.

Beverly's first step consisted of an external physical exam—an inch-by-inch journey down the length of the body, both sides, with multiple pauses to take notes on a pad as she went, noting every scar, mark, scratch, or bruise, regardless of age or size.

Then, scalpel in hand, she paused a moment as usual, looking down, seemingly torn between leaving nature's handiwork intact and visiting upon it her own meticulous, almost artistic talents. Inevitably, as always, she chose the second, unerringly drawing a V-shaped incision with her blade, from one shoulder down to the sternum, back up to the opposite shoulder. Virtually in the same gesture, she followed with a smooth slice from the sternal notch down to the pubis. It was soundless, effortless, and graceful—and because of the utter lack of flowing blood—seemed curiously benign. Indeed, in response, even Jane Doe appeared to slacken overall, one final bit, suggesting that she and Beverly had somehow conspired to finalize her release.

Beverly next reached into the incision with her fingers, and, while severing connective tissue with her blade as she went, lifted away each half of the outer torso—as if delicately opening the sides of a zippered sweatshirt—folding the diminutive breasts facedown on the table near the armpits and fully exposing the body's glistening pink rib cage.

This was always an autopsy's watershed moment for Joe, marking the divide between seeing a fellow human as someone's recently lost companion or child and simply discovering—piece by piece—what had once made it function.

Beverly's technique helped the illusion. She was gentle, soft-spoken, almost soothing, while she probed, cut, removed, and weighed organs, lending credence to the notion that she was more disassembling a complex and visceral puzzle than carving into a once-sentient creature.

She wrote down her findings as she went, or in this case, the lack of them, as she cataloged her way down the interconnected complex of body parts that nestle inside us all. One by one, the heart, lungs, major vessels, stomach, liver, and the rest were removed, placed on the scale, transferred to the dissection table, sliced open, and scrutinized. Periodically, per protocol, samples were collected and preserved in small, formalin-filled containers. They would be kept on file, in lieu of the body itself, in case further study was needed down the line. These were all medicolegal examinations, after all, open to court-sanctioned challenges and/or inquiries that no one could imagine right now.

Indeed, at the moment, Jane Doe was completely unknown to them, making this—on a forensic level—the ultimate blind date, with both parties shy and inarticulate.

Along those lines, Hillstrom hesitated after shifting from the exposed lower body to her patient's head and moving the metal block farther up accordingly. There, her masked face hovering over the dead girl's like a mother checking for a fever, she touched the cold, still forehead with her gloved fingertips, and observed, "She must be almost exactly Rachel's age."

Joe was surprised and moved by the comment. Rachel was the younger of Beverly's two daughters—unmarried, fresh from college, looking for a job. Joe had no children, although he'd aspired to as a young married man, long ago, while a rookie cop in Brattleboro, in Vermont's southeastern corner.

His wife had been taken by cancer, however, along with such hopes of normalcy. Life had progressed. There'd been other women, offering opportunities of fatherhood. But he'd never taken them; never even discussed the matter. That option died with the only woman he'd married.

Recalling his own appreciation of the dead girl's appearance, he looked at her anew, after Beverly had moved past her fleeting maternal gesture to the jarring contrast of peeling the body's scalp down over its face and removing the skullcap beneath. Joe's eyes drifted to the half-opened hands, thinking of all this young woman might have aspired to shape with them—the interrupted sculptor of her own destiny—and he suddenly experienced the pathos of this sterile setting as he rarely did anymore.

Cops, EMTs, medical examiners, and firefighters aren't so unfeeling as they're often portrayed by actors. Nor are they masking tormented inner souls that are raging against cruelty and injustice, as in other equally commonplace clichés. The middle ground of reality is more mundane than that. For the most part, they're simply overexposed to what the uninitiated refer to as the horrors of humanity. Like hunting dogs inured to the sound of steady gunfire, they tend to experience these moments on a practical level. It may be a defense mechanism, but more likely, it's just part of the job.

Which made the upswell of Joe's emotion startling and a little unnerving.

"Are you all right?" Beverly asked him.

He blinked at her unusually subdued tone and looked up, his eyebrows raised. "What?"

"I was wondering where you went. You seemed to have drifted off."

He glanced around to see if she'd been the only one to notice what must have been a more extended mental absence than he'd imagined. "Sorry," he said, sparing her the real explanation. "I was reviewing the case in my head." He indicated the exposed brain with a toss of his chin. "You find anything?"

Beverly's voice became businesslike again. She nimbly lifted out the brain after severing the spinal cord. "Serious impact trauma. Enough to have fractured the posterior of the skull." She pointed out the cracks with her pen. "In itself, evidence of either a fall or a blow." She switched their attention to the brain in her hand. "But as you can see from the lack of any contrecoup injury to the anterior—otherwise typical in a fall—I'll be ruling this a homicide, not that you're surprised by that."

He slid over beside her to observe the damage to bone and tissue she'd discovered, confirming the implication that their girl had been lethally struck from behind.

"A bat?" he asked.

She gave him a warning look. "You know me better than that. I will say the injury's consistent with a bat. And you should see this."

She led him back to the dissection table, which was serving as a generalized storage area for the collected samples. "I extracted bile, vitreous, pericardial, and cerebrospinal fluids as I went," she explained. "As well, I always throw in a test for human chorionic gonadotropin, or hCG. It was positive across the board, which confirms what I found physically."

"Okay," he said patiently, preparing for the punch line. For all her scientific and objective posing, Beverly was not beyond the occasional flourish.

"She was pregnant," she concluded. "Very early on, judging from the uterus, but undoubtedly."

"Can you get the fetus's DNA?" he asked.

"Absolutely."

CHAPTER TWO

Bromley Mountain's ski resort is historically known for being dreamed up by a scion of the Pabst Blue Ribbon beer dynasty, just before World War Two—a fact alluded to by several of its trails' beer-related names. Joe Gunther, however, typical of his often unorthodox take on things, saw something more subtle and poignant: Amid an impressively competitive, marketing-mad industry, lusty for out-of-state money, Bromley struck him as the Oliver Twist of recreational retreats. It was small, had been tossed around among several corporations like a neglected orphan, and rarely appeared on any hyperdriven ski aficionado's top-ten list. Perhaps because of that, it was one of Joe's favorites. In exchange for its lack of glitz, Bromley was among the friendliest of family mountains in the state, year-round.

An empathy only heightened by its having been callously used for an apparent body dump.

Back in the heady days of the ski business's childhood, when chairlifts were a hot new item and many of the early instructors fresh from wartime alpine units—both Allied and Axis—mountains like this were for hardy, dedicated, risk-taking adventurers, well used to hidden boulders, natural snow, and ungroomed trails. They came early in the season, put up with minimal amenities, stayed as paying guests at local farm-houses, and worked off some of the aggression that several years of com-bat had instilled in them.

That was a long time ago, as Joe was free to consider during his ride on the back of a young deputy's four-wheeler, an impromptu taxi service running between the base lodge and the peak. In these more consumer-sensitive times, resorts like this operated all twelve months, featuring everything from golf courses to condo villages to playgrounds, water parks, swimming pools, and tennis courts. About the only thing he could think of that none of them offered yet was deep-sea fishing.

As the four-wheeler ground its way up a threadbare dirt-and-grass ski slope that doubled as a summit-bound access road, Joe took in Bromley's far leaner offerings of a putt-putt park, a zip line, and a triple alpine slide snaking through the trees far to their right. Body or no, the business had to keep its customers happy. Along those lines, the crime scene up top had been cordoned off and the crime techs and cops asked to keep a low profile—not from consideration for the laughter and thrilled cries waft-ing on the warm breeze, but rather to avoid spooking any potential wit-nesses into leaving prematurely.

Everything about this case so far seemed steeped in incongruous contrast. Driving home the point, Joe twisted around to enjoy the hundred-mile view as the valley floor fell away during their journey. South, extending toward Stratton Mountain and Massachusetts beyond, it presented as a wrinkled blanket of ancient peaks and river-carved val-leys, surmounted by a cloudless blue sky that intensified and deepened as it soared overhead.

There were few times as rewarding to a New Englander as the asser-tion of early summer, taking over from an often stuttering, unstable, and unconvincing spring.

Joe got off the machine at the first yellow police tape barrier, thanked his chauffeur, logged in with a clipboard-equipped state trooper, and walked to where a large white tent stood over Jane Doe's last resting place.

This easy commingling of different uniforms was the new way investigations were being conducted nowadays, at least under ideal circumstances. Representatives from every relevant police agency—in this instance, the sheriff's office, the state police, the VBI, and the state forensic lab—were called out, inter-coordinated at the scene, and expected to get the job done.

Back less than a decade, a major case like this would have fallen solely to the state police. Actually, before the mid-1940s, the sheriff and local town constable were pretty much it, with results that explained the creation of the state police. Now, because of some almost-forgotten governor's stroke of a pen, the VBI handled most capital crimes, usually upon being invited by the prevailing legal authority—here, the Bennington County State's Attorney.

It had been an awkward transition in the beginning, with VBI agents and VSP investigators stalking one another like wary fighting cocks. But because the ranks of the former were largely made up of defectors from the latter—happy to be free of the tightly regulated, top-heavy state police—eventually a grudging truce was reached. It's also fair to say that in a state so thinly populated as Vermont, no agency was in fact big enough to bear much of an institutional grudge against another. Among Vermont's one thousand or so fully certified cops—grand total—there were just too many friendships that crossed company lines.

A small, striking woman standing outside the tent saw Joe approaching and came to meet him.

"Any luck with the ME?" she asked.

This was Samantha Martens, universally called Sam or Sammie. Unofficially, she was Joe's lieutenant, frequently functioning as such during his occasional absences. But that entailed more than it implied, given Joe's rank and responsibilities as VBI's field force commander, which in turn explained why Sam wasn't eager for any official title. She was happier, in her words, to remain a "street digger."

"She was whacked over the head and newly pregnant," Joe reported.

Sam made a face. "Great. That'll guarantee headlines."

Joe glanced to where the white-clad crime techs were putting away their equipment after hours of searching, taking photographs, collecting odds and ends, and creating plaster casts of impressions. "Any luck while I've been gone?"

"We've definitely had worse," she allowed. "They found a set of tire marks they believe correspond to a pair of boot prints near the dump site, which fits with the body being brought here on a four-by-four and dropped off by someone with a size ten-and-a-half foot. It ain't a confession, but it's something. The boot treads are worn and have the usual nicks and gouges we can match to the originals if we ever find 'em."

"Good," he said. "Anything from the canvass?"

"Yeah. That, too," she answered, holding up her phone. "Lester's on it, down at the base lodge. We got uniforms still knocking on doors and interviewing people who work here, but he's found something on video, from the mountain's CCTV system. You wanna go down and look?"

"You bet," Joe said, turning back toward where he'd come.

"Hang on, boss," she said. "I got a better idea."

She led them in the opposite direction, out of the trees, to a clearing above the mountain's two chairlift turnarounds.

"You know," she told him over her shoulder, "technically, you're walking on both the Long and Appalachian Trails right now. They overlap along this section."

He smiled. "I knew they hit a few of these mountains," he said. "Stratton, too, right?"

"A bunch of 'em," she confirmed, aiming for the older of the two lifts, the open-air model named the Blue Ribbon Quad. "Stratton, Bromley, Killington. After that, the Long splits off and hits Lincoln, Camel's Hump, Mount Mansfield, and Jay, among others, while the Appalachian heads for Maine. It's a real workout."

He laughed as they readied themselves to be swept off their feet for the downhill ride. "And you've done both, knowing you."

"I did the Long," she conceded, "before Emma and happy domesticity. I thought about tackling the AT, but I think that's behind me now."

Joe wasn't so sure. Sam did have a preschooler and lived with Emma's father—another of his cops, in fact—but she was fit and driven enough to be fully capable of taking on the Appalachian Trail at any time, including probably well into her retirement years.

Her recommended route proved a spectacular way of reaching the base lodge, even including a change of chairs halfway down the mountain. What he'd admired earlier by twisting around and craning his neck on a jolting machine could now be enjoyed from the comfort of a gently rocking padded chair, allowing him time and leisure to dangle before a panorama of natural beauty.

They were so used to working in such a wilderness-weighted part of the world, with its mud, foliage, and sugaring seasons, in addition to the standard four, that the two cops took the scenery before them in stride— if not for granted—by continually talking all the way down.

At the bottom, they cut between the alpine slide terminus and a cluster of heavily populated trampolines, crossed the equivalent of a fairway, complete with tents full of child-oriented activities, and entered the lodge.

As they walked, Sam phoned Lester Spinney and asked for directions, until she and Joe came to the entrance of a large room filled with electronics, flat-screen displays, and the sound of radio communications. A central map of the resort, festooned with LED indicators, monitored the health and activity of the mountain's mechanical heartbeat. With a year-round calendar of events, and catering to a particular form of high-risk recreation, Bromley—like most of its kind—had to be as aware of its operations as the average flight deck officer on an aircraft carrier.

A very tall, absurdly skinny plainclothes cop with short blond hair and animated features motioned to them from a corner of the room, which was otherwise occupied by serious-looking people moving from one station to another as they pursued their business, no doubt counting the minutes until the cops returned the mountaintop to its rightful owners.

Lester Spinney stood as his two colleagues drew near. He'd been sitting next to a lumpy man at a keyboard facing a tiered bank of TV screens.

"Worthwhile trip to see Hillstrom?" he asked, keeping things vague for the sake of the surrounding civilians.

"Yeah," Joe said, glancing at the screens. "What did you get?"

Lester resumed his seat, letting the other two look over his shoulder. "This is Barry, by the way," he said, to which the lumpy man held up a hand and twiddled his fingers without bothering to look back.

"Hey."

"Hey, yourself," Joe answered.

"Bring it up," Lester told him.

With the punch of a couple of keys, one of the monitors before them filled with the static image of a broad patch of rough-looking dirt road bordered by a pair of blazing overhead security lights. There was a digital clock in one corner, rhythmically counting off the seconds.

"This was recorded last night, at the bottom of two of the trails," Lester explained. "It's a road marking the western edge of the mountain face. They use it to bring equipment to the top, among other things. To orient you, the bunny slope and a condo village are just above here, to the left. After that, you get into the trees." He paused before adding, "Boss, that's probably how they took you up just now. Hang on, here it comes."

As they watched, a four-wheeler entered the frame, trundled across it diagonally, and disappeared, heading uphill.

"Back it up and hold it," Joe requested.

Barry did so, immobilizing the vehicle in midframe. The camera had a remarkably high resolution. Nevertheless, its angle caught the four-wheeler's driver from over his right shoulder, and thus didn't show his face.

Tellingly, strapped across the rear deck behind the driver, was a long, thin, plastic-wrapped package, the size and shape of a human body.

"Ouch," Sam said.

"You see what I mean," Lester said. "Doesn't look like anything normal, especially in the middle of the night."

"Do you have him coming back down?" Joe wanted to know.

"Show him what you got, Barry," Lester ordered.

Moments later, the same frame was filled with the four-wheeler returning from the opposite direction. The clock showed the time as twenty-three minutes after the first sighting. The rear deck now held only an empty, folded tarp.

More important, the driver's face was upturned and staring at the lens as he drove by.

"Can you print that?" Joe asked. "And a copy of the video itself?"

Lester retrieved a manila envelope from beside Barry's keyboard and handed it over—an example of his natural efficiency. Joe slid out an enlargement of the image before them.

"Guess we'll be wanting to talk with him," Sammie commented.

"You ever seen this man?" Joe asked Barry.

"Nope," came the terse reply.

Joe returned the prints to Lester. "And we couldn't get a clean shot of the registration?"

"Too dirty."

Joe tapped Barry on the shoulder. "Thanks." He gestured to his subordinates to follow him into the hallway, where, after looking around for privacy's sake, he said, "Let's get this out to everyone who's canvassing. There's got to be someone who knows this guy."

"Why's that a given?" Sam asked as Lester took back the manila envelope.

"It's not," Joe allowed, "but why else would he go through the bother of dumping a body up top, unless he was familiar with the layout?"

"On the other hand," Sam asked, "why dump it here at all? Why not in a ditch? This seems awfully convoluted."

"And crowded," Lester tossed in. "They've got things going on at night, too, a twenty-four-hour presence, and cameras. The killer was taking a big risk."

Joe nodded, saying almost as an afterthought, "He's not a killer yet. Let's find him first."

They fell silent as two Bromley staffers appeared from around a corner and walked by, chatting.

Joe extended his hand for the envelope again. "Did I see you had two shots printed?"

Lester gave it up. "The other's a long view."

Joe pulled it out and studied it carefully. "The four-wheeler's got some distinctive dents and markings, enough for an identification. Make sure you get that out, too. If people can't place the man's face, maybe they've seen the rig in the neighborhood. It's not like you drive those things long-distance. If we're lucky, this whole case'll be a local we can wrap up fast and easy, before the press gets into a lather."

"How do you want to handle them if they do get wind of it?" Sam asked.

"I called Bill Allard from the road," Joe said, referencing the VBI director, his immediate boss. "He said to refer everything to him."

"Should we get ahead of it and put out have-you-seen-this-person flyers for Jane Doe?" Lester asked. "No one could claim we were being secretive then, and it might get us something in return."

"I'll compromise," Joe replied. "Use the state intel center to issue a police-only Be On the Lookout. 'Seeking to Identify' or something like that."

"The OCME got nothing running her prints?" Sam asked. The OCME was shorthand for Office of the Chief Medical Examiner.

"No," Joe said. "Not too surprising, given her age." He shrugged, handed the envelope back to Lester, and added, "What we got is what we got, until we get lucky."

He then gave Sammie a closer look. "Where's Willy? I would've thought he'd be all over this."

She smiled ruefully. "How often do any of us know where he is?"

Willy Kunkle was at home alone, in West Brattleboro, in the house he shared with Sammie and their daughter, Emma, who was at that moment in preschool. It was a single-story, suburban-style bungalow, at the back of a horseshoe-shaped drive, which he'd purchased before he and Sam got together.

That helped explain why the house reflected so many of his unique peculiarities.

From the outside, it looked boring and stark, bereft of the usual visual softeners like bushes or nearby trees. It stood on its plot, bare and exposed, exuding the look of either a forgotten spec house—long out of date and perhaps never lived in—or the less comforting aura of a subtly disguised fortress.

For those who knew Kunkle, the latter was a foregone conclusion. Indeed, if asked, Willy freely admitted that the absence of vegetation allowed him an open field of fire, if it ever became necessary to mount a determined defense.

As a result, it was no surprise to find that the walls were reinforced, bullet-resistant, and fire-retardant; there was auxiliary power in the basement, an independent water well, a larder full of long-term provisions, a security system featuring cameras and detectors, and enough weapons under lock and key to hold off a small battalion.

As with Willy himself, none of this was evident at first glance. The interior was immaculately neat, rationally but sparsely furnished, and— given those walls—extraordinarily quiet. But even though this was a family home, with a small child, any visitor might notice an unusual feeling about it—not malevolent, necessarily, but certainly watchful and cautious in nature.

This was Willy's sanctuary, in the true sense of the word: as close to a place of comfort, safety, and sanity as existed for him. Sammie was fully aware of this, which had factored heavily in her agreeing to live here, instead of insisting on "a place of their own."

However, Willy wasn't feeling too comfortable right now, making of his retreat the hollow equivalent of a child's blanket pulled over his head for protection. He was in the worst pain he'd experienced in a very long time—searing, throbbing, unremitting, and resistant to any treatment.

Its source, to use his own blunt, unsentimental vernacular, was that he was a cripple, saddled with a limp left arm from a rifle bullet received in the line of duty many years before. It should have ended his career, and did interrupt it, until Joe, in those days his boss at the Brattleboro police, had intervened in his behalf. Such was Gunther's reputation, and Vermont's often creative approach to problem solving, that Joe's efforts had actually succeeded. The result had been a nontransferrable, quasi-unofficial, uniquely narrow blessing: Forever after, Willy could function as a cop only under Joe's aegis, regardless of what agency paid his wages. That meant that if the older man ever retired, Willy's choice of professions was most likely over.

Not that he gave a damn about any such considerations at the present. The pain in his arm was such that it had been all he could do to fake the morning family routine with Sam and Emma before closing the door to consider his options. He knew Sam had headed out to a probable homicide—usually Willy's cup of tea—but he'd lied by saying he had something else to clear up first.

Wishful thinking, of course.

Technically, that ancient bullet had destroyed the bundle of nerves at the shoulder that helps make an arm work as it should. The injury might possibly have been repaired immediately afterwards, but naturally, that's not what Willy had opted to do. He'd retreated—from the department, his colleagues, what few friends he could claim. Unbeknownst to all, he'd returned to drinking, ruining a years-long streak of sobriety, surrendering to his familiar and comforting sense of doom. By the time Joe Gunther smoothed a road back for him, medical opinion believed too much time had elapsed for the arm to be saved.

There had been occasional pain since, but always manageable, mostly not an issue. He had painkillers available, rarely used, and his doc and he had discussed their use, in light of Willy's past alcoholism. For a man of Kunkle's highly controlling nature, his self-discipline was something his physician paradoxically trusted to be reliable.

But something had changed recently. Willy didn't know how or why, but in just days, the pain had come on fast, hard, and was no longer taking a backseat to anything.

He stood now in his bathroom, his shirt off, before the mirror, staring at the useless limb as if it were the radiating agony within it. It made no sense to him how something this uncomfortable could look so banal.

He opened the cabinet and studied his diminishing choice of analgesics. He'd been hitting them as never before, trying to keep the onslaught in check. It was beginning to get tricky, figuring out how much to take without diminishing his performance. The last thing he needed was for people to discover what was happening.

The specter of his dependence on booze rose like a mist in his memory—its anesthetizing appeal, its easy availability, and the comfort of its rituals. He could sense, as surely as an outgoing tide, the ebbing dependability of his willpower.

It didn't help that he was running low on his prescribed alternatives.

He and Sam had side-by-side sinks, with hinged mirrors before each. He stepped over to hers and opened it, his eyes scanning the lipsticks, mascara, and creams, to where they rested upon a familiar-looking prescription bottle. She'd suffered an injury months ago, something minor and passing. He picked up the bottle, read the label, and shook it.

OxyContin—the strong stuff. More than half full. They'd joked when she stopped taking it that they ought to sell the rest for Emma's college fund.

God knows, they knew how and where to get a good price.

He opened the bottle with surprising dexterity, given the one hand, poured half its contents onto the counter between the sinks, replaced the container, and closed the mirror—almost in a single smooth gesture— willing his action to the immediate past.

In a show of respect to his fading resolve, instead of simply pocketing the pills for later in the day, he took his own bottle and loaded most of them into it, leaving a couple out. He returned the bottle to its place, feeling its renewed weight, and kidded himself that only a minor correction had just taken place.

Willy's primary care doc had once suggested the pain might worsen with time, or vary in intensity, and thus require intervention. So why would he begrudge his patient another refill a little before schedule?

Willy knew better than to believe his own fantasy, however. He'd heard that lie voiced by others, and in himself, too often over the years. But, he then persisted—in a cartoon parody of good angel versus bad—who knew his own body more intimately than he? Surely he was more deeply versed in the effects of addiction than any doc. And how many years had he been sober by now?

Still, he was torn by the debate's glaring false notes. Not to mention the practical considerations: how to duck any random drug tests that might be waiting down the line. Unlikely, but not impossible.

Because he was absolutely sure of one thing: If he got caught with the level of narcotics in his system he suspected he'd have at this rate—far above the therapeutic dose—it would take more than Joe Gunther to save his skin.

CHAPTER THREE

"We got a hit on the four-wheeler."

Joe looked up from his laptop. The crime lab had left the mountain-top, most of the police vehicles had dispersed from Bromley's parking lot, and in exchange, the resort had lent the VBI office space adjacent to the lodge.

Lester was standing in the doorway.

"What?" Joe asked him.

"The canvass turned up a lift mechanic who says it belongs to a friend of his." He consulted the pad in his hand. "Bud Thurley. Real name Thadeus, according to our database."

Joe was impressed. "Thadeus Thurley? His parents must've hated him. Why do we have him in the system? Or did that come from the DMV?"

"Oh, no," Lester clarified. "He's misbehaved. Not for anything overly dramatic. Three DUIs, including one where he hit a pedestrian—nonfatal. He did time for that. Two disorderly conducts, a receiving stolen property, some other stuff. When he's not acting out, he's a logger and runs a small lumber mill."

"He the guy in the video?"

"No, that would be too easy. The mechanic pegged on the machine only. No clue about the rider."

"We have a location on Thadeus?"

Lester grinned. "Right. Using that on him'll loosen him up, fer sher—remind him of his mother, probably. Yes, we do, and as suspected, it's not far from here."

Joe rose from his borrowed desk. "I promise to call him Bud."

"How's Sue enjoying her new job?" Joe asked as they got under way in Lester's car.

"A lot, so far," he answered. His wife had recently changed nursing jobs, after decades at their hometown hospital. "It's smaller than Springfield, so not as busy, but she's up for that, at long last, and she loves working for the woman who recruited her."

"Victoria . . . What was it, again?" Joe attempted.

"Garlanda. Wild name, at least for around here. They were BFFs in nursing school, and thick as thieves forever after, even though Victoria's a lot older. She's a bit of an overachiever, if you ask me, but a good egg, and a great friend to Sue. Also a mentor. She never got married or had kids, so it was all about the job. But she's distributed her good fortunes throughout, like this job for Sue, so I'm not complaining. Better pay, too."

Joe stuck his elbow out the open window and enjoyed the breeze washing through the car's interior. Summer for him was more catharsis than mere seasonal threshold. There were places with harsher winters than Vermont, but Joe imagined no one embraced this transition more happily than he. And he loved winter. He was a native born and bred, so it was in his DNA, and while people joked that guys like him preferred to vacation in Maine and die in Florida, he could envision nothing less attractive than a place without distinct seasons.

"How 'bout you?" Lester asked. "You and Hillstrom still getting along? We gonna hear wedding bells soon?"

Joe burst out laughing. "Right—from two workaholics whose jobs are as far apart as the state's boundaries. Very likely."

Lester cast him a glance. "You never know, boss. Don't forget that bumper sticker."

"'One Day at a Time'?" Joe quoted. "Never one of my favorites. Nah, we're good the way we are."

In the following lull, he wondered if Lester might be right. If he and Beverly continued as a couple with the same success as now, why not entertain an evolution of some sort? Neither of them was getting younger, nor could they work at the same pace forever. Joe was nevertheless surprised to be thinking along such lines, after a life increasingly resigned to an almost fatalistic bachelorhood.

It was more rule than exception that two people like him and Lester Spinney would prefer to talk about family and romance over how an anonymous young pregnant woman had been beaten to death and dumped by the side of a trail. Possibly such banalities shielded them against humanity's penchant for violence.

But more likely, it hinged on the fact that Joe had been operating at this investigative level long enough to have lost count of the homicides he'd worked. The empathy he'd experienced at Jane Doe's autopsy was transient, and rare enough to have struck him with the same startlement as Lester's comment about marriage.

The trip to Bud Thurley's mill was barely twenty minutes, which still brought them as far as imaginable from Bromley's world of leisure and entertainment. They found it at the end of yet another logging road, hemmed in by walls of impenetrable, freshly leafed-out trees. In a sudden clearing, they entered a rough-cut amphitheater of felled hardwoods capped by a broad, clear ceiling of blue sky and surrounded by haphazardly parked pickups, two rusty logging trucks, a dozer, log grapples, a skidder, and a construction trailer, all scattered across an equipment yard pockmarked with potholes, stumps, and rocks, and carpeted with shattered tree bark.

A chain-driven conveyor led into a large, dark, flimsy, open-walled shed, from which a howl of screaming generators, saws, splitters, and more poured into the air like locusts, sweeping up and out into the atmosphere. The entire clearing thrummed and vibrated as might the interior of an open-topped trash can of gigantic proportions, beaten upon by a thousand unseen metal bats.

In the South especially, during the timber industry's formation two hundred years earlier, this was the epitome of a peckerwood sawmill—a noisy, itinerant, often dangerous, and usually ramshackle operation that moved from one opportunity to the next, dependent on contracts and available source material.

Both men exchanged astonished looks as they emerged from the car.

"Jeezum," Lester said, approaching to shout into Joe's ear. "*This is nuts.* I hope whoever's in there is either deaf or wearing hearing protection. Good thing we're not OSHA."

Joe was thinking that OSHA might be the least of the place's problems, when the door to the trailer opened and a stocky man with a mean face appeared at the top of the aluminum steps and angrily gestured to them to approach.

"Who're you guys?" he yelled as they drew near.

Both men instinctively flipped open their jackets to reveal the badge each had clipped to his belt.

The man scowled and stepped back, leaving the door open.

Inside, they found him at a desk that wouldn't have qualified for a curbside FREE sign. His body language spoke of a preference to be manning a machine gun. As it was, he fiddled with a large, closed Buck Knife before him, turning it clockwise and counterclockwise with his stubby fingertips.

"Close the door."

Surprisingly, the noise abated significantly, to where a normal conversation could take place, assuming both parties stayed focused.

"What d'you want?"

"Maybe to be of service," Joe said pleasantly, eyeing a metal foldout chair opposite the desk before deciding to remain standing for the height advantage. "You missing a four-wheeler?"

The man stared at them, his mouth slightly open. His fingers stopped moving. "How'd you know that?"

"It came up," Lester answered vaguely. "What's your name, by the way? Mine's Spinney. He's Gunther."

"Bud Thurley."

"Date of birth?"

"Ten-fifteen-sixty-eight. And, yes, I have a record." Thurley's tone was contemptuous.

Les removed his pad despite already knowing all this, and slowly wrote down the information, thereby making his own show of disdain. "For?"

"Ran over a guy with my car. Flunked the breath test. Ancient history. Where's my four-wheeler?"

Joe changed his mind and sat in the chair, establishing that they weren't leaving anytime soon. By contrast, he kept his voice conversational. "Tell us about that. What happened?"

A veteran of past police encounters, Thurley was quickly deflated by Joe's gesture. When he spoke again, he was more resigned than pugnacious. He slipped the knife into his pocket. "I wish I knew. It's hard enough keeping everything running without supplying local losers with free equipment."

"How long you been in this location?" Joe continued. "I noticed the machine shed."

"Couple of years. I log and mill, both. The National Forest people like that. Very crunchy granola to them, and cheaper. It's a living, if barely. I'm not complaining."

Joe took his word for it. He reached back for the envelope Lester had brought in and slid a photo from it onto Thurley's desk. "This the local loser and equipment we're talking about?"

The sawmill owner leaned forward to study the print from Bromley's surveillance camera. "That's my machine. I got no clue who the guy is."

Joe frowned. "Not someone who ever worked for you?"

Thurley sat back. "It's not that big an operation. Who is he?"

"When did the four-wheeler go missing?" Spinney asked instead.

Their host looked from one of them to the other. "Last week," he said slowly.

"You didn't report it?"

"I don't got insurance on it and I don't like you people. It was a lose–lose, if you get my meaning."

Joe stood up. "I do. Mind if we talk with your employees?"

"Yeah, I mind. We're facing a deadline. I can't afford the downtime."

Joe turned to Lester and addressed him as much as Thurley. "Okay. We'll get out of your hair, then."

Lester hesitated, surprised by the easy capitulation. But he didn't resist being steered toward the door and into the earsplitting outdoors.

Back in the car, however, he unleashed his curiosity. "And we're just walking away because . . . ?" he asked.

"He don't got insurance and he don't like us people," Joe said, staring straight ahead and smiling.

He faced his partner as the latter started the engine, adding, "But I've got a notion he knew right off who was riding that four-wheeler. I doubt he was lying about the lack of insurance, though. My guess is he was stewing over this until we gave him the thief's identity."

Spinney did an awkward U-turn inside the uneven logging yard and began retreating down the access road. "So we stick a tail on him and see where he leads us?"

"Unless you got a better idea."

The spontaneity of Joe's plan meant they didn't know when Thurley might act—if he would at all—including immediately following their departure.

Thurley's past criminal history, as far as they'd researched it, certainly suggested a man with poor impulse control.

Lester therefore pulled into a spot from where they could watch the logging road's juncture with the highway, while Joe—after issuing the standard small prayer for cell coverage—pulled out his phone. In turn, he called Sammie and their dispatch to let them know what they were setting in motion. He wasn't going to get complicated at this point, hoping Thurley might act sooner rather than later, so he requested a two-car detail only, to last late into the night ahead. If things looked like they'd stretch out longer, then they could move to a plan B.

In homage to Joe's grasp of character, however, it was barely after quitting time when a string of the same pickups they'd seen parked at the mill began filing onto the highway—followed by the one registered to Bud Thurley.

Lester was watching them through a pair of binoculars.

"That him at the wheel?" Joe asked.

Les lowered the glasses and put the car into gear. "Yep, and he's alone. You really think he'll lead us straight to the thief?"

Joe shook his head, speed-dialing his phone. "Nope. If I were him, I'd wait till late. Catch the guy in bed, probably half a bottle into a self-induced coma. I could be wrong, though."

He updated Sam—now in a car down the road with Willy—on what Thurley was driving, and in what direction he was headed.

A mile away, Sam dropped the phone into her lap and relayed, "Older Ford 150, white with rust over the wheel wells, and a diesel fuel pump mounted behind the cab." She added the registration.

Willy Kunkle, in the passenger seat, reached up and adjusted the vanity mirror so he could monitor the traffic approaching from behind.

His arm was feeling fractionally better. The OxyContin had kicked in. "How solid is this?" he asked.

"It's a best guess," Sam said. "We don't even know if what was wrapped up on the back of the four-wheeler is our girl at all. But the driver wasn't an employee, the machine seems to've been stolen, the timing's about right, and Joe's thinking this lumber mill owner recognized the thief. Seems worth the effort, given what else we got."

"Here he comes," Willy announced.

As prearranged, they let both the pickup and Lester drive by before entering the road, all of them now heading south on Route 30, past Bromley.

"You set things up with Louise?" Sam asked, her eyes on the road.

Louise had almost become their live-in babysitter by now. An ex-cop herself, and a widow with children long out of the house, Louise was a godsend. She was dependable, affordable, almost always available, and a joy for their daughter to behold, to the point where Sam struggled, worried that Emma's affections were teetering more toward Louise than herself.

With Sam's checkered childhood, her prior poor history with men, and an emotional insecurity masked by a constant urge to overachieve, such concerns were inherent to her character.

"Yeah," Willy told her, shifting in his seat, hoping to become more comfortable. "I asked her to spend the night. She was good with that."

Joe turned out to have been prescient as well about Thurley's roundabout plan for the night, even if the man's destination was a surprise.

The string of them ended up in Manchester Center, among the wealthier towns in the state, and a place with a high gloss markedly at odds with the scrappy clearing in the woods they'd just left. This was a well-known, very commercial, heavily frequented intersection featuring an uninterrupted string of restaurants, bars, designer clothing stores, and—in Manchester Village itself down the road—some of the most exuberantly overpriced Greek Revival mansions available in Vermont, clustered prettily around a resort and spa the size of a landlocked ocean liner and frequented by suspiciously well-preserved people dressed in the carefully casual and high-priced offerings of the local Orvis flagship store.

As Joe and Lester's car drove by with the flow of traffic, Sam and Willy tailed Thurley into the parking lot of a diner on the edge of town.

"We'll wait out of sight," Joe said on his phone. "Enjoy dinner if you can keep a low profile."

"While we starve?" Lester asked him after he'd hung up. He was a man of regular eating habits, despite his emaciated appearance.

Joe reached into his coat pocket and pulled out an energy bar, which he handed over. "Perish the thought. Bon appétit."

Lester didn't hesitate, accepting the snack.

An hour later, the caravan started again, next following Thurley to a bar closer to the town center. There, the four cops rotated as customers, staying in dark corners and ordering ginger ales and seltzers, while keeping an eye on their target as he socialized with friends and strangers and failed to pick up any woman with low-enough standards to appreciate what he was offering.

That last ambition prompted Willy to send a text suggesting, "Don't know, boss. If he's trolling for mermaids, I doubt he's planning to roust our vehicle thief."

With Lester typing what he dictated, Joe responded, "He's got time to make trouble, regardless. Let's stick with him."

Thurley didn't take long to satisfy their curiosity. Staggering slightly, he stepped into the parking lot, rubbed his face with both hands, glanced around until he recognized his truck, and fumbled to fit his key into the door lock.

"We can just pull him over for DUI, if it comes to it," Lester said, preparing to follow.

Joe remained silent, watching the battered truck hesitate on the edge of the highway, and then begin returning north, along the road they'd used earlier.

"Headin' home?" Lester asked.

Joe doubted it. If he'd read his man correctly, he was not prone to delayed self-gratification. All they'd witnessed so far was a case of strategic timing. As he'd implied to Lester earlier, this slice of humanity was heavily populated by night owls who, when they finally collapsed for a few hours' sleep, did so without reserve. Joe figured Thurley was counting on his target doing just that.

Sure enough, just as their unwitting guide neared the Route 7 intersection on the north end of Manchester Center, he cut left, heading for the town's lower-rent area.

Not a mile on, he entered a trailer park by the side of the road. His followers pulled over and watched as his headlights lurched across the feeder road's rough surface before stopping halfway along, resting on a small, worse-for-wear single-wide before being extinguished.

"Close in from both sides," Joe ordered over the phone. "Block him in. No lights or noise."

It was done quickly and quietly. Less than a minute later, the four of them met up beside Thurley's empty truck, which was wedged against the same four-wheeler featured in the Bromley surveillance tape. There was one dim light on near the front door of the nearby trailer, and sounds of objects breaking toward the back, accompanied by a startled shout for help.

"That's it," Joe said as they rapidly donned ballistic vests retrieved from their car trunks. "Let's go."

Sam entered first with a 12 gauge, followed by Lester, Willy, and Joe. Trailers were nobody's favorite when it came to emergency breaches. Standard self-protective approaches were hindered by tight quarters and narrow corridors. Thus, the preference to fan out yielded to a high-man, low-man, two-person frontal attack—with the hope that the welcoming party wasn't equipped with either a shotgun or something fully automatic.

Instinct aids tactics, however, and not one of this team feared that

Thurley was either aware of their presence or awaiting their arrival. As they'd suspected from the start, he was angry and focused. By now, he was also drunk and fully occupied. They followed the sounds of a fracases down the length of a cluttered, smelly hallway into the darkened back bedroom, where, amid their own excited flurry of flashlight beams, they found Bud Thurley trying to throw punches at a skinny, half-dressed man who kept rolling away across a badly stained bare mattress, on which he'd been sleeping moments before.

The four cops fell on top of the pile, pulling the men apart, everyone yelling at once, until two separate clusters were huddled in opposite corners of the half-destroyed, dingy bedroom, each with a man pinned beneath it.

"Hit the lights," Joe called out to anyone who could find a switch.

An anemic fluorescent strip wrapped in cracked yellow plastic flickered alive overhead, making the scene look captured from a late forties melodrama.

Joe and Willy had the frail-looking homeowner, who appeared more exhausted than any of them. Joe released the man's arm and straightened, looking around for weapons or anything else potentially dangerous. He carefully retrieved from the floor the same large Buck Knife he'd observed on Thurley's desk earlier, its blade now exposed.

"What the hell d'you think you're doin'? Breaking into a man's house?" Thurley yelled. "This is private property."

The universal stare of astonishment he received stopped him from saying more.

Sammie, holding him in a painful armlock, shook her head. "You're shitting me," she said in an undertone.

"Take him up front and get a statement," Joe told her and Lester.

He turned toward their inadvertent host after the other three had left. "What's your name?"

The lighting didn't help, but the poor man looked truly awful. He was skeletally thin, jaundiced, sweaty, and haggard. The look wasn't helped by his being dressed only in a soiled, torn T-shirt and a pair of dubiously hued boxer shorts.

Sensing his weakness, Willy eased him onto the edge of the bed, still holding his arm, but now supportively.

"Mick," was the barely audible response, accompanied by a wet cough.

Joe sat beside him. "Keep going. Take your time, and keep in mind you're not in any trouble here. You're not in custody."

"Durocher. Mick Durocher."

"That stand for Michael?"

"Yeah. Michael. Sure."

"What's your birth date, Mick?"

Slowly, working around another cough, he gave it to them. Joe studied him more closely. The date made him forty-eight. He looked eighty.

Joe pulled out the security camera picture taken at Bromley and placed it on the bed between them. "This you riding the four-wheeler, Mick?"

Willy had retreated to the door, and gave his boss an inquiring look, his body language asking if Joe wanted to be alone. Joe released him with a subtle nod of the head.

Durocher looked at the picture and nodded. "Yeah."

Joe laid another print on top of the first, this one taken earlier, when the vehicle had been aimed uphill. "What d'you have strapped on the rear deck?"

"That's Teri," was the quiet, matter-of-fact reply.

The silence in the room encouraged Durocher to add, "Teri Parker. The girl I killed."

During this, Willy had backed into the narrow hallway, near the bathroom. At the far end of the trailer, Lester and Sam were interviewing Thurley, who was filling the air with protest. Seizing his opportunity, Willy eased into the bathroom itself.

It was a predictable pigsty, cluttered, filthy, the toilet unflushed and the shower reeking of mildew. While compulsively neat in his own life, Willy never reacted to how others chose to live. Having lived near the bottom of the heap through war, addiction, PTSD, personal loss, and more, he wasn't one to summarily condemn others. Criticize and bully when it suited him, perhaps, but rarely judge.

Besides, he had other things on his mind. Listening carefully to the conversations at both ends of the trailer, he stealthily opened the mirror over the stained sink before him.

As he'd hoped upon setting eyes on the ailing Mick Durocher, there were several orange prescription containers.

He selected the most powerful of the analgesics from among them, and slipped it into his pocket.

CHAPTER FOUR

The following morning, at their Brattleboro office, Joe waited for the last of his squad to settle down—Sammie, fresh from dropping off Emma at preschool. Recently, either she or Willy was the latecomer, since they alternated that duty. The only one without a child, Joe could only empathize with the admittedly happy responsibility his two cops had created for themselves.

It had been a long night for all of them, and they looked it, including—Joe found surprising—Willy, who routinely appeared untouched by days without sleep.

"Okay," he began, sitting on the edge of his desk. "I realize at best we've each maybe caught a short nap since processing Mick Durocher into jail, searching his trailer, seizing the four-wheeler and the rest of it, but has anyone had a chance to look into Teri Parker's background?"

Their small office occupied the second floor of the town's municipal building, an unlikely and minimally secure arrangement conjured up at the creation of the VBI, and never readdressed. Rumors were building that might change, especially since the police department, once housed downstairs, had moved into new quarters on the north end of town. Rumors, however, were all they'd amounted to so far.

Lester, while he'd dropped by his house in Springfield to take a shower and change clothes, had spent the rest of the night here, and spoke first. "Twenty-six years old, lived in Barre, on Prospect Street, according to her last Spillman entry."

Spillman was the older of two cross-indexed police databases that housed, in a perfect world, every citizen's encounter with law enforcement, criminal or not. If you were the backseat passenger in a car stopped for speeding, for example, the cop responsible was *supposed* to collect your name and date of birth, just so there was an official memory of the company you were keeping on that occasion.

It was, like most computer systems, as reliable as the people supplying its data.

"What's she down for?" Willy asked, shifting in his seat and wincing, the slight relief of the night before having evaporated.

Lester kept his eyes on his computer screen as he answered, oblivious to his colleague's pain. "All told? A couple of speeding tickets, an out-of-date inspection sticker, one prohibited act—"

"She was a hooker?" Willy asked sharply.

Lester held up a finger while he read further. "Never indicted. Picked up, but charges were dropped. Never printed, which would've been nice." He backed away from the screen. "There's more, mostly little stuff. Obviously, we'll go through all the involvements, check out who knew who. More to the point, boss, what did Mick have to tell you? He go into detail?"

Joe held up a thumb drive. "One of the most straightforward confessions I've ever gotten. After we all split up and I put him in the box, he went through Miranda and signed his waiver like he was applying for a bank loan."

They'd recently received a wall-mounted flat screen, interconnected with their computers, which allowed them to share a monitor without having to cluster around a desk. Joe plugged the drive into his laptop, entered a command, and sent the video to the display.

The camera angle showed the small windowless room that Joe had used at the Marble Valley Correctional Facility in Rutland, Vermont, not far from Manchester Center. It was white, stark, and equipped with a steel table, two chairs, and a waist-high bar attached to the wall, designed to keep prisoners cuffed in place.

As Joe escorted the faltering Durocher into view, sat him down, and ran him through Miranda, including the part where he forewent counsel, he did not bother shackling his prisoner to the wall.

He then recited Durocher's name, his own, and the date, time, and location of the interview before inquiring if his prisoner wanted anything to drink.

"No," was the response. "I killed her."

Joe, sitting opposite, studied him before asking, "Who did you kill?"

"The girl."

"What was her name, for the record?"

"Teri Parker."

"And how did you kill her?"

"With a piece of wood. A two-by-four."

"How long was it?"

Durocher thought for a moment. "Maybe four feet?"

"You don't know?"

"It was about four feet. I don't know exactly. It was a standard two-by-four."

"And where did you hit Ms. Parker?"

"The back of the head."

"How many times?"

"Once. Maybe twice. No, once."

"You aren't sure?"

"It was once, from behind. I was really pissed."

"Pissed, as in mad, or pissed drunk?"

That jarred what had been an almost robotic delivery. Durocher stopped and tilted his head, thinking back. "Both, I guess."

"What had you been drinking?"

"Beer."

"Was she drunk, too?"

"Sure."

"You guessing, or do you know?"

"She was drunk. That was beer, too."

"What brand of beer?"

Durocher stared at him. "What?"

Joe repeated the question.

"Who the fuck . . . ?" the man began, before yielding with, "Bud."

"Budweiser," Joe enunciated. "Not Bud Light?"

"Don't like it."

"How many beers had you drunk?"

His eyes grew round. "How'm I supposed to know that?"

"In six-packs, then? How many?"

"Maybe a case for the two of us."

Joe nodded for the first time, as if only now hearing something he liked. In fact, he was recalling that Teri Parker's blood alcohol content at autopsy was zero. "Where did this happen, Mick? Is it all right if I call you Mick?"

"Sure."

"Where, Mick?" Joe repeated, following a brief silence.

Durocher rested his head in one hand, his elbow on the table. "Near home."

"Manchester Center?"

"Yeah."

"Okay. Keep going. Indoors or out?"

"Out."

Joe changed positions, crossing his legs and scratching his cheek. "Mick. This is your statement. You're the one talking here. You made it clear you wanted this off your chest, and I want to honor that. But I can't read your mind. You gotta tell me what happened."

"Okay."

"Maybe we can approach it from another angle. How did you first meet Teri?"

Mick rubbed his forehead and straightened, trying to clear his thoughts. "In a bar. Manny's. I picked her up."

"Give me a break," Willy growled in real time, rippling across the tension in the squad room. "He couldn't pick up a dead cat."

"Quiet," Sam ordered.

Joe took the comment in stride. "When was this?"

"I don't know."

"Work with me, Mick. A week ago? A month? More?"

"A month," Durocher said, almost at random.

"Okay. Tell me."

"Well, you know. We hit it off for a while. Before things went bad. That's when I killed her."

"Good," Joe encouraged him. "Getting a timeline. That's helpful. Let's back up. Where's Manny's?"

"Windsor."

"You go there a lot?"

"Off and on."

"That's over an hour from your home. Why so far?"

Durocher suddenly jerked in his chair, making its legs squeal on the concrete floor. He slapped his hand on the table. "What the fuck, man?" he burst out. "Let's get this done. I killed her. She pissed me off and I whacked her."

Joe's voice sounded like a nurturing parent's. "Mick, you want people to believe you?"

Mick stared at him. "What?"

"How do we know you're not a nutcase who confesses to every murder he hears about? You see what I'm saying? We gotta make sure all the details add up, that you're the right man."

Durocher absorbed that. "Okay."

"Why were you in a bar in Windsor?"

"I had a job near there. In White River."

"Details."

"They ordered a demolition. A bunch of old factory buildings. I think it was an EPA thing, or maybe not. Anyhow, I got hired to help with the cleanup. Just shit work, draggin' stuff around. It was a huge job—more 'n a city block."

"Who'd you work for?"

"It wasn't exactly legal. A guy paid me under the table. As a favor."

"What guy?"

"Ted. That's all I got. I met him. We got to shootin' the breeze. He said he had this job and would I like to make a little cash."

"Where did you meet Ted?"

"I don't remember. Another bar."

"Manny's again?"

Durocher hesitated. "No. I don't remember. Probably near home."

"Where do you usually drink near home?"

"The Ski Pole."

"So it was there?"

"Maybe."

"Where was Ted from?"

"I didn't ask."

"How did you get to talking?"

"You just do, you know?"

"You talk to people a lot when you drink?"

"I guess. He's not gonna remember me anyhow."

"Why do you say that?"

"Like I said, it was under the table. The feds'll bust his balls if he said he offered me a job. He'll deny it."

Joe backed away from the topic. "So you got the cleanup job in White River Junction. Is that when you started going to Manny's, or did you already know about it?"

"I started then."

"There're no bars in White River?"

"I heard about Manny's, and I didn't want to drink near where I was workin'."

"About how many times do you think you went there, grand total?"

Durocher straightened from the slump he'd resumed. "Jesus. Who the fuck knows?"

"I sure don't, Mick. You tell me."

"Not many. Two, three. As long as the job lasted."

"Earlier, you said you went there off and on. Which is it?"

Mick's eyes narrowed. "You calling me a liar?"

Joe dropped it to keep him talking. "And you met Teri on one of those occasions?"

"Yeah."

"Tell me about that."

"Not much to tell. We hit it off, we fucked in my truck, I went home."

"Where did she live?"

"Don't know. Didn't ask."

"But you kept in touch," Joe suggested.

"Yeah. The next night."

"What happened then?"

"Same thing, only I brought her home."

Not a man given to self-admiration, Joe had been studying himself on the screen through all this, judging his own performance. Despite the hundreds of such encounters he'd conducted, not one had ever gone as he'd planned.

This was proceeding fine, for what Joe considered largely a piece of fiction on Mick's part. Believing that, and of course knowing how the interview went, allowed him now to daydream a little, if only for a moment, and drift back to his first encounter with Teri Parker, lying exposed on Beverly's autopsy table. Who knew then, seeing this slip of a girl—pretty, young, and momentarily without a history—what memories and experiences had died with her? He recalled how melancholy had been the revelations of her past, as he'd laboriously extracted them from purportedly the last man in her life.

He watched as he continued to ride herd on Durocher's narrative, getting him to explain, piece by piece, how Teri and he had begun an on-again, off-again relationship of "a few" weeks.

Joe had listened to so many such stories, of almost feral couplings largely free of shared dinners, or movie dates, or thoughtful chats about hopes and ambitions. Steeped in booze or drugs, unimpressed by consequences, and driven by a short-term hunger for pleasure and oblivion, the participants in these romances barely exchanged names, much less personal details. By the time Mick Durocher described hitting his lover across the nape of the neck with that two-by-four, in a deserted park-and-ride lot not far from his trailer, Joe found himself in the dreariest corner of human behavior in which his job so routinely deposited him, surrounded by the loss, waste, and malice of others.

He loved his job—the people, the puzzles, the pursuit of answers—but this particular insight was always the part he could live without, and without which he couldn't proceed.

He left his reverie behind as the interview changed topics.

"All right," he addressed his unhappy guest on the video. "You told me you hit her once or twice—you think just once. What happened then?"

"I got rid of the body."

Joe shook his head repeatedly. "No, no, no. Mick, just like we been doing. Step by step. What did you do with the two-by-four?"

Durocher sighed. "Christ Almighty. I dropped it. That work?"

"If that's what you did. We likely to find it there?"

The other man stopped short. "I don't know."

"Why not?"

"You leave stuff lying around, it gets stolen."

"Like a piece of wood in a parking lot?"

The reply was aggressive again. "*Yeah*, like that."

Once more, Joe let it be. "About what time was this?"

"Middle of the night. I don't know. I don't wear a watch."

"So, you dropped the piece of wood. Then what?"

"I had to move her."

"Why?"

Mick stared at him, his mouth slightly open. "What?"

"I asked why," Joe repeated, explaining, "You've told me several times you killed her. You can't seem to get this confession over fast enough. And yet you went to a lot of trouble to distance yourself from the body. Why?"

"I panicked. I mighta been able to get away with it, if she was found far from my home. I only copped to it after you busted me. It's not like I showed up and turned myself in."

"Fair enough," Joe accommodated him. "So, there you are. Teri's dead at your feet, you've dropped the two-by-four. What next?"

"I tried to figure out what to do with her. That's when I remembered the Run Around."

"What's that?"

"The trail on Bromley. That is where you found her, wasn't it, at the top?"

"Yeah, yeah," Joe answered, although his voice betrayed a moment's confusion. He hadn't known the mountain's proprietary name for the location. The police had referred to either the Appalachian or Long Trail. But he had also been thrown by Durocher's logic, given all the handy, out-of-the-way streams, ditches, and cellar holes between Manchester and Bromley.

Joe kept going. "How did you know about that spot?"

"I worked on Bromley once. Most people have around here, one time or another."

"Officially?" Joe asked. "Or was it like the job in White River?"

Durocher smiled for the first time. "Like that."

"How long ago?"

"A few years. I don't know."

"Who hired you?"

"He's gone—quit. I forget anyhow."

There was a pause before Joe resumed. "Okay, so you figured out where to put her. Why didn't you just dump her in your truck and take her there?"

Durocher seemed genuinely startled. "In that thing? It'd be tough enough in a four-wheel drive, but that heap can barely handle flat pavement. Plus, it's busted right now. I'm waitin' on a part. Nah . . . I knew how to do it. I just had to figure out the details."

"Meaning?"

"I had to get a four-wheeler. I knew where one was. Thurley always had a couple, mostly for scouting timber sites. And I knew where he kept the keys. I just had to put the pieces together."

"By which, you mean the body, the four-wheeler, and the dump site?"

"Yeah. I had to get to where the four-wheeler was."

"How did you know Thurley?"

"I worked for him, too."

"Why did that end?"

"He said I stole a couple of chain saws. I didn't. He was trying to collect on insurance to get new saws. He needed a bad guy. So he fired me to make it look good."

"How did you reach the four-wheeler?"

"Hitched a ride. Called a buddy and asked him to take me to Thurley's." He paused before adding, "Well, not Thurley's exactly, but close enough to walk there. I didn't want my buddy to know what was up."

"In the middle of the night?"

"Sure. Seth Villeneuve. You can ask him."

"You remember his name?"

"Why wouldn't I?"

"It's just unusual for you," Joe said. "Is that what happened? Seth drove you there?"

"Yeah."

"He didn't ask why?"

"Sure he did. I told him he didn't wanna know. That was good enough for him."

"All right. What happened next?"

"I walked up to the site, got the key, took the four-wheeler, and rode back for the body."

"Which you'd put where in the meantime?"

"By the side of the lot. I covered her with some brush."

"Brush you cut, or brush that was lying around?"

Again, there was that exasperation. "Lying around."

"What did it consist of? Old leaves, muck from the ditch, trimmed branches?"

"I don't *know*," he burst out. "Who cares? I just didn't want her seen, and it was only gonna be for a little while. I think it was branches."

"So you rode all the way from Thurley's back home to get the body, then back again to Bromley, then back home one last time, all in the middle of the night, and all using the highway?"

"Right."

"Anyone see you?"

A second smile, this one sadder. "They must've. Here we are."

Joe placed both forearms on the table and asked, "Speaking of that, didn't you know about Bromley's security system? Their cameras?"

Mick's voice sounded depressed. "I forgot. Till too late."

"When was that?"

"I saw a camera on the pole, right by the road I used. Guess I knew I was screwed then."

"Why didn't you move the body? Or at least return the four-wheeler? You could've called your pal to pick you up. That would've hidden your tracks better."

"It didn't matter," Durocher replied tiredly. "By the time I saw the camera, I knew it was over. I didn't mean to kill her. I just got pissed. But a couple of hours later, after all that runnin' around, and then seeing it'd been a total waste of time, I just didn't care no more."

"How do you think Thurley knew it was you that stole the four-wheeler?" Joe asked, pretending he'd never showed Thurley any proof.

Mick didn't hesitate. "I'd used it before. My truck breaks down a lot. After hitching a ride to the work site once, Bud said I could use the four-wheeler to commute if I was ever 'tween a rock and a hard place for transport. It didn't last. He's a jerk that way—later told me I was abusing his generosity and the deal was off. Sooner or later, I woulda been busted by some cop anyhow—that thing doesn't have plates."

Joe flexed his shoulders and twisted his neck to ease a crick before asking, "You're not a violent man, Mick. I checked your record. What made you so angry? And why were you and Teri down the road from your place, in that lot?"

"She was trying to get away."

"Why? Had you hit her in the trailer?"

"Yeah."

"There were no marks on her."

Durocher swallowed. "I pushed her. She fell onto the sofa."

"What was the fight about?"

"I don't know. What're they ever about? Total bullshit."

"Was it because she told you she was pregnant?"

Mick stared at him, his back stiffening. "What?"

"She was. Several weeks along."

"That's crap."

"Depending on your viewpoint, that means you killed two people."

In slow motion, Durocher slid back into a slouch, his hands in his lap, his shoulders slumped. "I don't wanna talk no more."

"We still have a lot to cover."

"You do it. I'm done."

In the squad room, Joe leaned forward and hit a button on his computer, freezing the picture there. "This actually goes on for another fifteen minutes or so, but with nothing new," Joe explained. "Impressions?" he added.

A moment's silence greeted him, followed by Willy saying, "I can't swear to it, but that may be the biggest crock of shit I ever heard. Pathetic. He didn't even try making it credible."

Sammie took that as a given and added in a businesslike tone, "Which means we got to find out who really killed Teri Parker."

CHAPTER FIVE

Lester Spinney pulled into his driveway in a leafy, middle-class neighborhood north of Springfield's downtown. He killed the engine and paused a moment to take in the view.

It wasn't a vista of undulating hills, populated with lush green trees under an azure sky. It was in fact his garage, attached to his modest suburban home, and probably due for a good washing, a coat of paint, or both.

But it was home, had been for a couple of decades, and represented his and his wife, Sue's, combined efforts to build a life, plant a spiritual flag, and supply a springboard for their kids, Wendy and Dave—the latter of whom seemed already well on his way, working for the local sheriff's office in law enforcement.

It wasn't much by the standards of a culture hell-bent on material possessions. But Lester had always been driven by other ambitions. Despite working with a head case like Kunkle, a quasi-obsessive workaholic like Sammie, and an Obi-Wan imitation like Joe, Lester comfortably saw himself as a regular guy. He'd lived in this town all his life, married his high school sweetheart, always been a cop, and was looking forward to enjoying a full career and a long retirement.

A knock on the glass by his head made him jump. His wife was looking at him, smiling but concerned.

"You okay?" she asked as he rolled down his window.

He poked his head out for a kiss. "Yeah. I was just taking in the homestead."

"Wanna replace it with something spiffier, like a trailer?" she asked, opening his door. "Be easier to maintain."

He took her in as he got out, trim and comfortably dressed in jeans and a work shirt. "I'm not used to seeing you out of your scrubs. You're lookin' good, girl."

She laughed and wrapped her arms around him, standing on her toes to reach his neck. The man was still surprisingly tall to her. "Get used to it," she warned him. "The new job's making me understand what they mean by 'banker's hours.'"

"You complaining?" he asked, resting his hands on her back and feeling her warmth beneath the fabric.

"God, no. I'm actually doing things around here. I was out back, laying out the garden, when I heard you drive up."

He nuzzled her hair. "I noticed you were kinda warm."

He circled his hands around to cup the sides of her breasts as he went in for a more convincing kiss.

She responded by pushing him against the car with her pelvis. "The neighbors're gonna enjoy this."

"More than we do their fights," he said, his voice slightly muffled. He slipped one hand higher and undid her top button. "The house empty?"

"Funny you should mention that," she said, breaking away and leading him toward the front door by the hand.

"So what *were* you thinking about in the car?" Sue asked him later in bed, daylight still showing through the windows. They'd remained entwined, and were slightly damp with sweat.

"Not this," he admitted. "I like the fringe benefits of your new employment."

She had worked as a nurse for almost as many years as he'd been a cop, the majority of them at Springfield's in-town hospital. But her friend Victoria Garlanda's offer to join her at Upper Valley Surgical Specialists, a short commute up the interstate, had been too good to ignore.

"I was mulling over a new case," he told his wife.

Sue propped herself up on one elbow. "The woman they found on Bromley?" she asked.

He rolled his eyes. "Unbelievable," he said. "The internet saying who did it, too? Might help us out."

She looked at him questionably. "No, but they're saying you have the guy in jail. Didn't you get the memo?"

Lester sighed. "Yes and no. We're thinking he didn't do it."

"Why'd you arrest him, then?" she asked, rolling out of bed to be presentable for their daughter's return from high school soccer practice. Lester shifted positions to take her in as she moved around the room, collecting her tossed-off clothing. In Lester's eyes, which he believed professionally objective, Sue remained as desirable and attractive as she'd been when they were first married.

"Looked like a slam dunk," he said, knowing she would treat everything he said in strictest confidence. "Including some glaring evidence. But his confession was crap. None of us take it seriously, meaning we spent most of the day backtracking through what he said."

She paused buttoning up her shirt. "What's that do to the case?"

"Good question," he allowed. "Finding out who really did the dirty deed'll be helped if we can prove this fella didn't."

"And the only thing you've got is that you don't like his confession?" she asked doubtfully.

Reluctantly, he, too, arose and began getting dressed, although in more casual clothes, like Sue's. "Remember the Sherlock Holmes story about the dog that didn't bark?"

"I've heard the saying. I wasn't sure where it came from."

"Well, I can't quote it," he confessed. "But it falls under the category of evidence sometimes being the absence of what you're expecting to find. With this guy—Mick Durocher—we had the body, pictures of him carrying it to the dump site, a confession, and his claim that he'd known the victim for the last month."

"Okay," she said slowly, taking her turn to enjoy watching him.

He caught her look, pulled on a T-shirt, and smiled, giving her another kiss as he opened the bedroom door and ushered her down the hall toward the kitchen.

"But his confession had holes from start to finish." He continued as they walked. "He said he met a contractor at a bar who set him up with a job in a town where he later met the girl. But he couldn't remember the man's name or anything about him, and the bar and the town were across the state from each other. Then he said he used to work at Bromley, except we'd already shown his picture around and got no hits at all, even from the old-timers."

They reached the kitchen, where he began to automatically prepare himself a cup of coffee while Sue opened the fridge door to find inspiration for dinner. "When he supposedly spilled his guts to Joe," Lester continued, "he went into how he and the girl had had a fight, and she stormed out, and he caught up to her in a parking lot down the road. Joe asked if he'd hit her—if that's what got her so worked up. Course he said, 'Yeah,' whereupon Joe said there wasn't a mark on her to show it."

"You cops are so manipulative," Sue said from inside the fridge.

"Whatever," he said. "So, he countered by saying he'd pushed her onto the sofa. First of all, give me a break!" he exclaimed, warming to his subject. "Why not say he hit her with a stuffed teddy bear? Second, I saw that sofa. We're not talking stretch Barcalounger here. It was completely covered with tools, bottles, and other junk. You toss somebody onto that thing, it would leave a mark."

Sue emerged from her explorations, holding a couple of items. She gave him a leery glance. "That sounds slim."

"Okay, I'll give you that," he said. "But you weren't there. It just *sounded* so wonky. I drove back to Manchester Center this afternoon, to check some of it out. No two-by-four, which he said he used to thump her on the head. No pile of branches, which he said he used to hide her while he got a ride to steal the four-wheeler. And no recollections by any neighbors about a noisy fight, a visiting girlfriend, or any guests ever being at his place. According to them—and I mean, all of them—Mr. Durocher might as well be a monk. They'd see him around, working on his heap of a truck, maybe, or just coming and going, but otherwise, not a peep."

"He friendly, at least?" she asked.

"Yeah," he answered. "Which is another thing. He didn't yell at people, never seemed angry. He just kept to himself. Nobody had a bad word to say about him. Not like most short-fuse lady-killers I know."

She came up to him with the two artifacts she'd extracted from the fridge. "And you know so many, too," she said sweetly, adding, "Last night's casserole? Or Tuesday's meat loaf?"

He hesitated. "Pizza?" he suggested meekly.

She smiled and nodded. "Done," she said. "But one of these gets eaten tomorrow."

"Got it. Oh, and I didn't mention the whole crazy thing about where he dumped the body—out in the open, where anybody could find it, but at the top, where he could be caught on video? *Really?* After driving up and down the highway on a stolen four-by-four in the middle of the night, *with a dead body on the back?*" Lester was laughing by now.

"And then," he added, "since it was late enough, I went to Mick's favorite watering hole to talk to the bartender as he was opening up. Young man, son of the owner, knew Mick well. There again, a completely different picture from what we were told. Mick said he met both the contractor and the dead girl at bars. Joe asked him specifically about that:

'Are you a chatty drunk or a recluse?' Or words to that effect. Mick painted himself as the former—at least enough that he got a job and got laid, both, on two separate occasions, which is more than I ever got back in the day."

"Poor baby," Sue cooed from across the room.

"But here's the kicker: The barkeep said Mick never says a word. Half the time, he doesn't even order; the bartender just knows to serve him a beer and keep 'em coming. He sits at a corner table, always alone, getting more and more depressed.

"Oh," Lester then added, almost spilling his freshly poured coffee in his enthusiasm, "and I forgot. He told Joe that he and the girl went through a case of beer on the night she died. I found a single six-pack of empties in the trailer. There were trash bags in the truck bed, for can deposits, but they were covered in dust kicked up from the road, so they'd been there awhile. You don't get two people smashed on six beers, especially not if you got a liver like Mick Durocher's, which'll probably end up in a museum. Plus, her tox results reported no alcohol in her system at all."

"He have any kids?" she asked out of the blue.

"A daughter. They're estranged," he replied. "At least according to one neighbor. Mick mentioned her, but she's never been by. Why?"

"Don't know. Just a mother's question, I guess. What about the friend who gave him a ride?" she asked. "That sounds worth looking into. 'Hey, Frank, I need to dump a body—help me out?' Might be something you'd remember."

Lester laughed. "It does, doesn't it? Why didn't I think of that?"

She gave him a warning look. "We could have meat loaf, after all."

"No, no. You'll be glad to know that great minds think alike—in this case, yours and Willy's. He got that assignment." Lester checked his watch. "He's probably dropping in on the man as we speak. We were told he'd be off work about now."

* * *

Seth Villeneuve lived in a section of Manchester Center that proved that even a town with its elitist reputation couldn't consist entirely of mansions and upscale businesses, regardless of its chamber of commerce's rosy portrayal.

However, Willy Kunkle was also not expecting any tar paper shack as he pulled to the curb. Indeed, the six-unit apartment complex in question was outwardly neat and inconspicuous, as tidy in appearance as all the homes on this admittedly backwater street.

He assessed his surroundings before leaving the car. According to his research, Willy thought Villeneuve should be home. This time slot fit the magic few minutes between when someone returned from work and felt the urge to hit the bars—if so inclined. Willy had looked into Villeneuve's past record, and knew for a fact that he was.

But Willy was an old drinker, too, whose recovery was partially based on not forgetting the yearnings and habits of yore—memories that were becoming poisonously corrosive now that his arm had caught fire and he'd started to make a diet of other people's pain pills.

He rested the nape of his neck against the car's headrest for a moment, watching the rearview mirror and the windows out of habit, but not with any focus—barely able to even push his thoughts through the pain long enough to address the task at hand.

That his well-known watchfulness—honed during years of active military service—was being undermined by this searing distraction only increased his distress. To his way of thinking, such vigilance had kept him alive in combat, and served him well in life. The fact that others often described it as paranoia in no way reduced its effectiveness.

Until now.

With a final push of self-will, he straightened, opened his door, and stepped out onto the sidewalk.

Villeneuve's apartment was on the first floor, a vulnerable location Willy never would have chosen. As he crossed the street, he saw that at least one of its lights was on.

He was in luck. The door opened to the second knock, revealing a tall, heavy man in a scruffy beard, jeans, and a Grateful Dead T-shirt. He was holding a can of beer.

"Yeah?" he asked in a neutral voice.

"You Seth?" Willy asked casually.

"I know you?"

Willy showed his badge. "Not yet."

Villeneuve stiffened and scowled. "What d'you want?"

"What d'you have to worry about?" Willy shot back.

"Nothin'."

"Then you won't have a problem inviting me in."

The big man hesitated.

"Will you," Willy stated, not as a question.

"No. I guess not."

"Then do it."

Villeneuve moved away from the door, leaving it open.

Willy followed him into a typically messy bachelor's pad, furnished no doubt by the landlord in Walmart colonial. A grease-stained pizza box was on the coffee table, empty cans were scattered across the floor, commingling with discarded clothes. Dirty glasses, old newspapers, unopened mail, plastic bags, and other domestic fallout decorated the counters and kitchen table. It was essentially a one-room apartment with a small bedroom to one side, beside the bathroom. Willy took most of it in with a single glance.

He pointed to the sofa. "Sit."

His reluctant host complied, asking in a belligerent voice, "What's wrong with your arm?"

Willy stood opposite him, looking down. He ignored the question. "How do you know Mick Durocher?"

"Who?"

The response was hardly original; the effect of it on Willy was startling and unexpected. As he shifted his weight slightly to reply, an excruciating bolt of pain shot down his arm.

He disguised its effect by violently kicking aside the coffee table, placing his foot between the other man's stockinged feet, pulling out his gun, and stabbing it between Villeneuve's eyes, knocking the man's head back against the wall behind him.

"*Answer the fucking question,*" Willy ordered him, his mouth half open to breathe through the torment, and his vision reverting to an earlier scene, decades ago, when he'd used this same gesture to extract information from an enemy soldier. The vision was so jarring and incongruous, he had to shake his head to beat it back.

Villeneuve gasped, his hands out to his sides, open in supplication. "Yeah, yeah. I know him. What the fuck, man? Who the hell *are* you?"

"Tell me about two nights ago," Willy said, pushing harder with the gun and trying not to follow his PTSD to its roots born in combat.

"You're no cop."

Willy drew back the gun, readying to strike Villeneuve across the face. In fact, he was in total agreement, bewildered by the same realization. But who *was* he right now? And what was he about to do? "*Are you stupid?*" he shouted. "Answer the question."

The terrified man brought his hands in for protection, cupping his own face. "I gave him a ride. That's all."

"Where to?"

"Up the road, beyond the mountain, on Route 11. Nowhere, man. I dropped him off by the side of the road. That's what he asked for."

Willy repeated his threatening gesture, desperately trying to stave off more flashbacks and return to the present. Villeneuve brought his knees up into a quasi-fetal position. "No, no. Wait. I'm telling the truth."

"He call you up?"

"What? Yeah. Outta nowhere, in the middle of the night. 'I'm in a jam,' he says. 'Ya gotta help me out.' So I did."

Willy started to recover. Villeneuve's voice and his own began to sound clearer in his head. "What kind of jam?"

"He wouldn't tell me. I asked, but he wouldn't say. Said it was better that way. 'The less you know, the better,' he said, and he asked me not to tell nobody. That's all I was doing. Just helpin' a friend."

Willy considered grilling him harder, hoping it might help him with his journey back to the here and now. But another jolt of pain brought him up short, frightening him with its potential. He was feeling so far outside the modern, hard-won identity he'd been projecting these last years that he had no idea what he might do next to this miserable man.

"Fuck it," he said out loud, speaking only to himself.

He straightened, holstered the gun, and strode toward the door. On a shelf, to the right as he crossed the room, was a half-empty bottle of vodka. He grabbed it as he went by.

"*Hey*," Villeneuve yelled. "Who the fuck you think you are, asshole?"

Willy stopped at the door and looked back at him, then glanced down at the bottle, there seemingly by magic.

He dropped it as if it had suddenly caught fire, hearing it thud on the floor as he answered. "Welcome Wagon."

He half ran across the street to his car, and drove away before Villeneuve was inspired to look out the window and record his registration.

The throbbing yielded slightly to the new environment, helping in his recovery. At least he could concentrate on the traffic and manage the wheel with his one hand, aided by the attached knob.

Of the whole event, the burning discomfort, the trauma-inspired trip down memory lane, even the pressure of his finger on the trigger hadn't been the most disconcerting, much less the terror he'd instilled in Seth Villeneuve. It was Willy's instinctive grabbing of that bottle that had shaken him most. The PTSD, the visions of combat-born violence and death, those he was used to from almost nightly flashbacks. But the feel of the heavy, smooth glass bottle in his hand, its contents sloshing gently, promising relief and temporary oblivion—that was something else.

Despite the odds and everyone's advice, he'd beaten his dependence alone, without help or guidance from the likes of AA. But this pain, this new and agonizing addition to an old disability—now compounded by a growing reliance on painkillers—had clearly led to a disorienting and stunningly self-destructive act he hadn't seen coming.

He was a man plagued by apprehension, which helped fuel his outer show of confidence. He questioned his worth as a father, a mate, a reliable colleague, a worthy member of society. His past lapses and addiction had all contributed to the orchestra in his head, making him no stranger to struggles with uncertainty.

But seeing that bottle appear magically in his hand, instead of merely sitting temptingly nearby, had shoved it all aside. Alcoholism was the closest of his devils. After putting it behind him so long ago, its leering reappearance—and in such a manner—had been a jarring, telling, deeply emotional blow.

Willy realized, absolutely, that he was in real trouble.

CHAPTER SIX

Bud Thurley had been put on ice in Rutland's regional correctional facility following his one-man, hang-'em-high vigilante routine at Mick Durocher's trailer. He'd been arraigned for two felonies, neither of which guaranteed incarceration in this often frustratingly lenient state, despite their having been witnessed by three cops. But he'd drawn a rare by-the-rules judge, and instead, he hadn't even been granted bail. He had been assigned a public defender, however, who'd agreed to a meeting between Joe and Thurley, having been assured by the AG that it would only benefit his client.

The setting was a replica of where Joe had spoken earlier to Mick Durocher, like so many other small, square, beige rooms across Vermont, and indeed the country, equipped with metal tables, wall-mounted restraint bars, and a red-eyed camera mounted in one corner.

Entering in cuffs, Thurley was sporting a predictable, tiresome, and conventional swagger, which looked faintly comical given his short, beer barrel physique. "The fuck do *you* want?" he asked as he recognized Gunther.

Joe indicated the chair across from him. "Just to talk, as I'm guessing your lawyer already told you."

Thurley didn't have much choice in the matter, given the agreed-upon terms. But he kept his attitude as he was seated by his escort and attached to the wall, to which Joe didn't object, and—interestingly—neither did Thurley's counsel.

The lawyer was in his late forties, with too-long hair, an awkward way of mis-coordinating his clothes—including a pair of clogs on his feet—and an expression suggesting that he'd rather be elsewhere. Joe got the impression that Thurley scared the man.

"I don't got to talk with you. Those're my rights."

Joe ignored him to shake hands with the lawyer, who introduced himself as Caleb Nulty.

"I'm not here to discuss the other night," Joe told Thurley, nodding his thanks to the corrections officer, who left them alone.

"Then I definitely don't got to talk to you."

"You don't. But as Mr. Nulty no doubt told you, you might want to," Joe assured him. "It can only be to your benefit."

Thurley frowned dramatically, acting like Nulty wasn't in the room. "How?"

"It could lighten your charges," Joe explained. "Right now, you're facing unlawful trespass, burglary, and aggravated assault."

"*Burglary?*" Thurley burst out. "What the fuck? He stole my stuff."

"Yes," Joe explained evenly, "and you broke into his place uninvited, with a lethal weapon and premeditated intent to harm. Ask him." He pointed at Nulty, who merely nodded.

"Altogether," Joe kept going, "those could cost you forty-eight years in here, or out of state, for that matter, and twenty-two thousand bucks."

"That's crap."

"Maybe, but it's the law, and what you did was witnessed by three police officers. That's a tough rap to beat."

Thurley scowled, but remained silent.

Nulty at last took the opportunity to say softly, "This meeting will help significantly."

Joe suggested, "Help yourself out."

"That fucker stole my shit and I only did what anybody would do in my place."

"That's for you to work out with Mr. Nulty and the prosecutor, Bud," Joe said. "Like I said, I'm not here to discuss that. I want to know about Mick Durocher, which is why what you say might reduce your charges."

Thurley crossed his arms, a bad sign in general, but asked nevertheless, "What about him?"

By his nature, Thurley didn't strike Joe as someone inclined to cooperate with anyone about anything. It ran against his culture and past experience. But Joe was hoping that in this instance, he also wouldn't see the harm. It wasn't like he'd been asked to implicate a buddy or violate an unwritten oath.

"Go ahead, then," Bud said tentatively.

"When did he come work for you?" Joe began, not letting the man deny that he'd ever met Durocher, as he had at their first meeting.

"I don't know. It's not like I keep records of guys like him."

"Meaning off-the-books workers?"

Thurley hesitated, to which Joe added, "It's not a legal question. Not with what you're facing. Let me put it another way: When did he stop working for you?"

Thurley smiled slightly. "Yeah, that is easier. That was just before the snow blew. I always lay people off around then."

Joe thought back. "So, this winter, around early December."

"Yeah, more or less."

"You didn't lay him off, though. You fired him, for theft."

Caleb Nulty looked up nervously, but was cut off by Thurley laughing. "That what he told you? He is such a fool. He tell you why?"

"You accused him of stealing a couple of chain saws."

Thurley remained amused. "Sure did. He was pissed. I even told him it was so I could collect the insurance on 'em. Classic, huh?"

"I'm not sure—" Nulty began.

Joe cut him off. "That's not what you did?"

"With my deductible? Nothin' to collect. I was just fuckin' with him."

Thurley suddenly sat forward, as if swapping stories with a pal. Joe half suspected he liked that Joe had been rude to his lawyer. "Stupid bastard couldn't figure out that I'd have to file a police report. What a moron. And then I'd have to tell 'em I'd been payin' him off the books."

"What did happen to the saws, out of curiosity?" Joe asked.

"Nothin'!" Thurley exclaimed happily. "I just made it up. I woulda laid him off anyhow, 'cause of the time of year, but this gave me a kick."

Joe shook his head in wonder. "Well, he's a believer."

Thurley took that as a compliment, which Joe used to become more conversational. "What was he like, generally? Chatty, quiet? A hard worker, at least?"

"Nah. Dumb as a box of rocks. Had to tell him everything three times. That's kinda why I fucked with his head—for fun."

"How 'bout during lunch break every day?" Joe persisted. "People shoot the shit, open up a little. Did you get to know him some?"

"Some," Thurley admitted.

"You knew where he lived," Joe suggested.

"Yeah, we went drinking a couple of times. He liked the Ski Pole. I think it's a dump, but it's what you do to keep your employees happy, right?"

Joe nodded, thinking Thurley was the last man on earth he'd consult about employee relations. "What did you learn about him?"

"Nothin' much. Usual. No wife, kid who won't talk to him. Life headin' nowhere. Same ol', same ol'."

"Where's the kid?" Joe asked.

"Massachusetts somewhere. He was a real pain in the ass about her. Goin' on and on about how bad he felt. How he shoulda done better by her. Best thing he ever did was lose her, I bet. Besides, what kid wants a father like him?"

"You get a name on her?"

"Nah. Well, maybe, but I don't remember."

"How 'bout an age?"

"She's grown. Could be married, even, have one of her own. It's all pretty vague. We weren't there to chitchat."

"Girlfriend?" Joe continued.

Thurley laughed again. "Mick? A girlfriend? Jesus, man. You seen him? An inflatable doll would cut her wrists before doin' him."

Joe took out the morgue portrait of Teri Parker and slid it across the table. "What about her?"

Thurley peered at it with interest, as did Nulty. "She dead?"

"Yeah."

He grinned and looked up. "She kill herself after meeting him?"

"No," Joe said evenly. "You ever see her? Anywhere?"

"Nah. Cute, though. I wouldn't've minded it."

Joe studied him a moment, considering, not for the first time, the company he so often kept.

Angie Hogencamp touched the visor of her hard hat from habit before giving a thumbs-up to the forklift operator and waiting for him to swap out his machine for a chair against the wall. She then mounted her own electrically powered, massive mobile battery puller, equipped with a steel exoskeleton frame, and quickly extracted the operator's drained, one-thousand-pound battery from the forklift's side, exchanging it for a fresh one she had ready to go on the platform before her.

The forklift driver returned to his recharged unit and sped away, beeping his horn quickly as he reached the corner and vanished from sight, while Angie trundled slowly down the twin-banked aisle of stacked batteries to place the depleted cell into a charging station and swap it with a newly energized one. Once she'd checked its fluid levels, she was ready for the next exchange.

GreenField Grocers was a billion-dollar-a-year business, impressive until compared to operations like C&S Wholesale Grocers in Brattleboro, Keene, and elsewhere, which had been quoted at up to thirty times that size. Nevertheless, GreenField employed hundreds of people, ran its own fleet of trucks, was renowned among lesser-skilled and -educated people like Angie for its liberal hiring practices, and considered a benevolent and generous financial force within White River Junction.

That, not surprisingly, was one of the primary reasons for GreenField having chosen this site, along with the railroad junction that many believed gave the town its name—actually due to the confluence of two rivers. As a bonus, there was the small but well-appointed Lebanon Municipal Airport just across the water in New Hampshire.

Angie, naturally, didn't pay heed to most of this. She was just happy to have a job that didn't involve being groped or stared at as she cleared tables or poured drinks. Here, she wore construction boots and a hard hat, had developed a limited but valued set of skills, and was mostly regarded as just another member of the general warehouse population.

Her specific job was battery changer, whereby she maintained the health of just under 150 electrically driven floor jacks, forklifts, hi-lows, and other so-called material-handling equipment, or MHEs. They, in turn, were designed to move the never-ending flow of laden pallets that entered, were stored at, and got shipped out of the huge warehouse.

Every one of these MHEs had big, heavy, lead-acid, deep-cycle batteries, each of which needed regular monitoring. Specifically, they needed charging, and to have their water levels checked, so that their volatile, sulfuric-acid-and-water electrolyte contents never got low enough to burst into flame. Given the size of the building—almost a half-million square feet by forty-five feet high—and its dizzying inventory—consisting of almost every item available at an average supermarket—any mishap would be disastrous.

Angie's job, mundane at first glance, amounted to a form of critical health insurance for every person within these towering walls.

She paused a moment to stretch her back as she readied to swap out the next four MHEs standing in line, and caught sight of a tiny flash of color high overhead, pressed against the distant ceiling like a bright orange moth silhouetted against a dark sky.

A "supe," as they were called—one of the supervisory staff that patrolled the warehouse—kept track, depending on your perspective, of either the vital functions of the place, or the performance of its employees. Angie was of the latter believers, having once been caught smoking inside the building.

She squinted at the tiny figure clad in a fluorescent safety vest, four stories above, looking down from a narrow catwalk, but she couldn't decipher a thing about it, including its gender. The distances in this facility were just too vast. It was like working in the Pentagon, but with all the floors and walls removed.

For his part, the supe in question was enjoying himself. You had to like heights to be up here. The catwalks were higher than even the tops of the innumerable steel pallet racks that stood like library shelves, rank upon rank, across the length of the warehouse. Indeed, the supe had only to casually reach overhead to touch the rough-textured metal ceiling.

Adding to the drama of the yawning space below was the fact that it was always almost completely dark. There were security lights, providing a permanent crepuscule, but otherwise, the illumination came solely from thousands of motion-detecting LEDs, flicking on and off in response to the endlessly scurrying MHEs. The constant succession of stuttering lights eased the supe's job in one way, letting him see what was moving far below, and in what direction. The small whirring vehicles made him think of lab rats in a maze, each equipped with a radio beacon.

His primary thoughts, however, were taken by other matters today, and his focus on Angie Hogencamp went beyond any supervisory role. Right now, he was not actually a supe, but merely posing as one, using his knowledge of the plant's layout and habits to achieve his goal, and using Angie's unwitting assistance in the process.

Her role was now completed, as far as he was concerned, and so he continued walking, godlike above them all, to a more centralized vantage spot. Floating up like a faint mist was the tinny piped-in music some HR dimwit had thought would placate the workers, and the endless rushing of electric MHEs on the run, accompanied by their steady chorus of nervous horn beeps.

His tension rising as the minutes ticked by, the counterfeit supe watched the rows of lights coming on as five freshly serviced MHEs in particular dispersed to various corners of the property, like spiders checking the perimeter of a mutual web.

Finally, he saw what he was looking for. A distant hubbub of shouts, corresponding with a cluster of overhead lights staying on in a far corner of the cavernous chamber, indicating an uptick in activity. He smiled, relaxed a bit, and rested his forearms on the catwalk's railing, watching and waiting, the lone spectator to his own play.

A fire alarm went off as a plume of smoke rose into view above the serried ranks of building-sized pallet racks, gently flattening against the ceiling at the supe's eye level, although far enough away not to be a bother.

The lights began spreading outward, mimicking the smoke. The hubbub increased and was transformed into loudspeaker announcements and alarms, making the whole mix an inchoate flood of reverberating noise.

The supe checked his watch and shifted position, strolling along the catwalk for a better angle. In the meantime, at the source of the first fire, he heard an organized response coming together. It wouldn't be long before the municipal fire departments from Hartford and beyond would be summoned as backup.

He stopped where he had a sightline along the axis of one of the aisles. At the end of it, as expected, some two hundred feet diagonally down from him, he saw a floor jack parked, abandoned and askew, its operator leaping from its steering platform and backing away from where smoke was spewing from its battery compartment.

"Come on, baby," he said softly to himself. "Do your stuff."

As if heeding his encouragement, the floor jack burst into flame, causing the operator to run yelling to the end of the aisle, waving his arms for attention.

There would be three more exothermic outbreaks, as the supe had heard them referred to in his research, and with them increasingly dangerous smoke, more firefighters, and especially, the cops.

Disappointingly, it had come time to leave.

CHAPTER SEVEN

"What's wrong with you?"

Willy looked up, startled that Sam had gotten so close to him unnoticed. For a man as twitchy about personal space as he, it was tantamount to having fallen asleep at the wheel.

He'd actually been leaning against the wall of their darkened hallway at home, immobilized by another of his paralyzing attacks.

"I'm fine," he managed.

"The hell you are," she countered. "You look like shit and you've been acting like a jerk."

Without warning, she reached out, peeled back his eyelid, and stabbed his pupil with the beam of a small light he hadn't noticed in her hand. He twisted away, making a grab for her wrist that she easily evaded.

"I thought so," she said bitterly. "Un-fucking-believable. What're you on?"

"Oxys," he said in a half sob, semi-blinded and yielding to the pain by clutching his limp arm. He folded over and slid down the wall to sit on the floor, his knees tucked up.

She stared at him, momentarily confounded, her fury blunted by his ready admission and sudden debility. This man, whom she'd known for so long and trusted so deeply, had never once exhibited such a degree of frailty.

She reached out again, this time to comfort, putting her hand on his good shoulder and crouching beside him. "What in God's name is going on?"

He took a deep breath. "It's the arm. It's killing me. Gotta be a nerve thing. I can't get away from it. It's like I wanna tear it off."

"Jesus Christ. We have to see a doctor."

He shook his head violently. "You do that and I'm done. I'm a gimp. The only reason I can work is 'cause of Joe's protection and his rep with the brass. I show up like this, that'll be all they need to fire my ass. You can't tell anybody about this, babe."

He looked up at her in the gloom pleadingly. "It would kill me. I mean it."

She knew he wasn't overstating the cost of losing his job, even if his wording was melodramatic. Sam may have had her own doubts and insecurities, but she was a realist about how other people could see the world. It was a large part of how she'd gotten to where she was.

They both heard a faint crying from down the hall—Emma, stirring in her sleep.

Sam shifted to the balls of her feet, but grabbed Willy's face in her hands to address him. "I got it," she said. "I believe you. Let me deal with her. Don't move. Don't leave. I got you, I swear."

She kissed his damp forehead and jogged down the hall to see to Emma. Now a preschooler, their daughter was precocious, intelligent, and curiosity driven, sometimes given to an overly active imagination. That could lead not so much to nightmares, as dreams that needed to be talked out.

Sam entered her bedroom, dragged a chair over to the bed, and rested her hand on Emma's chest, instantly quieting her.

"Tell me what's going on?" she inquired as the little girl curled her arms around a stuffed Eeyore that her father had predictably given her.

It didn't last long. It never did. Emma began explaining something about animals and the desert—details from a nature show that her dreaming had transformed into something less comprehensible. But her sweet voice soon trailed off, until Sam felt comfortable leaving her with her fantasies.

When she returned to the hallway, she was almost stunned to find Willy where she'd left him—truly a sign that things were seriously off-kilter.

She slid down the wall beside him and passed along what she'd thought of while tending to Emma: "Susan Spinney."

Willy stared at her. "What?"

"She's our friend—mine especially—she's inside the tent, and you know she won't say a word, even to Lester, if we tell her not to."

"But what can she do? She's not gonna steal drugs for me."

Sam gave him a gentle smack. "Such an idiot. You know anyone else in the medical field who could steer us the right way, off the books? She's been a nurse for twenty years. She knows her stuff."

His gaze drifted to the floor between them. "I don't know."

"Consider your options," she said simply. "Tell me what you come up with."

Both their pagers started vibrating simultaneously. Sammie didn't break off her gaze. "You got something better? And by the way, I know you swiped my Oxys a few days ago, just in case you thought you got away with that."

That brought a smile. Willy unclipped his cell phone from his belt and speed-dialed the VBI dispatch.

"What d'ya got?" he asked a moment later.

He listened a moment, said, "Got it," and hung up, explaining, "Arson in White River. GreenField Grocers warehouse. Multiple points of ignition. Jonathon Michael and his crew are already headed. Apparently, they're all dyin' for the usual clusterfuck, even though arson's not really in our wheelhouse. Wanna go?"

Sam had her own phone out. "I'll call Louise and see if she can come over." She paused and raised an eyebrow. "Unless you want to pass and stay here."

He awkwardly began getting up. "Only thing better than painkillers is the job. You know that."

Joe refilled Beverly's water glass from the restaurant carafe. Neither of them drank alcohol much, and only when they were sure they wouldn't be called to duty, so water had become their default beverage of choice. Joe had once been a Coke fan, but lately, the caffeine had been getting to him—not to mention the stern looks he'd been receiving from his physician companion.

They were enjoying an early dinner at a quiet place in Hanover, New Hampshire, home of Dartmouth College and just across the river from Vermont.

"Okay," he said as he replaced the carafe, stabbed his fork into the middle of his spaghetti, and began twirling. "I've done a spectacular job, I think, of containing my impatience. I've wined you—sort of—and dined you at your suggestion, ignoring the implication that you had news to impart, and have kept my counsel as we've discussed the weather, the fate of the Chicago Cubs, and studiously avoided mentioning the case. Would you—could you—please tell me why we're here?"

She was laughing and pointed her finger at him. "We have not discussed the weather or the Cubbies. Never have; never will. That is my pledge. I am devoted to our relationship never reaching such depths."

He sat back. "Hey. I know lifelong marriages that have thrived on that diet."

She tapped the back of his hand with her own. "We can do better. I know we can."

Of that, he had little doubt. He had the proof of time attesting to it. They may have been a couple for only a while now, but their decades-old trust, friendship, and closeness had created a foundation most married people could envy. Most of that time, Beverly had been married to a prominent Burlington lawyer—the father of her two daughters—and Joe had been sequentially committed to a couple of women following his wife's early death. But the dependability and ease of their connection had never faltered, finally evolving into something that could no longer be denied.

Once during those years, they had enjoyed a romantic interlude, after her husband had left her and, coincidentally, when Joe was between relationships. It had been the equivalent of sharing a life raft during a rough stretch—fortuitous, reaffirming, restorative, and temporary.

It had also been, unbeknownst to either of them, the planting of a notion not deemed worthy of serious consideration then—and yet which had germinated nevertheless. Whether it had been time's steady progress, the benefits of maturation, the dawning realization of happiness being so close at hand, or a combination of all three, he wasn't sure. But he'd never felt so settled in his heart, now that his appreciation of her had reached this point.

"All right," she was saying as he admired her sitting across from him. "Cards on the table. I have two pieces of news, the most exciting being that Rachel—in an undeniable demonstration of one's youngest child growing up—has landed her first full-time job."

"Well done," he replied, raising his glass. "Here's to her. What did she get?"

"This is the part you're not going to believe. In fact, I'm slightly nervous about how you're going to take it."

"Uh-oh," he said, smiling but slightly apprehensive. "Well, I am sitting down."

"It's a bit of a miracle, in a fashion," she continued. "It's rare when the very subject that so captures one's enthusiasm in college can be pursued in the real world. But that's what happened. She's been hired by the revamped *Brattleboro Reformer* to be their staff photographer."

That did catch him by surprise. The *Reformer*, whose Massachusetts flagship in the seventies had been mentioned as one of the outstanding small-town newspapers in the nation, had over the years slipped in prestige to become a merely average, run-of-the-mill daily.

That had been undergoing recent change, however. A group of hopeful business retirees had purchased it from its absentee corporate owners, and—much to the mixed emotions of old-timers like Gunther—a long-retired warhorse named Stan Katz had been lured back as the new editor.

"Holy smokes," Joe burst out. "This whole state is like a small-world joke sometimes. The *Reformer*? Working for Katz? I heard they'd brought him in from the pasture. Must be part of a total overhaul."

Beverly's smile faded slightly. "You know him?"

"Oh, yeah." Joe interpreted her expression and held up both hands. "Hold on. That's not necessarily bad, my lack of enthusiasm notwithstanding. He's one of the best, most tenacious reporters I know—totally at odds with what you'd expect of a paper that size. I mean, I haven't heard hide nor hair of him in years—not since the paper was sold to some midwestern outfit. But he used to be a dog with a bone. If he's still anything like that, he should be a terrific mentor."

She was clearly not impressed by his effusiveness. "You have never been so upbeat about someone, Joseph, least of all a reporter. What're you not telling me?"

He was amused by her use of his full name. Only his ancient mother did that, and, as with Beverly, only when he was under scrutiny.

"Hey," he confessed. "I'm a cop. How do you think Katz and I got along? If he was a dog with a bone, *I* was the bone. It was no fun at all. I was *delighted* when the paper changed hands and he left in a huff. That being said, his coming back'll be the best thing that's happened to that paper in years, and Rachel couldn't ask for a better leg up. I also don't doubt I'm gonna hate it."

He paused to take another bite and resumed with a question. "She does know her becoming a reporter is likely to put the two of us at logger-heads sometimes, doesn't she?"

"She said something like, 'Joe's not going to like this,' but I'm not sure that she does," Beverly said. "She is still a kid, after all. Saying something and believing it is often a stretch."

"Well," he said, trying to be hopeful, "she's likely to be more the police department's problem than mine, given her beat."

He suddenly shifted in his seat to check his pager, and then reached into his pocket to pull out his cell phone.

"You mind?" he asked her.

She smiled. "Of course not."

He dialed the same number that Willy had earlier, listened for a bit, replied, "White River? Really? Okay. Thanks," and hung up.

Beverly leaned forward eagerly. "Did I hear you say White River? Do we have a field trip as dessert?"

"I don't know," he said. "That's up to you. You invited me to dinner; I'm not about to start calling the shots."

She indicated the mostly empty plates before them. "We were almost done. If I'm invited, I'd love to come. Is it something I'm going to end up seeing on my table?"

He signaled to the waiter. "I don't think so. It's an arson at the Green-Field Grocers warehouse. Apparently quite a mess. Dispatch told me Sam and Willy are responding, and Lester may be on his way. And," he added with both eyebrows raised, "of *course* you're invited."

"I love it," she said. "You do know how to show a girl a fun time."

It wasn't until they were crossing the parking lot, heading toward their cars, that Joe turned to her and said, "You never told me your second piece of news."

"Oh," she said, shaking her head and getting out her keys, "compared to Rachel, it's pretty small bananas. I've been invited to teach pathology by the Geisel School of Medicine at Dartmouth, part-time."

He stopped in his tracks. "What? Talk about burying the lead. You're leaving the medical examiner's office?"

She chuckled. "No, no. Hardly anything like that. I'm simply cutting back a little to try a new opportunity. It's a yearlong trial to discover if it's a good fit—an experiment. I love my job too much to give it up, but, by the same token, I couldn't resist seeing how this feels. I hope it will be a win–win for everyone."

By now, they were standing between their two cars. They'd decided to drive separately to nearby White River Junction, in case Joe ended up being stuck there.

"Actually," she continued. "I was thinking it might be useful to Rachel, as well. If I were to buy a place somewhere halfway between Hanover and Brattleboro, she would have a place to escape to when she needed a break, while I'd have a pied-à-terre that could double as an investment. I'm hoping it won't turn into a typical mother–daughter nightmare, since—between being in Burlington half the week and working days at Geisel—I actually won't be there much."

Joe tilted his head slightly to one side and grinned at her. "Halfway to Brattleboro, huh? You know that's gonna be too close for me to ignore. In your calculations, have you allowed for the odd visit by a strange man, now and then?"

She laughed and unlocked her door. "I have, actually. Or at least, I was hoping to."

He turned her toward him and kissed her invitingly. "Count on it," he promised, feeling lighter in heart than he'd expected. "I think it's a terrific plan."

She tightened her grip of him before looking into his face, laughing. "Thank God," she said.

He tilted his head slightly. "What?" he asked.

"I didn't quite tell you everything."

"What?" he repeated.

"I've already bought it. A house. In Windsor."

His smile widened. "You're kidding. You own it?"

"Almost. I'm ninety percent along. It was too good to pass up, even if all I did was rent it out or resell it. Then, when the Geisel offer firmed up, I began thinking of it as something more than a good business deal."

His mind flooded with delight and doubt at once, both of them exciting. He was astonished at how happy he felt, despite his natural, inborn sense of caution.

He kissed her again. "You do know how to pull a rabbit out of a hat."

From the outside, as they drove into view, the fire scene resembled a training film. Response vehicles were there in droves, sparkling with lights and making the neighborhood pulse with LED strobes and deep-throated diesel engines. Of fire or smoke, however, there was not a sign—as if the special effects crew hadn't yet set those up. Instead, there was an enormous, hulking, blank-faced behemoth of a building, squatting like the base of a half-built, windowless skyscraper, making the largest fire trucks look like scattered toys. Running along its entire length—as far as visible—an uncountable string of closed truck bay doors stretched out in both directions, suggesting the purpose of this otherwise daunting structure.

Joe and Beverly parked well on the periphery, and walked together toward a white tent filled with uniformed people—the incident command center.

"I had no idea it was so big," she said as they approached arm in arm.

"A half-million square feet, I think," he said, taking it in. "And almost fifty feet high."

"And not a window in sight," she added. "A monument to single-minded purpose."

He laughed. "That about sums it up."

Joe was preparing for the ritual of introductions and sorting through echelons on his way to the incident commander—normally the chief of the primary fire company—when a voice called his name from among the dozens of haphazardly parked vehicles.

"Joe. My God. How long's it been? They had to burn down half the town to get you up here? Talk about being hard to get."

Joe stopped, his hand on Beverly's arm, and squinted into the blinding surroundings. Out from among the strobe lights stepped a narrow-hipped, broad-shouldered man wearing turnout gear stamped with the initials and logo of the Vermont State Police.

Joe stuck out a hand in greeting. "Jonathon Michael. I thought you'd be flying a desk by now. Or learning to fish in retirement."

Michael closed in for a half hug on top of the handshake, taking in Hillstrom as he did so.

Joe conducted the formalities. "Beverly Hillstrom, Jonathon Michael, of the arson unit. You still are, aren't you?"

"It's in my bones," Michael admitted. "I can't seem to do anything else. Nor do I want to, which is why I'm stringing it out as long as they'll let me."

He shook Beverly's hand. "And you brought the ME. Now, *that* was thoughtful, if a little pessimistic. You know something we don't, Doc?"

"No, no," she said with emphasis. "I'm merely a tourist tonight."

"We were having dinner nearby when the call came in," Joe explained.

"What happened?" Beverly asked.

Michael held up a forefinger authoritatively. "Aha. You happen to be asking the right person. At least, let's hope you are, or the rest of these guys're gonna wonder why I'm here."

He dropped his voice slightly to add, "And not to hurt any feelings, but if you'd like an insider's tour of the damage, don't go to them. Just follow me."

As they continued toward the colossal building, cutting between large trucks with engines idling, Jonathon kept talking, shouting over his shoulder as he led the way.

"Most of the crews are about to cut out anyhow. The fires are out, the structure is intact and fine, and the damage—considering what was at risk—was amazingly light."

"Mom?" a young woman's voice cut in, jarringly at odds with the circumstances.

The trio stopped abruptly. From the shadow cast by a truck, a young woman emerged, dressed in hiking boots and cargo pants, her torso crisscrossed by the straps of two cameras and an equipment bag.

Beverly was the first to speak. "Rachel? My God. What're you doing here?"

The girl looked slightly nonplussed. "I'm on my first assignment."

As the two women embraced, Joe explained to Michael, "Rachel Reiling, Beverly's daughter, newly hired as the *Brattleboro Reformer*'s photographer."

"And *Vermont Digger*," Rachel said, her eyes gleaming, shaking hands awkwardly because of her equipment, and adding, "They're why I'm here, actually, this being a little outside the *Reformer*'s turf."

"I wondered," Joe commented as he introduced their host. *Vermont Digger* was a recent journalistic innovation: an exclusively online news outlet that was gaining a good reputation and financial momentum, largely thanks to the fact that it needed no printing press, fancy headquarters building, or costly method of distribution. It had a bare-bones staff, but also called on stringers—like Rachel—whose services were made available by their employers.

"Congratulations," Joe said to her, giving her a high five. "How're you faring in this mess? Has anyone yelled at you yet?"

"Not so far. They've been really sweet. But it's not like I'm in the way out here, either." She jerked a thumb at the towering blank wall beside them. "All the action's been inside."

Jonathon laughed. "Ah. We got you, didn't we? Not enough doors to sneak through. Bummer."

He suddenly gave them a conspiratorial look and drew them close together to say, as quietly as he could in the surrounding noise, "If you promise to keep it under your hat, I think I might be able to give you a small welcoming gift."

Her face lit up. "Really? You'll let me in?"

He smiled broadly. "Briefly. You can step in, take a couple of shots, and step back out. It'll be worth your while."

Joe cautioned him. "You sure? You could be retired prematurely." Technically, this was breaching a crime scene. Not something to take lightly.

"Nah," Michael reassured him in an aside. "We're good. It's wicked dramatic inside, with the smoke and weird lighting, but nothing's really going on, at least not on the other side of that door. It'll give the kid a boost."

He stepped back, bowed slightly, and ushered them forward, adding to Joe, "Trust me. I'm a big cheese here."

"You said, 'fires' earlier," Beverly prompted as they resumed walking. "Assuming you can still speak freely."

He shrugged the notion off. "Oh, sure. Yeah. I've done hundreds of these investigations over the years, as Joe can tell you. And there've been times when I've really had to scratch my head, trying to figure out the cause."

He reached a surprisingly small door, given the context of the wall around it, pulled it open, and showed them through, instantly plunging them into relative quiet.

"This time, though," he finished, "a five-year-old could've nailed it."

He introduced them to their new surroundings with a wave of the arm. "Welcome to my crime scene. As for you," he addressed Rachel, "start shooting. You've got under a minute."

To his neophyte guests, what they were facing was nothing less than astonishing. The scope and dimensions of almost everything before them reduced their size to ants—an impression enhanced by how the thousands of tiny, distant, overhead LEDs barely dented the dark void of the warehouse's interior—or the somber fogbank of slowly thinning smoke that still hugged the ceiling and made each light radiate like a star.

The sting and odor of the recent blazes accompanied it all, making Joe think of some melodramatic rendering of hell.

Beverly had a different take. "It's like being in outer space," she commented as her daughter darted about to catch the best shots she could. "Completely cut off."

"It's actually brighter than usual," Michael told her. "All these lights are normally motion-activated, to save energy, so the lighting only works as you move. We overrode that to see better."

He turned his attention to Rachel. "You good?"

She straightened after one last picture, smiling broadly. "Better than that. This was awesome. Thank you so much."

He patted her shoulder. "Don't thank me. We never met." He reached behind her and opened the door again. "Now everyone'll wonder how the hell you got those. Have a great career. I don't doubt we'll run into each other again. It's that kind of state."

Rachel waved to them as she stepped outside, saying, "See ya, Mom. Thanks again."

After closing the door firmly, Michael walked to the middle of a large open area glistening with water, where, during regular operations, the shipping side of the enterprise readied pallets to be fed through the long row of truck bays and into an endless rotation of tractor trailers. He indicated the tall steel racks before them, reaching beyond their vision into the height and depth of the building.

"From what we've put together so far, five MHEs—floor jacks, forklifts, hi-lows, what they lump together as 'material-handling equipment'—were somehow rigged to burst into flames within fifteen minutes of each other, in five different parts of the warehouse. Luckily, all but one of those ignitions pretty much stayed put, consuming the vehicle only and releasing some sulfuric gas from the batteries. The one exception was a floor jack that went up beside a stack of lighter fluid. That made more of a mess."

He turned to smile encouragingly. "Still, given the options, between the sprinkler system, the overhead fans, the warehouse crew's initial response, and the fire guys reacting like Navy SEALs, management shouldn't complain. They may have lost some serious bucks because of this, but they should be up and running, at least partly, in pretty short order. In my book, it's a frigging miracle."

"You been able to isolate the mechanism of ignition?" Joe asked.

Michael smiled at Beverly. "Watch out. He's starting to sound nerdy and official. I hope you came by separate cars."

She laughed. "We did."

"Good," he replied. "'Cause we've barely begun. I'm putting money on somebody having monkeyed with the batteries of all five MHEs. How that was done, and especially by whom, I have no clue."

He looked meaningfully at Joe before adding, "That's what you and I are probably gonna spend the rest of the night trying to figure out. You got reinforcements coming?"

"I do," Joe said.

Beverly leaned toward him and kissed his cheek. "That's my cue, Special Agent Gunther. I will officially see myself out." She then surprised Michael with the same gesture—unheard of from a woman well known throughout law enforcement for her observance of strict procedure. "I cannot thank you enough for what you officially did not do for my daughter."

CHAPTER EIGHT

"Nice digs," Willy commented, stepping up into the mobile command center and looking around as he removed his latex glove with his teeth and opened the zipper to his soot-stained Tyvek suit. "Whaddya say we get one of these, boss?" he asked Joe over his shoulder.

Joe was following him in, mimicking his gestures, the second in a line of people who had just spent the past six hours inside the cavernous GreenField warehouse, conducting interviews, collecting evidence, taking pictures and video, and documenting the source of the multiple fires.

"Sure. Why not? I bet we've got that much in petty cash."

Next came Lester, Sammie, and Jonathon Michael, each one resembling an exhausted, trashed, Tyvek-clad Ghostbuster—minus the backpacks.

In turn, they settled down, making room for several technicians from the crime lab. By the time the door was slammed, the trailer, rigged with a long thin conference table between two opposing benches, smelled of hardworking bodies perfumed with damp smoke.

No one cared. Not only had they gotten used to their circumstances, they were beyond happy to sit down.

Joe readily conceded their shared exhaustion. "Jesus," he let out in a sigh while opening a plastic water bottle. "Talk about a workout. I thought we were the Sherlock Holmeses of this business. All brains and theories."

"Welcome to my world," Michael told him, wiping his face with a large red bandanna. "*Now's* when you get to do that, after you're too tired to think straight."

"I like it," Willy volunteered, massaging his bad arm, which he'd almost managed to forget about in the interim—and was struggling to do now. "It appeals to the geek in me."

That part was truthful enough. Running at odds with most people's perceptions of him, Willy was not exclusively dismissive, impatient, and action-driven by nature. He acted that way often enough. But to those who worked closest to him, he was known for watching, waiting, and pondering beyond the patience of the most stalwart fisherman.

"Me, too," Michael agreed with him, smiling broadly. "Rarely get enough of it, though."

"So, in the interests of time and a need for sleep," Joe suggested, "what did we get, all told?"

Sammie, predictably, had that in hand, spreading stained and damp field reports across the tabletop, including photographs they'd printed out in the general manager's office.

As she distributed them, Jonathon spoke. "Mostly, the hard part with arsons is finding the point of ignition. From there, you can identify the source, if you're lucky. After that, maybe you locate some evidence, and finally, you build your narrative of who did what, when, and by using what.

"In this case, we had more people than we could count tell us that the points of ignition were five separate electrically powered MHEs—specifically their batteries—which thereby technically created five different crime scenes. The unusual aspect became the randomly mobile nature of these retooled incendiary devices.

"Each of the teams we put out onto the warehouse floor," he continued, "came back with the same conclusion: None of the MHEs appears to have been sent to a target. Nor was the overall goal to burn down the building, notwithstanding the damage where the lighter fluid cases were. This then sent us to our sixth crime scene, the battery-changing station at the far north end of the warehouse, where we think each MHE was altered."

He held up a map of the warehouse floor plan, crisscrossed with red lines indicating the routes of the five explosive MHEs, each converging at the same spot that he now tapped with his finger. "The battery-changing station is where things were initiated, which is why, while most of you were digging through the debris at each ignition point, I focused my energies there."

Only now did he gingerly lift an evidence bag onto the table and lay it before them. Through its transparent sheathing, they could see what appeared to be a short, pale sausage.

"A TNT hot dog?" Spinney asked.

Michael smiled. "Kind of, yeah. It's made of two readily available dry materials—one of which is old-fashioned sugar—stuffed into the equivalent of a rubber balloon. These kinds of things used to be sold to kids in chemistry sets in the fifties and sixties. In simple form, you take the contents of this sausage, mix it with some sulfuric acid, and presto, you have an exothermic reaction."

"Or something that goes boom, in our language," said Willy.

"Exactly," Michael agreed. "Everyone knows how potentially dangerous car batteries can be—sulfuric acid, electricity, a hot environment, and the constant risk of a spark." He pointed to the evidence bag. "Well, add these missing ingredients, and you go from potential to guaranteed.

"The problem," he went on, "is that if you just dropped the contents of this so-called hot dog into the battery, the reaction would be instantaneous, which would screw up your getaway and singe your eyebrows, if you didn't die from the fumes. That's where the rubber casing comes in to save the day. In each battery, there's a thin platform below the filler caps which separates the opening from the inner cell plates and acid. This platform, like a flat sieve, has small holes in it to allow water and/or acid to be added, but prevents other objects from entering the cell chambers. All our arsonist had to do was drop one hot dog per battery onto that sieve, replace the filler cap, and let the subsequent vibrations and jostling of the MHE do the rest. A little acid inevitably splashes up through the sieve and eats through the rubber, the powder sprinkles onto the liquid below, and there you have it."

He snapped his fingers and threw in jokingly, "As the French say, 'Viola!'—assuming you don't speak French."

"Cute, Jonathon," Willy muttered before pointing at the evidence envelope and adding, "Since everything went blooey as planned, where'd you get that?"

"There were six batteries rigged," Jonathon said simply. "That one didn't make it into an MHE. I found it ready to go, next in line."

"How unstable is it?" Sammie asked warily.

"Without the acid to set it off? Totally safe."

"Any prints?" Joe inquired.

"The lab'll check it for that and DNA," Jonathon told them. "But a cursory exam showed nothing. Sounds reasonable that if you were putting all this together, you'd wear gloves."

"And you're saying," Lester summarized, "that whatever's in the hot dog could be had pretty much anywhere? Like the sugar?"

"Better than that," Michael said. "It's all available inside that warehouse. Our firebug didn't even have to go shopping."

"Did anyone check where those ingredients are kept?" Sammie asked.

"Yeah," Michael said. "Nothing to see."

"And," Willy threw in, "I spent several hours looking at the video files for suspicious activity. Nothing there, either."

"Meaning he either did go shopping," Joe suggested, "or he collected what he needed off the shelves much earlier."

"If the second is true," Lester said, "that implies our arsonist had or has free access."

"And knows how everything works," Sam added. "Including the recharging routine of the MHEs."

"That's an interesting point," Jonathon said. "Of the hundreds of people who work here, I would guess only a handful know enough to have pulled off this particular approach."

"Or had access to the internet," Willy said sourly. "I looked it up during a break from watching the surveillance footage. There're a dozen videos showing how to turn a battery into a bomb."

"Do we have an estimate yet on how much damage was done?" Joe asked.

"I spoke to the floor manager," Sammie said. "They won't know for a while, but it has to be a couple hundred thousand, with everything included. Maybe more, depending on lost revenue due to repairs. Anyhow, a shitload. They have another warehouse, in upper New York State, but this is their mother ship."

"Did he say he'd received a warning this might happen?" Jonathon asked. "Or mention any pissed-off employees or ex-employees?"

"No, but he referred us to his head of security, since he wasn't sure he'd have the latest on something like that." Sam referred to her notepad. "That would be Pat Smith."

"I know her," said Willy, who carried in his head an unimaginable number of contacts, from all walks of life. "Used to be VSP. Solid people."

"Never met her, but heard good things," Lester chimed in.

"What sticks with me," Sammie said, "is what Jonathon said about the nature of the attack. Why do all this if you don't want to burn the place down? Might help to remember that during any interviews."

"Good point," Joe said before stretching and placing his palms flat against the trailer's ceiling. "Okay. Why don't one of you get with Pat Smith and see what she knows. Sam, speaking of interviews, contact all our other squads, round up everybody not knee-deep in casework, and organize them into interview teams. We'll need to talk with everybody and anybody who works here or once did, and might have some insight into what happened. If that's not enough people at our end, ask the state police if they can spare anyone. We don't know who did this, or why, or if this was their only target. If it turns out to be the first of a string of arsons, I want to be able to say we already got a full team and then some working on it. Nobody died here, but that might've been dumb luck. Who knows what's next?"

He looked at Michael. "Jonathon, try to get anything you can out of that remaining hot dog—including any details about the casing. Did we get that whole battery-charging station fingerprinted?"

"The relevant parts, yup," one of the crime lab people said from near the door, "and we collected reference prints from the station operator, Angie Hogencamp, along with a sworn statement."

"Last but not least," Joe wrapped up, "and sadly, before we can hit the rack for some shut-eye, we need to have a word with local law enforcement to see if anyone saw anything suspicious or unusual over the previous twenty-four hours—loiterers near the warehouse, strange vehicular activity, whatever. I think we need to do that sooner rather than later, before memories fade."

Most often, Willy would have been the one to grab such an assignment. He was rarely known to sleep and always enjoyed catching up with his array of informants. But this time, Joe noticed that he seemed barely aware, staring instead at the floor, both arms gathered before him, his good hand slowly massaging his left shoulder.

"You okay, Willy?" Joe asked as Lester spoke simultaneously with, "I'll do that."

Willy looked up sharply and froze, while Sammie cautiously laid her hand on his leg. "Fine. Why?"

Joe hesitated, taking in their body language. "Nothing. Just wondered. Long night."

Lester quickly repeated, "I'll talk to the locals. I have the shortest distance to get home, anyhow."

"Thanks," Joe said before addressing the entire group. "It's been a long haul. We're all cross-eyed. Thanks for your help, everybody, and please pass that along to anyone you see who pitched in."

"Boss?" Lester asked, almost raising his hand for permission to speak. "Where do we put Teri Parker in the pecking order?"

Joe nodded and signaled to the lab folks and Jonathon. "You're good to go, guys. Many thanks. Catch some sleep."

He waited until only his squad members remained before saying, "Good call, Les. I'll take the lead on Parker, at least till the dust settles on this mess. Right now, there's no obvious suspect wandering around threatening the public, as there may be here, so my first order of business'll be to update the AG concerning our doubts about Mick Durocher's confession. After that, I'll go looking for his elusive daughter."

He pulled out his cell phone. "Much as I dislike these things, I think they'll be the best way to keep in touch for the next couple of days, since it looks like we'll all be out of the office. I won't be expecting your daily reports to be masterpieces of literature, but do enter the bare minimum, okay? It's crucial, now that we're running two major cases side by side, that everybody knows who's doing what."

"You sure about this?" Sam asked Willy. "We could sleep on it first."

"You called Sue, didn't you?" he pressed her.

Sammie rubbed her eyes. Her head hummed with sleep deprivation, and the last thing she wanted right now was to greet the rising sun on yet another mission. Home and bed and thoughts of Emma pulled at her like a raging thirst.

But that also gave her insight into Willy's present condition. She knew he was exhausted, too, yet he was more driven by his pain to choose this drive over the solace of a few hours' rest. Sam couldn't even imagine the level of his suffering.

More to the point, she also couldn't gauge—and didn't want to risk—how close he might be to completely yielding to old bad habits to remedy what was hounding him.

She started the car and headed for Sue Spinney's new place of employment.

Upper Valley Surgical Specialists was an experiment. Neither a full-fledged hospital nor an outpatient surgi-center, it was a consortium of independent surgeons, created partially to see if the almost-square wheel of modern American health care might benefit from what Sue had laughingly called a "boutique hospital."

That it was located in rural Vermont spoke indirectly of its unconventional birth. Its well-heeled founders had wanted an off-the-radar, minimally populated locale, benignly supported by a mostly progressive state government, which also had access to enough doctors willing to try something new amidst a little peace and quiet.

Neither Sam nor Willy cared about this, or how it was hoping to open a niche in the country's hidebound health-care system. Sue Spinney had simply recommended that they meet with her boss, Victoria Garlanda. Had she pointed them toward Mass General or the Mayo Clinic, Sam would have driven them there, instead.

As it was, they pulled into UVSS's parking lot within twenty minutes of leaving GreenField—a good thing, given how tired they were.

In contrast to their energy level, the morning was by then bright, cheerful, getting warmer, and accented with birdsong.

Willy groaned as he stepped out of the car. "Great. Ninety-degree weather on the way."

Sammie shook her head, expecting no less, but her worrying had undermined her usual tolerance for his grousing. "Maybe two months from now, if we're lucky," she shot back testily.

Having been called from the road, Sue met them outside the building's front doors, hugging Sam and giving Willy a critical and professional look. "Jesus, you're a mess."

"Nice manners," he told her.

"You should know," she replied, appraising them as a twosome. "Seriously, you both look like hell. You come straight from the fire Lester went to?"

"You got it."

She was impressed. "What's that? Twenty-four hours at full speed? You were working that homicide, otherwise, right?"

"You got it," Willy said.

Sue smiled. "But you wanted to see me so badly, you just couldn't stay away. That's really sweet."

"Believe what you want," he countered brusquely, his own impatience showing. "Where's your miracle worker?"

Sue's demeanor completely changed. Suddenly serious, she stepped up to him and studied his face. "You're in such pain, the standard ten-scale doesn't even apply. Is that close?"

"Let's say that if I headed home to quote-unquote sleep right now, it wouldn't be a success."

Without further delay, she ushered them inside.

CHAPTER NINE

Joe's meeting with the assistant attorney general occurred late on the same day that he and his squad had huddled in the command trailer after the GreenField fire. With what little stamina he had left, he'd driven to Beverly's house south of Burlington, crawled into the bed they usually appreciated for more amorous pursuits, and passed out.

How he awoke in time to make it to the AG's office in downtown Montpelier was beyond him. Certainly, as he entered her office and sat across from her, he didn't feel much more lively than a patient emerging from anesthesia.

Natausha "Tausha" Greenblott was "their" prosecutor, assigned especially to the VBI, much as the AG had made another of his Trial and Investigative Unit deputies responsible for the Vermont Drug Task Force. Back in Joe's Brattleboro Police days, he had reported to the county state's attorney. That was an elective office, however, responsible for every case brought to it from within Windham County. It was predictably under-funded and -staffed. Having Tausha Greenblott for their very own was another perk of being a specialized statewide agency.

Greenblott gave him a maternal appraisal, despite being an easy twenty years his junior. "Good Lord, Joe. You might want to consider scaling it back a notch. Have you had any sleep lately?"

"Thanks, Tausha. I just got up. Glad it shows."

She laughed. "I'm well known for my diplomacy. You here to update me about Michael Durocher, the GreenField fire, or something new? You folks are on a roll right now."

"Mick Durocher, and I'm afraid you're not going to like it much."

"Not the slam dunk we thought it was?" she anticipated without rancor. "Fire away."

"That's more your call than mine," he told her. "We've got the Bromley video of him transporting what appears to be the body to the right place at the right time; the four-wheeler found outside his home, complete with his prints on the handlebars; his boot prints next to the body, and the same boots in his closet; a confirmation from his pal Seth Villeneuve that on the night of the murder, he gave Mick a ride to near where the four-wheeler was stored at Bud Thurley's work site; Thurley's statement that Mick once worked for him, and that he suspected Mick of having stolen the vehicle; and—the kicker—Mick's sworn confession that he did the dirty deed. He denied knowing the girl was pregnant during the interview, but as a motive right now, that's also looking like a good fit."

Greenblott settled back, sensing that he'd just warmed up. It was a comfortable office, decorated with children's drawings, plants, and knick-knacks—a place in which she spent a lot of time, and liked reminders of her home life to keep her company. "I understand why you're nervous, Joe. Sounds very wobbly. I don't see how I could fly that in front of a jury in under three seconds."

Joe could only agree. "I know, I know. Bear with me." He paused to glance at the floor and rub his temples, hoping to clear his head a little. "I'll put it in chronological order. Then you can see how my doubts built up.

"Mick said he was hired under the table to do a job in White River Junction, cleaning up after a big building demolition over there, by a man he called Ted, whom he met at a bar in Manchester.

"We asked the barkeep there about the mysterious Ted. He said he's never seen Mick with anyone, man or woman; he's never heard of someone named Ted; and that Mick's a well-known loner. The bar, incidentally, is over an hour's drive from White River, making it an unlikely spot for someone hiring people for a White River job. And when we asked around about Mick having worked on the cleanup crew there, everyone denied knowing him. Mick said they would claim ignorance, since they don't want to be caught hiring illegally, but that doesn't explain why nobody remembers a man named Ted in a hiring position.

"Just for the hell of it, though," Joe continued uninterrupted, "let's say Mick was in White River. He told me that it was while working there that he met Teri Parker at another bar, this one in Windsor, named Manny's. Once again, nobody there has seen either one of them. Not only that, but Teri lived in Barre, and while we haven't dug into her past yet, there's nothing to indicate what she was doing halfway across the state in a bar, despite the implication that at least one of her occupations was as a hooker."

"Better and better," Tausha said. "Does the age of her fetus correspond with the time period Mick said they were dating?"

"It does. Point for you. So, moving right along, we now have Mick and Teri as totally unwitnessed lovebirds—making out in pickups and anywhere else that leaves no receipts or evidence—until Mick claims he finally took her to his trailer in Manchester on the same night he killed her. There again, we interviewed the neighbors, which was like hearing that first barkeep all over again—Mick kept to himself, was a nice and quiet loner, and, most tellingly, never had a girlfriend that anyone saw or heard about.

"Still, that's where he claims he had a knock-down-drag-out with her, including pushing her around, after which she stormed out, marched down to the parking lot at the end of the street, where he followed her and whacked her with a two-by-four."

"Don't tell me," Tausha suggested. "Which two-by-four you also didn't find? And I'm guessing he had no memory about what prompted the fight."

"Right on both counts. No bruises on the body suggesting a domestic, no neighbors reporting a fight or any shouting, no abandoned two-by-four, and no evidence of anybody having been stashed at the edge of the lot while Mick wandered the neighborhood, rounding up the four-wheeler.

"Last but not least," Joe concluded, "we have the video—the part juries love the most. That," he emphasized, "is where my objections to this cock-and-bull story get a little more psychological, and maybe in your eyes a lot less reliable."

"Oh?"

"What stuck in my craw from the start was, why complicate things with the four-wheeler? If I kill somebody in the heat of the moment, I don't hitch a ride ten miles to steal a vehicle and then drive back and forth, carrying around a dead body. I grab a shovel and bury the damn thing. And if I do opt for the four-wheeler, I sure as hell don't then drive it to the top of a mountain, so I can pose for the one video camera I think'll fit the bill.

"But," Joe kept going, amazed by how organized he was sounding, "that's exactly what I'd do if I wasn't too bright and being forced to conjure up a plan by the real culprit. Mick knew about the four-wheeler, the camera, who to call to hitch a ride, the various bars, and all the rest because they played a part in his everyday life—or he'd heard about them in the news, like that demolition in White River. The question therefore becomes: Why admit to the crime? Nothing in his record indicates that he has a habit of seeking attention. Mick Durocher is like a typical run-of-the-mill, all-American, self-destructive, underachieving loner. He doesn't have the passion to bash girlfriends on the head. Hell, he doesn't have the passion to *have* a girlfriend in the first place."

"I thought he has a daughter," Tausha reminded him, tapping on a closed file before her.

"An adult daughter, yes," he agreed. "I'd love to talk to her, among other people."

"Who?"

"I don't know yet," Joe answered honestly. "That's the problem. This was wrapped up so neat and tidy, there was no reason to do our usual background digging yet. I guess that's what I'm here asking for."

Greenblott seemed completely unperturbed. "Joe, if you're not happy with things as they are, by all means, go for it. I'd sooner have my own investigator find there's a bug in the soup than some headline-grabbing defense lawyer later on. And I sure as hell don't want this poor girl's real murderer on the loose, thinking he pulled a fast one. Screw that.

"I do have a suggestion that might help," she added. "One of your missing pieces concerns the fetus. You should round up a nontestimonial identification order and collect Mick's DNA to match it against Teri's baby. If you've got doubts about Mick's guilt, I would like to have that question answered. In fact, unless you have a driving need to do that yourself, I'll be happy to have one of our staff investigators chase it down for you." She smiled before adding, "Call it a personal show of faith."

"I'll take it. Mick's defense'll go for that?" Joe asked.

"They won't have a choice if we state in the application that we're going for motive. The trick will be to not even bring up the issue of whether you consider the fetus to be a human being or not, thereby implying its death is a homicide. Not that such a tactic would fly in Vermont anyhow."

The phone on her desk started ringing. She reached out and placed her hand on it, glancing at Joe. "We good? Or should I not answer this?"

Joe stood up. "Knock 'em dead, Counselor. Thanks for the help."

Sam was still holding her phone when its urgent vibrating startled her awake. Sue Spinney had parked her in one of the small hospital's coffin-sized break rooms—barely large enough for a bunk bed, a short ladder, and two reading lamps attached to the wall—where Sam, in denial, had passed out in the middle of writing a text.

She smacked the back of her head against the wall and blinked confusedly, trying to get her bearings. The phone screen revealed that the caller was Beverly Hillstrom—not someone Sam wanted to address raw-edged and sleep-deprived, her brain feeling packed with damp cotton.

Nevertheless, she cleared her throat before answering, "Hello?"

Hillstrom, despite having become an unexpected ally and friend, retained for Sam some of the attributes that a child might see in a powerful and exacting adult.

Something her trademark English teacher's perfect syntax didn't help to dispel.

"Samantha? It's Beverly. Are you all right?"

Sam straightened as best she could, being on the lower bunk without enough head room. "Sure. Sorry. Hi. Nice to hear your voice."

Hillstrom sounded crestfallen. "I woke you up. I was afraid of that. Joe came home after I'd left for work, and I believe he's already back at it. You people are making my old medical school hours look like the proverbial walk in the park."

Sam was trying to interrupt her, if timidly. "No, no, no, no. It's fine. I may have dozed off while I was writing something. It just surprised me, is all. Really, I'm awake. I mean, I was awake."

"All of you were at that fire where I left Joe last night?" Beverly asked. "In White River Junction? I was wondering if it might be an all-hands-on-deck situation."

An announcement came over the hospital PA system in the background. UVSS, despite its small footprint, nevertheless had many of the trappings of a traditional hospital.

"Yeah," Sam said, speaking over it. "It was pretty intense."

"You're not at home," Beverly said. "I know a hospital's public address system when I hear one. Are you all right? That's why I called. An instinct told me to contact you, for no reason at all. Was I correct—if I'm not intruding, of course?"

Sam was completely caught off balance—by the faintly parental words, the supportive tone, Beverly's instinct to reach out at just the right moment. She removed the phone from her ear to fight back a sudden, unexpected surge of emotion, but finished instead by bursting into tears.

"You are not all right," Beverly stated. "Where are you? Should I come?"

"I'm so sorry," Sam stammered into the phone, sniffling and wiping her nose with her sleeve. "I don't know . . . It's not me. I promise."

That did nothing to calm Hillstrom. "Is it Joe?" she asked, alarmed. "Are you in Burlington?"

"It's Willy," Sam said quickly. "His arm's—" She suddenly cut herself off, remembering Willy's concern about confidentiality.

"What? Did he get hurt?"

Sam tried backtracking. "It's just a standard tune-up, but we thought we could get Sue Spinney to do the honors this time. She's at a new place."

"I remember," Beverly said, sounding utterly unconvinced and thereby ramping up Sam's discomfort. "Is he in pain?"

"Oh," Sam spoke generally. "It comes and goes, but that's not it. We just wanted to get it looked at."

After a long and telling pause, during which Sam consciously relaxed her painful grip on the phone, Beverly said, "Let me say something clearly and unequivocally, Samantha: I strongly suspect that you and Willy are in trouble. I also suspect that it's of a nature you're not free to divulge. I honor that and will not pry. But hear me out. If at any time, for any reason, you think I may be of value—to either one of you—please do not hesitate to contact me. You two, and your extraordinary child, are doing an exemplary job under trying circumstances—not to mention that you both also practice a profession that by definition isolates you from most of the rest of civilization. Please do not include me in that isolation. And if my relationship with Joe makes you pause, let it go. I would treat any and all communications as strictly between us. You need not worry on that account."

Sam was speechless, crying again, her weariness only slightly offset by gratitude.

"I shall go," Beverly concluded. "You are tired and busy and need to keep focused. I only want to know that you heard what I just said."

"I did, Beverly," Sam said softly. "I promise, I'll call if I need you. I won't forget."

"It's not forgetfulness that concerns me, Samantha. It's false pride. Understood?"

"Yes, ma'am," Sam said automatically. "Thank you so much."

"You're welcome. I'll speak with you soon. Please take care of yourself, and that hardheaded lunatic you live with."

"I will," Sam said before realizing the phone was already dead.

She rested her head against the wall and wiped her face with her open palm, at once embarrassed and happy for the call. She saw Sue Spinney approaching through the narrow glass pane mounted in the door.

"How is he?" she asked as Sue stepped in.

"Sleeping like a log, like you should be, instead of making phone calls."

Sam waggled the cell in the air. "I was about to contact Louise. I wanted to find out how last night went with Emma. I so miss that girl when I pull an all-nighter. Louise is great and knows the routine inside out, but—"

"You're her *mother*," Sue cut her off, unknowingly mimicking Beverly. "Give yourself a break. Of course you want to know how she's doing. You can't be all things to all people. One crisis at a time."

Sam felt a bit overwhelmed, fresh from her meltdown and acutely aware of the effects of only two catnaps over two days. "How is this a crisis? Truly?"

Susan crooked her finger. "Follow me. Victoria's in her office. You didn't get to meet her when I threw you in here and dragged Willy off. It's time you did."

They walked down a long, white, wide hallway to a flight of stairs, where they arrived before an airy, large-windowed, nicely laid out office. The two-story building, once a small corporate headquarters, had largely kept its former layout: administration upstairs, and operations—literally, in this case—on the ground floor.

The woman who greeted them had arranged her desk so that it didn't face the door like the broadside of a gunboat, but at a more inviting angle.

She rose as they appeared, her tall and powerful build at odds with the gentleness of her face.

"You must be Sam," she stated, shaking Sammie's hand in a firm grip. "I'm Victoria. It's a pleasure to meet the so-called other half. How've you been holding up? I gather you've all been burning the candle at both ends recently—on top of what's ailing Willy."

"It's been a little busy," Sam agreed. "How is he?"

"In trouble," Victoria said bluntly. "From what I gathered during my interview with him, he's got an addictive personality and a propensity for going overboard. I'm sparing you the medical jargon because Sue told me you're both straight shooters. Correct me if I'm wrong, and I'll assume my best bedside demeanor."

"No, no," Sam assured her. "Please. Keep going."

Victoria indicated a circle of chairs away from her desk and made them comfortable. "He told me," she resumed, "that he'd dipped into your supply of Oxys and was hunting out others."

"Right," Sam confirmed grimly, surprised that Willy had admitted as much—another indicator to her of his level of despair.

Victoria leaned forward and tapped Sam's knee for emphasis. "I know you're all tough guys and there's nothing you haven't seen or heard, but dependency is not addiction. That's not just an inspiring phrase on a self-help poster."

Sam was unsure of what to say.

"Dependency concerns the body's growing tolerance of a medication and its corresponding need for more. Addiction involves a lifestyle sacrifice dedicated to the goal of getting more. The signs leading to both are similar: stealing meds, slips in neatness and hygiene, sleep disruption, routine becoming erratic."

Sammie was nodding throughout.

"*But*," Victoria stressed, "Willy is solidly in the first category, despite his history with alcohol."

Sam was trying to absorb all this. "He *told* you this stuff? He never does that. It took me years."

Victoria laughed. "I have my methods." But her face became serious again. "Look, he's in trouble. He knows it and I know it, but you and your daughter are way more the reason he opened up than I am. He doesn't want to lose you, and he feels that's guaranteed if he doesn't get ahead of this."

"But I don't understand what's happened!" Sam exclaimed. "He's had this injury for decades. It's ancient history. What's changed, all of a sudden? And what did you do just now to make him feel better?"

"Good questions," Victoria replied. "Last answer first: We talked, I gave him an injection, and Sue administered a session of craniosacral therapy, which almost freaked him out until he tried it. Fortunately, he finally just passed out. I doubt this is late-breaking news to you, but Willy Kunkle has probably the highest pain threshold of any human being I've met. So when he crashes, as he did with a little help, he goes all out. That same stoicism means, by the way, that he's been experiencing various levels of pain throughout the life of his disability, although never to this degree. That's the nature of such an injury. He just hasn't told anyone."

"So why now?" Sam asked.

"Things change over time," Victoria said simply. "Blood vessels, nerves, tumors, scar tissue, all of it interrelates in passive and active ways. It's what the body does. In Willy's case, after I consulted with a few people who know a lot about this, and reading up on it, I'm thinking he suffers from brachial plexus palsy, brought on by that bullet. The resulting scar tissue, or possibly a tumor, is impinging on his radial nerve, which in turn is sending a level-ten, nonstop pain signal directly to his brain."

"A tumor?" Sam repeated.

"Everyone thinks cancer when you say that," Victoria explained. "It doesn't make it so. All this needs to be explored and identified before it's addressed. The good news is"—she held up her hand and counted off her fingers one by one—"that you're here; the problem seems isolated to the arm; I've been rounding up solid opinions on a solution; and, most important, the science has been steaming ahead all the while. The therapies and treatments available now are much better than they were back when he wasn't open to them, anyhow."

"And he is now?" Sam asked skeptically.

"That's where you and Emma come in," Victoria comforted her. "He's here for your sake. He told me so just before I knocked him out."

"One reason we're here," Sam emphasized, casting a look at Sue, "is because he wanted to be seen under the radar. He's afraid they'll fire him as unfit for duty, since he's only employed now 'cause of a deal Joe worked out with the bigwigs. We're willing to pay for everything up front, even if it means taking out loans."

But Victoria was already shaking her head sympathetically. "I got that. He made it all perfectly clear. The first thing, right out of the gate, is actually to bring Gunther into the conversation. My counterargument, and Willy saw the logic after I talked myself blue in the face, is that the original injury is work related. Any cause for termination would have to have been made when Gunther struck the original deal about keeping him on the payroll. It's too late for anyone to reverse history—that would be grounds for a lawsuit. What I'm proposing medically is just an extension of everything that was done when the injury occurred, which includes the coverage."

She held up her hand again, lampooning the making of an oath. "I promise you, Sam. Nothing will be done without each of you signing off on it. I know what this means to you. But by the same token, you need to realize that Willy's facing a life-threatening crisis. One way or the other, this pain will do him in if we don't create a plan to combat it."

There was a reflective silence in the room, during which Victoria blinked a couple of times, reached for a small bottle on her desk, and administered a couple of drops of its contents into each of her eyes.

"Sorry," she said. "Dry eyes."

"What're you planning to do for him?" Sammie asked her.

There was a knock at the door, and a hard-faced, older nurse stuck her head in uninvited and asked, "I see you for a sec?"

Victoria frowned at the breach in manners, putting the bottle back down. "In a few, Lillian. This a crisis?"

"Depends on your interpretation."

"I'll be right there. I'll find you."

Lillian made a discontented face, muttered, "Whatever," and closed the door without apology.

Sam could tell from Sue's and Victoria's expressions that the unpleasant tone of the encounter hadn't been unexpected.

Sue rolled her eyes in partial explanation, adding softly, "Our token resident Oscar the Grouch. Seems like a workplace requirement, wherever you go."

"You asked what I was planning to do," Victoria resumed without comment. "Not much. I'm the go-between here. What I did for Willy just now is about all I can do. Sue and I got him off the ledge, for a few hours, and only because he was exhausted and desperate. But I can and will advise and guide you through the necessary layers to maybe get this permanently addressed. I'm talking about a neurosurgeon here, probably with orthopedic assistance—a complicated, touch-and-go operation. The works. Fortunately, you came to the right place, for whatever reasons. We have the people, the expertise, and the equipment right here. If I'm right, this thing is definitely feasible. But it is by no means guaranteed. There are a lot of people walking around with similar injuries who tried what I'm suggesting and got little to nothing out of it."

Sue reached out and squeezed Sam's wrist as the latter said, "So much for sugarcoating."

Victoria smiled thinly. "Speaking of that, I mentioned craniosacral therapy. That's Sue's department. Some people call it pseudoscience or quackery; others swear by it. It's a form of gentle touch manipulation of the cranium and skeleton—right on the border of hands-off therapy, but not quite. I'm not a believer in the science end of it, but I like the temporary results I've seen, like today. If the least we hope for is to do no harm, it certainly meets the standard, so why not? But if you want my opinion, and Sue told me earlier she agreed with me, it worked today largely because Willy was exhausted. Given his condition, it's a finger stuck in the dam, however, assuming it ever works again."

Victoria rose, indicating she was done. "You're more than welcome to hang around until Willy returns from Never Land, but I would urge you to go home and catch some sleep yourself."

She stuck out her hand, adding, "I'll try never to bullshit you. I'm hoping that's one reason Sue brought you here."

Sam considered that for a couple of seconds, returning the shake gratefully. "It is, and I'm on board. I'll do whatever it takes to get Mr. Grumpy there, too—although it sounds like you did that already. And I'll inform Joe and whoever else he recommends."

Victoria moved to her desk to fetch a business card, which she handed over. "Even knowing you as little as I do," she said. "I'd be willing to put money on your success. The only word of advice I'd add is to spur your superiors on. The injury may be old, but we're at a make-or-break moment. For Willy's sake and yours, move as fast as you can. He's like a man on a high wire, being blown by a growing wind."

CHAPTER TEN

"You see Rachel's pictures in the paper today?" Beverly asked. "They're online, too."

Joe smiled at the excitement in her voice. When they had first met, decades ago, she'd been cool, meticulous, unforgiving of sloppiness, and even more comically formal in speech and manner. Everyone, without exception, had been addressed only by title, rank, and last name.

Her quality of work had made these eccentricities tolerable, of course, not to mention that most cops are inclined to fatalistically accept their superiors being odd. In those days, they adapted by claiming bragging rights if Hillstrom didn't dress them down in some way, never mind handing out praise.

Her professional standards hadn't diminished any. But her sense of accomplishment had slowly allowed for the emergence of a more complex and open woman. The pure happiness and pride he heard now, even over the cell phone's marginal speaker, were testimony to how much freer she'd become with her emotions—contagiously, in fact, since she had helped him to open up in the process.

"I did," he told her. "I should've called, but I figured you'd be poised with a sharp knife over someone's chest."

"You figured correctly," she reassured him. "I didn't get to see them until an hour ago."

"They're really good," he commented. "Much more dramatic than I expected. She made it all look like something from an opera. Way over the top."

"Thanks to you, she did," Beverly praised him. "That was very sweet of you. I know your being there was a positive influence."

"It was still Jonathon's call," he countered. "I only hope it'll compensate for all the future times we'll be throwing her out of a crime scene."

"You sound like you're in a car," Beverly said, changing the subject.

"Heading to Massachusetts. Don't know if I'll get lucky or not, but I'm hoping to drop in on Mick Durocher's estranged daughter. I got her address from paperwork we found in his trailer."

"What can she tell you?"

"Damned if I know. Right now, it's just a rock I can't not turn over. I got the heads-up from the AG's office to unofficially treat this as an unsolved homicide, which basically moves me from proving Mick's a killer to figuring out who'd want to frame him and why."

"You're sure he didn't do it?"

"Only instinctively," Joe conceded. "That's why I'm stressing the unofficial nature of this. All the smoking guns here have his prints on them. I just think they're planted or circumstantial."

"Is there anything I can do?" she offered.

"Not so far. The AG's lining up a DNA sample from Mick, to compare it to Teri Parker's fetus. But unless you can come up with something more, I think you've already worked your end of this puzzle."

"How are things proceeding with the fire investigation?" Beverly asked.

"I touched base with Lester before I headed out," Joe reported. "He said he felt like the only cop directing traffic after the Super Bowl."

"That doesn't sound good."

Her response reminded him that her knowledge of professional sports rivaled a Martian's. "Believe me," he said. "It's not."

* * *

Lester sipped from his fourth mug of coffee as he stood before a large interior window overlooking the GreenField warehouse floor from forty feet above. He was in the general manager's borrowed meeting room, and behind him were two conference tables pushed together, covered with personnel files, organizational flowcharts, and three-ringed binders bulging with information about suppliers and customers of the business.

Also in attendance was a sharply dressed middle-aged woman with a practical straight haircut, short fingernails, and no jewelry, named Pat Smith. She was the GreenField security head Willy had spoken well of earlier, and another veteran of the Vermont State Police, like Lester himself.

Despite that, they'd never met, although the "troops," as they were generally called, were only about three hundred strong at any given time. He had heard of her as a serious overachiever, which in this case had been proving a real asset—even if it had pushed Lester to consume more coffee than he liked.

In truth, he wasn't supposed to be here right now, although he didn't mind. He'd caught a phone call from Sammie—usually the class workaholic—asking him to cover for her as she dealt with an unidentified personal emergency. He had a pretty good idea of what that was, especially since she'd added—parent to parent—"it's not Emma." It wasn't the first time Lester had contemplated what a handful Willy Kunkle must be as a partner. He hadn't pressed her for details, and she'd left it at that, but Les was perfectly aware that Willy had been off his game lately.

Smith and he were next door to what had become a virtual war room—larger, windowless, and as rough-hewn as a military barracks. Some eight cubicles had been set up there for interviews, each manned by an agent of the VBI culled from across the state, and each featuring a desk, two chairs, a video recorder, and a presumption of privacy wherein to conduct a nonstop series of employee interviews. The manager's smaller meeting room, by contrast, had been reserved as somewhere to reflect, strategize, and store the relevant paperwork for what was occurring one door over.

These two rooms crowned a four-story building-within-a-building—a freestanding, monolithic, plywood-walled stack of offices built on the warehouse floor to make communications between labor and management less of an effort. The company's executives, bookkeepers, and salespeople were in a large penthouse elsewhere—and harder to reach. The Castle, as this was nicknamed, was the equivalent of the field commander's headquarters, as stripped of artifice or pomp as a sentry post near a battlefront.

Pat Smith and Lester had chosen it to facilitate their daunting interview campaign, and to best process and monitor their results. So far, while they had collected almost nothing of worth, they had become privy to a minor avalanche of peeves, rivalries, illicit romances, resentments, crushed hopes, alleged improprieties, and several claims of criminal activity, from theft to sexual assault to sabotage to one case of someone who had copied the key to a food vending machine and was reducing his home grocery bill accordingly—if at the sacrifice of a healthy diet.

Lester, suffering from lack of sleep like most of them, believed he'd finally achieved the fantasy nightmare of being the only air traffic controller at O'Hare during a snowstorm. He understood the urgency Joe had placed on this investigation, and the fact that its unknowns were potentially more lethal than what they'd seen so far. But it remained an exhausting process.

"Let's step back a foot or two," he suggested to his colleague without looking back at her. "Tell me about the management structure here, from the bosses on down."

"Robert Beaupré," Pat began without questioning the request. "Originally French Canadian, or at least his family was. The name literally means 'beautiful pasture,' which is what led to GreenField. Most people think they made it up to fit a grocery business, but it's closer to the heart than that. Robert's old man was a farmer, and the son of a farmer. The father was kind of a socialist capitalist, if there is such a thing—he grew crops for income, but also distributed them far and wide to the benefit of the poor and less advantaged.

"The consensus is Robert smelled the Kool-Aid but didn't actually drink it. His GreenField is more along traditional lines: He distributes food but according to a capitalist model, although he does contribute more than most competitors to food banks and the like. He also caters primarily to mom-and-pop retailers, small markets, locally run chains, and even a few co-ops, although that's just a peripheral ploy. Bottom line is he can call himself the grocer of the little guy, shave a little off his profit line by being legitimately charitable, and still walk away at the end of the day with a few million under his belt every year. He's a tough negotiator—make no mistake."

Lester turned to face her. "That much? Just for him?"

"The margins in this business are ridiculously low, but if you counterbalance them with volume and efficiency—and you're as sharp as he is—there's a ton of money to be made."

Lester gave her a half smile. "For everybody?"

She didn't play coy. "I'm not complaining. I wasn't going much higher in the VSP, and this'll put my kids into better schools than before."

"Speaking of that," Lester segued, "what kinds of issues do you handle generally? I mean, whoever torched this place can't be your standard fare."

"Theft tops the chart," Pat replied. "No surprise there. Everything from filching something out of an open box on one of the aisles to rerouting entire truckloads. It's not rampant or crippling, and it's not unexpected, but it's what I deal with daily. There's just too much stuff moving through here. It's a temptation, and a lot of the people we employ—most of whom are terrific, and that's no bullshit—have led rough enough lives that they just don't have the wiring to resist taking what's lying around. It's like police work. If it weren't for that small inner core of dirtbag human beings that keep screwing up every system on earth, we cops would be unemployed. But they're the gift that keeps on giving."

Lester repeated the one item that had caught his attention. "Rerouting truckloads?"

She actually smiled. "We get a few that're that ambitious. I'm working to get management to equip every rig with a GPS, but it's more expensive than you'd think. They're interested, as are our insurers, but there's a long list of other good ideas waiting to be approved, too. For the moment, I try to control it through other means, but I would like to plug that hole."

"Other means?" Lester chuckled. "Almost sounds ominous."

She laughed with him. "Don't I wish. Nah, I'm just talking better inventory controls. It would be fun to be the head of a private army, but I ain't."

"All right." He stepped back from the window and sat across from her. "Back to the original question. Who's under Robert Beaupré? This an all-family operation?"

"Yes and no," she answered without pause. "There is family involved, but it's not strictly linear, and not strictly blood related. Robert and his wife have two sons and a daughter: Robert Jr.—called Bobby—Philip, and Elaine. Elaine's married to a man named Bradley St. John, believe it or not, who's actually not as stuck up as that sounds. Bobby and Brad do a lot of heavy lifting under Robert, whose hand is still very much on the tiller. Philip is more of a floater within the company, filling in on odd jobs here and there. Kind of a special projects guy. He played a big role in outfitting both warehouses with motion-sensitive LEDs, for example, which is saving us a bundle in utility costs. Elaine's not involved at all.

"Filling out the rest of the upper tier are nonfamily, run-of-the-mill professional management types. Finance, computers, development, sales, security, infrastructure, operations, and so on. All that's pretty standard. Also, a lot of the brass work out of our headquarters building in Colchester, conveniently near both Montpelier and Burlington, so you're not likely to see many of them around here."

"Would it be a big deal if they did show up?" Lester asked, looking down at the reams of files spread before them.

Pat shook her head. "Nobody would notice. For a building with no windows and only a few pedestrian doors, there's a *lot* of foot traffic coming and going every day. That's something you probably noticed staring at all that surveillance video."

"Somebody else did most of that," Lester confessed. "But I get your point."

"Also, we don't stand on ceremony here," Pat continued. "If Robert Beaupré wants to talk with somebody inside the building, he might call ahead, or he might just show up. I've found him leaning against my office doorjamb to ask a question, when I didn't even know he was in-state."

Lester scratched his head. "Okay. So, back to this fire. It was done for effect, carefully thought out, precisely executed, and apparently loaded with some kind of message. It also had to have been done by somebody still on the inside, not a pissed-off short-termer who got caught stealing pens."

"Seafood," Pat interjected.

"What?"

"Seafood, frozen steak, pallets of plastic razors, which are outrageously overpriced. Those're the high-end products where stealing a little generates the most cash."

"Okay. Well, whatever. You get my point. Plus, we're not talking theft, but arson."

She tapped the tabletop for emphasis. "But *my* point is that some of these items carry a bigger cash value than you might think. I don't want us missing a clever thief because we get obsessed with a superbrain bad guy driven by a mysterious agenda. You basically just said we don't know what we're dealing with, which means it might still be ongoing. These fires could be an opening salvo of some kind, with a big payoff we haven't seen yet."

Lester understood her point. By the same token, her focus on theft—her biggest daily concern—reminded him of who signed her paycheck. Cops—at least good ones—were guided by certain stolid shibboleths of the trade: every death is a homicide to start with; everybody lies; everyone's a suspect until cleared. It could sound close-minded and paranoid, but in fact, its all-inclusiveness was designed to keep an investigator sharp and open to suggestions. It was the practical, nonliterary, not-so-quotable thinking behind Conan Doyle's, "Once you eliminate the impossible, whatever remains, no matter how improbable, must be the truth."

In that light, it wasn't lost on Lester that he could very well be sharing this office with the person he was seeking—and who was only pretending to be helping him out.

He glanced at Pat Smith meditatively for a moment before sighing and saying, "Which still brings us full circle: Go through everything and everybody and see who stands out."

With that, almost on cue, a second VBI agent entered the room from next door, to deposit another thick pile of paperwork from yet another round of interviews.

"Having fun yet?" he asked, heading back out.

"Nothing but," Lester reassured him.

CHAPTER ELEVEN

Mandy Lawlor, Mick Durocher's presumed daughter, lived in Fitchburg, Massachusetts. "Presumed" only because the one document Joe hadn't found among Mick's trailer contents had been a birth certificate. There had been a handwritten, notarized will, listing her as Mick's only child, and bequeathing her all his worldly assets, although calculating those would probably prove a challenge. Joe's team had estimated that aside from a few small items, the bank owned the bulk of it, including the trailer and the broken truck.

Nevertheless, Joe was looking forward to meeting the girl, if not to prepare her for any anticipated bounty. In the few days since they'd found Teri Parker's body, Mick Durocher had become a shape-shifting presence, transitioning from suspect to confessed felon to something far less definable. Joe doubted Mandy would be a wellspring of information—all references to her in the trailer had reflected Mick's guilt and longing, but no sign of their having kept in touch. Research into Mick's true inner workings had to start somewhere, however, and clearly this young woman had played an important role.

Fitchburg, to veer close to political correctness, has been called a challenged town. Roughly forty thousand inhabitants strong, it often crops up in New Hampshire and southeastern Vermont law enforcement bulletins as a source community for drugs and related illegal activities that routinely spill across the northern border. Another classic example of nineteenth-century industrial might gone to seed, it is variously garnished with ancient architectural gems, down-at-the-heels strip malls, quirky Victorian-era artifacts, high unemployment and crime stats, and a museum devoted exclusively to toy airplanes. As Joe, a lifelong New Englander, drove into its embrace, he was reminded yet again of the entire region's struggles between the glories of its past and the uncertainty of its future.

Protocol dictates that if officers enter a town not their own on business, especially from out of state, first knocking on the door of the local "cop shop" is good manners and smart procedure. The logic being that if anything goes awry subsequently, the scene of the crime won't be where initial introductions are exchanged.

Joe had called ahead and so was anticipated when he stopped at police headquarters on Elm Street. Not surprisingly, the FPD was a busy place. When he presented himself at the front desk, instead of being invited up for the usual cup of coffee in some detective bureau, he was asked to wait in the lobby until a tired-looking man in a tired-looking suit appeared at the building's inner door and asked, "You the Vermont cop?"

"Yes." Joe approached with a smile.

"Al Danziger," the man said halfheartedly. "You lookin' for somebody down here?"

"Amanda Lawlor." Joe produced a piece of paper with Mandy's address on it. "She's the daughter of a suspect we have in jail on a murder charge."

"She a suspect, too?" Danziger asked.

"No. I just want as much background as she can give me on her old man."

"They were tight?"

"Doesn't look like it. From what we got tossing his place inside out, she might not even know he exists. The love seems to run one way."

"Guilty loser feeling sorry for himself?" Danziger asked with no real interest.

"Could be," Joe replied noncommittally.

Danziger crossed to the dispatcher behind the bulletproof panel and slid the scrap of paper through the slot at its base. "Run this, would you? Amanda Lawlor."

They didn't wait long. The dispatcher quickly returned with a printout that she passed through the same slot. Danziger glanced at its contents before giving it to Joe. "Seems like a minor bandit," he said. "Usual offenses: shoplifting, driving suspended, intoxicated, noise complaints. Nothing major, nothing recent, and mostly teenage crap, from the looks of it. She's also not coded for associations with known bad guys. I'd say you're good to go. Knock yourself out."

The man turned toward the building's interior, but then looked back to add, "But that's it, okay? No cowboying. You find her, talk to her, and leave. Or you come back here. I don't wanna find you facedown in our fair streets. You good with that?"

"Absolutely," Joe said.

"Have a nice day," Danziger told him as he continued walking away.

It wasn't unique in Joe's experience. The standard holds that detectives should travel in pairs, and a cop from another jurisdiction gets assigned a local babysitter, but variations were common. Danziger was an old-timer, he'd no doubt recognized in Joe someone of his ilk, and he'd gone with his gut to return to a caseload befitting a department with some four thousand calls for service every year.

Joe wasn't unhappy with the outcome. He'd been prepared for an escort, but was happier to have been cut loose. Willy Kunkle wasn't the only one to prefer working solo.

As with many towns like Fitchburg, the neighborhoods got tougher toward the city center. Reasonably, the PD was located appropriately nearby. Sadly, so was the address Joe had for Mandy Lawlor.

That was a three-story apartment building with the usual hallmarks of an affordable housing unit—a precisely calculated meeting point between what authorities demanded and investors were willing to pay for, measured in overall hardiness, paint quality, roofing material, and architectural flair. Or the lack of it. Joe left his car and crossed to the building's lobby, hoping life might reward him with Mandy being at home.

At least the address was correct. LAWLOR appeared under one of the buzzers mounted next to the mailboxes.

But as he'd feared, there was no answer.

A small, stooped, bald man appeared from out of the gloom of the lobby's interior. "Who're you looking for?"

Joe resisted saying anything beyond, "Mandy Lawlor."

It proved to be good enough. The man made an effort to study him a moment before announcing, "She's at the Wendy's on John Fitch. Till seven."

Joe nodded his thanks and left, grateful for the unpredictability of urban social mores—at moments cold and suspicious, at others so much the opposite as to be openly careless.

There was virtually no one in the restaurant lot when Joe arrived ten minutes later. And the place had only two people sitting by a far window. He approached the counter and a heavyset man whose cardboard hat was two sizes too small for his head.

"What'll you have?"

"I'd actually like to speak with the manager, if he or she's around," Joe said politely.

The man's expression went still. He straightened from propping both hands on the counter. "I'm him. What's wrong?"

Joe pretended to be tactful, glancing over his shoulder at the uninterested couple. He very quickly flashed the badge attached to his belt, fast enough to let it glimmer only—distinct but unreadable.

"It's a favor, really. Is Mandy working today?"

The manager scowled. "Yeah."

Joe lowered his voice so the man had to edge his gut onto the counter to hear him. "You could really help me out. I have some family news I need to give her. It's a courtesy we like to make whenever we can. Makes things easier."

The scowl eased a bit. "She's not in trouble?"

Joe's face showed astonishment. "Good Lord, no way. Not even maybe. I just want to steal her for a quick conversation—tell her what I got. Would that be okay? You'd be doin' me and the department a big favor."

The power of a little cheap and easy flattery. The fat man smiled magnanimously. "You kidding? Look around. Take your time." He then swiveled on his heel, bellowed, "*Mandy*. Up front," and faded back into the kitchen.

A young woman appeared, sporting the official Wendy's outfit and cap, her kind if wary face suggesting that experience had led—despite reasonable or rational expectations—to hopefulness instead of cynicism. It stood in jarring contrast to her worn, industrialized surroundings and uniform.

"May I help you?" she asked.

"Amanda Lawlor?" he replied, immediately taking a liking to her.

She shook hands tentatively. "Yes."

"My name is Joe Gunther," he explained. "I'm a police officer from Vermont. May I have a brief conversation with you? Your manager said it would be fine with him."

Her eyes betrayed what she thought of that permission, but her response was friendly and coconspiratorial. "Well," she said with a raised eyebrow, "then I guess we're blessed."

He chuckled and stood back, indicating the dining area. "We can sit at a table if you'd like, or my car if that's better."

She lifted a section of the counter and came out. "A table's fine."

He was struck by her lack of apparent concern. She seemed somehow settled internally, at ease with whatever calamity life might have in store. It was not a form of spiritual stillness he was used to.

As they sat far from the other couple, near a window facing the broad commercial boulevard beyond the parking lot, she commented, "My father lives in Vermont. I'm guessing this is about him?"

"It is," Joe said. "You're right." He suddenly looked around. "I'm sorry, would you like something to eat or drink? I forgot to ask, probably because of the setting. Threw me off my manners."

She held up a hand. "No. I'll pass, thank you. You probably shouldn't make that kind of offer to any fast-food employee, regardless of the brand. We're a little overexposed to what passes for nutrition. What's happened to my dad?"

"For starters, he's okay," Joe began. "I mean, he's not hurt. He is in trouble, though. In jail. He confessed to killing someone—a young woman."

Her hands rested in her lap as she shifted her gaze to the silently passing traffic. The air appeared to leave her body. "Oh."

Joe let a moment go by before asking, "Were the two of you in touch at all?"

"We weren't close," she answered indirectly.

"I thought that might be so," he said softly. "Going through his things, I didn't see much from you."

"No," she agreed. "You wouldn't have." She then looked at him directly and asked, "Did he do it?"

This wasn't the sort of question a cop normally addresses head-on. Natural instinct and normal procedure dictate evasiveness. But Joe was outside his comfort zone with this case, and needed help.

"He's saying he did. I can't take his word alone on it."

"I hope not," she said.

"Describe him to me," Joe requested. "I get that your life together wasn't the easiest road traveled, but if you wouldn't mind, I'd appreciate it."

She nodded, her eyes now on the tabletop between them. When she spoke, it was quietly, without bitterness—a voice recounting the plot of a documentary.

"My parents were probably like I was as a teenager," she began. "Pretty dumb and clueless. Happy to party and drink and fool around. I don't guess the apple ever falls far from the tree that way. You do what you see being done around you. Isn't that what they say?"

He knew better than to respond except to show that he was listening carefully.

"So my mom got pregnant with me soon enough," she continued. "That made her dad throw her out of the house. My own dad had no idea what to do. He was already getting into trouble with the law. I think they tried living together, mostly because they knew that's what was expected. But all they knew how to do was what they were already doing."

She smiled suddenly, glancing up at him. "I should probably count myself lucky I wasn't born with disabilities. I know my mom was drinking and smoking like a chimney when I was inside her. And probably a lot worse, besides. She was a serious doper. That's what finally did her in."

"She's dead?" Joe asked.

"Yeah. Years ago. An overdose."

"I'm guessing their living together didn't last long," Joe suggested.

"No," she said sadly. "I don't remember any of it, so I was a baby when they gave up—maybe even before I was born. I only know what I could piece together. My earliest memories were of living with my mom and seeing Mick every once in a while. He stood out 'cause he was the only man who came around who wasn't there for my mother."

She shifted slightly in her chair, easing into her narrative, which had maintained its even, sympathetic tone. "I'm not saying they never got it on when he came by. They still knew how to have fun. But he would pay attention to me. Bring me things. It wasn't a big deal. He had a short attention span, if you know what I mean. But he'd try. He was nice. He just wasn't there much."

Her voice abruptly grew an edge, as if she'd picked up a shield. "Then she died. Just like that. And everything changed."

"How old were you?"

"Thirteen. Great age. Hormones going crazy, stretching my wings, like they say, only my wings had feathers like razor blades. Of course, the state came into it right off, trying to figure out what to do with me. They probably got hold of my dad, to find out how suitable he was as a parent. That was a no-go. For all I know, he was in jail at the time. Pretty likely. Anyhow, I wasn't gonna be given to him, even if he had wanted me. My mom's dad was still alive, but his own past killed that option right out of the box. He was still the waste of time he always was."

She sighed before resuming, "So. It was off to a home for me. Foster care was the goal, I guess. That's what they tell you. And it was tried on me. A couple of times. But the people were in it for the money. Well, one couple was; the other were Bible-thumpers, and we just didn't get along. Anyhow, I washed out, and finally, I aged out."

She surprised him then by smiling broadly. "And that's when I had Julia, the love of my life."

"Oh," he said. "Congratulations. I had no idea."

She laughed. "Like mother, like daughter, right? That's what I thought at first. I was going to repeat all the same self-destructive shit my mom did. But I haven't so far." She waved her hand around. "I got this job and I'm taking classes at the college, and I make sure Julia knows who loves her and that I've got her back, no matter what. I'm not the great American success story, but I haven't become my parents, either."

"Nicely done, Mandy," Joe said. "I'm impressed."

"Thanks. It was hard at first. I was doing everything wrong. Getting pregnant is supposed to be the end of your life, if you're a person like me. But I guess that's what finally made me mad. I was going to show my daughter that she was the best thing that ever happened to me."

Joe admired the determination in her voice, and now understood the demeanor he'd noticed upon their meeting. She'd clearly appraised her situation, taken action as a result, and was making life happen, instead of being pushed around by circumstance.

"Did Mick know about Julia?" he asked, steering her back to why he was here. She'd deflected his inquiry about father and daughter keeping in touch. She'd said they weren't close, which wasn't the same thing.

For the first time, the girl's features became creased by emotion. She swallowed hard and stared back out at the traffic a moment, composing herself. Eventually, she reached for a napkin and dabbed at her eyes.

"Sorry," she barely whispered.

"Don't apologize," he said, struck by the sudden change. "I'm sorry to be stirring all this up."

That helped her recover as she shook her head. "No, it's fine. It's probably good. I worry about holding too much in sometimes. Yes. I told him about her—just recently—but I wouldn't let them meet. You have to understand: I didn't hate my parents, and I don't feel sorry about how I grew up. I don't blame anybody for any of it. I know who's an asshole and who's not. 'Shit Happens' is just half of what should be that expression. It ought to be: 'You Make Shit Happen.' When my dad asked if he could see Julia, I said no. Enough was enough."

"How did he take it?"

She pondered that for a moment before replying, "That's what hit me just then. He totally got it. He said I was right, and that he loved us both and always would, even if we never saw each other ever again."

She shook her head. "That was the crazy part. When he said that, it almost changed my mind. I think he knew it, too, 'cause in a later call he stressed that he'd stay away, that I should stick to my guns, and then he hung up, like to shut me up. That was a hard night—the last time we ever spoke—maybe a couple of months ago. I still feel bad about it, for his sake. His being sensitive like that makes me wonder what I missed by cutting him out. It sounds cruel now, what I did, especially after what's happened to him."

"Don't do that," Joe counseled. "Don't second-guess yourself. You were right, and he agreed with you. He gave you that, even if he gave you nothing else."

She was crying again, quietly, as was her style. "I know, I know. But his being arrested for what you told me—a murder. That's not the only bad thing that's happened. He's sick, too."

Joe studied her as she wiped her eyes again and blew her nose. "How do you mean? How often were these conversations?"

"Oh, just two or three this last year. Before then, virtually never. And it was the *way* he was talking that tipped me off. Not so much what he said. I got the feeling he was putting things in order. That's why his last call was hard. When you walked up and asked to talk, I was sure it was to tell me he'd died."

"Did he talk about what was going on in his life at that point?" Joe asked. "Who he was seeing, where he was working, anything like that?"

"No, and I wasn't very good about asking. The other times we talked, the questions were all from him. He was interested in Julia and me—I think that was real—but I got the sense that he didn't want to talk about himself, like he was embarrassed. So I never asked, and he never told."

"He never mentioned the name Teri Parker?"

"Was that the person he killed?"

"If he did," Joe said truthfully.

She shook her head. "No. Like I said."

"And you're pretty sure about his being sick?"

"He sounded really tired and old," she said. "But it was more than that—the things he said, the kinds of questions he asked. I thought about it afterwards, you know how you do? And I came up with 'resigned.' He'd been everything else in the earlier conversations—fake upbeat or apologetic or guilty. But this last time, it was like he'd run out of gas and wanted to make sure he said what needed to be said."

"Which was what?" Joe asked, adding, "In addition to your sticking to your guns about Julia."

"That he loved me, was proud of me. That Julia and I were the only things he'd ever done right in his life, which was a little weird. But I got what he was trying to say. That's what I mean. Normally, I might've given him a little pushback for saying something like that. But this was like a last will and testament."

"He did write a will," Joe told her. "There won't be much in it, but he was thinking of you."

"I know," she said mournfully.

Joe removed his notepad and slid it across the table with a pen. "You mentioned your grandfather—your mom's dad. Could you write down his name and contact information? He's married, I'm guessing?"

She spoke as she wrote. "If that's what you'd call it. I'm adding my grandma's name, but she won't tell you anything. Dumb as a rock. Only way any woman would stay with that man."

"Did you ever know your dad's parents?" Joe asked.

"No. They were never in the picture and he never talked about them. I always thought my dad came from somewhere else, like the Midwest or something, and that his folks were dead anyhow. But I don't know for sure."

"Any aunts, uncles?" Joe asked leadingly. "On either side?"

She shook her head. "My dad, I just said. My mom was an only child."

"How 'bout friends?" he persisted. "My mom has bosom buddies that're probably better than siblings. Did Mick have anyone close you know about?"

But she was already repeating her earlier gesture. "I wouldn't know. I can't think of anybody."

She looked more disappointed than he at the results on the pad before her. Which may have led to her looking up to ask sadly, "What does he look like?"

Joe hesitated, thinking the most honest answer was that Mick Durocher looked like death warmed over, which—with Mandy's revelations in mind—suggested a whole new line of thought.

Instead, however, Joe settled for, "Pretty much how he sounded on the phone."

He took a business card from his shirt pocket and slid it across the table. "Mandy, I am sorry to have brought so much of this back up. I know it's been tough. Do me a favor, though, would you? Let me know if you hear anything more from your dad?"

She touched the card without picking it up. "That's not too likely."

Joe hoped she was wrong.

CHAPTER TWELVE

Willy resisted opening his eyes. The pain was still there, pounding away, a nonstop tinnitus delivered by a live electrical cord plugged directly into his head. But it had lost some of its edge, something he feared the mere lifting of his eyelids might reverse.

"Willy?"

The voice was nice, oddly familiar, and comforting. Under normal circumstances, a stranger's voice from inches away would have caused him alarm. But not this time, which surprised him.

"Willy? It's Sue."

Okay. Now it was coming back to him. He opened his eyes slowly.

Above him, haloed by blond hair, was Sue Spinney, filling his field of vision with her smile and blue eyes.

He just barely resisted reaching out and touching her cheek. "Hey, Sue."

The pain notched up a click and made him wince.

"Still hurting pretty badly?"

"What did you two do?" he asked. "I feel like I been drugged."

"Victoria did give you an injection, but I also tried a massage technique that seemed to work."

He closed his eyes again. "I remember that. I thought it would be complete crap."

"And?"

"I apologize," he told her. "I'm not in great shape right now. I know that. But you did good. Thank you."

He heard a noise by his side, and a second female voice joined Sue's. "You're back," Sam said.

Willy smiled and looked at her, her face now hovering next to Sue's. This, he didn't have to think about. He reached out and laid his hand against her face. "Hi, sweetheart. Sorry I messed up."

He saw her register the endearment, maybe a first for him, or close to it.

Sam glanced at Sue. "You should give him that shit daily."

Joe punched in the code on the VBI office door lock back in Brattleboro and let himself in. It was rare that he got the place to himself at midday, and he enjoyed the solitude, standing in the middle of the room, absorbing the silence. But there was something more. As he surveyed the four desks and the walls covered with bulletins, reports, stat sheets, and the like, he realized that the other sensation he was enjoying was a lingering aura of industry—as if the air itself were redolent of past arguments, theories, questions, and responses.

Joe had progressed beyond simply loving what he did. The job and the people he worked with had fused with his spirit. He had no delusions that any of them could change the world for the better, or have a lasting impact upon society's behavior. It sufficed that they did good work, had a positive influence, and were of use to people in need. Cumulatively, it had become, in a phrase, the driving force in his life. Where those like Lester had a family and lived where they'd been born, and Sam and Willy a child they both adored, Joe was the one whose identity had gradually melded with what he did for a living, rather than who he was outside the job. His romance with Beverly was softening that, but he'd suffered from heartbreak before, and while hopeful now, as never before, he also knew they were still testing the waters together.

He moved to sit at his desk, his back to the room's one window, and dialed the phone.

"Marble Valley Regional Correctional Facility," was the response moments later.

"Walter Easton, please. This is Joe Gunther of the VBI."

Easton had worked as a supervisor at MVRCF for eighteen years. He was a born Vermonter, a Rutland native, and could have once evolved into your average woodchuck. Instead, upon graduating from the police academy, he'd magically transformed into a natural networker and student of correctional systems nationwide. Most members of his profession were dismissed as "guards," doing little more than shepherding inmates through their daily brain-numbing routines. Easton had recognized that among other things, jails contained among the highest concentrations of special-needs occupants shy of a mental hospital. Thus, his job, as he saw it, was to make his prison a safe and supportive environment in which all residents could treat their court-ordered time-outs as opportunities to do something beyond killing time. Walter Easton would've been the last person to label himself as such, but in many ways, he'd become if not a radical, then at least a devoted social engineer.

He was also well placed in Vermont, where the view of mental health naturally leaned in his direction, especially lately.

Joe was calling him not only because of all this—along with its implication that Walter would have an eye peeled for a sick inmate—but also because Joe had made it his business years ago to keep track of as many people in law enforcement as he could, if for no other reason than to have them available in times of need. This semi-closed community, in all its guises and jurisdictions—federal to local—was little different in terms of networking than most other professions. What you knew was an asset; who you knew was often the key that opened doors.

"Joe Gunther," came the familiar voice after a few minutes. "How long's it been?"

"Too long," Joe admitted. "I'd blame the fact that you're located on the far side of the state, 'cept that's only an hour away."

Walter laughed. "Too bad we don't live in Texas or Oklahoma, huh?"

"Nah, I'm good where I am," Joe replied.

"What can I do for you?" Walter asked. "I know in my bones this ain't a social call."

"Well, truth be told," Joe conceded, "I do have an ulterior motive. Are you aware of a newcomer to your population named Mick Durocher?"

Walter's response was immediate. "Hell yeah. Like we have so many murder suspects, we lose count of 'em. Funny he should come up, though. We're on the edge of shipping him to a hospital."

Even with his misgivings, Joe was caught off guard. "What's wrong with him?"

"Sick as a dog, Joe. I'm guessing cancer, but it's hard to say. He's refusing treatment, which puts the debate into tricky territory. We'll be okay in the long run, but we need a diagnosis and for him to sign the paperwork. After that, we'll just make sure he dies comfortably in the infirmary, but we've just started all that. Funny you should call now, though. Did you know this was happening?"

"I had my suspicions," Joe told him. "Do you have his daughter on his next-of-kin information? Mandy Lawlor? I didn't get the feeling Mick has anyone else."

There was a pause as Walter consulted a computer at his end. "Nope," he eventually reported. "Give me her particulars."

Joe did so, adding, "Could you keep me up to date on this? There are elements to the investigation that're ongoing, and Mick's health is relevant."

"Sure thing, Joe, and thanks. The way things're going, I'll be calling her and you soon."

* * *

Despite having done so too many times to count, Joe remained captivated by sitting quietly in someone else's living space. The sounds, smells, and surrounding landscape of another person's intimate environment reflect if not them, precisely, then certainly something fascinating to the interloper.

He was perched on a kitchen chair in Mick Durocher's trailer, studying the walls and surfaces as he might a museum gallery's. Like many tourists, he'd visited restored stately homes or colonial cabins, and sought to learn what their prior inhabitants had been like, taking in the furniture and artwork and tools—even the clothing, carefully laid out across the foot of a bed.

But the true essence of these ghosts had remained elusive, as they were now in the humming of Mick's refrigerator, the smells of aging food and unwashed clothes, even the sight of a field mouse gingerly making the rounds of crumbs and scraps wedged under the cabinet toe kicks. This was where Mick had lived, what he'd seen every morning, and—Joe was hoping—where he'd left evidence of what had brought him to everyone's attention.

Lester had earlier collected all the available paperwork. That's how they'd found the will and, later, Mandy Lawlor's address. But he'd left behind most of the personal effects, the few pictures on the walls, the food in the cabinets—now reflective of a man largely beyond their reach.

In response to Joe's hopes for inspiration, there was an unexpected knock on the trailer's flimsy door.

Smiling at the timing, he rose, crossed the narrow space, and swung open the door, revealing an older man in coveralls, a T-shirt, and an ancient, much-stained baseball cap, looking up at him.

"Can I help you?" Joe asked.

The man smiled back, if warily. "I was about to ask the same thing. Saw your car out front. Was wondering what you were doing."

His tone of voice was pleasant, but his proprietary interest was clear.

Joe revealed his badge. "I'm the police. You wanna come in?"

The older man hadn't been expecting that. "Well, I don't want to interrupt. It's none of my business."

"Maybe not," Joe said, catering to his visitor's self-esteem. "But you're clearly looking out for Mick's property. To me, that shows you're a good neighbor. Maybe even a friend."

He hoped to seal the deal by reaching out with an extended hand. "Joe Gunther."

The man responded in kind. "Ray Davis. People call me Reefus."

Joe stood aside. "Please. Feel free."

His impromptu guest hesitated no longer, and laboriously climbed the wobbly metal steps into the trailer.

"This look the way it usually did?" Joe asked, gesturing around.

Reefus followed his lead with a glance, nodding once. "Pretty much. Kind of a mess down the hall. I'd guess that's where the fight happened."

"You heard about that."

Davis chuckled shortly. "Heard? Hard not to. All of you yelling and throwing people around."

Joe nudged a chair with his toe so Davis could sit. "Yeah, the adrenaline gets pumping. Also, believe it not, it sometimes takes screaming our heads off to get people to listen. They can be pretty pumped up, too."

Reefus appeared to accept that, or chose not to argue. "What's happened to Mick?" he asked instead.

Joe began carefully, "Well, it turned out we interrupted his attacker's assault in the nick of time, so Mick didn't suffer too much there. But you must've noticed he's not been looking good lately."

Davis looked sympathetic. "Yeah. And feeling like hell, too."

"You were friends?" Joe asked hopefully, wondering if pure good luck wasn't about to hand him the prize he'd been seeking. For all their digging into Mick's paperwork and background, and driving for hours to interview his estranged daughter, the best source into his recent history might be the man next door.

"I guess so," Reefus allowed. "Nora and I only live a couple of units down. We and Mick struck it up a while ago for no reason I can recall. He's a nice fellow, so we sort of fell into sharing a cup of coffee now and then."

"You didn't want to tell that to the officers who went door-to-door the other day?" Joe asked, genuinely curious.

Davis shrugged. "They didn't ask. They wanted to know if we'd heard this or seen that, which we didn't. Nobody asked if we were friends."

Joe laughed, covering a pang of disappointment. "Yeah. Stuff like that happens more often than we like to admit. Still, here we are. You okay with my asking you a few things about Mick?"

Reefus gave him the kind of appraisal he'd received all his life from rooted, steady people like this—beginning with his own father.

"Depends on the things, don't it?"

Joe nodded. "It does. Sure enough. Well, let's start where you did, then. You said Mick was feeling like hell. What did you mean?"

"He was sick. Nora thought it was cancer, not that we asked. But he was losing weight and looked terrible. From how he handled himself, I'd say there was a lot of pain, too."

"He ever discuss it?"

"Nope."

"Ever mention a doctor, or seeking medical care?"

"Not that, neither."

"But you knew him in better times, so you could tell the difference."

"We could, yup."

"'Bout how long was that—that you knew each other?"

Davis paused to reflect. "Oh, I'd say maybe five years."

"That's good," Joe said. "Gives me something to work with. Let me ask what the other folks didn't: How would you describe him? What kind of man is he?"

"Nice fellow," Davis remarked. "Can't imagine he did what the papers are saying."

It had been slow in coming, and posed in the usual roundabout fashion, but now Joe was aware that his guest kept up with the news.

"It was a murder, Mr. Davis. There was evidence suggesting he committed it just down the street, in fact, in that park-'n'-ride near the main road, after Mick and his girlfriend had a knock-down-drag-out in here."

Reefus shook his head, removed his cap, and scratched his pale, bald pate, looking down at the unswept floor.

Finally, he replaced the cap, which suited him like a head of hair, and stated flatly, "Don't see it."

"I'm listening," Joe encouraged him.

"I'm an old man," Davis started. "Not educated, and not trained like you people. But I been around. I've worked farming and factories and most things in between, and it's not been too often that anyone's pulled a fast one on me. The way a person talks and acts, the way they work—that all speaks of what's inside."

"Okay."

"Well, what you're telling me don't make sense. I'm not saying somebody didn't kill your girl, whoever she was. But it wasn't Mick."

Davis reached up and pulled on his nose with his index finger and thumb, before shifting in his seat and repeating, "If I was you, I'd go back to that evidence and check it again."

"That's why I'm here, Reefus. I want to get it right. Maybe you could pass along a little of what makes you so sure he's not the one. What did you two talk about when he'd drop by?"

"The usual, mostly. Weather, sports, that useless truck of his."

"He ever refer to his daughter?" Joe asked.

"Mandy? Sure. He was so happy to hear she had a daughter. That was the worst thing that ever happened to him, his break with her." He quickly held up a hand. "Not that he complained. Don't get me wrong. He respected that she wanted to be free of everything that had gone before. Mick was straight about his problems—the drinking and the way he treated that little family. I know his ex-wife was no prize, either, but he never blamed her. And he was so proud of that daughter of his. His biggest regret was that he had nothing to pass along to her."

"We heard he was almost a recluse. Like a hermit. Did you ever see him with anyone? Man or woman?"

"That's what the other cop asked. Nah. There mighta been a friend who picked him up for work, now and then, on one of the times his truck would crap out, but that's about it. I don't know the friend's name, but I seen his pickup around town, so I guess he's local."

Davis rubbed his palm hard against his knee. "He was a loner. You heard right. And that's another thing, by the way: the way he was looking lately, the whole idea of his carrying on with some girlfriend is a joke."

"How often did you see each other?" Joe asked.

"Less, lately," Davis admitted. "Maybe once a week, maybe twice, and mostly 'cause I'd come by here. He was low, on top of bein' sick."

"He say why?"

"Nora says it was the cancer, but I think it was more like the weight of the world. Good news like Mandy having a child can cut both ways, you know? It's like there's no room in the world for you anymore. And he felt bad, like I said, that there wasn't something he could do for them."

"The man who attacked him the other night," Joe said, "was someone he once worked for, maybe five months ago. He was pissed Mick had stolen his four-wheeler."

"That was Thurley?" Davis asked flat out. "I know about him. Total crap artist. I didn't realize that. The four-wheeler was his? Son of a bitch. Small world."

"You've had dealings with Thurley?"

"Not directly. But I know some who have. Talk about a bad reputation. See? That's what I mean. Mick hated the guy, 'cause of his way with people—cheating everybody, treatin' them wrong. Mick was more stand-up than that."

"He did actually steal the four-wheeler," Joe pointed out.

"I'm surprised Mick had anything to do with that," Davis allowed. "Or Thurley, especially the way things went at the end. Thurley tried to get Mick tied into an insurance scam—something about stolen chain saws that weren't really stolen."

"What had Mick done before working for him?"

"This and that. Mick wasn't too proud to do anything that paid a wage. But that was another thing that made him feel so low, I think—the lack of a real job, with benefits and retirement and all that."

"He had that?"

"At one time, yeah. Not for a long time. Nothing ever lasted with Mick, but when he had it, it picked up his game. You could see it. He walked straighter, taller."

"When was this?" Joe asked.

"Maybe three years ago. For only about a year."

"What happened?"

Davis acted out holding a bottle and tilting it up. "The booze, like usual. He could never get ahead of it. That was really sad, though, 'cause that time, he finally felt like he'd caught the gravy train, and that he'd be able to help out Mandy."

"I see your point," Joe said softly. "Like having an elephant parked on your chest." He pulled out his notepad and asked, "What was the name of that company with the benefits and all? I probably ought to look them up."

"Oh," Davis replied, his eyes widening. "Big outfit. The commute was a bitch, but worth it to Mick. Talk about upward mobility. It woulda been a really good gig, if he'd only hung on to it. It was that wholesale grocer up in White River Junction. GreenField. You musta heard of it."

Joe closed the notepad, unused, and returned it to his pocket. "Yeah," he replied. "I have."

* * *

The supe was back, this time walking the warehouse floor, taking his time, pausing at the various locations where workers were restoring the fire-damaged pallet racks to their previous condition.

"Hey, J.R." one of them greeted him, glancing over his shoulder.

"Hank," J.R. acknowledged with a nod. "How's it going? Things almost up and running again?"

"Won't be much longer. The cops aren't helping. You been interviewed yet?"

"If you call it that. Pretty lame, if you ask me. If somebody on the inside did this, like they're sayin', I don't know how asking a bunch of dumb-ass questions is gonna get them anywhere."

"Yeah, right," the other man laughed. "The guy's gonna burst into tears at the first question and confess? I don't think so."

J.R. smiled in agreement and began moving along. "Hey, how smart can they be? They're cops."

But Hank wasn't quite finished. He put down the drill he'd been holding and approached J.R. in an almost conspiratorial way before asking softly, "Seriously, what d'you think's going on? People're saying something worse might happen next. I mean, what was the purpose of this?"

J.R. held both palms heavenwards. "Beats me, Hank. Maybe they're right—somebody we fired who got pissed off?"

Hank was unconvinced. "Pretty sophisticated way of doing it. Bypass all the security and set off a bunch of time-delayed bombs? Come on. There's gotta be more to it than that."

J.R. matched the other man's low tone to say, "I shouldn't say this, 'cause—well—it's bad for morale, but I think you're right. Between you and me, forget the company line or the cops. I think this was like a warning shot."

Hank's concern grew, his eyes widening. "Really?"

J.R. stood back. "Hell, you said it. I didn't. It doesn't make sense otherwise." He waved his hand around for emphasis. "I mean, some damage was done, but it wasn't a showstopper. What's that tell you? You ask me,

I think this is like the poor bastard in the crow's nest yelling at the captain in that *Titanic* movie, 'Iceberg ahead.' Right? You know what happened next."

And with that, he turned on his heel and walked away, smiling at the seed he hoped he'd planted.

CHAPTER THIRTEEN

"What?" Lester asked on the phone.

"Goddamn things," his boss muttered angrily.

"That, I heard," Lester said. "What did you say before?"

"Mick—" Joe's voice cut out again.

"I heard 'Mick,'" Lester told him. "What about him?"

"Shit—"

Lester laughed as Pat Smith cast him a look from across the borrowed GreenField office. He covered the mouthpiece and explained, "Gunther. He hates cell phones; always uses 'em where they're guaranteed not to work. Self-fulfilling prophecy."

But he knew the man well enough to simply hang on. Joe eventually came within reach of another cell tower.

"I said Mick used to work there."

"Stop the car where you are," Lester told him.

"Then why the hell do I have a goddamned mobile phone?" Joe countered.

"Point taken. Where did Mick used to work?"

"There. GreenField," Joe explained. "It was about three years ago, for maybe a year. Liked it a lot, but apparently blew it by drinking. It may be nothing—they employ a ton of people like him—but it's the kind of coincidence I don't want to let lie. Too close for comfort."

"No argument from me," Lester agreed. "You know Sam's been trying to get hold of you? Check your messages."

"I was in Manchester Center, at Mick's trailer. Met his neighbor and didn't want the cell interrupting, so I turned it off. Nobody asked the guy during the canvass if he knew Mick—only if he'd seen or heard anything. Turns out they were buddies."

Lester's heart sank. "That's my bad. Sorry."

"No big deal," Joe replied. "Just frustrating. We caught it. That's what counts. What's Sam want?"

"No idea. I just wanted to give you the heads-up. I don't think it's case related. Something personal, I think."

"Got it. I'll chase her down. Find out what you can about Mick, okay?"

"Got it. Happy motoring."

Joe didn't respond, which only made Lester laugh.

Sam and Joe met at the office, roughly midpoint from their respective spots of departure. Joe had succeeded in reaching her immediately after Lester's call, but all she'd said was that she wanted to speak face-to-face.

"Well, here we are," Joe greeted her from his desk as she entered. "I have a feeling this'll be good, since I just now checked the dailies and found that both you and Willy fell down a twenty-four-hour rabbit hole. What's cookin'?" His expression sombered as he read her face, and added, "Don't tell me it's bad news."

She sat at her own desk before speaking, clearly choosing her words carefully. "It's Willy, and it's a combination bad news–good news thing. It's fine now, before you ask, or at least everything's stable, so there's no crisis."

"Good," Joe said slowly and leadingly, encouraging her to explain further.

"It's his arm," she went on, switching her gaze from her desktop to him and back again. "Turns out that all this time, it's been hurting him. Not badly, and not all the time, but with twinges, I guess you'd call 'em. Or that's how he described it. Point being that it was related to some nerve damage, or scar buildup around the nerves."

"Can I interrupt for a sec?" Joe asked.

"Sure. Of course."

"Is he okay? Where is he now?"

"At Upper Valley Surgical Specialists, under a John Doe."

Joe sat up. "Jesus. Makes him sound dead."

"He's not. He's not. But the pain hit the roof, to where he couldn't function. It's that bad. He says it's like being hit by a Taser with no off switch."

"Awful," Joe remarked. "When did this start?"

"A few days ago," she said quietly. "I've been really worried, you know, what with his history. I hope this won't cause problems, but I even talked with Beverly about it, since she's been so good to us."

Joe waved that aside. "Of course that's fine. But all this was before we were working the homicide or the arson, right? Why is your other half such a hardhead? He was probably barely functional. He worked all night at the warehouse in this condition?"

"He said it helped keep his mind off the pain," she said, adding, "That's not all. It gets a little worse. The other way he was dealing with it was by taking Oxys. Lots of them."

Joe pressed his lips together before asking, "Is this where I don't ask where he got them?"

"If you wouldn't mind, yes," she answered sheepishly. "But here's the good news part: Sue Spinney admitted him into UVSS. She's just started working there and has a best friend who's head of nursing. Between the two of them, they got him a little more comfortable."

"All right," he said. "Then why the John Doe?"

"That's to do with billing and privacy," Sam explained, still sounding unusually meek. "Willy's worried that if word gets out the arm's acting up and he's strung out on painkillers, it'll cost him his job."

Joe scratched his forehead before responding. "He's half right. I'd chew him a new one myself if I catch him on unprescribed meds. But we already dealt with the disability. That's why he's on this squad. Why would any of that change just because some nerve's kicking up?"

"That's what Sue's friend said, too, but you know Willy. And given what a lot of people think of him, I'm not sure I blame the guy."

"Fair enough," Joe conceded. "So what happens now? Is it settling down again?"

"No. We're back in bad news territory. It's gonna take an operation. They have to open up the arm to fix it."

Joe scowled. "Damn. How do you fix something that's been damaged for so long?"

"I don't mean the arm itself," Sam said. "At least, I don't think so. My understanding is this is all about stopping the pain. Nothing more." She stood up abruptly and began pacing back and forth. "Look, I don't really know. So far, it's just been Sue and Victoria—that's her pal—who've been talking about what to do. The person who'll really know is an orthopedic surgeon—a specialist in hands, arms, and shoulders."

"That's a specialty?"

"So I'm told. In this case, the necessary doc is already on staff, and ready to discuss the details."

"So why'm I thinking there's another shoe about to drop?" Joe asked.

"'Cause there is, I guess. . . . Maybe," she replied. "We don't know who's gonna pay for it."

Joe stared at her, astonished. "I am trusting my life to children," he blurted out. "You people carry guns, for Christ's sake; deprive people of their liberty. *We* pay for it," he said loudly. "Jesus, Sam. He was shot in the line of duty. Maimed for life. How many times do you think that happens in this state? *Of course*, we'll pay for the operation, and assuming it goes well, and he's as good as he was before, *and* he chooses to return to duty, he'll be returned to full-time status. Does that statement eliminate any lingering doubts?"

In response, she circled his desk without comment and threw her arms around his neck.

Joe was as impressed as everyone by the panorama from the inner window. He stood at the doorway, ignoring the two people hunched over the large central table, transfixed by the vista of the warehouse beyond. Even with his previous visits to the building, he still couldn't get used to its setting—not to mention the drama of this particular view.

"It's like a sports arena, all hollowed out, isn't it?" he mused.

Lester and Pat Smith both straightened and looked at him.

"Hey, boss," Lester greeted him.

Joe crossed over to them.

"This is Pat Smith," Lester continued, gesturing to his colleague, who shook hands with Joe.

"We know each other," Joe said to her. "Although it's been a few years. Congratulations on joining this outfit."

"Thanks," she said. "It's good to see you. And thanks for the heads-up about Michael Durocher."

Joe glanced at the document-laden table. "He actually surfaced? I'm so used to him supposedly being places where nobody's really seen him."

"Nope," Lester confirmed, leaning over and retrieving a file. "They knew him here."

"Before we get into that," Joe suggested, "would you both please tell me that as a result of this aha moment, you checked to see if Teri Parker ever worked here, too?"

Pat laughed. "We did, and she didn't. Les brought me up to speed on the weird connection. Speaking as GreenField's head of security, I'm guessing there's no point arguing that our arson and your murder could be a coincidence, given how many people we hire and the overall shallow employment pool."

"You can argue it all you want," Joe said. "But you know we can't think that way. Until we can prove otherwise, the murder of Teri Parker is absolutely tied to this mess. Sorry."

Pat merely looked rueful. "No apologies needed. I had to ask for the record."

"Your boss gonna have a cow?" Lester asked.

"Beaupré?" she replied. "Not a chance. He's a good guy. He'll understand once I spell it out."

"Okay," Joe resumed. "I just wanted that out of the way first. Did you two have a chance to do more than pull Mick's file?"

"We read it," Lester stated, "but that's it so far."

"I gotta say," Pat added, taking the folder and leafing through it. "He doesn't come across as your run-of-the-mill murderer. Not that there is such a thing, but you get the idea. We do quarterly reports on employees here, in part because we know what level of society we often hire from, and he consistently rates terms like friendly, eager, helpful, a team player."

"Not the sullen recluse we got from the barkeeps and Thurley," Lester said.

"That was probably recent history," Joe told them. "According to the neighbor I interviewed, the dark stuff came later, after he washed out. I don't think it's unreasonable for both portraits to apply. One thing I'm wondering, just so we don't forget it later: Did something here push him back into the bottle?"

"There's no mention of it," Pat said, scanning the pages more carefully. "But having read my fair share of these, they're not necessarily accurate biographies. A lot can happen from one quarter to the next, and the supervisors who write the evals aren't Ph.D.s in psychology. Politics play a role, too. Sometimes a rating's better or worse than it should be because of something personal going on. This whole place is a soap opera now and then."

"What was his job?" Joe asked.

"He began conventionally enough," she said. "Without using our in-house terminology, he went from someone who prepares pallets for shipment—that includes operating the big shrink-wrappers that keep everything from shifting en route—to running a jack. That's a nice move up the ladder in a short time, but not unheard of. What is a little unusual is that he got tapped to drive the big chief around in his pickup. That usually takes longer."

"What's that mean?"

"It's one of Beaupré's quirks," Pat replied. "And it works, which kind of amazed me at first. Bob Beaupré reaches into the company on a revolving basis and taps the high performers among the rank and file to drive him around for a while."

"A chauffeur?"

"I suppose, technically. But that's not how it comes across. It's like what they said about Sam Walton of Walmart fame, who, in the early days, used to show up at stores in his pickup truck and jeans. Beaupré just likes other people to do the driving. It's still a truck, and he's also dressed down, but the way he does it, he gets to use the phone on the road if he needs to, or shoot the breeze with his driver if not. He finds out how things are on the floor, and he leaves a good impression with the driver, who takes that back when he cycles out of the job."

"Huh," Joe grunted. "There's always some new wrinkle. How long's each cycle last?"

"It's not set in stone. Not every matchup is made in heaven. Bob never makes a big deal out of it when he doesn't like his driver much, but they'll be out in a month or so. Where there's chemistry, it might last longer."

"It's like the governor's security detail," Lester commented.

"Yeah," Pat agreed. "But friendlier. No guns or suits."

"All right," Joe returned to the topic at hand. "So you're saying Mick got this perk with less than a year on the job. And it's a reflection of performance, is that right?"

"Yup. The final choice is always Bob's—after management gives him a selection—but that's the pool he selects from, and it's popular. It's gonna be a ton more fun to drive the chief around than schlep pallets in a dark warehouse at high speed. And the word's out that the boss is a cool dude. It's the proverbial win–win."

Joe sat opposite them at the big table. "Unless it bends either one of you out of joint, I'd like to chat with Master Bob about Mick."

In response to them both shaking their heads, he continued, "Have you found any connections between Mick and the people you've been considering for this arson?"

"It's early yet," Lester answered realistically. "You only told us about Mick an hour ago. But we did start overlaying his old schedule and his coworkers with the people who're still around. If nothing else, it'll give us a narrower field than we had before."

Pat laughed. "Yeah—like almost the whole company."

Joe looked at them in surprise. "You must've cut down the suspects list more than that."

"Not as much as you think," Lester told him. "That was the genius of the battery balloons. They could've been put in place anytime, not just the shift when the fires broke out."

"Which opens up the pool almost exponentially," Pat followed up.

"It's true that we have people with past criminal records or on-site poor performance evals," Lester went on. "But that doesn't mean we can ignore the others. Having a record just means you were caught. We all know that's probably not the majority of people out there who are misbehaving."

Joe once more cast an eye across the files spread between them. "Swell," he said, getting back up. "If you can stand it, I'll try to come back to lend a hand after I chase down Bob Beaupré."

Lester smiled tiredly. "We'll be here."

* * *

Abigail Sumner was Willy's kind of doctor: the precise opposite of the upbeat, hand-holding, sympathetic type he couldn't stand. She entered the exam room where he and Sam were sitting, gave them a perfectly friendly if just serviceable smile, and forewent all handshakes or chitchat in favor of placing a laptop computer on the elevated treatment table lining the wall opposite them.

"I'm Dr. Sumner," she said, glancing over her shoulder quickly, while typing in commands. "I'll have the privilege of untangling the mess in your arm and giving you your life back. At least the one you were used to."

She straightened as an image appeared on the screen, and stood back to reveal it.

"These are the results of the MRI we made earlier," she explained. "To the layman, they're borderline incomprehensible. To me and my consulting neurology colleague, they represent a predictable picture of our biology's frequent tendency to not leave well enough alone."

Almost comically on cue, Sam and Willy both leaned forward to better see what they'd just been told they wouldn't understand.

Sumner dutifully played along, taking a pen from her lab coat pocket and using it as a pointer, manipulating the images via the touchpad with her other hand as she went.

"First things first," she began. "What have you been told so far, so I can address your fears and misunderstandings from the start?"

Willy sat back. "Ask her." He jerked a thumb at Sammie. "I've been out of it so much, you don't wanna know what I remember."

"Victoria thought it might be a palsy, I think," Sam said. "I'll get it wrong, but it was something involving the plexus, and that it might be a tumor, although she said not to get excited about that word, because they aren't all cancerous."

Sumner sat on the edge of the high, padded table. "Close. Willy's suffering from brachial plexus palsy."

Sam nodded. "That was it."

The doctor smiled thinly. "Right. I'll keep this simple. When that bullet entered your shoulder, it did two things: It smashed the clavicle—what most people call the collarbone—and its shock wave drove microscopic bone fragments into the brachial plexus like a shotgun blast. The brachial plexus, which sounds like a Los Angeles interstate junction, is actually an interwoven complex of nerves—large and small and all entangled—that originate from high on the spinal column and work their way down your arm."

She shifted around slightly to bring up a much more simplified anatomical image of the shoulder. "At the time of your initial repair," she continued, "the surgeons exposed the damage, almost from neck to shoulder, and conducted a debridement and lavage procedure, removing bone and bullet fragments and pieces of clothing, and washing the area out. I know all that because I've accessed the medical files you made available to me through Victoria. Then they applied a clavicle wrap and a sling, and let Mother Nature do her thing."

She returned the screen to its original image. "So far, so good. Given the times, they did good work. You lost the use of your arm, but you weren't otherwise disabled. And I imagine you dealt with whatever pain arose later through Tylenol or Advil or some other analgesic. Is that more or less accurate?"

Willy kept things moving, rushing this forward to its promised relief. "Yup."

He was also by now embarrassed and irritated by his near-miss relapse into substance abuse, the devastating consequences of which he knew all too well.

Sumner smiled appreciatively. "Nevertheless, those good old days are where your current complaint was born." She used her pen to stab at a small array of tiny objects with no meaning to her audience. "These are a few of the bone fragments they missed," she said. "And this opaque stuff here and here and here is representative of the scar tissue that formed around them—all of it impinging on the architecture of the brachial plexus."

"How did they miss that?" Sammie asked, her frustration clear.

"They couldn't see it," Sumner replied calmly. "That's what I was saying. When this all occurred, MR imaging didn't exist. We had little better than the X-ray technology dating back a hundred years. All this activity—" She emphasized by tapping the screen in multiple places. "—is essentially invisible to the naked eye. I generously referred to it as bone fragments. Actually, that's what they did extract. What we'll be going after could be called bone dust."

Willy scowled. "But it's been there all along."

"Yes," she agreed. "Slowly stimulating scar tissue, which then began to contract. There's the irony of this particular tale: While the initial expansion caused no pain, as it moved in the opposite direction, it finally hit the radial nerve in a way that blew the top of your head off—neurologically speaking."

Willy snapped his fingers. "But it happened overnight, damn near."

"As it will," Sumner said simply. "Nerves are like that."

Sammie was transfixed by the complexity before her, the science of it edging out the suffering and loss the imagery represented. "That's really him?"

"In exquisite detail," Sumner answered. After a moment's pause, she added, "Keep in mind that MRIs can be a little misleading until you learn to read them. If you consult a road map, the pavement is highlighted in red or blue, and the things lining or covering that road, like ditches, skid marks, rumble strips, paint striping, gouges, and the like don't even appear. Not so in an MR image. Everything shows up. To the untrained eye, it can be a little daunting."

"How will you do it?" Willy asked.

"Same as before," she answered. "We'll make an incision along the axis of the brachial plexus, divide the clavicle, wheel in a microscope to help me see what's what, and look to reverse the neuropathy."

"Which is what?" Sam asked.

"Neuropathy? The dysfunction of nerve tissue. That's what all that dust and scarring has done. What I'll be doing, Willy, is essentially running along the length of the nerves—roughly a foot, grand total—stripping each of its fibrous scar buildup, and removing each of those specks of bone dust as I go."

"Oh," Sam reacted. "A foot? That sounds much better."

Willy was less sure. "How long does it take?"

"About fourteen hours."

Sam's mouth fell open. Willy ignored her. "You said, 'Dividing the clavicle.' That doesn't sound good."

Sumner did look a little rueful. "Yes. If the clavicle's moved out of the way, it makes my life much easier. It also increases your chance of success. Look on the bright side: It'll be a much better healing process than after the bullet shattered it."

"Meaning that afterwards, I'll be in a sling and swath like before," he suggested.

"Correct. You could be up and about in a week or so, but the knitting of that bone, and the need for you to keep the region immobilized, will take closer to six weeks—if you behave."

He smiled at the small editorial addendum. "You must've heard about me."

"I have," she said.

Sam had recovered from her earlier shock, at least partly. "Given all this time and effort, going nerve by nerve, will you be able to return his arm to normal?"

Sumner shook her head. "As I said at the top, at best, I hope to return things to the way they were before this onslaught of pain. If everything goes as anticipated, you may end up more pain free than you've ever been, but as for functionality, it's just been too long. There is nothing for the restored nerves to connect to. That's all atrophied away."

"I don't care," Willy told her. "That, I'm used to. When do we start?"

Sumner stood up. "This is the part you'll like. Tomorrow morning, if you're willing."

"Willing and able," he said.

CHAPTER FOURTEEN

Pat Smith had been correct about Bob Beaupré's pickup. Joe discovered it—suitably dusty and utilitarian—parked on the edge of the pea-stoned dooryard fronting the house. Right beside the Cadillac Escalade and Porsche Boxster GTS, both of which were being needlessly washed, it appeared, by a man in dark blue utility clothes, outside the five-door garage.

Joe was in Colchester, Vermont, north of Burlington, and a fifteen-minute commute from GreenField's corporate headquarters, in front of a home of—if such a term existed—rich, rural excess.

It was probably called a log cabin by its owner, and it appeared to be built of felled trees. But that's where this and any notion of what Jeremiah Johnson might have called home parted ways.

It was large enough to make Joe stand and stare for a while, soaking it in.

"Nice, ain't it?"

Joe turned to see the car washer watching him, the hose in his hand still dripping.

"You probably see a lot of people with their mouths open," Joe said.

"Fair share," the man said. "It's not the kind of place most're used to. Not around here."

"Reminds me of those tourist lodges you see out West," Joe observed. "Yellowstone or somewhere. How big is this?"

"Seven thousand square feet."

"Damn."

Joe studied the man more carefully—less the clothes and more the way he carried himself—before asking, "How long ago did you build it?"

Bob Beaupré chuckled and laid the hose on the ground, wiping his hands on his pants to dry them. "Busted. Most people just walk by me. Course, you're not them, are you?"

"That can be good or bad," Joe said, shaking hands. "Joe Gunther."

"Call me Bob," Beaupré requested, not bothering to answer the question. "You're the one who phoned. You like to come in?"

"Absolutely."

With Beaupré preceding him, Joe stepped into a home with decor deserving of Newport, Rhode Island. The lobby's arched and timbered ceiling lofted overhead, anchored by a chandelier made of an enormous stripped and lacquered tree trunk, festooned with lights running along its spider-leg-like roots, but modestly sized in these surroundings.

Joe's host took him through a dining hall big enough for the Round Table, and into a library out of *My Fair Lady*, complete with two-story bookcases, a second-floor gallery running around its periphery, and a wrought iron spiral staircase in one corner.

Joe kept his counsel about all of it, but his expression was obviously not so guarded. Beaupré caught his look and smiled. "I know," he said. "I went a little nuts. I saw too many musicals. Have a seat." He gestured to a pair of leather armchairs before a movie-screen-sized row of French windows revealing what the massive house had been blocking: a broad wooden deck with a view of Malletts Bay, looking out onto Lake Champlain—comparable to something Joe imagined might be visible from the bridge of the *Queen Elizabeth*, as she was about to set sail.

"You want coffee or something?" Beaupré asked, settling in and looking like the groundskeeper taking liberties in the boss's absence.

Joe noticed that he'd left a trail of wet footprints upon entering the building.

Beaupré began predictably, taking an educated guess at Joe's motive for coming. "I appreciate your dropping by to meet face-to-face. I heard an hour ago that we're almost back to normal at the warehouse. You folks gotten closer to finding out who did it?"

"Not in any way that would make you happy," Joe told him. "But to our way of thinking, we're making progress."

"What's that mean?"

"Basically, we make algorithms in cases with so many suspects. Lists of people who were in the right place at the right time; with past criminal records; who've stood out for what they've done or said against the company; with knowledge of the battery recharging process; and so on. Generally, after a while, patterns start showing up. It takes time, but it works well in the long run. Speaking of which, have you thought of anyone who might've wanted to kick your shins this way?"

"By burning me to the ground?" Beaupré asked in a surprised voice. "You must have one hell of a pair of shins."

"I don't think that was the intent," Joe said. "The brains behind this were more than capable of destroying the whole place. What happened was a choice to do otherwise. That suggests a complicated motive."

Beaupré didn't respond, instead staring sightlessly out through the French doors.

"Right now," Joe resumed, "we're pursuing typical leads: disgruntled employees, oddball personalities, even pissed-off competitors. But we don't have your insight into a lot of potential bad actors. You know best about past contracts gone sour or people who've felt stepped on. Yours is a highly competitive business. You've got farmers, producers, and suppliers all lined up with similar goods, clamoring for attention. You've got other wholesalers trying to undersell or outperform you, and you've got customers complaining about pricing and contracts and lack of attention. The list goes on."

Beaupré had begun shaking his head. "I know. Believe me."

"Well, that's my point," Joe stressed. "We've got a big crew on this, but we could stand any help you can provide. I heard about how you regularly reach into the organization to get a driver, and I'm sure you know more people and more details than anyone else in the company. Green-Field is part of your DNA. What I'm asking is for you to run it through your mind—way outside the box we're working in—and see what you might come up with."

"I have been mulling it over," Beaupré said, looking at Joe directly again. "It occurred to me this might be personal. But so far . . ." He left the phrase unfinished.

Joe broached his other subject of interest. "Speaking of that," he began, "I was wondering if you remember a man who once worked as one of your drivers, named Mick Durocher?"

Beaupré's response was instant and positive. "Mick? Oh, sure. Good guy." He paused and asked, "You're not thinking of him for this, are you? Your algorithms need work if you are." He looked around the room somewhat restlessly. "You sure you don't want something to drink? A lemonade or iced tea or something? I'm thirstier than I thought."

He rose and moved to the oversized desk that dominated a corner of the library and pushed a button. "Why has Mick's name come up?" he asked. "You know he left the company years ago."

"Why was that?" Joe countered instead of answering. "He reads like the perfect employee." Joe noted that Beaupré had either not made the connection between the murder in the headlines, featuring Michael Durocher, and the man he knew as Mick or he wasn't owning up to it.

Beaupré snorted as a maid entered the room and stopped near the door. Her boss gave one last look at Joe, who shook his head. "I'm all set."

"One lemonade, Mary," Beaupré requested. "Thanks."

He returned to his seat, crossing his legs and getting comfortable once more. "In a word? Drinking. Mick was the perfect employee until he opened a bottle. I wish I could say that was rare among my employees, but I can't. It sort of goes with the territory. We actually set up a program to fight it a few years ago. Brought people in who knew what they were talking about as counselors. It's still up and running, having some success, I hope. But Mick wouldn't get near it."

"How long did he drive for you?"

"A few months. That's the usual. I try for a regular turnover, 'cause I know what it means to the troops."

"Do you remember what you talked about when you were together?"

Beaupré's eyebrows shot up. "Talked about? Who the hell knows? Sports, the weather, maybe local politics, although probably not with him. Family comes up with these guys. I think he had a daughter he felt badly about. I don't remember her name."

"From what I heard," Joe said, "he was chosen for driver duty earlier than most. Why was that?"

Beaupré laughed. "I wouldn't know—for exactly that reason. If I'm suspected of playing favorites, that would turn the process on its ear, wouldn't it? Somebody in HR picks 'em out. They end up in a pool of deserving employees who work hard, don't take too many sick days, have the least accidents, all the rest of it. I only pick from that pool, pretty much at random."

Joe opened his mouth to speak as the other man cut him off, adding, "That's not to say I don't sometimes ask for one or two of them to stay longer if I like 'em. I am the boss, after all. But that's the only favoritism I show, and believe me, it's totally self-serving. Some of these success stories are so dull that getting a good one is worth his weight in gold."

The lemonade arrived. Following a token sip from his glass, Beaupré asked, "You never answered my question. Why the interest in Mick?"

"He came up in another investigation," Joe answered, deciding not to enlighten him. "We just noticed he'd worked for you once. Interesting coincidence."

"Oh. Well, I hope that's all it is. I liked Mick. Worked hard, mostly kept his mouth shut, which I appreciate when we're on the road. When he showed up drunk at work—after his stint with me as driver—I don't think there were any hard feelings when we had to let him go. He was always a straight shooter, and if my memory's right, he took it like a stand-up guy. Like so many others with that problem, they aren't bad people. They have a sickness. That's why we set up the program. But you know what they say: Ya gotta hit bottom before you can pick yourself up. I guess Mick wasn't there yet. I'm sorry to hear he's in trouble."

"So you haven't been in touch since he left your employment?" Joe asked.

Beaupré shook his head. "Nope. You wouldn't tell me what he's done, I guess."

"It'll come out sooner than later," Joe said. "But I'll let the prosecutors and the press decide that."

Beaupré nodded. "Understood." He placed the otherwise ignored glass on a nearby side table and stood up. "Was there anything else?"

Joe joined him, speaking as they returned the way they'd come. "Not at the moment. I'll be sure to keep you up to date as things proceed."

"And I'll give some more thought to who might've done this from my perspective," Beaupré said. "I could sure live without any more crap like this."

He took Joe to the front door. "Good luck, Mr. Gunther. Don't hesitate to reach out if you think of anything else."

It had been a perfectly civil, almost bland exchange, from start to finish. And yet, Joe strongly suspected that it would be resumed in the near future, where the pleasantries might be lacking. Call it instinct, or what younger types like Lester referred to as "Spidey sense," but there was something going on in this oversized Lincoln Logs pile that made Joe think he'd be back to talk with its owner.

"This is the second house I've stared at from the outside today," Joe said.

Beverly turned to look at him. "Really? Are you house shopping?"

"Not a chance," he laughed. "It was Bob Beaupré's, in Colchester. It sure didn't look like this. And it sure wasn't this sweet."

They were standing before a small, immaculately restored Greek Revival on two acres of land near downtown Windsor, overlooking the local lake. It was quiet, very pretty, and bucolic, while within easy reach of Main Street.

"Bigger?" Beverly asked.

Joe pointed with his chin. "This whole place would've fit into his garage, with minimal customizing."

He didn't add that her own house south of Burlington struck him as being almost in the same class. But that, he knew, had been purchased by her ex-husband, a high-priced lawyer with a penchant for flashing cash.

"You like it?" he asked her.

They'd been inside already, and had walked the property. He thought it was great, but hadn't yet said a word.

He bumped her with his hip. "I love it. You dun good."

The front door opened and Beverly's daughter stepped into the sunshine, a smile on her face. She crossed over to them and gushed, "This is awesome, Mom. Were you serious about my using it sometimes?"

"Yeah, Mom," he mimicked her. "Were ya? Huh, huh?"

She laughed and pushed him away, pointing at them both. "You two are impossible. Of course I was."

"*Cool.*" Rachel exclaimed. "I can't wait to throw some parties here. It would be like *Risky Business.*"

Beverly gazed at the house, sighing, "What a horrible child. Where did I go wrong?" She wandered off toward the right, her attention caught by some detail.

"Have you already moved to Brattleboro?" Joe asked the girl. "And I meant to compliment you on your warehouse shots. They were terrific. I know Katz didn't benefit directly, since they didn't run in the *Reformer,* but I hope he's giving you high marks for making him look good by proxy."

Rachel beamed. "Oh. Thanks. You made those possible. I would've been screwed without your being there. And you're right: Katz was really impressed I got in."

Joe raised his eyebrows. "Ah, the immortal Stanley Katz. I was telling your mom how I thought his was a name I'd never hear again. How is he as a boss?"

"I like him," she said. "He's old school and grumpy, but like a TV sitcom. He's also got a memory like nobody I know and a neat way of making sure you asked all the right questions. I think he's cool."

"So, back to my first question: You're an official Brattleboro resident now? I should've offered to help you move."

"Are you kidding?" she said. "All the junk I own fit into my backseat. Took me fifteen minutes to settle in. I found an apartment over Main Street. Fourth-floor walk-up. I'm right across from the bagel shop. When I shower, I can see Wantastiquet Mountain out my bathroom window."

He knew almost exactly where she was describing—what he and his colleagues would call a dump.

"Nifty," he said. "I'll have to come visit."

"You probably will," she said brightly. "I'm pretty sure at least one of my neighbors is dealing drugs. He's nice, though."

"Swell," he said, at once admiring her broad-mindedness and taking note of her neighbor's approximate address.

A dozen or so miles from Beverly's future second home, Willy Kunkle slowly became conscious of a small orchestra of muted electronic noises and hushed voices.

He remained utterly still, assembling the functional pieces of his brain like a rake gathering leaves, until he felt collected enough to glance through barely opened eyelids. It seemed like he was doing this a lot lately.

The acoustic ceiling tiles did the trick, jogging his memory enough to revive a images of doctors, nurses, IVs, the short journey down a hallway to an operating room.

He closed his eyes again, at least having recognized where he was, if not the overall state of the immediate world. He could almost feel the presence of foreign substances in his bloodstream, hard at work at their assigned tasks, but at the same time making him even more aware of his vulnerability.

That, unsurprisingly, triggered his ever-present paranoia, along with an upsurge of anxiety. What had they done to him? Had it worked? What if it hadn't, and he was now a cripple on the verge of unemployment and substance addiction—because that was going to be the next stop. He knew that as a stone-cold fact. That he'd avoided slipping back into the bottle, via the pills he'd already started taking, was a miracle. Doing so in the face of this operation's failure would be all but impossible.

He knew himself that much at least.

But there was something else in all this panicky thinking. Something missing. Something of substance and meaning that had pulled him to safety the first time.

He smiled, which gave him away.

"Willy," he heard. "You awake?"

He opened his eyes wide this time, to take in Sam's face, hovering above him once more. "Yeah," he said, barely feeling his lips.

She kissed him, long and gently. "Yeah, yourself."

"Guess what?" he slurred, startled by his own discovery—coming like an announcement via an intercom in his head.

"What?"

"No pain."

Her eyes widened. "What do you mean? They sliced you open."

"No, not that," he said, his smile broadening to where he looked like a vaudeville drunk. "That's nothing. The other one. The two-twenty line into my head. It's gone."

"It's better? It worked?"

"Not better. Gone," he repeated. "Like they hit a switch."

Another face came into view next to Sam's.

Willy smiled. "Hey, Doc."

Abigail Sumner's expression barely responded in kind, although her voice, when she spoke, more than compensated. "Did I overhear a happy customer?"

"You did. I can't believe it's gone, like that." He tried snapping his fingers, but he had a blood oximeter attached to one of them. "Well, you get it."

"As I said, nerves'll work like that sometimes," she repeated from earlier, her eyes drifting across his left shoulder—as much as was visible under the dressing. She also scrutinized his lower arm for circulation, color, and warmth.

"I hope you're experiencing some pain, nevertheless," she said. "If you're not, we have a serious problem."

"No," he reassured her, his voice sounding slightly clearer. "It hurts, all right. But it's localized. Like it should be. That makes sense."

"How long will it last?" Sam asked.

Sumner straightened, satisfied. "You'll probably never find out from him," she said, as if Willy were in another room. "His tolerance is high and his willingness to give you feedback nonexistent." She glanced at Sam. "But I doubt I'm telling you anything you don't know. As I said when we first met, he'll take a few days flushing out the medications we gave him. Then he'll be up and about, bound and in a sling. After that, he'll quickly become a pain in the neck as he denies that it takes six weeks or so for his particular clavicle to knit. But mark my words: The more he screws around, the longer that process will take." She returned her gaze to her patient. "Just so you both understand."

She shook Sam's hand and patted Willy on his right wrist. "Unless all hell breaks loose, I'll see you then, in six weeks. Good luck."

And she was gone.

"Cold fish," Sam said under her voice, giving him a repeat kiss.

He reached up and stroked her hair, smiling. "I like her."

CHAPTER FIFTEEN

Beverly adjusted her plastic face shield, thinking back to when autopsies were done with little protection beyond a rubber apron. She didn't argue with the protocols involving multiple layers, double-gloving, face and eye protection, and even booties. But she did miss the sense of ease she'd once enjoyed, wearing far less. Another price of progress.

"Top of the day to you, Todd," she greeted her diener. "Would you like to make the introductions this morning?"

Todd, similarly adorned, had been in the procedure room for a while already, preparing their first case. Also present was their law enforcement liaison, who for the moment was back in a far corner, filling out something on his portable computer, his fingerprint kit open on the counter beside him. That was it at the moment. The usual gaggle of med students was not in attendance, probable victims of an ever-changing class schedule.

"Good morning, Doctor," Todd said, his words muffled by his mask. "Today, we have William Larabee, aged forty-eight." Todd paused to retrieve the report that had been sent electronically from their regional investigator. "He comes to us from Upper Valley Surgical Specialists, where he was a patient for only a few hours."

Beverly took her eyes off the naked man on her table to cast Todd an inquiring glance. "Upper Valley Surgical Specialists? Did he die prior to surgery? He doesn't have a mark on him."

"Yeah. That's explained in the narrative. It was a mutual aid kind of thing. A little murky, but it seems with the best of motives. Mr. Larabee was found in his motel room, sick as a dog, after a couple of days during which they honored his Do Not Disturb sign, meaning that when they brought him in, he'd become unresponsive. Despite not having an emergency room, per se, UVSS was nearby, and the next hospital's ER was suffering a temporary power outage, so they stepped up. So much for good intentions."

Beverly frowned to herself and surveyed the body. "Reading between the lines," she said, "I'm guessing no known medical history, local physician, next of kin, and probably no meds in the room, since that would be far too helpful. Is that about right?"

"That is exactly right," Todd concurred, still scanning the report. "The local cops and our investigator are scrambling as we speak, but so far, nothing."

"What did the scene tell us?" Beverly asked. "Any blood, anything in the toilet or sink, stained clothing? A cell phone, perhaps?"

"Yes, on the phone, which is where they're putting most of their efforts, along with his credit card. We got his name from his Maryland driver's license, so that's another lead."

This was not unheard of. It wasn't even rare. Cases arrived fairly often with little more than a wristband and most of the open slots on the report form labeled "pending."

She studied what she'd been given, therefore, without prejudice or foreknowledge, as had often been the case in school, where the provenance of cadavers had also been occasionally murky.

"All right," she began, at once writing points down as she went and speaking aloud in order to use Todd as a sounding board, much as a pilot does her copilot. "We have a one-hundred-and-seventy-pound white male, approximately five feet ten inches in length. He has about a three-day stubble, and appears to be of average fitness and proportions. Upon first glance, he doesn't seem to have any gross abnormalities or disabilities, nor any signs of trauma."

Together, they rolled him over to examine his back and buttocks. "Similarly," Beverly continued, "the posterior appears equally unremarkable, with lividity fixed and appropriate given the circumstances."

Beverly walked around her patient after returning him to the supine position, taking in and cataloging his features. "Two small observations: There are some minor purpura of the lower legs and petechia of both conjunctivae, consistent with sepsis, but no hemorrhaging from any natural orifices."

She put her hands on Mr. Larabee at last and started pushing him about, in order to access some of his more remote nooks and crannies, talking all the while as Todd assisted. In the meantime, the state trooper had quietly set to work taking photographs and lifting fingerprints.

Finally, she picked up her scalpel and repeated the procedure Joe had watched her perform on Teri Parker days earlier, ending with the removal of the man's sternum with the aid of a pair of adapted brush cutters.

With the lungs and liver now lying in full view, Todd knew enough to comment, "Well, he sure as hell ain't your cut-and-dried heart attack victim. That looks bad."

Beverly removed the lungs, weighed them, palpated them, and moved them to her cutting table to look inside.

"Definitely hemorrhagic and edematous. No frank blood, but very frothy and blood-tinged."

"Still sepsis?" Todd asked.

"Could be," she said, slicing some more. "The spleen is soft and bloody, which would fit. We're absolutely ordering slides on Mr. Larabee, though. I have no idea what's going on."

The liver was next, which she declared soft, somewhat necrotic, and etched with reticular hemorrhaging. The kidneys, sections of the bowel, and the brain all eventually showed signs of swelling and bleeding.

An hour later, Beverly stretched her back, stepped away to allow Todd to wrap things up, and asked, "Not that they had a reason to, but did UVSS do a GI workup?"

"Nope. And blood cultures were ordered but aren't completed, for obvious reasons. Fast-and-dirty analysis revealed he had an elevated white count, which supports sepsis, but from what, they had no clue. His coagulation labs were also off."

"What did he do for a living?" Beverly asked. "He's got good teeth and nails, well-cut hair. Seems like a man who took care of himself—definitely not our usual type of customer."

Todd was shaking his head. "Details at eleven, Doc. Sorry."

Beverly sighed. "That's fine, Todd. We'll get it sorted out. Let's start by getting those samples packaged up. I'll tell the state epidemiologist to expect them and contact UVSS's attending and medical director, just to see if there was anything that didn't make it into our investigator's field report."

She checked her watch. "Good. Early enough to actually get something rolling. I hate it when these things occur late in the day."

She crossed the room and opened the biowaste container prior to removing her gloves, mask, and gown. "Thomas?" she inquired of the trooper.

"Yes, ma'am."

"I don't usually bother you with things like this, but if you could tell whatever department is handling the investigation concerning Mr. Larabee that I would greatly appreciate any extra effort they can apply. I don't want any avoidable delays on this."

The trooper, although new to the liaison post, was both used to her formal syntax and aware of her having high expectations of everyone around her. Or else.

"You got it, Dr. Hillstrom," he said quickly, crossing to his computer to look up the appropriate phone number.

Beverly looked at the floor to hide her smile. Her amusement, however, was directed solely at his response. Otherwise, she wasn't the least bit entertained by what might have killed the late Mr. Larabee. Unlike most people, she didn't like mysteries.

"Talk about déjà vu all over again," Joe commented, looking at Willy's bulky shoulder dressing.

Willy reached up and self-consciously touched the bandaging, also recalling when he'd first incurred this injury years ago and was facing an uncertain future.

"You drop by to gloat, now that I'm down?"

Joe let out a snort, having anticipated as much. "Yup. That's me. All about the gloating. You know me well."

Sam, on the other hand, did all she could not to rap Willy on the forehead with her knuckles. She did, however, growl, "Jesus," under her breath.

Joe breezed past it. "Actually," he told them, looking at the door, "I thought I'd ruin your goldbricking by having a spontaneous team meeting."

Like clockwork, although actually running five minutes late, Lester Spinney entered the private room.

"Sorry," he said.

"Perfect timing," Joe reassured him. "Willy was about to complain of being bored."

Lester addressed his bedridden colleague with characteristic empathy. "Hey, partner. Did it work? Did they get the pain?"

To Willy's credit, or perhaps responding to his long-awaited relief, he answered openly and genuinely. "Totally. I haven't felt this good since before that son of a bitch shot me in the first place."

"When do you get out?" Lester asked.

"Not for at least a week," came a female voice from behind them. "Maybe more, considering how ornery this one is."

All four of them turned as Sue Spinney joined them, addressed her husband with a quick kiss, and stationed herself beside Willy in order to take his vitals.

"He's got an unstable clavicle and a ginormous wound that needs monitoring. Plus, we still have him on painkillers and meds. He may look fine to you people, since you've gotten so used to him, but I'm here to tell you that medically, he's at death's door and one step shy of the loony bin."

Willy laughed. "Jeez. With that style, you should ask to work with Joe's girlfriend."

"Speaking of girlfriends," Sam asked Sue, "is Victoria around today? We wanted to thank her for getting the ball rolling, or helping you get it rolling."

Sue looked up briefly from what she was doing. "Oh, sure. She was really pleased the way things turned out. Actually, she's fighting a stomach bug or something. Took a sick day." Sue hung her stethoscope back around her neck and stepped back. "I'll let her know, though. Okay, that ought to do it. You'll live for another few hours, until the arsenic kicks in. See ya, everybody."

She patted Les on the butt as she walked out, closing the door behind her.

"And they say American health care ain't what it should be," Willy said, shifting slightly in his bed and wincing.

Joe sat on the windowsill as Sam took the edge of the bed and Lester the one guest chair. As with so many Vermont hospitals and clinics, the scenery out the window was of trees and distant hills instead of the usual urban clutter—a definite plus for positive patient outcomes, in Joe's prejudiced view.

"We got some strange doings with what we're juggling," he began.

"And the stranger they get, the more I was thinking we were overdue for a spitballing session." He eyed the reason they were meeting here. "Willy, all horseshit aside, are you up for this? I want you back sooner rather than later, so I don't want to mess things up by pushing too hard now."

Willy took him seriously. "I'm good, boss. I do take a lot of naps, but right now, I'm okay."

"Thank you," Joe said. "All right. This started straight up and narrow: one dead girl, one quickly confessed killer. It's been going sideways ever since. Any arguments that the supposed killer ain't what he says he is?"

No one said anything.

"Good. That makes the first fork in the road a split between who really did kill Teri Parker and why is Mick Durocher taking the rap?"

"And did he even know her?" Willy added.

"Right," Joe agreed. "We have footage of him dumping her body, but no one we've found can tell us they were ever alive in the same room at the same time. In addition, I heard from Mick's daughter, his neighbor, and just lately his jailer in Rutland, that he may be about to die of cancer."

"Making whatever murder charges they throw at him null and void," Lester said.

"Correct," Joe agreed.

"Very convenient," Sam commented.

"Mick's a designated fall guy?" Willy asked.

"It's a theory," Joe said. "Which just got more convoluted when we found that he used to work for GreenField Grocers, and for Bob Beaupré personally."

"Really?" Willy blurted out. "Amazing what you can miss in twenty-four hours."

"He was the boss's chauffeur for a few months," Joe explained. "Beaupré has a habit of plucking high performers off the line and rotating them through this assignment. Makes him look like one of the boys, and makes the rank and file talk about him in glowing terms. He even has an especially beaten-up pickup he uses for the job."

"Nobody sees through that?" Lester mused.

"Jesus, Les," Willy scolded him, clearly not close to needing a nap. "Such a socialist. This is God handing out favors from on high. It's not something you question. Get with the program."

"Mick washed out in under a year," Joe went on. "Hit the bottle again. But that was a few years ago and, as far as we know, when all contact between Beaupré or GreenField stopped. But it's a hell of a coincidence, and not one I'm willing to take in stride."

Sammie addressed Lester, "You gotten anywhere on the arson?"

Les shook his head. "Not the way I'd like. We got a good system and we're flushing everybody through it, but so far, nuthin'. The gap left by our not knowing exactly when those time bombs were planted has not been helpful, nor the fact that the one Jonathon Michael found turned out to be free of fingerprints or anything else. Plus, even with the employee badges and CCTV, there are still ways a complete outsider could've bypassed security."

"Yeah," Willy argued, "but we're not going there already, are we? I mean, it makes sense that it was an inside job."

"I know, I know," Lester agreed. "I'm just sayin'."

Joe reached into his pocket and pulled out his vibrating smartphone. He read its screen and reported, "Interesting timing. That was the crime lab. The AG collected Mick's DNA and submitted it for analysis, as promised." He slipped the phone back into his pocket. "It doesn't match Teri Parker's fetus's, and they didn't get a computer hit off CODIS."

"Perfect," Willy said. "We gonna ask everybody to spit in a cup next, just to see if we get lucky?"

Joe wasn't going to turn down any suggestion outright. "If it comes to it, we might."

"Going back to the arson for a sec," Sam said. "We've been looking at it like it was a grudge of some sort. What if it was a competitor? Some other warehouse trying to gain an advantage?"

"Pat Smith and I have been working under that premise, as well,"

Lester replied. "There are competitors, for sure, but according to her, the northern New England market—where GreenField has the biggest investment—isn't stuffed with them. C and S, in Brattleboro, for example, may be the Goliath up around here, but it doesn't do that much in Vermont. They're more a national outfit, and GreenField and they don't bump into each other much. The irony is, it's more likely GreenField who'd be firebombing them for a bigger share. Not the other way around."

"What more did we get out of Teri Parker's past?" Willy asked.

"That's my next stop," Joe said. "What with Mick's slam dunk going south, your arm crapping out, the warehouse fire, and our trying to figure out what the hell's going on, I asked the Waterbury office to drop by her place early on and seal it till one of us could give it what it deserves. That time is officially overdue."

"We're getting nowhere fast," Willy said sourly.

Joe couldn't say he was wrong. He looked at Sam and inquired, "You good with leaving Mr. Chipper to heal on his own for a while? Field trip to beautiful downtown Barre?"

"Can't wait," she replied with a smile at Willy.

He tilted his head back to look at the ceiling. "You guys go have fun. You heard Sue anyhow: Won't be long before the arsenic kicks in."

CHAPTER SIXTEEN

Across blue-collar New England, in neighborhoods tucked away from historical downtowns filled with Victorian mansions of bygone magnates, there are clusters of other antiquated buildings—featureless, purely functional, and drab—whose sole purpose from birth was to house the working class. They could be considered the architectural version of the tired, proud oldsters bearing flags at parades, often outfitted with canes and nasal cannulas, who refuse to let people forget what went before—and of its cost.

A few towns have whittled away at these eighteenth-century proletarian enclaves, converting them or tearing them down—a form of urban renewal most northern New England communities can't afford. More often, civic leaders have allowed Realtors and landlords to bring such buildings barely up to code and stuff them with renters struggling to survive.

From Brattleboro to St. Albans, Bennington to St. Johnsbury, there are thousands of these marginally maintained structures, their entryways festooned with mailboxes, indicating the multiple families within. It boggled Joe's mind to think of how many people had paced their floorboards over the decades, hoping for any opportunity to live elsewhere.

Neighborhoods of this nature were sprinkled across Barre. Where next-door Montpelier was the state capital and well known for politics and business, having evolved gradually into its current trendy, hipster incarnation, Barre better represented a place more stamped by a stalled industrial past.

Not that the town wasn't still well known for what had put it on the map. "Barre granite" remained renowned worldwide for its fine-grain and handsome appearance. But the days of using this stone to build entire downtowns—from buildings and bridges to monuments and cobblestone boulevards—had withered. Limited demand persisted, and supply remained ongoing—rumors were that the granite bed ran ten miles deep—but the area's heyday was past, and with it the economic vibrancy that had once made it shine.

"Shades of Washington and Canal Street," Sammie echoed Joe's thoughts, invoking Brattleboro's version of where they were entering, a stroll from Barre's city center.

Joe had called ahead, and Perry Craver, a VBI agent stationed nearby in Waterbury, emerged from his car as Joe and Sam walked up the sidewalk.

They exchanged greetings before Teri Parker's old residence, a factory housing unit built when Barre's population quintupled at the end of the 1800s—the granite business's glory days.

"I asked the local PD to sit on it, more or less, ever since we sealed it," Perry was explaining as he led them up the front steps and into the lobby. "Since we figured we had the doer in jail, nobody was thinking along chain of custody lines, so that probably means the PD did an occasional drive-by, just to see if they saw lights on inside." He looked directly at Joe as he added, "I'm sorry if I screwed up there."

"Not a problem." Joe set him at ease. "We were all thinking that way, plus we suddenly got a little shorthanded."

They were clomping up the old wooden staircase to the second floor as Perry added, "I did check when I got here just now. If anyone has tampered with the seal, they're really expert, 'cause I couldn't see any-thing different from when I set it in place."

"Relax," Joe said, patting him on the shoulder.

By now, they were at the front door of a street-facing apartment, at once padlocked and sealed with yellow police tape, which Craver indicated with a showman's flourish. "Ta-dah."

Without comment, Sammie sliced through the seal with a switchblade that had mysteriously appeared in her hand as Perry opened the padlock with a key from his pocket. This he handed to Joe.

"Has anyone been interviewed about her?" Joe asked him, taking the key.

Perry locked troubled again. "No. Like I said. We thought it was a done deal. We talked about it at the office, figuring if a trial date ever came up for Mick Durocher, we'd do some backup interviews then. But with his confession, that seemed unlikely."

The agent let out a sigh. "I know you keep saying it's no big deal, but I feel like I dropped the ball."

Sammie left them talking and entered the apartment. Her silence told Joe, and perhaps subliminally Perry, that she would have interviewed neighbors, coworkers, family members, and anyone else—regardless of presumed slam dunks—had she been the agent in charge. That level of thoroughness was second nature to her.

"You didn't," he reassured Perry one last time. "Everything's fine, and it does seem the place hasn't been touched since you were here, so give yourself a break."

He half stepped across the threshold and gave Perry a wide smile. "We'll take it from here, and let you know if we need any more help. If we've got time, we'll drop by the office, but in any case, say hi to every-one."

Craver nodded, only slightly mollified, and took his leave.

Joe entered on Sam's heels and closed the door behind him. "He's beat-ing himself up," he said sympathetically.

"He should," she replied. "He fucked up."

Joe didn't argue. He valued her tenacity and work ethic. If it came equipped with a little harsh judgment now and then, so be it.

As was his habit—and hers, too, he being that much of an influence—Joe stood quietly by the door for a while, studying the room before them section by section, more absorbing its information than cataloging it.

It wasn't big. An efficiency with a separate bathroom. Kitchenette in one corner, closet in another, two dirty windows, side by side. The walls and floor were bare and dirty, the mattress lacking a box spring or frame. Piles of clothes, indiscriminately clean and soiled, were spread around haphazardly. There was a chest of drawers, a cheap armchair, a clock radio and a lamp on the floor beside the mattress, next to a couple of fashion catalogs, and little else. Unusually, there was no TV.

Sam spoke first. "Talk about sparse."

"Not counting what you could collect from a yard sale," Joe agreed, "the rest would fit into one suitcase."

Slipping on latex gloves, they set out to explore different parts of the room in detail, each imagining Teri Parker living here—eating, sleeping, getting ready to go out, coming home after a long day. In their minds, they tried to make the place come alive—to visualize every item they handled being used by her in context.

Sadly, in the end, it amounted to very little.

Plus, more suspiciously, there were gaps.

"Check this out," Sam said, holding up a thin electrical cord.

"Recharger?" he queried.

"I'd say for a phone," she reported. "We never found one, did we?"

He frowned. "No—not with her, not at Mick's, and not where he said he killed her. We also found no records in her name associated with any Vermont cell carriers."

"Something else," Sam added, holding up a second wire.

"What's that?" he asked from across the room.

"To either a laptop or a tablet," she said. "The charge cord's different than a phone's."

"Two for two, then," Joe mused. "I'd call that a clue."

He entered the dead girl's bathroom and surveyed her belongings. "This is clearly where she spent her quality time," he announced over his shoulder.

Sammie appeared in the doorway and let out a low whistle. "No kidding. Look at all this crap."

There were lotions, shampoos, creams, nail polish bottles, ointments, aerosol cans, stacks of various soaps, and sundry other so-called beauty supplies lining every flat surface, including several makeshift shelves, and along the baseboard.

"Her history implied she'd been a hooker, at least off and on," Sam recalled. "I guess some of this makes sense. Gotta take care of the assets. Seems a little much."

Joe smiled to himself, doubting that he'd seen a hint of makeup on Sammie in all the years he'd known her.

"Interesting," Joe said, reaching down and holding up a pregnancy test kit. "Looks like a new box."

Sam crouched by the full trash basket and began extracting its contents with a gloved hand, until she found the item she was hoping for. She brandished the same sort of plastic chemical strip that she'd used herself years earlier, when discovering the happy news about Emma.

She had her doubts that Teri Parker's reaction had mirrored hers. She showed it to Joe.

"Positive?" he asked.

She nodded.

A thin, hesitant voice reached them through the apartment's outer door. "Teri? Hello? Is somebody in there?"

Joe glanced at Sam and raised his eyebrows. "This might be useful."

Both cops moved into the other room. Sam stood to one side of the door as Joe carefully opened it. "May I help you?"

The chunky young woman outside took a startled step back, her mouth half open. She was dressed in leggings and a tank top with too much cleavage, exposing much of her brassiere, as was the fashion among many. "Who're you? I heard voices."

Joe showed her his identification. "My name's Joe Gunther. I'm from the Vermont Bureau of Investigation."

"You're a cop?" she asked. "Where's Teri? What's happened?"

"What's your name, miss?" he asked gently.

"Dot." She gestured generally down the hall. "Dorothy. I live next door."

"Dot what?"

"Naylor. What's happened to Teri?"

"You didn't notice she's been gone?" Joe asked, pointing at the remnants of yellow tape still sticking to the doorframe. "Or that the apartment was sealed?"

Naylor seemed to take that in for the first time and rubbed her forehead with her palm. "I sorta been out of it for a couple of days. I been sick."

A door slammed upstairs. Joe looked up and gestured to the woman. "Why don't you come inside? Maybe you can help us."

She complied hesitantly, startled anew to see Sam standing by the door, who then closed it behind them. Technically, the apartment was a protected scene, and shouldn't have served as an interview room, but given the exchange with Craver earlier, and the lack of ready alternatives, Joe wasn't overly concerned.

"This is Special Agent Martens," Joe introduced her. "Dot Naylor."

The two women nodded to each other without comment.

"Would you like to have a seat?" Joe asked Dot, indicating the one chair.

But their guest was staring around the room. "What did you do?"

"To what?" Sam asked.

"This," Dot said, indicating the whole apartment. "You messed everything up. Why'd you do that? What'd she do to you?"

"We found it this way," Joe explained. "How was it normally?"

Dot spread her hands out to both sides. "She was no neat freak, but it was never like this."

"Did she have a computer or a smartphone?" Sam asked.

But answering that was too premature for Naylor. She stared at Sammie. "A computer . . . ? What's going on? Why're you here? I heard voices and people walking around. Where's Teri? Did you people lock her up?"

Joe took her supportively by the elbow and guided her to the chair, where she sat. "We've got some hard news, I'm afraid," he said. "Teri's died, and we're trying to find out why. We're terribly sorry."

Dot looked from one of them to the other, bewilderment stamped on her features. "What?" she asked softly. "How?"

"We can't go into details," Joe continued. "But it would help if you could tell us a little about her. There are so many things we'd like to know."

Joe crouched beside the chair and took Dot's hand in his own. "Such as: Did she have a computer?"

Naylor still appeared in shock. "Sure. Who doesn't? She didn't use it much. It was a hand-me-down from an old boyfriend."

"She preferred her phone?" Joe suggested.

"Yeah. She was on it all the time." She wiped her nose on the back of her free hand and mumbled, "I can't believe this."

"You were close?"

"We were friends," she replied. "Ever since she moved in. We hit it off."

"How long ago was that?"

"Couple of years."

"She have a job?"

"A bunch. Same as me. At the bottle-recycling place, bagging groceries, a week or two at McDonald's. She didn't like that. She was on unemployment a few times. She was a chambermaid for a while. I forgot that one. . . . I don't know. Stuff like that."

"You're leaving out the hooking," Sam stated flatly.

Dot stared at her, appalled. "You're mean."

"That doesn't make her wrong," Joe said quietly, with a small and encouraging smile. "It also doesn't make Teri a bad person."

Dot cast her eyes down, despite her outrage and sorrow. "Maybe she did a little, when she needed to."

Joe's knees were hurting by now, so he rose from his crouch, stepped back, and began pacing the room slowly, speaking as he went.

"Okay. Tell us about her friends, who she hung out with, what she did with her free time. Draw us a picture of what you two did together."

Dot scowled. "Why? I don't get it. If she's dead, why do you care?"

Joe stopped a moment to ask her, "How do you think she died?"

"I don't know. OD?"

"Did she use?"

"Doesn't everybody?" The familiar refrain.

"What, lately?"

"Heroin, but not much. When it suited her."

Joe reapproached but remained standing, looming above her. "Teri was murdered, Dot. Beaten to death."

Dot's face crumpled in on itself and she started crying. Both cops waited her out, not offering comfort. In time, she stopped, wiped her eyes and nose on her sleeve, and took a deep breath.

"Who did it?" she asked, sniffing.

"That's why we're here. You know anyone who might've wanted to hurt her?"

"She have a boyfriend?" Sam specified.

"She saw a bunch of people."

"Anyone named Mick, or Michael Durocher?" Joe asked.

Dot looked surprised. "Mick? No. I never heard that one."

Joe tried a more general approach. "Of the guys you know about, who stands out?"

She considered that a moment before saying, "She had a sugar daddy she was milking."

"What was his name?"

"She never said. He was particular about that."

"You ever see them together?"

"No. It's not like they went to Burger King and hung out. He bought her the phone you're looking for. Over-the-top fancy. She had a way of finding the rich ones."

"You never heard her on the phone talking with him?" Joe asked.

"Nope."

"Who was the phone carrier?" Sam asked.

"Don't know."

Of course not, thought Joe. "Anyone else? You implied Teri was seeing several men."

"I can't say he stands out, like you said, since I never met him neither, but there was another one who was kind of a hot ticket."

"What makes you say that?"

"Maybe 'cause she talked about him? I don't know. There were a lot of guys I didn't hear about."

"What did she say?" Sammie asked. "Good things? Bad?"

"He never hit her," Dot said, her tone brighter.

Sam and Joe glanced at each other. This was high praise in some circles.

"Okay," Joe urged her. "Where does he fit in? Were Teri and he a current item, at the same time as the sugar daddy, or are you talking ancient history?"

"Oh, no," she replied, her earlier grief having drifted off. "It's recent. Kind of."

"What's that mean?" Sam asked.

"You know love affairs," Dot stated philosophically. "Up and down, all the time. This one had its lumps, but she really liked him."

"Can you give us details?" Joe wanted to know.

But there, she let them down. "Nope. Nuthin'. Teri wouldn't tell me a word. That was like a law between them: Keep your mouth shut. Just like with the sugar daddy."

"Why?"

She laughed. "Like I know? Beats me. She just said he was superprivate, and she was okay with that. Plus, she didn't want to screw things up with the older one, either, so it paid to be . . . Whatever."

"Discreet?"

"Right. That."

"How did they meet?" Sammie asked.

"Dunno. One day she just said she'd met this guy. That was it. She was in love and wouldn't tell me anything more."

"Did the sugar daddy—or the other one, for that matter—buy her anything else?" Joe asked. "We noticed she had a lot of cosmetics."

Dot's face brightened. "Oh, yeah. That was wild. And it was the younger guy. Boxes and boxes. She said he had an inside source. Could get her anything she wanted."

"Where from?"

There, she drew a blank. "I dunno. She never said and I never asked. It was good stuff, though. She gave me more than I'll ever use. I sold a bunch of it. She didn't care."

Joe straightened slightly. "You still have some?"

"Sure."

"Can you show us?"

She looked at them doubtfully. "Really? They're just bottles and stuff, like at a store. There's nuthin' to 'em."

But she was rising at the same time, and led them down the hallway to her apartment.

It was a near copy of Teri's, if more crammed with belongings than a

Salvation Army store—cheap furniture, clothing, stuffed animals, boxed and canned food, and random items like a cluster of sparkly whirligigs hanging from one wall and a fluorescent-hued feather boa draped above a window.

With no choice to do otherwise, they proceeded single file through to the bathroom, where Dot swept aside the shower curtain to reveal stacks of cardboard boxes in the tub, the uppermost of which had been opened to display a dizzying array of the items she'd described.

Joe glanced at her in wonder. She seemed clean and reasonably cared for, but for all this bath product, it was obvious she didn't use much. And now he had to wonder about her access to the shower.

"What's in the other boxes?" he asked.

She pulled a few onto the floor to reveal the contents of those below, speaking as she did, "Mac and cheese, cans of soup, there's one full of aprons here. There're some cleaning products. . . . All sorts of shit."

"And you didn't ask for any of it?"

"Nope. Some of it comes in handy. But like I said, I sell the rest if I get a chance."

Joe and Sammie stared at the booty for a few moments before Sam read aloud the one label most common among the boxes: "GreenField Grocers."

"Yeah," Dot said without interest.

"Did Teri give this benefactor a nickname, maybe?" Joe asked. "The younger of the two, right?"

"Yeah. Sure," Dot said. "She called him J.R."

Joe nodded a couple of times before indicating the boxes. "I hate to say this, but we're going to have to keep those for a while."

CHAPTER SEVENTEEN

Joe and Sam were driving back from Barre after spending two more hours with Dot Naylor, grilling her for ever-smaller scraps about the late Teri Parker. They were worn out and frustrated with their lack of results. The mention of the mysterious J.R. notwithstanding, the indications had been clear that somebody—the sugar daddy, J.R., or someone else entirely— had most likely cleaned out Parker's apartment of any incriminating evidence before the dead girl's body had even been found. On the basis of that possibility, Joe got hold of Perry Craver and told him to chase down every person who'd had anything to do with Teri Parker, and to interview them about any and all of her past boyfriends.

"At least we got one line to pursue," Joe said hopefully, looking out the front passenger-side window as Sam took them east through the time-worn Green Mountains on I-89, following the prehistoric tracings of millennia of waterways.

"The all-too-elusive J.R.?" she asked.

"He's a big one," Joe agreed. "We should give that tidbit to Les and see if the initials match any of his GreenField suspects—or anyone nicknamed Junior. It sure looked like J.R. was ripping them off to impress his girlfriend. As for the sugar daddy . . ."

"Yeah," Sam filled in the silence he'd left. "Not much to go on there. Too bad the phone was stolen. That could've been a gold mine."

Joe's own cell went off on his belt. He pulled it out and read the screen.

"Beverly," he announced, and hit the answer button. "Hey, there," he said. "Are we on the same road, heading in the same direction for once?"

Beverly laughed tiredly. "Don't I wish. I know we were hoping to meet up and give the Windsor house another visit, but I've been delayed by a case."

He knew she routinely conducted her autopsies in the morning. It was now nearing late afternoon. "Oh? Bad one?"

"Mysterious might be a better word, with 'bad' waiting in the wings. I'm in deep with the state's epidemiologist, the CDC, and an attending at Upper Valley Surgical Specialists on a possible infectious disease death."

"Good Lord," Joe reacted. "Mind if I put you on speaker? I'm in the car with Sam."

Beverly sounded surprised. "I don't mind at all, but why?"

"Willy's a patient there," Joe told her before hitting the speaker button and laying the phone on the console between them.

"Hey, Doc," Sam called out.

"Samantha," Beverly acknowledged her. "I hope your boss is treating you like the talent you are."

"He bows to me all the time," Sammie told her. "It's starting to get creepy."

Joe brought her up to speed: "Beverly just told me she's dealing with a possible infectious case from UVSS."

"You're kidding me," Sam said, her smile collapsing. "That mean something serious?"

"Probably not," Beverly reassured her. "Have you noticed any unusual activity there? Staff looking nervous or hurrying off to sudden meetings?"

"No," Sam said. "What would that tell us?"

"Just that their tranquil world has been ruffled. Hospitals can lay on the melodrama sometimes. The attending I spoke with had no idea what

I was talking about, and I swore him to secrecy, but I was curious if you'd noticed anything out of the ordinary."

"Nope. Can't say I have."

"How's Willy progressing?" Beverly asked, her interest less in Kunkle than in Sam. Her burgeoning friendship with her did not include Willy, whose tactics and manner Beverly usually found abrasive, if not offensive. "I didn't realize he'd had his procedure done there. I would have presumed Dartmouth-Hitchcock. Joe's been very tactful about discussing this, which I applaud, by the way."

"You know Willy," Sam said as Joe smiled in response. "Lester's wife works there, as of recently, so I think that helped persuade him. That and the pain, of course. He wasn't into shopping around."

"He's feeling better now?"

Sam laughed. "He said it was like a miracle. That's not the kind of word he uses."

"Don't I know it," Beverly deadpanned. "Wish him Godspeed from me."

"Will do."

"Do you want us to poke around UVSS ever so gently?" Joe asked. "At least see if we notice any heightened activity?"

"No, no," Beverly reassured them both. "As I said, this will no doubt prove trivial. Counterinfection protocols exist for good reason, but they rarely yield anything alarming."

"When will you find out?" Joe asked.

"Difficult to say. Perhaps as early as tomorrow afternoon or the day after. In wild, untamed Vermont, as ironies have it, we often get results more quickly than in the civilized world. A lack of urban gridlock. Any analysis still takes time, however."

"But you're not worried?" Sam asked, her voice calm but her mind definitely considering the unstated risks.

"I'm conservative," Beverly replied. "I'll await the results."

"Yes, Doctor," Joe said, laughing, both of them unaware of Sam's growing concern.

"While I have you both on the line," Beverly continued unexpectedly, "I was wondering about your take on the lab results from Michael Durocher's buccal swab not matching the sample I extracted from Teri Parker's fetus."

"That's all we heard," Joe said. "Speaking scientifically, and since you've apparently read the fine print, there's no doubt about that, is there?" Joe asked.

"None. I am sorry," Beverly said sympathetically.

"No problem," Joe said. "All part of the process. Keeps life interesting."

"That it does," she agreed. "I better get back to work. The phone's lighting up. Good luck, and—again—apologies about tonight."

"Don't give it a thought," Joe reassured her.

"Good luck to you, Beverly," Sam said, falsely lightheartedly, as Joe's finger hovered over the phone's off button. "Don't hesitate to let me know if Willy's about to be quarantined."

They were silent for a few moments following that conversation, before Sam finally asked, putting her anxiety on hold, "Who're you putting money on as the father? Sugar Daddy or J.R.?"

"Yeah," Joe said slowly, adding, "And which one of them set up Mick Durocher to take the fall? And why?"

Bob Raiselis was a happy man. Through a neat alignment of coincidences, he'd just celebrated his twenty-third anniversary, received a raise from GreenField for ten years of faithful service, and gotten a text that morning from his daughter announcing she'd just gotten the promotion to head teller that she'd convinced herself she wouldn't.

Bob took special pride in this last bit. Not only did he think the world of his daughter—and believed her to be the brightest child he'd ever known—but he'd also been the one to cajole her into applying for the bank job in the first place.

It was enough to swell a father's proud heart.

Raiselis adjusted his sunglasses, took a sip of his coffee, and checked his mirrors. He'd been driving big rigs for twenty-seven years, and derived the same pleasure from being high above the road as a cowboy does in the saddle or a pilot at the controls. The array of instruments, knobs, levers, and shifters—even the noises and vibrations informing his senses—was as delicately familiar to him as the intricate contents of a clock to an horologist.

Tractor trailer drivers had once been termed "knights of the road." The phrase hadn't weathered well, but the big rigs themselves still attracted the occasional compliment, if mostly from among young kids in awe of their sheer size.

The fact that Bob's work environment was seventy-three feet long, over eight feet wide, thirteen-and-a-half feet tall, had eighteen wheels, and weighed about seventy-three thousand pounds was merely something he took in stride. The similar wonderment with which he'd first approached such a monster had long since been replaced by a technician's obsessive concern with equations, balances, weights, and measurements—and road and weather conditions—not to mention the arcane, ever-changing federal and state regulations that monitored his livelihood.

People often thought truck driving was restricted to big and beefy types, because of its dependence on brute strength. More accurately, skills in math and interpreting closely worded statutes were increasingly in demand.

He was just settling into his "day at the office," as he termed it to his family, having left the White River warehouse forty-five minutes earlier with a load of produce destined for Hartford, Connecticut. He was approaching Brattleboro, the weather was sunny and comfortable, the road clear, dry, and thinly traveled, and he'd just come off a good night's sleep.

It was, as pessimists like to say, the perfect setup for a disaster.

It began slowly. A sense of unease, followed by something more palpable—the slightest of shimmies, from far back in the rig.

Bob's eyes automatically dropped to his instrument cluster, then to his mirrors. In the left one, he couldn't be sure, what with the speed and glare, but was it smoke?

He looked ahead for an escape route or a pullover, feeling a single sharp tremor as he lifted his foot off the accelerator. That drew him again to the mirror, like a man transfixed by a snake too close to avoid.

The smoke had burst into a blaze, the tremor into a chassis-rattling malfunction. He touched the brakes to little effect, began working the shifter to slow things down, but even as he methodically enacted his emergency procedures, one by one, he saw in that infernal mirror how his load was beginning to slither out across the lane, flames spewing forth and tires smoking like gas-soaked campfires.

He could feel his influence over events disappear as the cab began screeching and howling in protest, as metal, roadway, and tons of momentum swelled up next to him, flooding the air like an all-encompassing tidal wave. The surrounding glass began to crack and burst, gravity itself altered beneath him, and even the horizon ahead—so predictably reliable after so many decades—shifted, tilted, and finally vanished altogether amidst a concluding crescendo of explosive noise.

There was still smoke in the air when Rachel crested the rise. Avoiding the streets feeding into the blocked interstate ramps, she'd parked at a distance and begun cutting across people's properties, climbing fences, ducking under clotheslines, and once outsprinting an outraged and thankfully aging terrier, until she'd wriggled over a final chain-link barrier and found herself, as hoped, poised directly above the mangled wreck.

It was spectacular in scope. Every photographic element she could have wished for was there. Ambulances, police cruisers, fire trucks, and wreckers, all sparkling with different-colored lights. The bitter stench of burned rubber mixed with the delicate scent of wildflowers on the hill at her feet, which she immediately captured on camera by crouching low and placing the blooms as a foreground to the tangle below. There were skid marks, gouges in the pavement, a tractor trailer ripped apart as if by a giant can opener. Fluids poured toward the ditches—dark oil, gasoline, viscous runoff from pallets of smashed fruit cans.

And blood.

Toward the head of the truck, which lay on its side like an exhausted whale, a smear of blood extended from inside the flattened cab and across the crumpled hood, dripping onto the roadway like melting ice cream.

Rachel used her longest lens to capture that image, even knowing that the paper wouldn't run it. But the adage was no less true now than it had ever been: "Film is cheap." Even if film was no longer involved.

She found her mind clear, calculating, filled only with concerns for angles, lighting, focus, and framing. She saw the driver's dead hand protruding from a window—pale and crimson-stained, dangling above the black paint of the truck's door—and photographed it as coolly as she might have a senior posing for the yearbook.

Multiple shots later, she worked her way downhill, taking portrait after portrait of firefighters, EMTs, police officers, and others immersed in their work—faces grim, eyes narrowed, voices low and direct. This was a demonstration by professionals, much practiced and trained for, by people in their comfort zone. Given the lack of visible emotion on display, she might have been documenting the construction of a dam site instead of the disassembling of a gory and fatal vehicle crash.

And there were other injuries. The truck had swept across both lanes like a windshield wiper, collecting several cars in the process and launching them into the ditches and ledge without effort. She took pictures of a paramedic starting an IV line on a dazed pickup driver, and another of a small child sitting quietly on the bumper of an ambulance, watching her mother being bandaged nearby.

"*Hey*," came a male voice from behind her.

Rachel turned to see a Brattleboro police sergeant approaching, his expression stern.

That softened as he drew close enough to recognize her. "You're shitting me. We heard about you. How'd you get here?"

She glanced up the nearby hill and smiled apologetically. "No one said I couldn't."

He chuckled and lowered his voice. "Very clever. You're Hillstrom's kid, aren't you?"

She awkwardly stuck out a hand, slightly tangled in her camera strap. "Rachel. Hi."

He reciprocated and looked around. "You work for the paper now?"

"Yeah. Just started."

"Right," he said. "Saw your shots of the warehouse fire. How the hell did they let you in there?"

She just looked at him. He laughed after a prolonged and suggestive silence, and gently slapped his forehead. "Nobody said you couldn't. Of course. And you look like such a sweet young girl. You are a chip off the old block."

"You know my mom?" she asked.

He shook his head in wonder. "Your mom is a legend. Tough as nails and tenacious as hell—no disrespect. Very cool."

"None taken. Are you gonna throw me out?"

The sergeant pursed his lips. "I should."

Again, he checked to see if anyone was watching before saying, "You got fifteen minutes. Grab a safety vest out of the back of that SUV over there, so you blend in better, and don't do anything that'll draw attention. And do not throw me under the bus if you get caught."

He seemed embarrassed by that last comment, and added, "Not that they won't wonder where the hell you got the vest."

"Can you tell me anything about what happened?" she asked, putting her camera on the ground in order to slip on her semi-disguise.

He laughed quietly. "God, you are a natural. I'll have to spread the word. No, not really." He patted her shoulder before moving off. "That means, Miss Rachel, no comment. And remember: fifteen minutes. Tops. Have a nice day."

He turned his back as if they'd never met and moved away.

She resumed her assignment, careful to take his advice about the vest and heed his warning. She was discovering the delicate ground of this new profession—the need for discretion, politeness, a little charm—and how not to be shy about using her pedigree.

She was under no delusions about how her mother would receive that last part, which added to her wanting to be very careful right now.

She angled up to the huge truck, seemingly so much larger lying down than it might have been simply parked in a lot. There was considerably more activity near the cab, where people were discussing how best to extract the driver's body, so she worked around to the rig's wounded rear wheels, highlighted against the sky. She composed several shots, including the remnants of retardant foam still clinging to the charred chassis.

"Who the fuck're you?"

Great, she thought. Here we go again.

This time, however, it wasn't a cop. Nor was there any hint of accommodation. This man's voice spoke only of anger and entitlement.

"Rachel," she said quickly, finishing her shot.

He eyed her vest as she turned to face him, which was labeled POLICE, but ran at odds with the rest of her.

For her part, she saw that the hat above the mean face was stamped with the GreenField logo—same as the truck.

Damning the risk, she stuck her hand out to shake. "Hell of a mess. Sorry for your loss. You know the driver?"

It caught him off guard. His narrowed eyes widened a fraction. "What? No." He shook hands halfheartedly and stepped back a few paces, indicating the truck. "You should watch out," he said. "This could be unstable."

She suppressed a smile, unable to imagine anything less unstable than this flattened, oversized paperweight.

"Thanks," she told him. "I will."

He scowled, unsure of what to say next, before being saved the need by another man in a similar hat, rounding the truck's corner and calling out with relief, "Damn, J.R., you're a hard man to track. The accident-reconstruction guy wants to talk to us."

The angry man was visibly stumped, wanting to make sure Rachel had been dealt with, but not knowing how to do it.

He finally ducked his head and turned away, muttering, "Fine," to his companion.

Rachel stood alone for a moment. She was pleased with her bit of theater, but aware of her lack of authority here.

It was time to savor her gains and make herself scarce.

Still, she turned one last time to study the truck's underbelly, discerning the burn pattern as it snaked around and between the axles, brake lines, and wiring.

Even to her untrained eye, it didn't look right.

She took one last shot and walked away.

CHAPTER EIGHTEEN

Willy studied his daughter's profile as she bent to her work, crayon gripped, guarded by two stuffed animals and a miniature pillow that went with her everywhere. She was sitting in the hospital bed beside him, nestled in so that his good arm could curl around and still reach the pad she was drawing on.

It was a team effort. Instead of using a standard coloring book, this one had been blank. Willy drew the outlines, and Emma filled them in.

The results were much better than what might be imagined. Two nurses had already commented on the fact. Yet another of Willy's closely guarded attributes was that he was better than a good draftsman. He was, in truth, a master with a pencil. Joe had stumbled upon this many years ago, when he'd approached Willy unnoticed while the latter was on stakeout. To pass the time in those days, Willy attached a pad to his steering wheel, and, rather than simply observe the scene before him, would draw it. With remarkable precision and artistry.

It had once been a solitary and private activity, and Willy, upon Joe's discovery, had sworn his boss to keep it that way. Now, however, as with so much else along Willy's turbulent life journey, this talent was finding a peaceful and constructive outlet. That Emma was the beneficiary made it that much sweeter for her father.

Sue Spinney entered without a sound, not wishing to disrupt the artist's concentration. Willy, aided by his self-protective nature, had of course seen the first tiny motion of the door's hinges, and even recognized her tread approaching from down the hall.

He was therefore easy with her appearance. "What d'ya think?" he asked. "The next Georgia O'Keeffe?"

Sue cast the work a critical eye. "At least," she said. "Maybe better. How's the pain level?"

"All things being relative? A walk in the park," he reported.

She checked his vitals, loosened his johnny enough to glance at the dressing covering his left shoulder, and ran a temperature probe across his forehead.

"Something up?" he asked.

She smiled distractedly. "No. You seem A-okay."

"I know how I am. I was asking about you."

She looked surprised. "Really? What about me?"

He smirked. "If you ever take up poker, please challenge me to a game."

She conceded the point, if partially. "Oh, you know hospitals. Even small specialty shops like this one. I shouldn't have let it show. Sorry."

"It's what I do," he said. "What's up?"

"One of the nurses. She's bad-mouthing Victoria because she's out sick, and making cracks about how she left the chain of command."

"Don't tell me," Willy said. "She put you in charge?"

Sue laughed. "God, no. That's one reason I got out of Springfield. I like being a grunt. But she did tap somebody with fewer years than the woman bitching."

"Who is . . . ?"

Sue glanced at the door, as if anticipating a large ear to appear, and dropped her voice accordingly. "You met her, sort of. Remember when you and Sam were in Victoria's office the first time? A nurse stuck her head in?"

"Yeah," Willy replied, he of the machinelike memory. "Face like a battle-ax. Victoria called her Lillian."

"Damn," Sue reacted. "That's creepy. Well, she's the one. This place only started up a year ago, so we're all more or less on the same footing, but Lillian walks around like she's God's gift. Seen all, been everywhere, and resents the bejesus out of anyone giving her orders. The rest of us, she just dislikes."

"Why don't they can her?"

"Easier said than done. She knows her job. That's the problem. She'll never be head of nursing, like she thinks she should, but she never does anything to warrant being fired. Rock and a hard place."

"How's Victoria doing? She was out yesterday, too, wasn't she?"

"It's a flu, for crying out loud," Sue replied. "That's the other thing that pisses me off. Lillian never had a sick day? She smokes like a chimney, coughs all the time, can barely climb a set of stairs. She takes her share of days off. Who's she to cop a 'tude?"

Willy checked Emma's progress, which was ongoing, before returning to Sue. "She's really got you cranked."

Sue made a face. "It's not just that. Something's going on and nobody's talking. I hate it when they pull that crap."

"What crap?"

"Secret stuff. Hospitals do that more'n people realize. Somebody gets a call or an alert from the CDC, like back when Legionnaires' was a big deal, or anthrax. It's never real—not in Vermont—but the brass likes to pretend it might be. I'll grant we should be prepared, and we are. Don't get me wrong. I've even taken a bunch of the courses on how to handle the dangerous stuff. But everyone always ramps up the drama instead of just telling us what they heard and what we're gonna do about it."

"So what do you think it is?"

"Me? Nothing. That's my point. And if it is nothing, we'll never hear anything, which is dumb. It's like they think if they tell us, we'll imme-diately blab to the patients, or get on Facebook, or who knows what, and make the hospital look bad."

She suddenly did a double take and burst out laughing, admitting as she did, "And here I am, blabbing to a patient."

Emma looked up then and gave them both a wide smile.

"Joe? It's Bill."

Joe had recognized his boss's phone number on the display screen—one feature of modernity he didn't mind. "Hey, there. How's life among the big brass?"

Bill Allard was the director of the VBI, whereas Joe was its field force commander. In an autonomous, thinly staffed, self-directed outfit like the Bureau, most of its five statewide offices worked pretty indepen-dently, managing their assignments without much interference from above, which was rare in the bureaucratic, sometimes nitpicking world of law enforcement. Gunther appreciated that, and that Allard, located near the state's capital, was also such an adept traffic manager and dip-lomat, at once shielding his people and coordinating VBI's efforts with other agencies.

"Peachy," Allard said in response to the question. "You hear about that ten-fifty in your hometown, on the interstate, yesterday?"

"How could I not?" Joe replied. "Huge photo spread in the paper today, taken by none other than Beverly's daughter. Not to mention that traffic was at a standstill for hours. You got something for us on that? I heard the truck driver didn't make it."

"That's why I'm calling. State police're kicking it to us, based on what their crash-reconstructionist suspects."

"Which is what?"

"Sabotage. Somebody planted a device that blew off a small but cru-cial part of the truck's rear end. Weight and momentum did the rest."

Joe absorbed that before commenting, "That was a GreenField rig. I wondered when I heard about it."

"Yeah. That crossed my mind, too. How're we doing on the arson?"

"Not great," Joe told him frankly. "Spinney's pulled people from three other field offices to help him out, but it's slow going. We've got no trace evidence and only a vague idea that somebody either called J.R. or with a name ending in Junior might've been involved. Turnover's predictably high at GreenField, and they hire a lot of folks with past records. Good for the little guy with a chip on his shoulder; not so great for us who now have to pore through the chips."

Joe could hear Allard's other line ringing in the background. "Hang on a sec," his boss said before returning moments later. "I gotta take this, Joe. Sorry. Maybe the reconstructionist'll have something for you. They hauled what was left of the trailer to the state highway garage, north of Brattleboro. I think he's still fiddling with it there. You might want to drop by."

"Thanks, Bill," Joe said. "Will do."

As with so many such places, the Department of Transportation truck depot and servicing garage between Brattleboro and Putney on Route 5 was notable only for its lack of distinction. Pragmatic to a fault, consisting of a semicircle of truck-sized sheds facing a large concrete apron, it occupied a slope of land that fell away from the road toward the interstate some twelve hundred feet away, paralleling the Connecticut River and including a significantly sized sand, rock, and gravel pit.

All but unnoticeable from the road, aside from a sign and small Department of Motor Vehicles building, it was a perfect example of architectural discretion—useful, available, and yet tucked out of sight—so that admirers of Vermont's sylvan charms wouldn't have their sensibilities jarred.

There, inside one of the metal-sided sheds, Joe discovered a scene better suited to a monster movie than a highway maintenance yard. Mounted onto the back of a flatbed trailer, surrounded by glaring work lights, and resting on its side—as found—was the looming, harshly shadowed rear axle assembly of the destroyed truck from the day before. The tractor was missing, and the box had been largely cut away, leaving behind the entire rear section of the undercarriage, including eight burned and torn rubber tires, its axles and related hardware, and the truncated wires and hydraulic tubing that had once serviced them. As it was all positioned five feet off the ground on the flat bed, and thereafter loomed an additional eight feet overhead, it was an imposing sight inside a windowless, otherwise darkened garage.

Before it, wearing headlamps, green coveralls, and work gloves, were two men with STATE TROOPER stamped on their backs. They were standing on the transport trailer, deep in discussion and virtually entangled in the semi's rear axle assembly.

Joe immediately recognized one of them.

"Jonathon," he called out. "I didn't know you did this and arson, too."

Jonathon Michael turned to face him, inadvertently bringing his headlamp to bear directly into Joe's eyes.

Laughing, he hit the off switch and jumped down. "Joe. I had a feeling one of you guys would show up. And in answer to your question, no, I do not do reconstructions. But I do incendiary explosives, and that's what we got here."

He turned to indicate his colleague, still on the flatbed. "Leslie Martens—Joe Gunther, from VBI."

Joe waved to the other man, saying, "Martens? How do you spell that?"

Martens laughed. "Like Sam does. Distant cousin. I get that all the time. Call me Les, if that makes it easier."

Joe shook his head. "Another one of my guys is named that."

"William's my real first name. I don't like it, but if it'll make it easier for you . . ."

Joe waved it off. "This state is way too small." He looked again at Michael. "You saying this was firebombed? Like at the warehouse?"

"Different setup, but, yeah—including signs of a GreenField insider's knowledge."

Joe stepped up and rested his hands on the truck bed, staring at the twisted mass of metal above him. "Huh. How so?"

Martens took over, moving to one of the axles, preparing to reveal the prize behind Door Number One.

"I won't bury you in techno-speak," he began, pointing to a soot-blackened smear near his head. "But a timer-equipped device was placed where it could defeat the trailer's safety features and lock up her brakes in a single shot. Once that happened, it was road physics one-oh-one: static friction became sliding friction, burning the tires, the trailer jack-knifed, and the unit crashed because it had no other choice. The driver couldn't have known what the hell was going on."

"Did the device survive?" Joe asked.

"Not in so many words," Martens told him. "That's what we've been doing all this time—rebuilding what happened based on residual evidence, which was spread, by the way, along almost a mile of roadway, from where it first went off to where the truck ended up. Unfortunately, the sheer violence of it all, not to mention its thermodynamic properties, pretty much cooked everything we could collect. If we were in a *CSI* show, of course, we'd be two beautiful women in dramatic lighting, and get the job done in forty-three minutes with commercial breaks. But we ain't. Sorry."

"That's for the hardware, though," Michael corrected gently. "As for signature issues—call 'em psychological fingerprints—we may have more to go on."

Martens chuckled. "That's why we bring Jonathon in. He's more the artist than I am."

"What're you talking about?" Joe asked his old friend. "You mentioned insider knowledge."

Michael leaned against the flatbed. "I did, although you could argue that's a stretch. I threw it in because of the double coincidence of Green-Field and an explosive device. That being said, it's interesting to me that both scenarios involved specialized vehicles—an eighteen-wheeler and an electric floor jack—and something that either caught fire or went boom. That sure as hell suggests we're dealing with the same bad guy, not to mention that the best time to rig a truck with a device is when it's backed up to a warehouse and everybody's attention is distracted."

Joe was nodding by now. "So for our psychological profile, we can safely overlay GreenField, knowledge of industrial vehicle mechanics, and pyrotechnics."

"And smarts," Jonathon added. "Whoever this is has got brains. He's a planner, he's patient, and he's clearly pissed off." He held up a finger to make one additional point. "And, before you ask, he or she also knows the GreenField security camera setup. Soon as I got here and saw what they had, I called up to Spinney and company and had them check the footage for when this truck was in the bay. Because of its location and the other rigs blocking the view, Lester said he couldn't see a thing."

Joe made a face. "Good thought. All right, so who's this nutcase mad at? Bob Raiselis? From what I heard, the man might've been a saint. Not even a speeding ticket. And if he was the target, then why burn the warehouse? And if Mr. Mystery or J.R. or whoever the hell he is wanted to burn down the warehouse, then why did he do such a surgical job of only scorching it? And then why kill Raiselis? I just keep going in circles on this damned case. It's not giving me anything."

"I'd say the truck driver was collateral damage," Martens volunteered from his perch.

"I think so, too," Jonathon said, "chosen more for where he parked than who he was."

"All the worse for poor Bob's family, then," Joe concluded. "Blown to pieces because of a camera angle."

"I'm not saying I'm right," Jonathon argued, switching gears perhaps out of sympathy. "Maybe Raiselis was in witness protection for being a triggerman for the Mob."

"I'd quit while I was behind," Martens counseled him.

Joe had begun walking alongside the stacked trucks, his footsteps echoing in the large space. "The common link's GreenField," he said. "I think you are right about Raiselis. Wrong place, wrong time. We'll check him out, of course, but . . ." He didn't finish the thought.

"GreenField's a middleman operation, isn't it?" Jonathon asked. "Suppliers on one side, retailers on the other? What if one of them is out to ruin it?"

"What's that do to your insider argument?" Joe wanted to know.

"Maybe nothing," Jonathon said. "Wouldn't be the first time allies were created out of mutual convenience. Your doer could be somebody else's cat's-paw. Maybe a payoff's in the mix, making your saboteur a mercenary."

Joe was still going back and forth, his chin tucked. "Too many loose ends," he muttered. "We need a couple of them to interconnect."

CHAPTER NINETEEN

"Have you done the dirty deed?" Joe asked. "You said you were ninety percent there."

Beverly gave him an amused look. "Do you mean, Joseph, have I concluded the purchase of this fine property?"

He laughed. "Yeah. That, too."

She looped her arm through his. "I have. Actually."

Once more, she, Joe, and Rachel were in Windsor, revisiting the house on the water. Like the previous time, it was quiet, pleasant, and soothing on the senses.

"Yay," Rachel said, giving her mother a thumbs-up.

"I take it," Joe suggested as Rachel wandered off toward the lake, "this also means the Dartmouth teaching job is a sure thing?"

"It is," Beverly said, her mood tellingly contented.

Joe was equally pleased. Old bachelor that he'd become—and since his initial elation—he'd been considering how he felt about her moving near Brattleboro. He'd been slightly fearful that it might change their personal dynamics, but the more he'd pondered the question, the more he liked how it felt. "Looking forward to that, are you?" he asked, his inquiry more loaded as a result.

She rolled her eyes. "Am I ever. And if I ever needed confirmation, this week was it."

"That infectious case you were talking about? Anything new?"

"Tomorrow," she replied. "At least, I think so. That's when the first of my answers will arrive."

"Who from?"

"It's less a person than an object. I'm referring to the histology slides I ordered. Studying them should give me a heads-up on the poor man's cause of death. I'm hoping the state epidemiologist will follow up twenty-four hours afterwards, to confirm whatever I find."

"This sounds like a bigger deal than I thought," Joe commented. They started walking toward the house to take a more proprietary tour, now admiring it in a different light. This was promising to become where he would spend a good deal of time. Unconsciously, he slipped his hand into hers, taking in the skylights, many windows, and especially the small, silolike turret that formed one corner of the house—all very appealing.

"It might be," she said carefully. "Which certainly means the absence of any similar cases so far is heartening. Of course, I have to consider the possibility that their discovery has merely been delayed. But if we are dealing with something infectious, it could be cause for alarm. That's in part why I've been both distracted and unavailable. I'm grateful now that I started buying this place so long ago."

Joe smiled. "You probably would've been safe. I don't think Windsor's under threat of a land rush quite yet."

She jabbed him in the ribs. "You are so harsh sometimes. I love this town. It's a little rough around the edges. You can be, too. But I love you."

He slipped his arm around her waist as they entered the foyer. "I love you, too, Dr. Hillstrom."

He looked around and gestured with his free hand. "It look different, now that it's all yours?"

She broke away enough to face him. "Let me ask you that. I'm hoping it's about to be ours, in a way."

This, of course, was the topic they'd avoided openly discussing, being at once respectful of each other's privacy and perhaps a little shy. "Keep going," he encouraged her, realizing they'd been privately thinking along similar lines.

Her manner was characteristically precise. "Do you see this as somewhere you might want to spend more than a night now and then?"

"I have been thinking about that," he replied.

"And?" she urged him.

He considered simply blurting out what she wanted to hear—and what he'd been feeling earlier. But his connection to this woman, the foundation of trust on which it was built, demanded a more nuanced and thoughtful response. "It's very attractive," he admitted.

"But?" she seemed to enjoy escorting him through this process, like an usher taking a patron to his chair.

"Well," he resumed, having hoped for such a reaction, "you've created a very seductive scenario for a self-protective loner and workaholic like me. From what I understand, you'll be here half of every week, and maybe weekends?"

"Two days a week, yes," she confirmed. "And some weekends. Not every one."

"Which'll give me three days a week on my own, down in Brattleboro. If I'm correctly reading what we're dancing around, you wouldn't be averse to our sharing this place while you're here."

Her half smile broadened. "You're dancing well, Special Agent Gunther. And I did just mention how not all my weekends would be here. I should add that the Geisel School will no doubt have me committed to an evening class or two, further opening up that timetable. And none of that takes into account your own often insane and spontaneous schedule. We could go for weeks without seeing each other."

She leaned forward and rested her hand against his chest, putting her face close to his. "Joe, I value you the way you are. I love your company and want to see more of you, but you're not the only one to have become comfortably single in your way. I don't wish to threaten that, for either of us. I'm suggesting a gentle experiment, to see what we enjoy and what we may find too claustrophobic."

He kissed her and stroked her cheek. "I'm in," he said. "I have never been so sure of anything."

Joe left Beverly to take room-by-room measurements of the house's interior, and went to find Rachel outside. She was shooting close-up photographs of a nascent blue flower. His agreement to share a roof with Beverly had in the same breath stimulated an unstated contradiction they both instinctively understood. New Englanders—born or transplanted like Beverly—were famous for guarding their privacy and feelings. He therefore honored that her invitation had not included his playing a role in how the place was to look. This was her house, hers to furnish and decorate. Not only that, but he wanted to give them both a moment to savor the decision they'd just reached.

"I hope you're getting its good side," he commented to Rachel.

She straightened at his approach. "I'm not actually into this kind of shot, but I've been told to keep an eye out for filler material. What better than an early summer bloom?"

"True enough," he said, taking a seat on a weathered wooden bench facing the water.

Rachel joined him, her camera in her lap. "Mom casing the joint?"

"Oh, yeah. My guess is she'll have everything but blueprints ready in an hour. How's the job going, by the way? You did great work on that truck crash."

She turned to him, her expression eager. "Wasn't that amazing? I know I've been spoiled rotten so far, what with the warehouse and the crash coming right on top of each other, but it's so much better than I expected. People told me to be resigned to garden-club lunches and ribbon cuttings, and I haven't had either yet. Even the sports stories have been neat, and I barely know one sport from another."

"How's your boss?"

"He's fine. He says hi, by the way. Told me to make a crude comment to you when we next met, so you'd know it came from him."

"Consider it done," Joe said, reminiscing about how he and Stan Katz used to tangle back in the day, when Joe worked for the local police and was therefore of particular interest to Katz.

Rachel was still speaking. "He talks a lot about how things used to be, when the building was packed with people, and they were transitioning from typewriters to computers. It does sound like it was a lot of fun."

Joe nodded, gazing ahead at a bird gliding low, in search of fish. "It was a different world," he said quietly. "More one-on-one, less pessimistic and angry than it seems now."

"That's what Katz says."

He glanced at her. "What's it like now? Just the two of you? You must be like two BBs rolling around inside a boxcar."

"Kind of," she conceded. "There're one or two reporters who come and go. I actually don't see Katz much. He doesn't come in till the afternoon, and I'm more in my car than at the office."

"How's the average day play out?" Joe asked, genuinely interested. "In the old days, photographers were at the beck and call of their editors." He laughed, adding, "Almost like dogs fetching sticks."

She joined him. "Hardly. I'm guessing I come up with about half my own assignments, and just hand them in. There's a ton of independence."

He was surprised. "Really? How do you do that? You're new to the area. I'm impressed."

She held up her large iPhone. "Don't get carried away. I have a regional scanner feed. Dozens of people wandering around, posting what they're seeing. It's not like it used to be. In school, they told us you had cherished sources you cared for and nurtured—probably like you do in police work. But with this, I just keep my eyes peeled and go after what looks interesting."

She tilted the screen toward him so he could see an endless crawl of one-liners scrolling by in real time. He tried to decipher what was being said.

"Wow. Some of that looks moronic."

Rachel gave him a rueful look. "Yeah. Well, knowing how to interpret it helps. You should've seen this when the truck crashed. That's when you just turn it off and go yourself. Gets too crazy otherwise. Speaking of that," she said slowly, "was there anything suspicious there? I was going to call you about that."

Joe turned to her, diplomatically wide eyed. "Suspicious? How do you mean?"

"I heard rumors."

"Yeah," Joe said slowly. "Well, you will. Something like that will get people talking."

"Funny that it was the same company as the warehouse fire. You think someone has it in for them?"

"It bears looking into," he said lightly, at once wary and impressed by her persistence.

"Implying the truck was fooled with."

He stared at her in surprise. "Look at you. You have been hanging out with Katz. How in God's name do you get that from what I said?"

She kept her eyes fixed on his, her expression studiously neutral. "I've been hearing more than just that."

He chuckled, thinking of all the men who'd populated the crash scene, and been involved—including as eavesdroppers—in the discussions about which truck part to preserve and transport to the state garage, and why. Rachel was attractive and knew how to handle herself, as she was making clear now. It was no stretch to imagine that she'd gotten a source to give her more than he might have intended.

Assuming it hadn't all been lifted from her ever-handy phone.

Either way, it was a pretty old game. Young Rachel was proving a fast learner.

"You better tell me what you got," he therefore said. "So we're both on the same page. I don't want to miss a good tip."

That shifted the burden. He saw her play for time by lifting her camera and scrolling through its archive. She showed him a shot of the trailer's undercarriage. "That's what was attracting all the attention, as I bet you're not telling me."

He loved the end of the sentence, with its invitation to confirm or deny.

"I'm surprised you're interested," he commented, steering for safer waters. "You did your job, didn't you? Photographing the scene? Don't you move on to the next assignment now?"

She didn't take offense, which he'd worried she might. "It used to be that specialized," she said instead, in a lightly indulgent tone. "Like what you were saying about editors making photographers fetch. It's a new model now, with so few of us on staff. Katz told me that if I find something interesting, like this crash, I should chase it down like a reporter, as well as take the shots. I think he's actually angling to make me more a reporter than a shooter in the long run. More and more editors aren't even hiring photographers."

Joe wasn't as thrilled by this as he knew he should be. Her response positioned her even more in potential opposition to him. Suppressing a sigh, he steadied the camera with one hand and took a closer look at the image filling its small screen. "Hard to see anything. I wasn't there, of course. I did wonder how you were able to get that close."

Endearingly, she blushed, which he figured would be a short-lived reaction if she continued in this profession. "I got lucky," she confessed. "And nobody threw me out." She gestured with the camera again. "So, was there something funny with this part of the truck?"

He pretended to squint again, hiding his reaction, and even pressed the control that enlarged parts of the picture, before finally pulling back and apologizing. "I'm sorry, Rachel, I can't make anything out. The state police are handling the crash reconstruction. They'd really be your best source."

She didn't hide her disappointment, adding to his discomfort. While the cop in him was happy to thwart the press creatively, the mentor in him wished he could impart what he knew. He liked this young woman, outside of her being Beverly's daughter. He'd known her for several years, had employed her once as a videographer at a crime scene, and had even dealt with her in the context of a couple of criminal cases. She'd always come off as thoughtful, smart, considerate, and resilient—character traits he highly esteemed.

It was frustrating to now play avoidance games with her, bordering on lying, when her curiosity was merely imitating his own.

But of course, it was where the fruits of their separate curiosities would end up that defined the barrier between them. Not just legally, but also philosophically, Joe questioned the press's judgment when it came to the famous "public's right to know," thinking that often enough, the reporter's ambition was more at stake than any citizen's ignorance.

That obviously wasn't the case here, but, unlike when he'd helped smuggle Rachel into the warehouse, Joe was going to leave her in the dark on this particular issue. He knew her boss, after all, and things were complicated enough to make the extra aggravation of a hyped-up media an unpleasant distraction.

Joe's phone went off in his pocket, and—as if illustrating the divide between them—he stood to pull it out and moved away from the bench for privacy. The screen told him that his caller was Walter Easton, the corrections officer from Rutland.

"Hey, Walter."

"I'm on the run," Easton said, "but I wanted to give you the heads-up. Mick Durocher just died in the infirmary. That's a mandatory autopsy, per statute, but there's not much doubt it was cancer. Just thought you'd want to know."

"Thanks, Walter. Appreciate the courtesy."

He hung up as Rachel looked at him inquiringly. "Everything okay?"

He nodded and checked his watch. "Yeah—a bit of news I was waiting for. Speaking of which, I guess I better start heading back. Never a dull moment, as they say. I'll go see how your mom's doing."

Rachel stayed behind, camera in her lap, once more studying the flat water before her. She was really happy her mother and Joe had hooked up. She found him kind and decent and in many ways superior to her own father, whom she did truly love, despite his flaws.

But she'd just discovered her first stumbling block with Joe.

She'd always known him to be a man who happened to be a cop. In this last conversation, for the first time, she'd encountered the cop holding sway over the man.

She understood it. She represented the opposing side, even the enemy. Intellectually, she knew the divide between a free press and the law to be a chasm of necessity. But finding herself on the wrong side of it right now, frustrated and empty-handed, hurt her feelings and made her a bit angry.

She accepted it was childish, a reflection of her immaturity as a journalist. Stan Katz had already described this challenge as a battle of wits—something to relish.

But she wasn't there yet. Nevertheless, she was learning. She knew Joe had been holding back, for example. She, too, hadn't volunteered that she'd sniffed out a lead during her visit to the crash site—that she'd seen both unhappiness and something less definable stamped on the Green-Field representative who'd found her studying the truck's undercarriage. More important, she remembered that his colleague had referred to him by name.

Now alone, she scrolled back several shots from the picture she'd shown Joe, to a scowling man wearing a traffic vest—almost out of the frame—rounding the corner of the upended truck.

She smiled at the recalled moment. "Hello, J.R.," she said thoughtfully.

* * *

Unusually for midweek, Beverly chose to spend the night at Joe's that night, taking advantage of Brattleboro's proximity to Windsor over the longer drive home to greater Burlington.

It was also a welcome change for her: In contrast to the rambling, high-ceilinged, many-roomed, wedding cake mansion she lived in, Joe's rented carriage house was just shy of a garden cottage. You had to duck to pass into the miniature kitchen, half crawl up the ladderlike staircase to the sleeping loft, and from at least one corner of the wood-walled, intimately cozy living room—beside the door to the attached woodworking shop—you could take in the whole place in one glance.

It also, surprisingly, had a blue/silver cat named Gilbert Gumshoe, who'd arrived in Joe's life unexpectedly and never left, and whose companionable independence perfectly suited the two humans in the house.

Beverly loved the place's simplicity, its peacefulness, its lack of pretension so reflective of its owner, almost as much as she enjoyed making love to the man himself on the couch before the fire, which they did shortly after a light dinner of soup and sandwiches.

Sadly, as was too often the case, given their respective professions, that's about all they got to exchange on this night. Just as Joe returned from the kitchen with a container of Ben & Jerry's and two spoons, Beverly's phone went off.

He knew it was a wrap as soon as she read the small screen. Her face hardened slightly, her voice dropped as she answered, and her eyes began seeking out where she'd earlier dropped her clothes.

He was already handing her some of those items as she rang off. "Bad?" he asked.

"Could be worse," she began cryptically, "but I do hope it doesn't go there."

That caught his attention. "What happened?"

"Remember the infectious death I mentioned? One of the things I set in motion—along with collecting samples, ordering slides, and speaking with various authorities and docs—was an investigation into the decedent's background."

"Yeah," he replied, retrieving a shoe from under the couch, which Gilbert immediately made an attempt to take back. "You thought all that wouldn't show up until later."

"The lab stuff, yes," she corrected him, struggling with some buttons. "I had no idea about the background search. Well, that just came back. Mr. Larabee was a private commercial pilot, flying Learjets and whatnot for high-priced executives. Shortly before he checked into the Upper Valley Surgical Specialists in a near-comatose state, he'd been to Germany on a job."

"Okay," Joe encouraged her, wondering where this was heading. Gilbert jumped up onto the couch between them to see how he could impede Beverly's progress.

"It turns out," she continued, close enough to returning to a daytime appearance to ruffle the cat's ears, "that our pilot was a man-about-town when on the job, like the proverbial sailor with a girl in every port."

"He caught something," Joe suggested.

She gave him a worldly smile. "And how. Give a round of applause to your brothers in arms, Joe. My law enforcement liaison—that was he on the phone—dug deep enough to discover that Mr. Larabee's bedmate of that night—just back from Africa—died earlier today in Munich, of what later killed her flyboy lover in Vermont. Her cause of death—and therefore his—is about to put everyone here into a well-deserved tizzy."

Joe prepared for bad news.

She stood, fully dressed, looking down at man and cat, and tilted her head in an equivocal way. For the first time since he'd known her, Joe read uncertainty on her face.

"She and Larabee died of Ebola, Joe. I've got to get back, confirm the finding, shut everything down, and hope that's where it will stop."

CHAPTER TWENTY

Before leaving for Burlington, Beverly had reassured Joe that the protocols for dealing with an exposure like this—long ago created by the public health community and reviewed on a routine basis—were already in motion. As long as word didn't get out until after everything was under control, there would be no hysteria beyond a number of post-event, appropriately blaring headlines.

Statements like that reminded him how much messier and chaos-driven his world was than hers. After kissing her goodbye, he wasted no time putting back on his rumpled clothes, abandoning Gilbert to refreshed bowls of dry food and water, and getting into his own car to head directly for Larabee's last known address: the same hospital Willy Kunkle was still calling home.

Ebola, Beverly had informed him, was in fact pretty hard to catch, especially in the circumstances surrounding the late Mr. Larabee. He'd checked in virtually at death's door, and the hospital's standard handling of him included barriers like gloves and masks that would have defeated routine disease migration, to use her phrase. Also, she'd added for good measure, virtually every factor that encouraged the spread of Ebola in Africa was nonexistent here.

Joe should keep all that in mind.

He did, and he was, during his high-speed drive up the interstate late at night to be by his colleague's side, updating Sammie by phone as he drove.

Truthfully, he'd heard what Beverly had politely implied: Do not contribute to the problem here. What's done is done, the proper response is in motion, and wherever this goes, it will soon be brought under control.

He got that.

What she couldn't have addressed was that part of his extended family was at risk, Joe felt responsible for them, and he needed, if for emotional reasons only, to be among them.

They met up, he and Sam, in Upper Valley Surgical Specialists' waiting room, finding, much to their surprise, Lester already in residence.

"What're you doing here?" Lester asked, standing as they entered. He checked the clock on the wall. "It's after midnight."

Joe settled into an armchair. "I'm your boss. You first."

Les and Sam sat next to each other on a couch opposite. "I'm here with Sue," he said vaguely. "She got called in for an emergency, and I figured I'd tag along."

Joe glanced around to make sure they were alone and that no one was within earshot. "The same infectious disease that did in Mr. Larabee?" he asked obliquely.

Lester sat forward, his approach suddenly more open. "Yeah. Ebola. How'd you hear about it? I thought it was hush-hush."

"Beverly was staying over when she got the call," Joe explained, adding, "She wanted me to tell people it's not as contagious as in Africa. That's why I drove up here. Apparently, the better the overall hygiene, the better everyone's chances. It's harder to catch than the common cold. She compared its publicity to the bad old early days of AIDS, when the rumors were that death was a handshake away."

"Yeah," Lester said, unconvinced. "Well, if she survives, you might want to tell that to Victoria Garlanda. She's the emergency we're here for—along with the fact that Willy's been breathing this polluted air for days. Not to disagree with Dr. Hillstrom, but I think we're beyond the common cold."

"You check on him yet?" Sam asked anxiously. "I didn't want to barge in, since I know just by approaching his room, I'll wake him up."

"Way past that, too," Lester went on. "This is as far inside the building as you're going, and only because of Sue's influence. They locked the place down. I talked to Willy on the phone," he added, holding up his cell. "He's fine. Couldn't care less. He's the only one, though. Everybody else is staring at each other like they're about to sprout horns. They're waiting for the brass to tell them what's gonna happen."

Joe backed the conversation up a bit. "Talk about Victoria. What's that about? I thought she was an administrator."

"Who's been out sick for a couple of days," Lester replied. "Ebola apes the flu early on, so the flu's what she thought she had. When word went out that Ebola had killed Larabee, and everybody was ordered in or contacted personally, Sue immediately thought of Victoria and put two and two together like that." He snapped his fingers. "So, while we beat feet up here, they sent an ambulance to pick her up."

"She here now?" Sam asked, having pulled out her phone and moved toward the door to call Willy from outside.

"No way. Not with what she's got. That's Dartmouth-Hitchcock material. She's in isolation up there, supposedly at death's door."

"For what it's worth, Sam," Joe called out to her as she was about to leave, "Beverly also said the shelf life's really short. If no one's come down with it in the last twenty-four hours, chances are it's been contained."

Deeper inside the building, Sue Spinney entered Willy's room, finding him peacefully reading a gun magazine.

"How're you feeling?" she asked.

He looked up and gave her an almost pitying look. "The same way I told the other five people who asked me that. I promise if I start feeling shitty, I'll have my lawyer spell it out in our lawsuit."

She stopped in her tracks, uncertain of how to respond.

Without changing his expression, he said, "Joke. Take a breath."

His phone rang. He glanced at it, held up a finger to Sue, and then answered it. "Hey, babe. Sue just walked in. I'll call you back."

He waited a moment, added, "Got it. I'm fine. No sweat. We oughta make Louise part of the family. Later."

He hung up and smiled, explaining, "Babysitter. Gift from God. Came over in the middle of the night, just so Sam could cool her heels in the waiting room. You know when things'll settle back down?"

"No." Almost from habit, Sue checked his monitors and vitals as she spoke. "Anyone tell you what was up?"

"That there'd been an infection down the hall and they were being extra careful about making sure it was contained and exterminated. Love that word."

"It's Ebola," she said bluntly, knowing her audience. "A patient who died a few days ago just got autopsied by Beverly. I guess he'd had contact with someone from Africa."

"Cool," Willy said, showing no concern. "Same question, though: When's normal coming back?"

"It's not over," she said, her voice remaining grim. "Victoria got it, too."

That brought him up short. He looked concerned. "How is she?"

"Don't know. They took her to Dartmouth."

He scowled. "How the hell did she catch it? She doesn't mess with patients."

"She does, but not that one," Sue said, looking helpless. "That's what's really bothering me. I can't figure it out. Even without knowing what that patient had, it shouldn't have mattered—our routine practices should have prevented contamination. It doesn't make sense. And that's doubly true for Victoria. She never even set eyes on the guy."

Sue stared at the floor, clearly overcome.

Willy couldn't do more than to say sympathetically, "She'll probably beat it. She's a healthy girl."

Sue looked up, her chin trembling. "There's no cure. You either live or die on your own. It's like a lottery."

He was left speechless.

She took a breath before saying sadly, "She's my best friend—the whole reason I came here."

Before he could think of something to add, she turned on her heel, said, "Sorry. Don't forget to call Sam back," and left.

Joe handed Lester a cup of coffee from the vending machine. Through the window, they could see Sam walking back and forth in the parking lot, talking to Willy on her phone.

"I suppose being here is kind of dumb," Lester commented, accepting the cup.

Joe sat back in his armchair. "What the hell else are we going to do? Both our better halves are out saving the world. We might as well sit here drinking bad coffee as stare at the ceiling at home."

Les took a sip and wrinkled his nose. "True."

"Anything new in the GreenField archaeological dig?" Joe asked.

"Nothing startling. It helped getting the J.R. reference. Maybe throwing that into the mix'll do something. That truck sabotage was out of the blue, wasn't it?"

"I sure didn't see it coming," Joe admitted. "It does raise the question: Is our bad guy just warming up?"

"You think he meant to kill the driver?" Les asked. "Raiselis?"

"Yeah—I was going to ask Sam to poke into that," Joe said. "Jonathon Michael did a once-over-lightly on his background, and only found a poster child for the decent, hardworking middle class. No record, solid marriage, good kids, boring finances. From the outside, it looks like knocking him off was just to add to GreenField's misery. That's what got me thinking that both the fire and the truck sabotage might be opening moves only. After all, somebody *could've* died in the fire, as well. There was no effort to safeguard human life. In that way, they were lucky."

"To what point?" Lester asked. "You may be right, but the fire still wasn't meant to burn the building down, and if the intention is to destroy the company, blowing one truck off the road, or even killing a few people as collateral damage, isn't gonna do anything, either. What's this guy want?"

Joe considered that, not for the first time. "I wondered at first if ruining the company's reputation was the goal, but that would be better served by spoiling food or introducing a toxin—something implying that Green-Field's quality controls are faulty. If anything, these two events've only stimulated sympathy."

"They cost GreenField a bunch of money," Lester mused out loud.

"Which insurance'll probably cover."

"What else, then?" Lester asked.

"Stress," Joe suggested. "You don't know when your workplace'll catch fire, or your truck'll be blown up, or Christ knows what else. That would stress *me* out. It could be psychological warfare."

Lester showed his frustration, understandable given the time he'd spent chewing on this problem. "But why?" he burst out. "You don't do all that planning for shits and giggles. There's gotta be a purpose."

Joe was unperturbed. In fact, this was one of the first times he'd fully reflected on the matter—something he should have done much earlier. He was actually enjoying himself—the puzzle master facing a worthy challenge.

"You're right," he agreed. "So why *do* you conduct a campaign like this, if it isn't to kill particular targets or ruin the business? It's gotta be that you're a terrorist."

"Great," Lester grumbled. "I don't know why they do it, either."

Joe thought a moment before suggesting, "To scare you, to undermine your confidence, to divert your resources, to advertise that even though you feel like Goliath, you're surrounded by Davids."

"But he's not advertising any of that," Les protested. "Wouldn't that be the whole point?"

"Not to us, he's not," Joe replied. "Maybe there's someone inside the company who knows exactly who this is."

That brought Lester out of his funk. He blinked at Joe, caught by surprise, before saying, "Jesus Christ. I never thought of that."

"What're you picking up about their management?" Joe asked. "When I met with Bob Beaupré, we mostly talked about Mick Durocher. This is making me think a revisit might be in order."

Lester's enthusiasm, rarely gone for long, was back. "I like it, and there's even a 'Junior' who might fit, which I feel like an idiot for not remembering. One of his sons," he explained quickly, seeing Joe's inquisitive look. "He's never referred to as that, and I was too buried in rank-and-file records to give the big brass much thought."

He held up a hand to count off the players, reaching back in his memory to recall what Pat Smith had told him. "Robert, the old man, has a wife and three kids: Bobby—he's the J.R. I should've thought of—Philip, and Elaine. Bobby and Philip work for the company, as does his son-in-law, Bradley St. John. Elaine's not involved."

"Tell me about Bobby," Joe requested.

"He and Brad are numbers two and three, under Robert," Les told him. "I've been learning more about them, through exposure to management's nuts and bolts, which is what makes me extra embarrassed about dropping the ball on Junior."

"Let it go," Joe urged.

"Okay. Anyhow, in simple terms, Bobby is essentially operations, and Brad is finances. Philip could be called a floater—troubleshooter, idea man, sounding board. Bobby's the eldest by eight years. I don't know why the gap in ages. Philip, the next oldest, and Elaine are only a year apart.

Bobby's married, with three kids, lives in Stowe, in a suitably large mansion, and has the personality of a desk lamp, so they say. Same rumors say that Philip supplies most of the creativity and energy, while Bobby's got the carry-through that his little brother's too impatient to mess with. That makes 'em a good team, in company terms—and probably in the old man's eyes, who set up the structure—even if it doesn't make great buddies out of the two brothers."

"Bad blood?" Joe asked.

"From what I heard, that's too strong. Just totally different styles. Pat Smith told me it actually works pretty well. She said it was like watching one player pass a ball by leaving it in the middle of the floor for the other player to pick up. It functions fine—they just don't have much to do with each other."

"What about Bobby when he's not at the office?" Joe asked. "He bet the ponies or chase women?"

"Not that I heard. Rumor has it his missus wouldn't mind if he chased her a little. He's said to be a workaholic. Even his father's ordered him to cut back and enjoy the family. Of course, he should talk."

"What's that mean? I thought the old man was father-of-the-year material."

"Paternalistic might be a better fit. I think the early days weren't so warm and fuzzy. He's like a combination of his two boys—Bobby's work ethic and Philip's imagination. You're right if you're talking about the 'working man made good' image. I think that's legit, and it may be what's missing from his kids, who were all born rich. But as a family man, Robert Sr. was probably better with his coworkers than he was with the rug rats back home. That's not unusual."

"Okay," Joe said, conversationally taking a step backwards. "Let's put Bobby—or J.R., if you prefer—into the context where we first heard of him."

"I read about your and Sam's interview with Teri Parker's neighbor," Lester said. "According to her, J.R. was 'hot' and Teri was in love."

"And superprivate," Joe added, "to use her words."

"As was the sugar daddy. Did I get it right that he gave her the fancy phone?"

"Supposedly," Joe agreed. "But Sam and I got the feeling Teri considered J.R. the alpha dog, and the sugar daddy just a source of amusement and toys."

"So which one removed the phone and the tablet?" Lester asked.

Joe smiled and suggested, "Keeping in mind that it may've been neither of them."

"Meaning your informant's lying?" Lester mused. "One thing's for sure. She didn't make Teri pregnant."

Joe pushed out his lips meditatively, staring at the floor. "I think it's time we found a way to start selectively collecting a little DNA."

CHAPTER TWENTY-ONE

The saying is that familiarity breeds contempt. For J.R., it was breeding a much appreciated inconspicuousness. Despite the extra security, cops pawing through records in the general manager's office, and a heightened sense of wariness affecting everybody since Bob Raiselis's death, Green-Field's warehouse remained an open turnstile for older hands. People like J.R. were coming and going without notice.

It wasn't just that his was a familiar face. GreenField, like large shipping operations everywhere, was more ant farm than plant. The number of employees at desks was small, compared to those moving product. And the latter were constantly on the move—walking, riding jacks, shifting pallets, loading racks, and filling tractor trailers. One side of the building received product, the other half shipped it out, and it got stacked, sorted, picked, and packaged in between—nonstop, around the clock—by an army so numerous that, finally, all anyone paid attention to was not getting run over by a forklift or a jack. It got to be like dodgeball, where the last thing you focused on was the face of the person aiming in your direction.

And aiming was what J.R. had in mind.

This time was going to be his best yet, a fitting progression to what had gone before. If he pulled it off to expectations, Bob Raiselis would become a footnote, and the holy name of Beaupré would receive the kind of scrutiny it deserved. The years-long benevolent image of the corporate paterfamilias constructed from whole cloth—the pickup-driving hayseed-done-good—would be torn away, revealing the hypocrite beneath.

J.R. proceeded casually through the overall bustle, reducing his visibility by avoiding contact and pretending to be preoccupied. He was headed toward what they called the cooler—a room big enough to be a building wing—in which GreenField stored its frozen goods. Here, regardless of the season, workers performed the same duties as those outside, but dressed in arctic garb. To J.R., they looked like lost Inuits, dumped from a train and wandering through the world's largest, coldest railroad terminal.

He didn't pass through the cold cavern's curtain of hanging plastic strips, however. Instead, checking over his shoulder to make sure he was unobserved and in one of the camera system's blind spots, he cut behind a wall of boxes, worked his way to the bottom of a vertical ladder stretching straight up to the catwalk forty feet overhead, and started climbing.

An industrial refrigerator like the cooler is built on the scale of an ocean liner. Every aspect of it has been enlarged to where the people responsible for its care and feeding are reduced to Lilliputians. However, just as the workings of an old-fashioned fridge appear as a crisscrossing of tubes covering the icebox's back wall, so GreenField's cooler was serviced by a tangle of pipes resting on its top, some of them big enough to contain a human body. Finally there, breathing hard, just under the warehouse ceiling—and literally surrounded by miles of pipe—J.R. envisioned himself as the only human amid a vast, intertwined nest of dormant pythons.

The threat of lethality was enhanced by the boldface signage stamped upon every surface, even here, high above the casual onlooker. Wherever he glanced, J.R. saw virulent yellow labels cautioning against the pipes' contents.

Which was, of course, what had drawn him here. In the ever-progressive search for affordable, effective, and efficient coolants, refrigeration engineers had in some cases returned to the quasi-antique solution of anhydrous ammonia. It met all the above requirements, with the small additional inconvenience that it was incredibly toxic.

Anhydrous means "without water." Any contact of the gas with a human body—consisting of 60 percent water—causes a catastrophic transference of fluid, dehydration, and severe burning, especially of a person's lungs. Death is agonizingly painful.

Careful maintenance of such systems is strongly encouraged. Green-Field practiced that, naturally, and the state's inspectors made sure of it.

Except, for what J.R. had in mind, none of it was going to matter.

He gingerly traversed the field of pipes, toward where the cooler's roof almost met the building's far wall. In that way, the cooler was a box within a box—like a fridge inside a home. The design was so that if any inspections or repairs were called for, they could be conducted in normal temperatures, away from the frozen goods inside and the workers shuffling them about.

Reaching the edge, J.R. lay on his stomach and peered over. Below him was a straight drop down the equivalent of a four-story building, at the bottom of which was a convoluted knot of control valves and panels—isolated, camera-monitored, and accessible only to a select few, if something were to go wrong.

Which it was about to.

He carefully pulled a .45 semiautomatic pistol out of one jacket pocket, a long and bulky sound suppressor from another, fitted the two together, and took careful aim at the metallic tangle far below.

Four quickly discharged subsonic slugs did the trick, their reports all but consumed by the surrounding hum of machinery. Instantly, a white, heavier-than-air plume began spreading across the floor, seeking more space, fed by J.R.'s four spontaneously created, jetlike nozzles.

J.R. separated the gun from its suppressor, retreated across the cooler's top, and as the first alarms began piercing the air, slipped through a small overhead service door onto the pitch-black, night-washed warehouse roof, where he jogged over to a previously anchored throw-and-go doubled rappel rope. He peeled off his jacket to expose the climbing harness beneath, and backed over the edge of the roof.

At the bottom, he retrieved the rope and crossed the darkened service road to where he'd left his car. In under two minutes from having punctured the pipes, he was driving away, leaving behind a nondescript anchoring bolt on the roof of a building now filled with screaming people.

GreenField's corporate headquarters were located in a tree-ringed industrial park off I-89's exit 16, in Colchester. That placed it next to Burlington and a mile from the airport. Joe Gunther was there because that's where Robert Beaupré had told him he'd prefer to meet.

No more casual chats around the pickup.

Whatever GreenField's mystery nemesis was hoping for, he had certainly brought the company to the brink of disaster. Beaupré's tone on the phone, when Joe called him for this appointment, had been frosty and distracted.

It had good reason to be. From an underplayed fire emergency at one of the firm's two warehouses several days ago, GreenField's headaches had raced through a headline-grabbing fatal truck crash to conclude last night with a major industrial accident including five dead, twenty hospitalized, and the primary warehouse completely shut down. Everyone from the EPA, OSHA, several insurance companies, multiple law enforcement agencies, lawyers beyond counting, and more had been consulting Google Maps and booking nearby motel rooms.

At least Joe hadn't needed a map.

He also didn't have to worry about standing in line to meet Robert Beaupré. Upon entering the crowded, tension-filled GreenField lobby and announcing himself to the receptionist, he was immediately escorted down a hallway to a conference room and introduced to three men in suits sitting side by side at a table so massive, it could have doubled as a yacht club dock.

Joe didn't catch the names of the two outliers, lawyers both. He was more taken by the dull-looking man between them, Robert Beaupré Jr.

No one rose upon Joe's entering. Nor did the table's width allow for handshakes. Instead, there were awkward head nods, gestures, and muttered greetings followed by Bobby Beaupré stating, "Mr. Gunther, I know you were expecting my father. So, I'm sorry you've made a long drive to end up with just the three of us."

He issued a self-deprecating smile before resuming. "Nevertheless, we're hoping that I and my colleagues can answer at least some of your questions."

"Is your father refusing to meet with me?" Joe asked sternly, choosing his phrasing purposefully and sitting across from them.

One of the lawyers put on a pained expression. "No. You can only imagine how busy he is right now, what with this latest setback. He was hoping you'd understand, as do we."

"I understand that I'm conducting a multiple-homicide investigation," Joe countered, his voice hard, additionally irritated by the lack of a heads-up phone call. They'd obviously had enough time to compare schedules and book a conference room. "Your warehouse right now is a closed crime scene, where no repairs or business can take place. Surely, you'd like that property back as soon as possible, no? After the funerals of your employees, of course."

"Of course," the other lawyer echoed, not to be left out. "But you can't be suggesting that Mr. Beaupré is a suspect in all that. And if it's facts that you're after, the three of us may actually be better suited to supply them. Mr. Beaupré Jr., here, is in charge of operations, after all."

"I heard that," Joe said, deciding to join them in ignoring whatever human costs they'd just suffered. Add that to the list of lost causes. "I also heard that your younger brother was the primary idea man and that the two of you avoid each other's company. How does that work?"

Bobby opened his mouth to speak, but once more, it was one of the others who answered.

"How do any unfounded rumors have anything to do with your investigation, Mr. Gunther?"

"How could it hurt to ask?" Joe shot back, satisfied that he'd chosen the right tone for the conversation. "Unless I'm to conclude that I've stepped into sensitive territory with my very first question."

"It just caught us unaware," Bobby said, again with a smile. "We've been so knocked over by all this that we didn't expect you to ask anything about the family. We're all grieving, after all."

"You watch any TV or go to the movies, Mr. Beaupré?" Joe asked.

Confusion creased Bobby's face. "What? Sure. Some."

"Then you know from the cop shows that the first person we look at in a domestic murder is the spouse."

"Okay . . . ," Bobby responded doubtfully.

"The situation's much the same here," Joe explained. "Whoever's going after your company could be someone random, but chances are it's not. These attacks speak of insider knowledge, revenge served hot and full of passion, and that's been building for a long time."

Bobby's face darkened. "And that therefore makes you go after my brother and me? What a crock."

One of the lawyers laid a hand on his wrist, which he angrily shook off, continuing, "People have died here, Mr. Gunther. Good people. People who have been with us for years. We're not a bunch of corporate hacks trying to cut corners and milk the company. Our goddamned name's on the sign outside. To say that we killed those folks because of a family squabble is nuts. You're the guy watching too much TV."

"What's the squabbling been about?" Joe asked, his own quiet voice now making Beaupré's seem shrill.

Bobby stared at him, transparently fighting the urge to leave the room.

Joe placed his forearms on the table and returned the look. "You need to understand something, Mr. Beaupré," he said. "In the middle of the circus that's descended on this building, I'm the only one looking for a murderer. I don't care about insurance issues, or regulatory loopholes, or civil and/or criminal lawsuits. I also don't care about hurting your feelings. Just as you may be sensitive about your company being under siege, I am equally thin-skinned about being considered a nuisance by you and two lawyers claiming to care for the people who died in their employ.

"I can get to my feet right now and leave the building, as you'd love me to do, but then I'll make it my driving ambition to bring every resource at my disposal—municipal, state, and federal—in to finding out why you chose to be both huffy and coy today. Are you absolutely sure that's the strategy you want to take with me?"

The three men were momentarily silent. Joe imagined—rightly or not—that they'd been caught off guard by his unexpected aggression.

"No," Bobby said slowly. "I apologize."

"What I need to know," Joe continued, at last softening his tone, "is what you folks are thinking at the top. Somebody is incredibly pissed off— way beyond having been fired for showing up late or stealing some frozen shrimp. This all speaks of someone feeling fundamentally betrayed. By now, your losses have got to be running into the millions. We have spent hundreds of hours going through your contract and personnel files, and have interviewed a majority of your employees, past and present. We've developed leads and have a couple of possible scenarios, but as with all complicated cases, the more intel, the better."

Joe was hoping his dramatic rendition of the bully becoming a team player would encourage Beaupré to cooperate, if not his two Dobermans.

"What's the scuttlebutt among the brass?" Joe rephrased his earlier question. "And, more pointedly, among the family?"

Bobby was doing a good job of appearing hapless. "You keep imply-ing my family's involved. None of us are wilting violets. I admit that. And my brother and I have very different styles—from each other and from Dad, for that matter. He's the one who encouraged that. But we work to-gether, and have for decades. What you're saying doesn't make sense. Philip and I would've just walked away if this company wasn't in our blood. And you're right about Philip, by the way. The rumors have some truth, as usual. He is the creative one. He's also the one who makes the most mistakes as a result. That's his process, just as it's mine to keep things organized and running smoothly. As kids, I made my bed every morn-ing. Philip's room looked like a rat's nest. It's just who we are. We may not be buddy-buddy. We never were. But we're each part of what makes GreenField a success."

"Until now," Joe said, nevertheless impressed by Bobby's speech.

Beaupré rejected the notion. "We'll get past this," he said forcefully, trying to turn the tables by pointing at Joe and saying, "Assuming you can do your job. To me, your being here now, throwing accusations at me instead of beating the bushes like you should, is looking like you're frustrated by your own lack of progress. I would suggest you let us put the company back on its feet, while you get busy arresting whoever's doing this."

Taking his own cue, Beaupré rose to his feet, adding, "In fact, come to think of it, don't let us slow you down any more. Best of luck."

With that, he led the other two in a short procession out the door, leav-ing Joe in his seat, staring out the window.

He wasn't alone for long. The double glass doors to his right revealed a man of medium height, build, and appearance, dressed in a dark suit and sporting a close beard, who tentatively poked his head into the room to ask, "Are you the policeman?"

His surprisingly squeaky voice prompted in Joe an instinct to respond in like language with something from *Sesame Street*. Willy Kunkle rubbing off. Again.

He rose instead. "Yes. Joe Gunther. VBI."

The intruder's face cleared. "Hi. Brad St. John. I'm the CFO here. I heard you were in the building."

Joe motioned him to the seat beside his, wondering what to expect next, and seriously doubting the serendipity of Brad's appearance. "You must be a busy man right now."

St. John chuckled. "You could say that. You meet with Bobby?"

"Yeah. He said your father-in-law was too busy."

St. John didn't argue. "He is that. You can only imagine."

"I imagine lots of things," Joe said in a neutral voice.

The CFO smiled politely. "I guess that's true. So, what's your take on what's happening to us?"

Joe repositioned his seat slightly and crossed his legs. "That's why I'm here, Mr. St. John. I wanted to ask you people the same thing."

The man waved one hand dismissively. "Please, call me Brad. And how did you fare with Mr. Beaupré Jr. and his minions?"

"You knew about them?"

"Sure," he replied without guile. "We had a meeting about how to deal with you."

"We?"

"Robert, Bobby, me, a few of the senior staff. That's why Robert went missing and you got Bobby and the boys."

"And now you," Joe filled in.

Brad put on a slightly embarrassed face. "Yeah, well. I'm not really here."

"So why are you?"

"I didn't agree with the plan. You're on our side, trying to end this nightmare. Showing you the corporate stiff upper lip seemed wrong to me."

"You're not worried about breaking ranks?" Joe asked, amused by this variation of the traditional good cop–bad cop routine he was so used to enacting himself.

"I'm CFO and married to the boss's daughter, and she actually likes me," Brad said, his eyes wide. "They're not about to fire me, if that's what you mean. It was just a business decision. I think it's crap. That's why I'm here—to ask if you got what you wanted, despite their united front."

Joe absorbed that, wondering where the truth lay. First, the old man said he'd meet and then ducked; then his son with the two watchdogs and their bluster; now the affable and renegade wizard of numbers. For all St. John's denials, the front was in fact looking well united and orchestrated.

"Okay," Joe told him. "I'll play. No, I didn't get what I was after, which was to get your opinion on these assaults, along with some insight on the reputed dysfunction among GreenField's brass."

Brad looked surprised. "Dysfunction? Here? Give me details. I'll see if I can shed some light."

"I was told the two brothers don't entirely see eye to eye, or at least that they give each other a lot of room."

Brad shook his head slightly. "Right on both counts. Give me a company that doesn't have some of that, and I'll show you a place with no imagination, energy, or future. What you're calling dysfunction, I've been calling creative differences since I met those two. I mean, I know them both. How different could two guys be? Stands to reason they'd be like Itchy and Scratchy."

"I actually don't know Philip," Joe admitted.

Brad took that in stride. "No surprise. He's never here. He's not here now, and all hands've been ordered on deck. The old man doesn't hold him to such decrees. I think that's one reason Bobby doesn't like him much."

"Because he's treated differently?"

"Among other things," Brad allowed. "He's also the fair-haired boy.

Robert and Martha thought they could have only one child, and had pretty much conceded the point when Philip arrived eight years later."

"But your wife's younger than Philip," Joe observed.

"I know. They got lucky. Bam, bam—two in a row. After Elaine, they chose to stop. I always thought Bobby felt a little robbed by the competition, and he sure as hell gets his nose bent out of joint when Philip gets praised for flitting around while Bobby's spending his life at the grindstone."

"I thought Philip had a good rep—the ideas man."

"He does, and he is," Brad confirmed. "But it's never that simple, is it? Especially when you add sibling rivalry. Ask me about Philip, and you'll get a different opinion than if you asked Bobby. Look, everyone likes to pigeonhole other people. The rich are no different. Consider the hundreds of folks who work for us, from all walks of life and past experiences. They could just be considered warehouse grunts, but I bet you know better than most that's not true. The Beauprés are just as complicated, except that because of their status, they're seen as black-and-white cutouts. Bobby and Philip may be polar opposites, just like so many other employees, but they haven't made the company dysfunctional. Like I said, I'd argue just the opposite."

Joe hadn't missed the way St. John had awkwardly transformed the issue of sibling rivalry into a hackneyed statement about the nature of being human.

"Okay," Joe moved on, "then what about the other question: Why do you think you've come under fire?"

St. John shrugged. "What else? We hire people, we fire them. And some of them carry a lot of baggage. I heard about the guy you arrested for killing that girl, for example. I guess he was one of ours at some point. I'm not saying our people are murderers, but we got our share of oddballs. Who knows what might make them lash out?"

"So, given your particular expertise, all this doesn't make you think money's a motive?" Joe continued.

Brad looked stunned by the notion. "A motive? Like from an investor trying to drive the stock value down or something? We're privately owned. Who among management would benefit from ruining the company?"

"Somebody who hates it and you," Joe suggested simply.

To pay him credit, Brad St. John didn't instantly dismiss the idea. Instead, he sat back in his chair, seemingly disappointed, and allowed, "I guess I see what you mean, from an outsider's perspective. But given how well I know everybody here, I think you're barking up the wrong tree. I could be wrong, but . . . Well, I don't think so."

It was the sort of reaction Joe had been expecting all along, which only made him more deeply suspect that something darker and complex may have stimulated the overproduced dog and pony show he'd just been presented.

Confirming such misgivings, Joe received a phone call forty-five minutes after leaving the GreenField headquarters. It was from Mandy Lawlor, the late Mick Durocher's only daughter.

"Hey, Mandy," he answered, pulling over to the edge of the interstate. "What's up?"

"You asked me to call you if anything happened," she said, her voice tense.

"I did," he said, not having believed she ever would. "Are you okay?"

"I'm fine," she answered quickly. "That's not it. I just got a package dropped off, not by mail. I mean really dropped off—left at my door. There was two hundred and fifty thousand dollars in it. In cash."

Joe was still for a moment, his brain teeming with questions, especially given the nest of millionaires he'd just left.

"What should I do?" Mandy asked.

"I'd find a qualified financial advisor and a tax expert and ask them the same question," he told her.

"Really? But I don't know where it came from."

"I think I might," he reassured her. "And if I'm right, you and Julia are all set. I'll let you know if I find out differently."

"But who's it from?"

Good question, he thought, troubled by the possible dilemma her honesty had created: Revealing this delivery opened it to being seized as evidence, unless he could run some sort of compassionate—and legal—interference. "I'll see what I can find out, Mandy. In the meantime, I think I'm on safe ground telling you that your father probably played a role in it. For all his faults—and I'm not excusing any of them— he loved you very much."

"Thank you," he heard her say, her voice choked by emotion.

"Take care of yourself," he therefore said before hanging up. "Thanks for telling me this, and just in case it comes up, and unless you've already thrown it out, do me a favor and save the packaging the money came in. It might be useful later."

CHAPTER TWENTY-TWO

Rachel had been too busy to exclusively focus on J.R. and his relationship to GreenField. The ammonia leak at the warehouse, the related stories concerning its fatalities and survivors, the ripple effects on White River Junction and its emergency response crews, and her regular assignments, including—at last—an actual garden-club lunch, had ganged up to keep her a prisoner of her car and a slave to her camera. For several days, she had been eating from gas stations, changing clothes from a duffel bag, taking catnaps in rest areas, and shooting pretty much nonstop up and down the Connecticut River valley, regularly uploading her images to either the *Reformer's* website or her own, where she kept an archive of surplus shots. In the end, her car looked lived in because it was.

The effort was paying off. *Vermont Digger* and AP were buying her images, Stan Katz was grudgingly paying her an almost constant hourly wage, and when she was awake enough to appreciate it, Rachel was enjoying having her bank balance and her reputation swell simultaneously. In almost no time, she had become the go-to photojournalist in Vermont's southeast quadrant.

Most significant, several of her pictures were featured in an article that went viral, first in local papers, and then over the internet, titled, "Who's Got It In for GreenField?"

It was in the throes of this activity that she found herself in Brattleboro's Brooks Memorial Library, staring at screenshots of endless pages of murky newspaper print, in pursuit of historical information concerning Robert Beaupré. As had almost everyone else, it seemed, she'd been bitten by the bug to more closely examine this hitherto little-known clan. More to the point, she'd been asked by Katz to find something beside official GreenField portraits to illustrate the *Reformer's* ongoing features chronicling the company's struggles. The story wouldn't die, he wanted fresh head shots, and it turned out the Beauprés were instinctively camera-shy.

She'd been at this endeavor for over an hour, collecting photographs of family members at sports events, ribbon cuttings, press release photos, and the like, when she came across a high school yearbook picture featuring a young, fresh-faced Robert Beaupré, proudly holding a trophy at the front of a small group. She was about to move on, dissatisfied with the shot's quality, when her eye caught the caption listing the attendees.

"Holy cow," she said softly, and hit Print.

Willy Kunkle opened his eyes without altering his breathing or moving a muscle. It was his habit to surface from sleep covertly, in barely noticeable stages, so that he might have the advantage over anyone nearby.

Nine times out of ten, it was a wasted effort—either no one was there, or it was someone who didn't matter, much less pose a threat.

This time, however, despite being in a private hospital room in the dead of night, he had not one but three guests, as silent as he, and as far from being threatening as he could imagine.

"Hey, there," he greeted them.

Sam and Sue were huddled by the far window, their heads together as in prayer, and Emma was fast sleep in a portable crib in the corner.

Both women looked up at him.

"Hey, yourself," Sam responded, rising to kiss him. "I've never seen you so unconscious."

"Painkillers," Sue spoke up, smiling. "I spiked 'em with something extra. You shouldn't be awake now, given what I gave you. Typical."

"Don't complain," he said. "They worked. Best sleep I've had in living memory." He indicated the crib and his child. "I thought this place was quarantined for the plague. You toughening the kid up?"

Sam punched his good shoulder, which still made him wince slightly. For all his bravado, he was appreciative of Sue's unrequested help. His surgery was hurting like a bastard.

"They got the all clear," Sam explained. "The whole staff passed muster, including the ones on vacation. Me, I was sick of running between here and home, and I thought you'd get a kick out of seeing her when she wakes up."

"I will," he said. "Thanks. Speaking of running around, Sue, you're not supposed to be here, either, are you?"

Sue Spinney was looking tired, and dressed in her street clothes. "No," she admitted. "But Lester's working, the kids take care of themselves nowadays, and I needed some company."

"What's up?"

"It's Victoria," Sam said gently, sitting by his side.

"She's worse?" he asked their friend.

"She's not better," Sue reported. "I went up to DHMC to check on her. They still have her in isolation, so we couldn't talk. It wouldn't have mattered anyhow. She might as well be in a coma. She just lies there, a sack of meds and bad bugs duking it out. God only knows what's happening inside her."

She suddenly reached into her pocket and pulled out her cell, glancing at the screen. "Crazy," she said, and typed something out quickly.

"What?" Sam asked.

"It's Rachel," Sue said. "She wants to know where I am and can she come by."

Both Sam and Willy checked the wall clock. It wasn't as late as Willy had imagined earlier, but still after normal working hours for a small-town reporter.

"You say yes?" he asked.

"Yeah. She was already headed to my house, so she's almost here. I can't imagine what she'd want with me. I don't really know her that well."

"Nice kid, though," Willy said unexpectedly. "Got her mother's perseverance. I like that."

"You would," Sam chided him. "And speaking of which, when she gets here, remember: She's press now, even though she only takes pictures. Her job's to fish for quotes, ours is to shut the hell up." She glanced at Sue and added, "With all due respect."

"No, you're right," Sue said. "I forget about that."

Sue glanced at the clock and moved toward the door. "Well, given that, I'm going to hit the ladies' and check on a couple of things. Be back in a bit."

Willy reached for Sam's hand as soon as they were alone and asked, "How've you been holding up, babe?"

Sam looked into his face, caught by the tenderness in his voice. "I'm not sure I know," she answered honestly.

"What do you mean?" he asked.

She shrugged. "Like right now. Your asking me that. You don't do that. You've been a roller coaster lately. It's been hard."

He nodded. "Yeah."

In the pause following, she added, "I thought you'd gone off the far end, and that Emma and me were gonna have to sort things out on our own."

"Sorry."

She pulled her hand away. "Me, too. Now that it seems you're getting better, I gotta tell you it's been a bitch. You're not the only one carrying a load, but sometimes that's how you act. You've got us all trained by now—Where's Willy? How's he doin'? Oh, don't worry, it's just Willy bein' Willy."

She pointed to the quiet child, fast asleep in the crib, and said, "Well, fuck Willy bein' Willy. You need to grow up, for her sake if not mine or your own. You're not alone in the world anymore, like it or not."

"I know," he barely whispered.

She startled him then by leaning forward and slipping her arms awkwardly around his neck.

"I know you know," she said in his ear. "I can see how you're trying. That's what I meant about what you just asked me. You want to know how I'm holding up. You never would've asked that before. I love you for that."

He caressed her back. "I love you, too."

She straightened just as abruptly. "And that," she said, staring at him. "You love me? How many times have you told me that?"

He didn't answer, unsure of what to say.

Her face softened as she touched his cheek, a gesture he usually shied away from, given trauma-laden personal space issues dating back to childhood, but this time he held still. "I'm not saying I don't like what's happening," Sam reassured him. "It's just been hard as hell. You asked."

He smiled ruefully and kissed the back of her hand. "I did that."

It wasn't fifteen minutes before there was a light tap on the door and Rachel stepped into the room, carrying her camera off her shoulder.

"Oh, gosh," she said, taking them all in, including Emma and Sue, who'd returned from her walkabout. "They told me where to find you, Sam, but I didn't realize you were all hanging out. Maybe that's good, though."

Willy snorted. "That's a first, if you're including me."

Rachel glanced at him uneasily, never sure what to make of him.

Sue almost asked her how her mother was coping with the post-Ebola scare at the morgue, when she recalled Sam's warning about what Rachel might or might not know—and what she might potentially do with what anyone told her. It was an inhibitive sensation that left her ill at ease.

As a result, Sue asked cautiously instead, "What did you want to talk to me about? It sounded urgent."

Rachel didn't seem to have noticed her discomfort. Spurred on by the question, she eagerly dug into the bag hanging from her other shoulder, saying, "You know I've been working on the GreenField story. Well, my boss asked me to find some old pictures of the Beauprés, dating back to before the business—to add a little flavor to the stuff I've been reporting, you know? That meant scrolling through newspaper files at the library, where—" She extracted a sheet of paper with a flourish. "—I found this. I was wondering if you knew anything about it. Isn't she the friend who's been helping you out? I thought I over heard that from one of you."

Sue took the printout of the group photo Rachel had found earlier and brought it over to Sam and Willy so they could see it at the same time. Standing next to a very young Robert Beaupré Sr. was Victoria Garlanda.

They silently exchanged surprised looks, no one daring to be the first to react.

Willy broke the ice. "That's the thing about this Podunk state," he said. "Everybody knows everybody else. You ever know she went to school with old man Beaupré?"

Thereby unleashed, Sue felt free to concede, "She told me a long time ago he'd been the love of her life."

Everyone greeted that with raised eyebrows.

"Really?" replied Rachel, visibly pleased.

"No shit," Willy said more thoughtfully, working through as many permutations as he could.

"What happened?" Sam asked.

"She never told me," Sue said. "But she made it clear he was the reason she never married."

"What did she say?" Sam pursued.

Sue tapped the photo with her fingertip. "They were a hot item. High school sweethearts. What I read between the lines was that she was more serious than he was. His big deal was to be successful."

"But he did get married," Sam pointed out.

Sue remained scornful. "Yeah, well. Victoria knew Martha, too. Called her a good broodmare. I guess Robert got what he was after, 'cause they had a kid right off."

"Wow," Rachel said, taking back the printout. "That is one amazing coincidence. How's Victoria doing, anyhow? She still sick?"

There was another stilted silence, which this time Rachel correctly interpreted by smiling broadly and saying, "Guys—I know about the Ebola. I take pictures; it doesn't mean I'm clueless."

"Her condition's unchanged," Sue said shortly.

Rachel shook her head sympathetically. "That's too bad. I guess you're close. That is wild, though, isn't it? That all this bad stuff is happening to Beaupré, and now his old girlfriend is horribly sick. I wonder if it's connected?"

Willy's voice was disarmingly dismissive—despite his thoughts paralleling hers. "Oh, hell. Coincidences do happen. Pretty big jump to go from arson and sabotage to Ebola, don't you think?"

Rachel seemed to consider that for a moment before agreeing, "I guess. It is a reach when you say it out loud."

"It would also be a risk if you tried reporting it," Sam said supportively. "Assuming Katz would even let you. We'll check it out. If we get a notion that fact is stranger than fiction, we'll let you know—just like we smuggled you into the warehouse after the fire."

That was frankly manipulative, and a little mean, reminding Rachel of the debt she owed them. Whatever its influence, however, the moment was interrupted by Rachel now being the one distracted by a phone text.

She read its contents quickly, pocketed the device, and collected her things before heading for the door, saying distractedly, "Okay, I gotta go. Thanks, everybody."

It suited Sam and Willy to have her gone, of course, but it prompted Sam to ask, "That was fast. Wonder what fired her up?"

"Don't care," Willy replied bluntly, back on keel and looking at Sue. "I wanna know more about Victoria."

"Not much more to tell," she responded.

But Willy turned scornful. "Not about their coochie-coo. I'm talking about if there's any linkage between Beaupré's problems and her getting sick."

"You think somebody gave her Ebola?" Sam asked.

He stared at them both. "What do I know? Sue, you were the one who said she couldn't've caught it from the pilot. So how else did it happen, when nobody else got tagged? I mean," he added, pointing to the room's far corner, "that's why the heiress to my worldly possessions is snoring in this nest of microbes, isn't it? 'Cause none of us was ever at risk."

Sammie sighed as Sue reassured him, nevertheless comforted to see the old Willy back. "Yes, yes. But I still don't know of any contact between Bob Beaupré and Victoria since way back when. She hasn't even mentioned him in years."

"It could be like you told Rachel just now," Sam suggested to him. "You said it, if only to throw her off track: Real coincidences do happen. All the time."

"Yeah, yeah, yeah," Willy grumbled, utterly unswayed. "But then let's treat it like we do a real case—get out and collect the evidence."

"Of what?" Sam asked.

"What's the first golden rule?" Willy asked her. "Anytime we're called out? It's a homicide till proved otherwise."

"You think somebody infected Victoria on purpose?" Sue asked him, the horror clear on her face.

"I'm saying we should rule it out," Willy stated.

In the following silence, Sam said in a low voice, "He's right."

"How?" Sue wondered.

Before he could answer her, Sam's iPhone went off.

"Your hubby, Sue," she reported, reading the text. "He's asking me for backup at the warehouse."

She glanced instinctively at the crib, but it was Willy who quieted her concern.

"I got it, babe. Leave her with me. God knows I'm not goin' anywhere, and if I get in a jam, I'll call Louise."

"I'm standing right here," Sue reminded them. "Mother of two? Hello?"

"Okay, okay," Sam conceded, giving Sue a hug and Willy a kiss. She crouched by the crib and touched her daughter's head. "Night, night, sweetie pie."

She threw them a wave at the door, and was gone.

Willy resumed, undeterred. "What were Victoria's primary bases of operation around here?" he asked Sue.

She blinked a moment before answering, bringing herself back on topic. "Really only her office. Otherwise, she moved throughout the building."

"Making the office the best place to set a trap," Willy proposed.

"You make it sound like a trip wire," Sue said.

"Exactly," he replied, and wincingly began shifting his legs to dangle over the side of his bed.

"What're you doing?" she demanded.

"Give it a rest," he told her. "You're off duty."

"And you're still recovering."

He gave her an exasperated glare. "Oh, for Christ's sake. 'Time for your walk,' 'Time to get some exercise,' 'Don't give PT a hard time.' That's all I hear around here. Well, I'm ready to exercise. Where's her office?"

He rose carefully, trying to hide his discomfort, and allowed Sue to adjust his sling. He gestured to her to precede him out the door. She glanced at Emma's sleeping form as they did so, to which he only said, "A bomb wouldn't wake her up, and I'll tell the nurses."

Garlanda's office was one flight up, large, light, pleasantly decorated, and as neat as when Willy had first met her there with Sam.

He approved, although—typical of the man—his own demonstrations of similar neatness were restricted to his home and car. In a classic display of misdirection, he pointedly kept his office desk a mess, so that most people would think him a slob.

Victoria had no such need to disguise a monumentally complicated psychology. She was simply tidy.

"I don't know what you're going to find," Sue said, hitting the lights to enhance what was coming through the glass partition overlooking the central hallway.

Willy didn't answer, touring the room like an art patron at an opening, albeit dressed in a gown with its back flapping open. He eventually took Victoria's seat behind the desk.

"This the way she usually kept it?" he asked.

"Yup. Nothing's been changed. People may have come in for a file or something. That's possible. But she's only been out a few days."

"Good," he said, surveying the scene as its rightful occupant would have every workday.

He sat forward and rested his good arm on the edge of the desk, studying the retro leather desk pad; the twin silver pen holder; the elegant, feminine antique clock; the red stapler and tape dispenser. He reached out and handled one of the sharpened pencils above the pad, pretending to take a note. Fulfilling the gesture, he then pulled a Post-it notepad toward him, although he wrote nothing.

He touched the box of tissues with a fingertip, the small replica of an ancient Greek recumbent figurine—reworked as the handle of a letter opener—and a porcelain dish of paper clips.

Finally, he pointed to a small bottle parked beside the multibutton phone. "That her eyedropper? I saw her use something like it when Sam and I were here."

Sue made to reach for it.

"Don't touch it," Willy requested quietly. "Just tell me about it. Why's it not labeled?"

"She thought buying it was wasteful, when it's just saline and we have bags of the stuff in the dispensary. They charge a bundle for it at the drugstore. So she got hold of a generic bottle and just refilled it as needed."

"Huh," he said. "How does she transfer it to the bottle? What's the process?"

"Pretty straightforward, for a nurse. You spike the bag, like you would for a patient, but instead of starting an IV, you put the drip straight into the bottle—run it wide open till it's full."

"And the bag?"

"If it's still got fluid left, you shut off the drip. If not, you just throw it out. Like I said, they're really common around here. Almost every drip set we rig begins with a bag of saline."

Willy was silent, lost in thought. His next question, however, caught her by surprise. "Didn't they decontaminate this office after she was diagnosed? I woulda thought they'd strip it clean."

Not knowing where this was going, she explained, "They did swabs and ultraviolet. It's not my area, but the experts went all through here, including this office, and gave us a clean bill. They sure convinced me they knew what they were doing. Maybe it was just those suits they wear."

"Swell," Willy said, virtually to himself. "You have any gloves on you?"

She didn't, but opened a nearby drawer and extended a box to him without comment.

He extracted one, slipped it on his good hand, and picked up the bottle, shaking it slightly.

"About half full," he said before dropping it inside a second glove, which he handed to Sue. "You have a twisty or a rubber band to close that off?"

She circled the desk to stand beside him and opened the drawer at his waist to locate a rubber band, asking, "Where're you going with this?"

"Literally? To the lab. Figuratively? I'm playing twenty questions in my head about everything I've learned while I've been staying here, trying to come up with who tried to knock off your pal."

Sue pointed at the bagged eyedropper with her chin. "With that?"

"If I'm right, yeah. Everybody's been saying how ya gotta have fluid contact with Ebola to catch it." He held up his prize. "Well, how 'bout self-administered spiked saline, right into her own eyeballs?"

Sam found Lester holed up in his new permanent residence, the Green-Field conference room he shared with Pat Smith. Pat wasn't there when Sam arrived, however, since by now, it really was getting late—which made her all the more curious about his request for assistance.

"Guess who I found?" he asked her as she entered, his enthusiasm at odds with his haggard expression.

"Who?" Like everyone before her, she crossed to the interior picture window and looked out into the dark, and now empty, interior space beyond.

"The ever-elusive Philip Beaupré," he replied. "For days, I made it crystal clear we wanted to interview him, especially after Joe missed seeing either him or his father on his trip to Colchester headquarters. A couple of times, I was even told that he'd come and gone right here without my being told. But this time"—he raised an index triumphantly—"I was not only given the heads-up he was coming, but—one minute before I texted you—confirmation that he'd arrived. He's supposedly in the executive offices on the top floor right now."

At that, without Sam saying a word, Lester's face fell slightly, revealing how tired he was.

"I'm really sorry," he said. "I should've asked, what with Willy sick and Emma needing a babysitter. Shit. Not thinking straight. I just didn't want to question him on my own, not after all this anticipation. I'm getting a little punchy."

Sam left the window and patted his shoulder, struck by not just his show of consideration, but also how it reflected their squad's instinctive interdependence and support. "Let it go, for crying out loud. Emma's fast asleep on the floor of her father's hospital room—with your wife, no less. What can go wrong?"

His split second of confusion made her laugh. "Come on," she told him. "Don't answer that and lead the way."

As she followed him toward the aforementioned executive offices, located in the penthouse suite, Sam found herself bemused by her colleague's excitement. She, too, was interested in speaking with Philip, he being the one family member they had yet to meet. But she'd also had the advantage of watching the variable components of this convoluted case behave like bumper cars at a country fair. Lester almost hadn't been out of this building since he'd been assigned to it, buried among its files and flowcharts, rumors and facts, legends and lore. The huge, all-encompassing edifice had become a world unto itself. She half wondered whether, in that light, the place hadn't become an empire where its missing prince—the wandering Philip—had taken on mythic proportions.

For her, Philip Beaupré was no more than just another player, with no more or less involvement in this mayhem than anybody else—including the one guy—now dead—whom they'd arrested for a murder it didn't look like he'd committed, and whose demise, according to Joe, seemed to have generated a quarter-million-dollar payoff.

She only hoped that leaving her daughter yet again—not to mention a healing Willy, whose testimony of love had left her stunned, happy, and understandably nervous—would be worth the guilt and disappointment accompanying this outing. Could Philip even remotely live up to Lester's expectations?

Personally, she doubted it.

CHAPTER TWENTY-THREE

Rachel sensed she'd been given the runaround. The person who'd texted her in Willy's hospital room, "I got what your after," had been coy from the start, not to mention grammatically challenged, and was now clearly missing in action.

As she'd explained to Joe earlier, journalists of her generation were as tied to their smartphones as their predecessors had been to police scanners. But the difference exceeded technology. The scope of her sources had become virtually endless, since texting, tweeting, emails, and Facebook knew no boundaries. Everybody with a device and the urge to broadcast was a potential source of information. And people's near compulsion to publish every thought and observation, in all circumstances, greatly favored news reporters.

The problems, however, went from the obvious to the more nuanced. This information overload meant that Rachel's phone never stopped receiving, needed constant housekeeping, and ran the risk of becoming addictive. Along those lines, it also meant that, if she wasn't careful, she could become like a puppy chasing treats—too distracted separating worthy morsels from trash to ever lift her head and develop a story based on a more thoughtful, measured, and penetrating approach. Investigative journalism—still rightly or not the crown jewel of the profession—had once been a painstaking business, often conducted through the meticulous, lengthy nurturing of reliable informants. This hadn't necessarily changed, but too many reporters were opting for the less taxing option of sorting through easily acquired online garbage in search of a rare nugget of gold.

All of this was alive in Rachel's mind because she'd proceeded straight from the hospital to GreenField's White River warehouse in the hopes of locating just such a nugget. That's what she'd been hoping her source meant by "what your after." Unfortunately, that little bird was known to her only as SuperStacker, which "handle" implied that he or she worked inside the plant, but withheld the logical next step, like a phone number or a real name. This was a definite disappointment, now that Rachel found herself empty-handed. She had circulated her interest in talking with anyone about why and from whom GreenField had come under such fire, and SuperStacker had been the only one to volunteer something beyond an uninformed opinion.

But no one had shown up where SuperStacker said they should meet, leaving Rachel with few options beyond texting, "Where are you?" to no effect. She was tired, unwashed, with her stomach complaining about her steady fare of fast food, making the ease and regularity of simply snapping pictures of Rotary meetings look increasingly attractive.

And there was an additional concern, arising in the wake of her adrenaline collapse. Stan Katz had warned her at her job interview about the number of dead ends that lay ahead of her. He had not detailed the pitfalls of traveling late at night to meet with mysterious sources promising much-desired intelligence. Perhaps he'd assumed she'd have common sense enough to figure that one out for herself.

In any case, as she looked around the gloomy edges of the remote, poorly lit, gigantic recycling area she'd been directed to, it occurred to her to move to a more populated part of the property, rather than wait any longer.

That didn't mean she was giving up. Her mother's everyday dogged determination hadn't been lost on her over the years. If SuperStacker had veered off, it didn't mean that his information hadn't had merit. And even though Rachel was now on the building's outside, she sensed its security to be in disarray, and was thinking that she could do worse than to hunt for the story on her own. SuperStacker had implied there was something to be found. Why not try to turn a setback into something more rewarding?

Lester had been to the executive offices before, and thus better appreciated his and Pat's Castle aerie as a result. He'd wondered at the time if the intent had been to park the visiting investigators in such hardscrabble environs, hoping they would tire of the lack of the penthouse suite's soft lighting, wall-to-wall carpeting, and clean and shimmering walls, complete with artwork.

But in fact, the fancier digs struck him as sterile and disengaged, indistinguishable from any offices inside a bank or insurance company. His opinion was that he'd gotten a better feel for the organization from his rough-and-tumble perch and—he could only hope—the vengeful menace in its midst.

Nothing about the area he and Sammie now entered spoke to him that viscerally.

Reinforcing the notion, they were met at the elevator by a woman in high heels, silk blouse, and a business suit—an unusual sight in Vermont to begin with—holding a seemingly prop clipboard and wearing a broad and vacant smile. Connecting her and this setting to the dark and now abandoned black vastness below demanded a serious stretch of the imagination.

"Would you like to follow me?"

Lester's instinctive response was, Not really, quickly overridden by his desire to both succeed where Joe had not—in having a conversation with

Philip—and in doing something slightly outside the paperwork slog he and Pat had been bound to for so long.

"Lead the way," he therefore said, gesturing politely with one hand.

Their receptionist took them down a long, quiet hallway, no doubt bustling during normal operations, and even now containing the odd figure working before a computer or a copier as they passed.

"Must be hard, working here with everything shut down," Sammie said conversationally, in fact thinking of how bizarre this woman appeared, dressed to the nines just so she could wander around a largely empty office with no apparent purpose.

But their hostess appeared unfazed. Glancing over her shoulder, she smiled brightly and suggested, "You get used to it."

This was neither insightful nor comforting to her two visitors. Nor did it lessen Lester's feeling of having dropped into some futuristic fantasy.

Their destination, however, when they reached it, turned out to be not much different from similar offerings downstairs. Rather than ushering them into an office befitting both her outfit and the corporate surroundings, their guide took them into a small break room equipped with microwave, fridge, sink, several tables, and one man in worn jeans and a soiled T-shirt who was halfway through a cup of coffee. The walls were covered with bulletin boards, safety notices, and those painfully sincere framed posters advising people how to properly spell "team."

"Hey," the man said in a friendly voice, lightly kicking an empty chair with a booted foot. "Take a load off. Want some coffee?"

As the two newcomers looked around, the woman in the suit mysteriously vanished.

Sam spoke first, crossing to the coffee machine. "Sure."

Lester took his cue from the casual greeting and dialed down the official standard approach. "You Philip?" he asked instead, sitting down and stretching his legs.

"Yup." Beaupré took a sip of his drink. He was almost self-consciously good looking, Sammie thought, dressed as if he'd thrown on whatever had been littering his bedroom floor, but with what she recognized as a two-hundred-dollar haircut, carefully tousled, and—she suspected—highlighted to complement his green eyes.

Lester jerked a thumb at her. "Sam Martens. I'm Lester Spinney. Thanks for meeting with us."

"Don't thank me," Beaupré said. "I happened to be here; somebody mentioned you were hot to talk. I figured it couldn't hurt."

Sam turned with a mug in her hand and asked in a hard voice, "What couldn't?"

He smiled. "You the bad cop? He's certainly the nice one. I thought that was just a TV thing."

"How could talking to us hurt you?" Sam continued, ignoring the comment. "We're here to find out who's trying to shut you down."

Philip's expression didn't change. "It's an expression. People say it without thinking. But if you want to get into it, I'm old school, Detective. I figure everybody's up to something they won't admit. Cops, especially."

"Ouch," Lester reacted. "That mean you're going to be evasive with us?"

"No, it's just human nature," Beaupré answered. "Some avoid being straightforward more than others. It's no big deal, at least most of the time. I'm just assuming you got more on your minds than catching a firebug."

"Who's killed several people," Sammie reminded him, staying at her station by the counter. "This isn't a parlor game."

Beaupré shrugged. "Could be to the guy you're after."

"You have insight into that?" Lester wanted to know.

The man chuckled and sat back, cradling his drink. "Ooh. Very crafty. Give me a break. This is psychology one-oh-one. It doesn't make me a suspect to imagine that whoever's doing this has an ax to grind. And if that's true, then he must be enjoying both the fruits of his labor and your lack of success in catching him. It's what kids do, and psychotic fuckups. That's all I'm saying."

"How bad is the company hurting?" Sammie asked, grateful that

Lester had asked for her to be here. Philip Beaupré was turning into one unusual interview.

"You can cross-examine Brad about that," was the quick response.

"No one at corporate is being exactly forthcoming," Lester told him.

Philip shook his head. "I'm shocked. Shocked. Imagine: a bunch of suits who don't like cops poking into their business affairs."

"So?" Lester persisted.

"It's hurting," Beaupré conceded. "How could it not? People think it's all insurance covering the losses and fat cats taking a slight hit at the end of the year, but the margins in this business are pathetic, and competition is literally cutthroat. Have you looked into that, by the way? It's where I'd go to find who's out to get us."

"Anyone in particular?" Sam asked.

"Nope. It's just what I'd do."

"What's your job at the company, Mr. Beaupré?" Sam continued after a pause.

"Call me the special projects man."

They waited for more, but Beaupré took another swig of coffee instead of elaborating.

"Meaning what?" Lester prompted him.

Philip leaned back and eyed the acoustic ceiling thoughtfully. "You know much about wholesale groceries?"

"More than I ever thought possible," Lester admitted.

"Then you know it's not a breeding ground of creative innovators, even though it's built on the ideas of those exact kinds of people."

Lester saw an opening. "Like you, and your bringing in motion-sensor LEDs to cut electricity costs. I heard it took forever for you to get that through, and now it's an industry standard."

He'd actually heard no such thing, but it sounded right. Beaupré dropped his gaze to stare at him in surprise. "Yeah. Exactly like that."

Sammie maintained her stance by the coffee machine—distant, purposefully hostile—not that she was having a hard time with that. She didn't like this man. "Must piss you off, being ignored. It would me," she said.

Beaupré gave Lester a look. "She always like this?"

"You always avoid answering direct questions?" Lester asked in response.

Beaupré was still pondering Sam's comment. "Yeah, it makes me mad—sometimes. Same as you, I guess. We all buck the system now and then, if we have any brains."

"It could make you a malcontent," Sammie observed, momentarily flashing on Willy in this context.

"That why you're so grouchy?" he shot back. "Look, how many businesses you know that would take a guy like me—even though I'm family—and create a special slot for him instead of throwing him out or buying him off? Do I get frustrated sometimes? Sure. But it's never been a deal breaker."

"Who's your biggest opposition?" Lester asked.

"We interviewed your dad, Bobby, and Brad," Sam added. "Not one of them came across as an innovator. Maybe your dad, once upon a time, but your older brother? The heir apparent slash Mr. Grind? And the guy who married the boss's daughter? Hardly."

"Don't sell the old man short," Philip told them. "He may be laying back more nowadays, but he still calls the shots, and he's still got the instincts. There was no extra room for something like GreenField when he started it. C and S was already going full guns, as were United Natural Foods and Associated Grocers of New England. People said he didn't stand a chance. But we're doing okay. Better. At least until this freight train hit us."

"Which only tells me it's Bobby and Brad who routinely throw a wrench in your works," Lester concluded.

Philip shook his head sorrowfully. "God. You people are relentless. How the hell *do* you solve crimes? No wonder you been running around in circles."

"We solve crimes through evidence and interviews," Sammie told him. "Which means that people like you, in a position to help, do more than hand us crap like you've been doing."

It may not have been textbook interviewing, but she was hoping it would work on a self-professed maverick like Beaupré.

She got lucky. He chuckled and said, "Wow. I like your style after all. Okay. Granted. The problem is, I still don't know what to tell you. Before this started, I thought we had a happy company. We're good to our employees, get high marks from our suppliers and customers, play nice with our competitors, and keep the banks happy by meeting our payments. We even make a point of hiring people with backgrounds that other companies wouldn't touch. And those folks reward us—for the most part—by not screwing us over. There are exceptions. Your homework's told you that. But somebody with the know-how to do what's just happened? Beats the hell out of me."

The tone in the room shifted slightly with this, to something at least sounding more collaborative and less cagey. Sam considered toning down her antipathy, if only to see where it led.

"We've also been checking the historical picture," she said. "Going back a few years, looking for anything that's been festering. Did you ever know a man named Mick Durocher? He didn't work here long, but was good enough to rate one of your father's chauffeur gigs."

Philip laughed shortly. "God. Spare me. I told him once it was like bringing the field slaves into the mansion for a breather. Not one of our better conversations."

"Durocher?" Sam repeated.

But he shook his head. "Nah. Doesn't ring a bell."

"You don't read the papers?" Lester asked. "He's the one we arrested for killing that girl they found on Bromley Mountain."

Beaupré looked surprised. "He drove my dad around? Damn."

There was a long silence as both cops eyed Beaupré's innocent expression.

Lester decided on a long shot. "Since we're talking ancient history, how 'bout Victoria Garlanda?"

Philip's face completely switched to what looked like genuine astonishment. "Whoa. You have been digging. That's amazing."

"You know her?" Sam pressed, equally caught off guard.

"I know *about* her, sure," he said. "She and my dad were an item, back in the Stone Age. I never met her."

"Give us details," Sam requested.

"Not much to tell. They were sweethearts in school and things didn't turn out. Pretty common story, I guess."

"How do you know about it?"

"By accident. I was in my dad's office as a teenager, messing around in his desk, looking for something innocuous, and I found a photograph of her, just when he walked in. I gave him a little shit, like a kid'll do. Something like, 'Ooh, holding out on Mom?' or whatever, and he got really worked up. I thought he was gonna hit me. Surprised the crap out of me. It's probably why I remember her name. Plus, it is a little hard to forget—you gotta admit. Garlanda—crazy."

"What did he say about her?" Lester asked.

"He got real sentimental. Course, he started with 'You know I love your mother,' and all that, but then he fessed up that Victoria had been the love of his life and the one that got away and all the other one-liners."

"Sounds like you weren't too impressed," Sam commented.

"You think I'm cynical now, you shoulda seen me then. Still, I *was* more impressed than I'm making out. Watching his face and hearing how he talked about her, it was pretty clear he'd fallen hard."

"How did he explain not marrying her?"

"He didn't. Not really. I think he said something along the lines that he and Victoria had a falling-out and then he met my mom. I was dubious enough that I did a little math afterwards. You ask me, the old man knocked up Mom with Bobby. That's why he didn't marry Victoria. He may or may not have had a falling-out with her, but I figured he was screwin' around on the side, regardless. That's much more his style."

"I thought you liked your father," Sam said.

Philip couldn't repress a quick shifting of the eyes before saying in a dismissive tone, "I do, but boys'll be boys. He was a young man, for Christ's sake. I can't hold that against him."

But to her, it was a tell—something revealing that he'd let slip unintentionally.

A knock on the open door stopped all conversation and brought their attention to a uniformed security man looking awkwardly at the three of them.

"What?" Beaupré asked.

"Sorry to bother," the man said. "With the heightened security, we didn't know how you wanted this handled, and we knew you and the police were in a meeting, so maybe you'd be the best to deal with it."

Philip gave him an unpleasant, indulgent smile—at odds with his friendly hunk physique. "You do realize you're talking gibberish, right?"

"What happened?" Lester asked more supportively.

"We caught a prowler, maybe trespasser. Don't know what you'd call her. Anyhow, she claims she's a newspaper person and said we can't interfere with freedom of the press and shit like that. Sorry."

"It's okay. Keep going."

"Well, we weren't exactly sure what to do, and like I said, we knew you were all up here, so we thought that since you're the police and management, combined, we'd ask you."

"Press?" Sammie echoed, irritated by the interruption. "What's her name?"

The man checked a small pad he was holding. "Rachel . . . Renning?"

"Reiling," Sam corrected him, having sensed as much. "You have her with you?"

The security guard jerked his thumb over his shoulder. "My partner's got her by the elevators."

Sam didn't bother consulting Beaupré. "Bring her here. You did the right thing."

Their visitor left as Philip ruminated, "Who knew a wholesale grocery business would attract so much attention?"

Sam didn't fault Rachel's perseverance. She'd been accused of the same character trait herself more than once. But the girl's timing could have been better.

Rachel appeared in the doorway, flanked by her escort. She gave Lester and Sam a smile tinged at once with pleasure and embarrassment. "Hi, guys."

Sam was preparing to chastise her delicately, when Rachel's gaze settled on Philip Beaupré.

"Hey," she said to him. "We've met before, not that you'd remember. At the GreenField truck crash in Brattleboro. You're J.R. I took your picture."

Both cops stared at Beaupré as if he'd suddenly sprouted horns, which, in a manner of speaking, he just had.

CHAPTER TWENTY-FOUR

"You're J.R.?" Sam asked, looking hard at Beaupré, the collaborative glow of moments earlier reverting to sudden suspicion.

He shook his head, his semipermanent smile looking pasted in place. "How does that work? Bobby's the Junior of the family. Not me."

"It's what the other guy called you at the truck crash," Rachel reiterated. "I've been looking for you ever since." She slipped her camera off her shoulder and began manipulating its controls.

"Why?" Lester asked her.

"He was really angry when he found me near the truck's rear wheels, like I was seeing something I shouldn't."

She held out the camera so both cops could peer at the photo of Philip on its screen.

"We'd just lost one of our drivers," Beaupré protested. "Of course I was upset. Not everything's a news story. People's lives are involved. He had a wife and kids."

"Quiet," Sam told him before addressing Rachel. "You just said he was angry, not upset. Which was it?"

"Angry," Rachel affirmed.

"Why do they call you J.R.?" Sam asked Philip.

"They don't."

Lester spoke, no longer the nice cop. "We're in your building, dummy. All we have to do is walk down the hall and ask."

Beaupré pursed his lips. "It's a nickname. I don't like it. That's all."

"What's it stand for?"

"Who cares?"

"What's it stand for?" Lester repeated.

Philip put on a show of exasperation. "This is stupid. It's a bad joke. It stands for 'Junior' because some of the guys think I'm better to take over from the old man than Bobby, even though he's the senior executive and the next in line. He's a cold fish. People don't like him. So they insult him behind his back by calling me J.R. That's it. No big deal."

"And you allow it because you don't like Bobby either," Sam suggested.

He started to respond to that, before Sam interrupted him with an upheld hand and ordered, "Hang on."

She turned to Rachel and said shortly, "Thanks. You're off the hook. You might as well head off."

Rachel stared at her in disbelief. "What? I gave you this."

Sam remained adamant, feeling the unmentioned presence of Beverly looming up between them—the supportive friend of one and the loving mother of the other. Nevertheless, Sam didn't yield to favoritism or sentimentality. "It's not a lead and this is not a story, Rachel. It's a criminal investigation. We need to do this without a reporter in the room possibly getting cited down the line as a witness. If any of this ever went to trial, the defense would have a field day with it."

Rachel's expression went from shock to fury before settling on betrayal, making Sam's discomfort all the keener. At a virtual loss for more words, Sam maintained her intractable position silently, trusting her body language to substitute for any repetition. Both men in the room merely watched.

"Wow," Rachel conceded, shaking her head finally. "Who knew?"

Without further comment, she turned on her heel and left.

Shunting aside the guilt with effort, Sam returned her attention to Philip Beaupré, her voice studiously deadpan. "Tell us about Teri Parker," she told him.

He was flawless. His eyes widened slightly, his chin lifted half an inch, both followed by a thoughtful frown. "Never heard of her. Who's she?"

"You tried that stunt when we mentioned Mick Durocher," Sam said. "You claim to be the hotshot special projects guy, fast on his feet and quick with the solutions, and yet you're totally clueless about the state's most sensational murder case?"

"You keep up on forensics?" Lester asked, apparently at random.

Beaupré played along. "I guess. As much as anybody. DNA and the rest?"

"It's getting creepy good," Lester continued. "Wearing rubber gloves to a scene no longer cuts it. People leave clouds of microbes behind, wherever they go—right here in this room, for example—and now we're starting to pick them up and backtrack them to their owners. It's amazing—evidence so small, it stays floating in the air."

"Cool," Philip said, unimpressed.

Sam filled in the missing detail. "Maybe not for some of us. We've been to Teri's apartment, where her phone and computer were removed. You ever meet her next-door neighbor?"

Beaupré smirked. "Hard to do, since I didn't know her."

"Right. Well, the neighbor knew about you. Turns out girls'll be girls, you know? Get together, talk about boys. Not only that, but you gave Teri so much stolen stuff from your own warehouse that she passed a few boxes on to the neighbor."

"Original GreenField boxes," Lester added conversationally. "Complete with the fingerprints of everybody who'd handled them."

"Hard to remember to wear gloves every time, isn't it?" Sam asked.

Beaupré wasn't close to the verge of tears, ready to confess, but his self-assurance had lapsed into watchfulness. Both his interviewers could almost hear the gears grinding in his head.

In fact, in conclusion, he checked his watch, rose, and announced, "Good story, guys, but it's got nuthin' to do with me. It's also getting late and I'm tired—no offense intended."

Almost daring them to stop him, he crossed somewhat warily to the door before turning and concluding, "Good luck. I hope you get off this crap and back to chasing the real killer. My people call me J.R. 'cause I'm well liked. I'm not the one trying to bring their world down around them. You oughta try focusing on who'd benefit from all this. The company goes belly-up, I'm out of a job. Hardly a great motivation."

With that, he stepped into the hallway and vanished.

"You like him?" Lester asked his partner.

"I love him," she answered. "But your cloud of DNA microbes aside—or whatever the hell you were talking about—it's gonna be a neat trick tying him to this mess, even with his fingerprints on some boxes."

"Assuming there are any," Lester agreed. "I know you and Joe grabbed them as evidence, but did we even order them printed, considering how many people must've handled them?"

"We will now," she said with a grim smile. "Not that it'll count for much anyhow. It's no smoking gun for an employee to have his prints on a box with the company logo on it."

Compensating for that statement, however, she nodded toward Beaupré's abandoned coffee cup. "That, on the other hand, I'd like to add to the mix, for prints *and* DNA. Joe said he wanted to start a collection. Might as well be obliging."

Philip Beaupré was not surprised when Rachel walked up to him in the parking lot outside the warehouse. He did look unhappy with the cell phone she held in her hand.

"We meet again," he greeted her warily.

"We do," she stated, indicating the phone. "Formally, too. On the record, I'm Rachel Reiling of the *Brattleboro Reformer*. This is a recorded conversation, being sent directly to the paper's website for safekeeping, and this interview is with Philip Beaupré of GreenField Grocers, who is also otherwise known by the nickname of J.R."

Philip resumed his by-now-familiar lazy smile and pointed at the phone. "Is that supposed to protect you from being attacked by a nutcase? It's not gonna happen, Miss Reiling. Having a nickname doesn't make me a homicidal maniac. I'm one of the many victims of what's happened to GreenField Grocers. For that matter, I have a bigger interest than most in wanting the cops to find this man as quickly as possible."

He resumed walking across the lot, heading toward his pickup truck. Rachel fell in beside him, recorder still running.

"Mr. Beaupré," she went on. "You've just been interviewed by the police concerning your possible involvement in the recent attacks against GreenField. What did they want to know from you?"

"You'd have to ask them. I was just doing my best to be as helpful as possible."

"Why were you at the truck crash in Brattleboro? Is that part of your job for the company?"

"Everything's my job. I'm what you'd call an executive-level jack-of-all-trades—the one who's called on at a moment's notice to solve problems and address emergencies."

"Is that what you saw when you found me examining and photographing the obvious sabotage to the truck? A problem? You were certainly angry when we met."

Beaupré paused in midstride, his voice maintaining its polished, practiced, impervious tone. "Absolutely, I was angry. You were in a restricted area, an unauthorized member of the press wearing police identification, contaminating a crime scene, taking pictures, and—I learned later—using your connection to your mother, the state's medical examiner, as a means to penetrate the security cordon. If you don't think that's a bigger news story than my being at the crash site of one of my own company trucks, then you should go back to newspaper school and bone up on both your priorities and the letter of the law."

He left her rooted in place and continued to his truck, where he swung in behind the wheel, started up the engine, and added through the open window as he pulled out, "Share that with your boss at the *Reformer*, Miss Reiling. I'm pretty sure he'll recommend that you cool your jets and do a little homework before ambushing innocent people on private property in the middle of the night."

Philip concentrated on negotiating White River Junction's feeder roads to the interstate, channeling his slowly fading anger.

He'd done well with the pip-squeak reporter. That had felt good. It was the least he could do for her outing him, not that a nickname was going to truly do him harm. He and Bobby—the real Junior—already knew where they stood regarding both each other and their pecking order within the company.

But talking with the cops had been a wake-up call. Despite his care and attention to detail—including referring to himself only as J.R. to Teri Parker—something had slipped through to catch their interest.

That was unfortunate for a couple of reasons. Philip had begun this vendetta reactively, from pure emotion, and largely without a plan—aside from not getting caught. He was a man prone to impulse. It's one of the reasons the old man had cooked up his special projects job description. Took one to know one, his father had said at the time, and he'd been right in more ways than he'd known.

Mixed blessings, as they say.

Since his initial action involving the firebombs, however, a strategy had begun to develop, one Philip had warmed to in part because it had slow-cooked, and thus grown in value in his mind.

But that had clearly now been derailed. The bitchy cop's partner had been right. He hadn't attended to everything, much as he'd tried, and their mention of Victoria Garlanda proved how thorough they were being. And now that they were onto him, considering their resources, he was going to have to reach for an improvised, cruder, and far less satisfying conclusion to all this.

Such a shame. But then, "shame" was the operative word.

CHAPTER TWENTY-FIVE

"Take a breath, honey," Beverly counseled her daughter on the phone, wriggling her toes under Joe's thigh as they sat on his couch in Brattleboro. He had just returned from taking a shower, was dressed in sweats and drinking a mug of coffee. He silently mouthed, "Rachel?" to which she nodded and rolled her eyes, mouthing back, "Work drama."

He'd guessed as much, hearing Beverly's soothing voice through the bathroom door a while ago. In truth, he'd always been charmed by this nurturing aspect of her, given her sometimes stern exterior. He'd been impressed, witnessing her support of not just her daughter, but Sammie Martens, too. It had come as confirmation that he'd done well to open his heart to someone one last time, considering how close he'd been to simply abandoning thoughts of further romance.

Tonight, however, was probably not going to hold much proof of its fringe benefits. Despite their both being at his small house on Green Street, he'd gotten home only twenty minutes earlier, she'd been on the phone throughout, and the way events had been unfolding recently, neither one of them was going to escape being paged soon.

"I love you, too," she eventually said, and put the phone down with a weary smile.

"Troubles with her love life?" he inquired, massaging the cat, who'd mysteriously appeared on his lap.

Beverly laughed. "Don't I wish. That child has no love life at the moment. But she is having a crisis. I'll give her that."

"What's going on?"

"She's been in mad pursuit of the whole GreenField fire, truck crash, gas leak story that's been consuming you all, but she's stuck in a quandary because now—officially, at least—she's more press than family. I'm afraid we got her used to eavesdropping—even participating—in some of our past cases. Getting the cold shoulder because of her new job has come as a shock."

"Who did that?" he asked. He knew what law enforcement company Rachel had been keeping lately, and suspected bad tidings.

"Sammie tossed her out of the sandbox. Something to do with her being told to leave when Sam and Lester were interviewing Philip Beaupré."

She shook her head and chuckled, adding, "And I can fill in the details because, just before my real daughter phoned, my surrogate daughter did the same, to unload about the same encounter."

"Sam?" he exclaimed, startling Gilbert enough to make him leap for safety. "Oh, that's not right."

She dismissed it with a shake of the head. "Oh, it's fine. I'm glad they feel free to reach out. Better that than bottling it up. They love each other, in their way, and Rachel's new job has put them at odds. I'm happy to be the go-between."

"What did Sam say?" he asked. "If that's not being indiscreet."

"It's not. Hers was actually the simpler complaint. She was just beating herself up for being such a hard-nose. I told her that she'd acted professionally and correctly and that she had a good heart—things that often run afoul of each other."

"Why was Rachel's problem more complicated?"

Beverly's face became more serious. "It didn't stop with Sam's banning her from the room. It turns out my intrepid daughter intercepted Mr. Beaupré in the parking lot after the interview, and challenged him, recorder in hand."

Joe stiffened. "He didn't do anything to her, did he?"

"It depends on your meaning," she explained. "He threw in her face that she was using her relationship to me and her connections to the police to violate the rules, and maybe the law, to gain unethical access to sources."

Joe looked pained. "Ouch," he said. "I guess that makes me guilty, as well. Yes, I smoothed her way into the warehouse that night, and I know she pulled some strings to get those truck crash shots. Beaupré's probably right. Why all the hoopla about him, though? As far as I know, nobody until now had even put an interview into him. She say what Sam and Les found out?"

"Yes," she said. "That's at the heart of the drama. They were chatting with him at the warehouse tonight when Rachel walked in and identified him by his nickname. That apparently lit a fuse under both your folks. Up to then, they'd been ignorant of it."

Joe furrowed his brow and reached for his phone, which he'd left on the coffee table before them. He knew Sam would have updated him by text with any news of importance. "She say what the nickname was?"

"J.R."

He stopped in midmotion and stared at her. "Really?" he asked. "At the rate she's going, your daughter may be pursuing the wrong profession. She should become a cop."

Lester glanced at the clock above the nurse's station as they walked by. They'd just arrived at the area's health-care behemoth, Dartmouth-Hitchcock Medical Center. "You sure this is a good idea?" he asked halfheartedly.

Sam didn't look back at him, nor did she break stride—a woman on a mission. "Hey," she said. "Where's the downside? People in hospitals don't have normal sleeping hours, and chances are she's still in a coma anyhow. And weren't we in the neighborhood?"

He couldn't argue with that. White River Junction was just one town south of where Victoria Garlanda was struggling to survive her Ebola virus. He also couldn't deny his own curiosity about why and how Garlanda kept surfacing in the context of the GreenField case.

As it turned out, they were in luck. When they paused at the window separating Garlanda from the rest of the world, they saw that she was not only awake, but talking to an industrially gowned and masked Susan Spinney, as well.

"Great minds think alike," Sam said, rapping her knuckles on the glass, to the alarm of several nearby nurses. "You and your wife oughta talk more often," she kidded Lester.

Sue looked up and came to their rescue, quickly approaching the window and gesturing to one of her DHMC counterparts to pick up the intercom on the counter near the door. The nurse did so, exchanged a couple of sentences, and handed the phone to Sam.

"Hey," she said.

"Hey, yourself," Sue answered.

"How's she doing?" Sam asked.

"They're saying she beat it. You want to talk to her?"

"That's okay?"

"Since she's still pretty weak, you'll have to gown up. That's what I was telling them, assuming that's what you want. I told them you two're on the access list, given the circumstances. Just let that nurse know."

Sam glanced at the woman who'd handed her the receiver and nodded, smiling. The nurse gave her a thumbs-up and retreated to fetch the proper clothing.

Fifteen minutes later, Sam and Lester were in with Sue, looking like stand-ins for a bioterrorist training. They shuffled awkwardly over to the bed, whose occupant was looking remarkably good, given her recent adventure.

"I know you can barely see who we are," Sam said by way of introduction, "but it's Sam Martens and Lester. How're you feeling?"

"Terrible." Victoria smiled weakly. "And that's great. Believe me. Sue was telling me you wanted to talk."

Sam, despite her earlier desire to confer with Victoria after their interview of Philip Beaupré, was now embarrassed by her own good fortune. The poor woman looked precisely as though she'd just escaped from death's grip, blunting Sam's ambition to put her through a grilling—all because of what might turn out to be a coincidental happenstance.

Nevertheless, here she was. Plus, what with her drubbing of Rachel and subsequent mea culpa to Beverly by phone, Sam's self-esteem was close to the basement. Why not give the third degree to someone fresh from a coma?

"Okay, I'll try to keep it short, but there're just too many times your name's come up for me not to want to ask a couple of questions."

"My name?" Victoria asked wearily.

"Well, yeah. In addition to what put you in here, we're running a second, maybe related investigation." Sam awkwardly maneuvered to sit on the edge of the bed, absurdly hoping to introduce an element of friendly intimacy despite her bulky garb. "Let's start with that, in fact, since we're on it. Tell us about Robert Beaupré."

Victoria was completely taken aback, her astonishment tinged with sadness. "Bob? Why are you asking about him?"

"You knew each other?"

She thought for a moment before answering simply, "I wanted to marry him. He was the only man I ever loved."

"What happened?"

"He married someone else," she said. "Why are you asking about him?"

Sam ducked the question. "Let me ask you first, have you two kept in touch?"

"No. I haven't talked to him in years—decades—not since it happened."

"What was it like? The breakup. Were threats made?"

She scowled. "I was heartbroken, not angry. I don't understand this."

Sam reached out a gloved hand and took hold of her wrist, stroking it gently. Garlanda was crying, quietly, without fanfare.

"Victoria, I'm so sorry. It seems to be my day for upsetting people. It's just that we've discovered what happened to you wasn't by chance. The Ebola you caught was introduced into your eyedropper bottle."

Garlanda wiped her eyes with the back of her free hand and stared at her. "My eyedropper? That's crazy. Who would do that? You're not saying Bob Beaupré, are you?"

"We don't know who it was," Lester said from beside his wife. "That's why we're here. We lifted fingerprints from the bottle, but they don't match anything on file."

"I asked you about Bob," Sam resumed, "because your name came up in the GreenField investigation. It just seemed too much of a coincidence, especially since we learned that what happened to you wasn't accidental."

"Who would do that?" Sue echoed her friend. "We all love Victoria."

It was a generalized question, not directed at anyone, but Victoria answered it: "Lillian Wuttke."

Her three companions looked at each other in confusion.

"Who?" Lester asked.

"Lillian?" Sue echoed. "Why?"

"It was the last thing she said to me before she left on vacation," Garlanda said tiredly. "And before I got sick."

"She threatened you?" Sam asked pointedly.

"No. She told me we all get what we deserve in the end."

No one said anything, prompting Victoria to explain, "I know. It doesn't sound like anything, but we'd crossed swords before, when she told me she should have gotten my job. She's made it her mission to undermine me whenever possible, but always indirectly enough to avoid getting herself fired. It's become a joke of sorts among management."

"Some joke," Lester said, looking around at the hyperclean environment.

"I'm not saying she did this," Victoria said quickly. "You asked who might have. Combining her anger with me and her nurse's skills, she's the only one I can think of."

Sam had headed toward the door. "Don't worry about that. I'm going to call right now to have somebody drop by her house."

"She's on vacation," Victoria repeated.

"That's what she told you," Sam responded.

Rachel had her window down and the radio up, hoping the combination would keep her awake. It wasn't just the long hours. Ever since childhood, she'd used sleep to escape from stress. And stress, right now, was the driving emotion.

Her mom had been great when she phoned her a half hour earlier. As usual, calm, a good listener, and a thoughtful advisor, she'd done everything right. And it hadn't had the slightest impact.

Rachel was in an emotional turmoil of her own making. She knew Sam had been within her rights and acting protectively when she'd asked Rachel to leave; she also recognized that slimy Philip Beaupré had been utterly and self-servingly manipulative by challenging her youth, competence, and integrity. But both encounters, taken together and ramped up by exhaustion, had exacted their toll.

Any such realization, however, didn't reduce the resulting anger, frustration, or guilt. Rachel wanted to do good work, to be considered apart from her hyperaccomplished mother, and like most people at her career stage and age, didn't want to screw up. She was unusually levelheaded, compared to her peers, perhaps due to her prior exposure to trauma and loss. Earlier, while still in school in Burlington but living off campus, she'd taken in a young woman on the spur of the moment, who'd turned out to be a runaway from Albany, New York. Unbeknownst to Rachel, she'd had some very bad people on her tail, resulting in the girl being assaulted and killed in the apartment. Rachel had woken up in time to chase the assailant away, but too late to help her newfound friend.

But whatever the leavening agents in her maturation, the result had been an unusually rational insight into her own weaknesses and strengths.

However, any such armor is vulnerable when the subtext of an accusation—no matter how crudely delivered—smacks of the truth. Rachel could handle Sam's rebuff. It was humiliating, but quickly balmed by time and understanding. Beaupré's comments, conversely, rankled deeply, striking at Rachel's own burgeoning self-worth. Was she a child of privilege and connections, using both to navigate the real world under false colors? Had she earned her job at the *Reformer*, or had it been her mother being the state's chief ME? Certainly her ease of access with cops spoke for itself. She'd interpreted that earlier as simple good luck, but with Beaupré's sneering words in her ears, it morphed into entitlement, which as a socially conscious young woman, she found repellent.

All of which helped explain her present single-minded conviction that she'd found a way out of her humiliation: His taillights were ahead of her right now.

Mr. Beaupré may have hit the nail partially square-on, but that didn't absolve him of his own misdemeanors. He was a rat. Rachel knew it in her gut, and was convinced the police shared her opinion.

But where they were constrained by procedures and rules of evidence, she was free to discover what she could about this man, and expose it for all to see.

CHAPTER TWENTY-SIX

They all took their time. From what Sam had said on the phone, Lillian Wuttke was, "most sincerely dead." And given the circumstances behind that condition, no one was entering her house until Beverly arrived and issued a thumbs-up. Cops as a rule aren't too crazy about the deceased. The unknown factors, not to mention the accompanying odors, made that easy to comprehend. Adding a possible exposure to Ebola, however, pretty much sealed the deal.

Chief medical examiners rarely did fieldwork anymore. They had once. That was in part how Beverly had established her no-nonsense public presence, keeping overalls and a pair of barn boots in her car trunk just in case.

Situations like this, however, were the wrinkle that proved the exception. And one she actually enjoyed, despite the situation and the stifling equipment required to explore it. Bioexposure scenes like what Sam had uncovered were, in Vermont, the exclusive realm of a truly tiny cadre of experts, Beverly among them. If you had a body, possibly killed by lethal contagion, she was on the call list.

As was her diener, Todd, who was now suiting up beside her in the postdawn coolness, next to their official van, in view of Wuttke's small house.

It had been cordoned off with gently fluttering yellow police tape, and the lonely, narrow street it fronted blocked by police vehicles. The only people present were there by necessity, and—aside from Todd and Beverly—keeping their distance, as if the virus inside were watching at the windows, coiled and ready to strike anyone foolish enough to get close.

Beverly, of course, knew otherwise. Her training had informed her of Ebola's life cycle, habits, and abilities. It was highly unlikely that simply entering this house was going to expose anyone to much of anything, and that wasn't factoring in the protective clothing she was donning with Todd's help. That was dictated by protocols, not because it was actually necessary.

These were total isolation suits—white, bulky, cumbersome, and awkward to walk in—made a cliché by overexposure in the movies. They came equipped with their own breathing apparatus, allowing the wearer to enter most toxic environments with impunity.

But comfortable, they were not.

To Beverly, that merely heightened her sense of purpose. Despite her knowledge of the risks involved, putting on the suits—as she imagined had been true of a knight's armor of old—served to sharpen the wearer's focus.

At last, with a final tap on his back, she informed Todd that he was as secure as he'd just finished making her.

He turned to look at her, one face mask to another, and gave her a thumbs-up. "You hear me?" he asked over their closed-circuit radio.

"Loud and clear," she replied. "Ready?"

He stooped like a white bear, uncomfortably balanced on his hind legs, and retrieved a large equipment case at his feet. "Sooner the better. I'm already dreaming of getting this thing off."

The house was locked, an obstacle Todd solved by immediately smashing a small side window with the corner of his case and reaching in to work the door handle.

"You've had practice at this, Todd?" Beverly asked, easing the tension.

"It's called preplanning, boss," he said grimly, pushing open the door.

Probably because they were seeing the world through plastic-lensed hoods, with the sound of their own breathing resonating in their ears, they couldn't deny the dread of what lay ahead. They'd been briefed that Lillian Wuttke's remains were in a back bedroom, visible through her window. Nevertheless, they hadn't been trained in self-protective police tactics, and the house, while presumably empty, hadn't in fact been officially cleared. Lastly—all rational thinking aside—there loomed in the surrounding air the mythologized specter of Ebola, eager and ready to kill them.

In fact, Beverly reassured herself, not only was this virus not airborne, but the standard isolation of U.S. patients infected with it consisted mostly of shutting their doors to outside visitors. All this hoods-and-air-tank riga-marole notwithstanding.

She brought her attention back to reality. Wuttke's house was modest, aging, dirty, and cluttered, forcing both visitors to pick their way slowly between boxes, bags, old product containers, and piles of clothing lining the opposing walls. It wasn't a hoarding environment per se. Beverly was overly familiar with that phenomenon. But it suggested one.

"You okay?" she asked Todd, whom she could hear breathing hard behind her.

"I'm good, Doc. It's just hard running an obstacle course in this getup."

Beverly reached the bedroom door and said softly, "Well, it's all but over now. I think we can tell the others that a preliminary diagnosis of Ebola is within reason. You have that body bag in your kit?"

He drew up behind her and looked at the ravaged woman spread out on the bed before them, mired with all the gruesome end results usually attributed to the disease. "Damn. Yes, ma'am, I do."

"Then we better start buttoning up what's left of her," she said, stepping forward.

"I seriously doubt you're here with your doctor's permission," Joe addressed Willy. "But welcome anyhow."

"From my mouth to your ear, I've been officially cleared for duty," Willy came back, carefully settling into his office chair so as not to jar his slinged arm. He finished by leaning back and propping one foot into an uppermost drawer, as was his habit.

Lester laughed outright. "That's the most equivocal statement I've heard in a while."

All four of them were assembled in the Brattleboro squad room, the first time in some time, given how often they'd been pulled afield by recent events. Daily reports had been appearing in the unit's online log, but Joe—along with the rest of them—had always preferred face-to-face meetings. It was by now late in the day, which had begun with the discovery of Lillian Wuttke's remains.

"Seriously," Joe followed up, delaying protocol for the moment. "How're you feeling?"

Unusually, Kunkle did not respond with something dismissive. "Seriously? I wish I'd had this done years ago. Except for when I had an arm that actually worked, I've never felt better."

Joe nodded in acknowledgment. "Can't ask for more than that." He shifted his attention to the team in general. "Okay. Over the last twenty-four hours, I thought we've had enough jackrabbits jump out of the hat to warrant an actual in-person brainstorming. But before we get into that, I want to rule on whether the poisoning of Victoria Garlanda had anything to do with the assaults on GreenField. Who's got the goods on that?"

Almost from tradition, given how long these four had been together, Willy spoke first. "No connection, despite her having been Robert Beaupré's high school squeeze."

"Arguments?" Joe asked the others.

"What's Beverly say about Wuttke?" Sam asked.

"She couldn't do the autopsy herself," Joe reported. "Her office doesn't have a high enough biohazard rating. But I heard half an hour ago that Ebola was confirmed."

Lester added, "And the lab weighed in on her fingerprints being on the Ebola-laced eye-drop bottle Willy found in Victoria's office."

"Outstanding," Joe commented.

"How did Lillian get infected?" Sam asked.

"Can't say for sure," Lester answered. "The theory is she had no more clue than the rest of them about what was killing the pilot when he arrived at UVSS. She just knew he was wicked sick. The thinking is that she swabbed his mouth, mixed it with a small amount of saline, dumped it into the bottle, and waited to see what would happen. Given that, they think she must've wiped her eye or rubbed her nose, and Mother Nature did the rest—she was infected. She probably wasn't wearing gloves, 'cause you don't walk around the hallways like that—it looks suspicious."

"What I don't get is why she didn't come in once she started showing symptoms," Sam said. "She was a nurse—good, bad, or indifferent."

"She was an arrogant crap artist," Willy argued. "I bet she thought she could beat it. Like Les said, nobody ID'd Ebola. There's no reason she thought that, either. Probably figured she'd caught the flu. Before I snuck out of there, I asked the hospital administration why they hadn't chased her down when she didn't answer their heads-up. They showed me the email she'd sent them. It said she was on vacation, out of state as planned, and feeling fine—probably lying to keep people at bay. Not much they could do with that."

"To a notice that she might have been exposed to Ebola?" Lester asked incredulously.

"That's not how they worded it," Willy corrected him. "They didn't want to put that out there, so they called it a serious infection threat, or some crap. She died never knowing."

"And we're sure all this is because she wanted Garlanda's job and was pissed about being passed over?" Joe asked for confirmation. "No doubts on anyone's mind?"

"No doubts from Victoria," Sammie said. "She says Lillian made it crystal clear. Keep in mind that for Lillian, probably none of this was intended to go where it went. By putting that germy shit into the eyedropper bottle, she was just hoping Victoria would lose her sight, or get too ill to keep working. Nobody I talked to believes she had homicide in mind. How else could she've been considered next in line for the position? And that was her rationale—she was that deluded about her qualifications."

"Guess that's been taken care of," Willy said quietly.

"Which still leaves the fact that Victoria and Robert Beaupré were sweethearts," Joe stated. "Is Willy right about that being a coincidence?"

"We got nothing more to go on," Lester said. "Victoria herself is our best source, and she says she and Robert haven't been in touch in decades. We can keep the door open a little, but I doubt there's anything left to it. Consider it a false lead."

No one argued the point. Joe finally bobbed his head once. "Okay. Moving on."

"J.R.?" Sam inquired hopefully.

Joe wouldn't bite. "Not yet. I want to end with him, so we don't overlook anything else we've got on our plate."

"Mick Durocher," Willy suggested.

"Good," his boss agreed. "We now know unequivocally that he isn't a match to Teri's fetus. We also have no witness or evidence even connecting the two of them—"

"Except the surveillance shot of him carrying the body up the mountain," Willy interjected.

"Granted," Joe agreed. "But the neighbors drew a blank, no bartender we could find saw them together, nor did his buddy Seth Villeneuve, and Mick's so-called confession was a joke."

Once more, nobody said anything, allowing Joe to add, "Finally, there's the money Mick's daughter received—a quarter million bucks of untraceable cash, delivered after her old man's death."

"Payment for the false confession of a terminally sick man with nothing to lose," Sam proposed, "and a daughter he feels guilty about?"

"Payment from a very rich real murderer," Lester suggested. "Of which we have several candidates to choose from."

"Is that true?" Willy asked, understandably not quite as up to date on the smaller details as the rest of them.

"Yeah," Lester explained—their resident GreenField expert. "For tax reasons, the old man set things up so that management gets some seriously impressive compensations. Bobby, Philip, Brad, and even Elaine are the big winners, but there are others in the millionaire category. Not sure what the advantages are to doing that over stock options, or inheritance, or whatever, but that's how he structured things."

"I didn't think Elaine even drew a salary," Sam said.

"She doesn't, not as such. She gets a stipend, like an allowance. And Brad pulls in a bundle."

"For that matter, so does the rarely mentioned Mrs. Beaupré," Joe mentioned. "The mother of the clan."

"Any of them lose two hundred and fifty thousand bucks recently?" Willy asked.

"No way of knowing," Lester answered. "If we were a TV show, I could just call up their financials." He waved at his computer. "Unfortunately, the law makes that impossible till we get a judge to agree to it.

"Speaking of which," he added, "Sam got a warrant for that coffee mug Philip Beaupré left behind, making us so legal, we squeak."

"And?" Willy asked leadingly. He then glanced at Joe theatrically, saying, "Uh-oh, don't wanna get in trouble with Dad. Okay to mention the five hundred-ton, J.R. elephant in the room?"

"It is," Joe acquiesced.

"Nothing on the prints," Sam reported. "But we did get enough touch

DNA to create a profile, which might help us out with Teri Parker's baby."

"Is it a match?" Joe asked.

"Not quite. There are familial markers, but he's not the actual father."

"Jesus," Lester said. "This is relentless."

"Leaving Bobby and the old man," Willy mused, ignoring him.

"We have no DNA on file for either of them?" Joe asked, already knowing the answer.

"No reason for it," Sam answered.

Joe was unfazed. "It's still enough to apply for nontestimonial warrants, just like the AG did for Mick's DNA."

Willy was the only one in the room whose enthusiasm wasn't ramping up. "Let's say we do nail down who's dear old Papa. So what?" he asked. "Maybe it gets us a little extra to apply pressure, but it still doesn't identify who used the two-by-four on Teri, or killed those poor bastards in the warehouse, or the truck driver. That's the bug I wanna step on. Boss, you just mentioned old lady Beaupré—"

"Martha," Sam injected.

"Whatever," Willy resumed. "She should have an ax to grind—knocked up and married to a guy who loved somebody else. What d'ya wanna bet she knew all about that?"

"And now she strikes all these years later?" Lester argued.

"Far as we know," Willy said with a smile, "only Robert or Bobby are left as Teri's sperm donor." He eyed Sammie. "What was it you reported Philip said about Daddy Dearest?"

Sam was nodding in support of where Willy was heading. "He said he thought his dad impregnated Martha with Bobby, which is why he and Victoria didn't get married. What Willy's talking about was what J.R. said right afterwards, when he bet his father was generally screwin' around on the side, anyhow. The exact quote was, 'That's much more his style,' using the present tense."

"That's it," Willy announced. "We have no frigging clue what's going on inside that family. Buncha gerbils, you ask me, and I think it's sexist if you exclude Martha."

Sam burst out laughing. "Oh, please."

But Willy was only half joking. "Philip clearly has a love–hate thing goin' on with Dad. Why wouldn't Martha, too? That's all I'm sayin'. Somebody planted those Beaupré wigglers inside Teri, but it's not necessarily the person who caved her head in. I think we have the makings of a daytime drama here, and I bet the evidence'll support it."

"Or a Greek tragedy," Joe said quietly.

CHAPTER TWENTY-SEVEN

Rachel jerked awake, hitting her hand painfully against her steering wheel and swearing. She was sore, hungry, smelled of body odor, and needed to pee. As she worked her tongue across her teeth, she also suspected that her breath could melt paint.

And she was beginning to seriously doubt what she was doing.

Perhaps to restore her motivation, she looked out the dirty windshield at the car parked in the driveway an eighth of a mile down the road.

Her subconscious must have jarred her from her nap. The darkened house she'd been watching—where Philip Beaupré led her the night before—had sprung a light over its front door, illuminating the source of her interest as he keyed the lock before heading for his car.

Rachel realized she'd have to relieve her bladder later. The game, as the familiar phrase had it, was afoot once more.

The pursuit of that game, however, was becoming harder to justify, even fueled as she was with admittedly ebbing humiliation. She'd started out after Philip Beaupré with an ill-defined sense of revenge. Surely he was crooked, she'd reasoned, and definitely arrogant and rude. Also, he'd smoothly sailed out of the warehouse after talking to the police, indicating that they'd had nothing on which to hold him.

That left her, so she'd reasoned, with using her mandate as a reporter to independently assist the legal process. Not only would it be a good story, were she successful, but a moral and personal victory as well. She'd even cooked up an explanation for not calling Joe or Sammie to update them: So doing would make her an "agent" of the police—per the law—and perhaps taint whatever evidence she'd be able to deliver.

That was the theory—which had sounded better twenty-four hours ago—before she realized that all she'd done is tail Philip to his own house, in the meantime forgoing all her other obligations.

The day just past had therefore not been easy. Nor had it been easy to stave off napping, fearful as she'd been that she'd awake to find his car gone.

But all that now vanished in a rush of adrenaline as she watched Philip back into the street and head off for parts unknown. Even if this was another goose chase, at least she was back in motion.

As it turned out, they didn't travel far. Already in Colchester, they drove some twenty minutes to the log-built mansion that had so impressed Joe—the home of Robert Beaupré.

"Okay," Rachel said to herself softly. "What now?"

She killed her headlights at the turnoff to the long driveway, grateful for a full moon and a cloudless sky, and happily discovered that the road opened up onto a parking area vast enough to allow her to stop in the shadow of some ornamental trees that almost completely shielded her from the house.

Moving fast, she grabbed her camera and cell phone and swung out of her car, running along the parking area's edge toward the house, hoping Philip's arrival had been distracting enough to anyone inside to give her cover.

As far as she could tell, it worked. She wound up in the bushes lining the building's front, in time to see Philip reach the entrance and enter. She noticed that he hadn't rung the bell and no one had let him in.

She hesitated, unsure of her next move and, frankly—if a little late—surprised by what she'd done. Unlike last night, when she hadn't even left her car, now she was skulking on private property, camera in hand, wondering how to illicitly access the house.

That realization made her reconsider why she was so devoted to this cause. It went beyond immaturity and hurt feelings. There'd been something about Philip himself that had also encouraged her—an underlying fury when he'd lectured her in the parking lot—and just now, as he'd marched purposefully from his house to the car—that spoke of a man having readied himself for battle.

She shifted gears more confidently on that premise, and started checking for an unobtrusive way to follow Philip's progression inside.

The building, though gigantic, was hardly aglow with light. As she circled its perimeter, at once taking in the layout and peering through its many windows, she was struck by the general stillness. The house may have been designed to accommodate an army of guests, but it seemed virtually empty tonight—a notion that only heightened her curiosity and growing concern.

Whatever Philip's reasons for waiting this late to charge unannounced into his father's darkened home, when combined with his single-minded determination, they increasingly convinced Rachel that his intentions were passionate and dire.

In time, on the far side, facing a view of moonlit mountains and tiny lights from distant communities, Rachel came to an expansive deck with chairs and tables and well-tended planters spread out before a long row of brightly lit French doors, only one of which—unfortunately several units down—was half open.

She cautiously leaned forward to peer through the nearest windowpane, and found herself looking into a two-story-high library jammed with books, paintings, statuary, and two men. One was Philip, angrily pacing across a string of oriental carpets as he spoke and gesticulated. The other was his father, Robert, whom she recognized from her research. He was sitting casually in a leather armchair near a cold fireplace, the lord of the manor, striking a pose of indifference, aside from the grip he was exerting on the arm of his chair.

They were talking, especially Philip, but about what, Rachel couldn't make out. She glanced along the row of glass doors to the one ajar through which their muffled voices leaked out into the night, and tried calculating her chances of reaching it unseen.

The deck underfoot posed no problem. Relatively new, and clearly built to carry the weight of several trucks, it was soundless and smooth. The challenge was the light flooding its surface, laying a series of bright trapezoids through which she'd have to travel to reach her target.

Her advantage was that Robert was angled so that he'd have to shift in his seat to see her. That made Philip the wild card, restlessly marching about the huge room like a worked-up automaton.

Rachel readied herself, stood slightly away from the wall, and watched Philip's body language like a hunter.

Window by window, as he spun on his heel and briefly showed her his back, Rachel flitted down the row of doors, praying she'd anticipated any and all pitfalls ahead, especially among the dark strips of shadow falling between each of the windows.

Finally, her heart pounding, breathing through her mouth with excitement, she got close enough to the open door that the voices became clearer and, at last, comprehensible.

She pulled out her smartphone and hit the Go button on its recorder function.

Rachel heard Philip speak first. "It never crossed your mind that instead of some delusional father figure, you were coming across as the white Massa lording over the plantation?"

Robert answered, "Oh, come on, Philip. What the hell? That again? *Gone with the Wind*? Really? This crap is all in your head. Nobody else would have the ghost of a notion what the fuck you're talking about."

Philip did another of his jittery, about-face pirouettes, momentarily vanishing from Rachel's sight, as he'd been doing throughout. "Jesus, Dad. I spend more time with the people who work for you than anybody else. Don't you think I know how they see you? All that bullshit about the rotating drivers, chauffeuring you around in an old pickup? Are you on drugs? Everyone knows what you really drive, what this palace looks like, what you pay your family versus the lousy wages they all get."

Robert Beaupré's voice was hard and angry, not matching the casual pose she'd earlier misinterpreted. "You're a fine one to talk, you privileged little prick. The schools I paid for, the cars I bought you, the clothes I put on your back, the shit I put up with when you copped an attitude about the corporate life and how it was beneath you. Who's really on drugs here, you little turd? I have carried your sorry ass for years, not because of some magical way you have with people and problem solving, but because your mother told me I had to protect you. You've been a loser pain in the ass from the day you and your bloodsucking useless sister came out of her womb."

"*Loser?*" Philip screamed. "*You slept with my goddamned girlfriend, Dad!*"

Rachel never saw it coming. She looked up from her phone, making sure it was functioning, to stare right into the face of a flushed and startled Philip Beaupré, who'd gone from striding back and forth just out of sight to abruptly appearing in the middle of the doorway, not five feet before her.

"*What the fuck?*" he exclaimed, reaching outside, grabbing her by the shirtfront, and dragging her into the room.

Robert was startled out of his royal pose, and half rose to his feet, his expression stunned.

"Who is this?" he demanded.

"I'm Rachel Reiling," she said quickly, brushing away Philip's hand and smoothing her shirt.

"She's press, Dad," his son interrupted, snatching the phone from Rachel's hand. He held it up. "And she's been recording every word."

"I just got here," she said meekly, sensing the idiocy of the statement as soon as it left her mouth.

Robert approached them, his face stiff with rage. "Then you heard how this ungrateful little bastard turned his hatred of me into a killing spree of innocent people?"

Rachel stared at them both. "What?"

Robert was unfazed, stopping within reach. "You missed it?" He held out his left hand to his son. "No matter. Give me that."

Instinctively, Philip passed over the phone. Robert checked its screen, confirmed it was still recording, and returned it to Rachel.

"He's who the cops are after," he said, nodding toward Philip. "He just told me he set the warehouse fires, rigged the truck crash, and punctured the cooler pipes to poison all those people." He pointed his finger accusingly. "He's the mass murderer everyone's looking for, all because he got his feelings hurt."

The older man suddenly reached out and patted Philip harshly on the cheek. "Poor baby. All because Daddy didn't love him enough."

Philip snapped, as his father had designed, and lunged like a fencer to land a punch. Rachel leaped forward and pushed him, throwing him off balance and making him miss his aim, while Robert, despite his age, gracefully stepped back and to one side, and presented from behind his right leg a hidden fireplace poker he'd brought from across the room. In one fluid, jarring sweep of the arm, he brought it down sharply against the nape of his son's neck.

Philip continued falling to the lavishly carpeted floor, landing as solidly and motionless as a wet bag of sand.

Rachel stared in stunned disbelief, overwhelmed by how all sound and motion had stopped, as if cut off by a guillotine.

Robert Beaupré almost gently reached out and pried the phone from her hand, holding it before her face and blocking the sight of the body stretched out on the floor between them. "You might want to put this to proper use," he suggested calmly. "I'm sure the cops'll want a heads-up."

CHAPTER TWENTY-EIGHT

Sammie Martens found them on the screened porch facing the lake. Mother and daughter were half caught by the light of a single candle secured to a small plate on the card table between them. The black water, beyond the lawn, reflected a shimmering, distorted image of a full moon.

They were at Beverly's new house in Windsor, about which Sam had heard, but which she hadn't yet visited. Not that she would have done so now, so long past midnight. But Beverly had asked for her, as a favor to Rachel, and Sam wasn't about to quibble. Besides, the truth of the matter was that, despite the hour, most of the squad—minus Willy, who'd retired to be with Emma—was still at the office when Beverly called.

"Hey," Sam said softly, stepping onto the wooden floor. The house was still largely unfurnished, the closing having just occurred. The rooms she'd walked through had featured a few token chairs and tables, oddly making the place look emptier than had they been absent. In the gloom of night, it struck Sam less as a home about to be inhabited than a place freshly abandoned.

But that was likely just Sam's mood. Aside from Victoria's complete recovery and Mandy Lawlor's good fortune, there weren't many aspects of this case that had turned out well for its participants.

And from the tone of Beverly's voice on the phone, that also applied to the heralded "hero of the hour," Rachel Reiling, whom the early internet blogs were already crediting with having "broken the case wide open."

Beverly rose and gave Sam a hug. "Thank you for coming. I appreciate it as an extraordinary gesture of friendship, not taken lightly."

Sam was embarrassed. "Jeez, Beverly. It's not that big a deal. I'm happy to help if I can."

She sat in the chair indicated, noticing that Rachel had barely glanced at her.

"Hey, Rach," she said, touching the girl's shoulder.

Rachel turned to give her a brief, wan smile before resuming her gaze into the middle distance.

"What's goin' on?" Sam asked generally.

"Rachel and I have been discussing what occurred, but being her mother is perhaps less helpful than I'd wish. I was hoping your perspective might be more useful."

Sam hesitated. For all her good qualities, including those of friend and mother, Beverly remained at her core a scientist, and Sammie suspected that the more she neared a high-voltage emotional situation, the more she was inclined to seek the familiarity of pure analysis.

That's certainly the way it was sounding. Sam now understood why she'd been summoned.

"I hate to ask this," she therefore began, "but would you mind if Rachel and I just talked alone for a while?"

The girl's mother in fact looked relieved, and immediately rose to go. "Not at all," she said. "I completely understand. I'll be trying to organize the kitchen."

"Thanks," Rachel said listlessly once Beverly had retreated.

"No problem," Sam said. "What's up?"

It was all she needed to say. The young woman looked at her, the candlelight accenting her distress, and asked, "You know what happened?"

"Most of it, I think," Sam said. "We've been squaring away all the legal bits and pieces most of the night. I'm sorry you had to be there when the shit hit the fan."

Rachel's expression contorted. "I *caused* it," she said. "That's what Mom doesn't want to hear."

Sam pursed her lips. "You interfered when Philip went for his father to hit him. Is that what you mean?"

"Yeah," Rachel said mournfully.

"And throwing him off balance allowed Robert to whack him with the poker?"

"Yeah."

"A poker that he'd brought from across the room, and hidden from view till he needed it?"

Rachel had been staring into the flame, and now shifted back to Sam's face. She blinked a couple of times. "Yes," she said softly, thoughtfully.

"You get it, don't you?" Sam asked. "Philip was gonna die."

Rachel didn't answer.

Sam had another point to make. She was fully aware of Rachel's recent trauma involving her murdered roommate. She had been the lead investigator on the case, and had joined Beverly in doing what she could to smooth Rachel's recovery.

That had taken some dealing with, in part by Sam's stating her genuine belief that the worst had come and gone, and that at least from now on, Rachel could look forward to happier tidings.

Until now.

"The real point is, it's happened again, hasn't it?" Sam broached the subject, sharing the loss of her former optimism. "Another person's been killed right in front of you."

Rachel wasn't crying. She seemed too hollowed out for that. "You see that a lot," she stated.

"Not like in the movies, but more than you will again, I hope," Sam agreed. "It doesn't alter the bigger point that how you're feeling makes sense. If you didn't think you could've changed the outcome of a bad situation, that would make you a pretty shitty person. Don't you think?"

Rachel absorbed that for a slow count before commenting, "I really hated him."

"Philip?"

"Yeah."

"For how he made you feel?"

"He was right."

"I read Joe's interview of you after the dust settled," Sam said. "You told him you felt humiliated because Beaupré said you used your connections and influence to better yourself. The implication being you don't deserve the breaks you've gotten."

Rachel's voice was just above a whisper. "Yeah."

"You know that's baloney," Sam stated. "You *feel* bad because you're a decent human being, and you don't want statements like that to be true, but what about the messenger? Why do you think Philip did all those terrible things, and said that to you?"

The deflection seemed to work. A small crease spread across Rachel's forehead as she asked, "What *was* that all about? I got that his father had betrayed him terribly—"

Sam put it more bluntly. "He knocked up his own son's girlfriend."

Rachel nodded without comment.

"Look," Sam continued, "we're talking Shakespearean tragedy here. Love–hate, privilege run amok, zero impulse control. I come from a screwed-up family, but this one's the bomb. There's nothing from this bunch you can take as a life lesson, Rach, and you sure as hell don't need to pay any attention to what Philip said. What you did was try to interrupt a violent act. You had no idea what the old man was planning. Nobody would've seen it coming."

"Did you interview him yet?" Rachel asked.

"Joe and Lester did."

"Why did he do it? I understand Philip being mad because of his girl-friend, but Robert?"

Sam understood the question, as she did Rachel's need to make sense of something so disturbing.

But there was a legal problem, and she hated how it threatened to re-peat recent history between them.

She hesitated, glancing away toward the moon-rippled water for in-spiration.

But salvation came from closer by. Rachel reached out and laid a hand on her forearm. "I'm sorry, Sam. I'm doing it again, aren't I? Making you choose between friendship and breaking the rules." She squeezed Sam's arm for emphasis. "I promise on my mom's life that none of this will go anywhere. I'm not a reporter here. I just want to make as much sense out of this as I can to get past it. The whole newspaper thing doesn't apply. It's still your choice—I know that—but I wanted you to know."

Sam smiled in appreciation. "I was wondering how to deal with that. I know I pissed you off last time."

Rachel waved that away. "I have a lot to learn."

Sam went on a slight segue as a result, however. "Speaking of the news-paper shtick, what's it like to suddenly be the headline and not the re-porter? What's your boss gonna do in tomorrow's paper? I read some of the early online stuff. That's gotta be awkward. I can't even imagine the story's lead."

"No kidding," Rachel admitted. "On top of everything else, I had to explain to him what I was doing there."

"He think you were working for us?"

"Sure he did. We may not have your legal restraints—probable cause and the rest—but there are rules. He let me know pretty clearly what he thought of what I did."

"But . . . ," Sam suggested leadingly.

Rachel laughed. "Yeah, you're right. I did get the story. Not pretty, but hard to argue with."

Sam shook her head. "God, what a racket. Okay. So, I'll tell you what I know if you promise not to tell anyone, including Joe or your mother. Deal?"

"Deal."

"The thing between Robert and Philip began with Philip's birth. In a nutshell, while Bobby was an accident, having his two siblings was all Martha's idea, according to Robert. Plus, Philip and he just didn't like each other. There was as much envy as hatred between them. Joe guessed they each saw what they didn't like about themselves in the other guy."

Sam sighed before continuing. "That's what I meant by it being a Shakespearean tragedy: We only have Robert's word for it, of course, but he said his whole family was a source of resentment, from the moment Martha announced she was pregnant, forcing Robert to give up Victoria.

"By dumb luck, Bobby ended up fitting in, 'cause he's basically a grind, and Elaine was written off as a girl and therefore deemed useless—plus she brought in Brad St. John, who turned out okay. But Philip became the symbol of everything Robert had lost by marrying Martha."

"My God," Rachel said.

"I know, right?" Sam smiled in wonder. "They ended up like alpha dogs, competing for everything and pretending it was all cool. That's what got Robert chasing after Teri. She must've been stunned by her good luck, having both of them on the line—before Robert got her pregnant and sealed her fate. The man just never learned to keep it in his pants.

"In the end, once Philip found out, maybe from Teri herself, he went after everything Robert had built—hitting the old man where he thought it would hurt most, consequences be damned. We found Philip's house full of research materials on how to build explosives and rig trucks like the one that blew apart on the interstate. And he had the tools—welding equipment, a metal shop. You name it. Handy guy."

"So, Philip really loved her?" Rachel asked. "I thought she was just an opportunist."

Sam shrugged. "She may've been, but like I said, Robert's the only one left talking. And let's not forget, he didn't just sleep with Teri. He killed her out of rage and paranoia and then exploited some other poor slob's guilt over his estranged daughter to take the fall. Talk about an opportunist."

Sam's voice saddened as she explained, "Turns out Mick Durocher approached Robert a couple of years ago, asking for whatever help Robert could provide Mick's daughter after Mick was dead and buried with cancer. He'd just been diagnosed and remembered how much he and Robert had got along when he worked for GreenField. Mick hit a blank wall then, but when Robert found out he was about to be an inadvertent papa yet again, opening himself to a raft of problems, he got back in touch and made Mick an offer he couldn't refuse."

Rachel was surprised. "Mick didn't kill Teri?"

"Nope. We were good with that theory, especially given Mick's supposedly mild nature. All Robert had to do was let us keep believing it— or steer us into thinking that Philip pulled Mick's strings somehow. But he just copped to it instead. Joe thinks killing his son released something inside him—described it as the same kind of trigger point that unleashed Philip when he heard about Teri and his dad. It was an oddly similar crisis for both of them, in a way—neither had anything left to lose anymore."

"Like father, like son?" Rachel wondered.

"Crazier things have happened," Sam conceded. "And Robert definitely killed her. Mick was the garbage man—using his words. I guess when you're talking about psychopaths, everything becomes doable.

"But in the end," Sam returned to a previous thought, "who knows what's true and what's not? Did Philip really love Teri? Or did he just *think* he was avenging her, when he was only using her as an excuse to lash out at his father? They were sure as hell cut from the same mold."

She shook her head. "In a way, it reminds me of Lillian Wuttke going after Victoria. All she had to do was look outside her own little world for three seconds to realize she was living the dream, being a marginally competent nurse in a good work environment with a great boss. Instead, all she could think about was resentment, envy, and vengeance. Every day, I'm amazed by how self-absorbed people are."

"I still don't understand how Robert could go that far—kill his own son."

Sammie had been mulling it over, as well. "I've started to think that inside Robert's head, he was doing an honorable thing. Could be he rationalized killing Teri to save the company, since he saw it and himself as one and the same. And then he additionally compensated for it by honoring his contract with Mick Durocher, sending Mandy Lawlor the money—the ultimate good-guy gesture. With that logic, I could see him also paying homage to his murdered employees by executing Philip. We all laughed about Robert's routine with the rotating chauffeurs, but he saw that as a kind and generous effort—his way of showing his workers— his real, chosen children—how much he thought of them. Call me crazy, but I've ended up seeing his sacrificing Philip—and therefore himself— as no weirder than some Bible story."

"Abraham standing over his son with a knife in his hand?" Rachel asked with a sad smile.

"Yeah," Sam said, adding, "Except there was no God, or at least no messenger to intervene. As usual, it was just us humans, stumbling around."

"And that's it?" Rachel asked rhetorically.

Sam hitched one shoulder, leaned forward, and blew out the candle, allowing the moonlight to assert itself fully over the porch.

"It's where I put my faith," Sammie told her. "I got a kid to bring up, and a man who keeps fighting to stay sane, sober, and useful—despite the odds against him. I try to do the right thing, and surround myself with people like you and your mom and Joe and Lester. Who cares if the rest of the world is acting like a bunch of loonies?"

She leaned forward and tousled Rachel's hair. "All of whom'll give you something to take pictures of and write about. Think of that, and don't let the bastards pull you under. It's the best I got, corny as it is."